A VALIANT
DECEIT

Books by Stephanie Graves

OLIVE BRIGHT, PIGEONEER

A VALIANT DECEIT

Published by Kensington Publishing Corp.

A VALIANT DECEIT

Stephanie Graves

KENSINGTON
PUBLISHING CORP.

www.kensingtonbooks.com

KENSINGTON BOOKS are published by

Kensington Publishing Corp.
119 West 40th Street
New York, NY 10018

All Kensington titles, imprints and distributed lines are available at special quantity discounts for bulk purchases for sales promotion, premiums, fund-raising, educational or institutional use.

Special book excerpts or customized printings can also be created to fit specific needs. For details, write or phone the office of the Kensington Special Sales Manager: Kensington Publishing Corp., 119 West 40th Street, New York, NY 10018. Attn. Special Sales Department. Phone: 1-800-221-2647.

The K logo is a trademark of Kensington Publishing Corp.

Library of Congress Card Catalogue Number: 2021945743

ISBN-13: 978-1-4967-3152-4
First Kensington Hardcover Edition: February 2022

ISBN-13: 978-1-4967-3158-6 (ebook)

10 9 8 7 6 5 4 3 2 1

Printed in the United States of America

For my aunt and uncle, Ellen and Sandy,
who saw me through my year at
The Ohio State University

IN WARTIME, TRUTH IS SO PRECIOUS THAT SHE SHOULD
ALWAYS BE ATTENDED BY A BODYGUARD OF LIES.
—*Winston Churchill*

THE COURAGE OF A LION, THE HIDE OF A RHINOCEROS AND
A CAPACITY SO GREAT THAT IT COULD NURSE THE WORST
FORM OF TYPHOID OR START A FROZEN CAR.
—*Sir Arthur Stanley, Head of the British Red Cross Society,
referring to the women of the FANY*

Acknowledgments

To all the usual suspects: my editor, John Scognamiglio; my agent, Rebecca Strauss; the wonderful coterie at Kensington Books that has taken Olive under its collective wing to make her fly. Particular thanks to Larissa Ackerman, Alexandra Nicolajsen, Lauren Jernigan, Robin Cook, and Rosemary Silva.

To all the wonderful booksellers, librarians, and readers who warmly welcomed Olive into their cozy reading nests. I hope you'll enjoy her latest adventure.

To so many authors whose work on myriad subjects has directed and inspired my own writing, notably, Julie Summers, Janie Hampton, Giles Milton, Gordon Corera, Ben Macintyre, Leo Marks, Jon Day, and, of course, Agatha Christie.

To the bear and the bunny, the giraffe and the cheetah, goddesses all.

Chapter 1

Pipley, Hertfordshire
16 August 1941

"I'm beginning to wonder if you have even the tiniest bit of experience with this sort of thing," Olive said tightly, her clenched fists strategically hidden by the full skirt of her cornflower-blue dress.

"What sort of thing?" Jamie said, oblivious.

In the weeks she'd been gone, she'd forgotten how his unruffled demeanor could spark her irritation. He needed, she decided, a thorough ruffling, and when she had a moment, she would certainly deal with the matter. But right now really wasn't the time.

"With *romance.*" Her voice caught on the second word, and she put a hand to her throat, momentarily at a loss. But she quickly rallied, crossing her arms, hugging them tightly against her chest, and ruthlessly jerking herself free of her tetchy mood. Her gaze whirled round the room, taking in the flirty Victory Red smiles and the put-on glamour of the evening, courtesy of wartime ingenuity and, in a few notable cases, the black market.

In the centre of it all, the bride and groom were grinning besottedly at each other, and while Olive was delighted that Margaret and Leo had found that sort of magic in each other, she couldn't help but feel a little stab of envy. Because here she stood, tethered indefinitely to a make-believe relationship with her superior officer, Captain Jameson Aldridge.

It had only been a few months since he'd shown up at her dovecote to assess her pigeons and her character. Upon inspection, he'd been seemingly unimpressed with both. In the end, he'd grudgingly enlisted her to work for a hush-hush government organisation, one so secret it was known to insiders only as Baker Street. She'd been conscripted for Station XVII, in particular: the special training school for sabotage, housed at nearby Brickendonbury Manor. Olive had had occasion, during the manor's previous incarnation as the Stratton Park School for Boys, to walk those hallowed halls as its sole female student, and she considered this a serendipitous return.

Jameson Aldridge, however, was another matter entirely. He was brusque to the point of rudeness, distrustful and disapproving, and utterly irritating. In fairness, he'd grown on her a bit in the intervening months, but his dark-haired resemblance to the object of a short-lived love affair, and her own damnable curiosity on that score, had kept things from being strictly comfortable.

Perhaps worse still, ever since Jamie's appearance, she'd been the envy of the village. From Girl Guides to spinsters, they'd all been taken in by his broad shoulders, commanding presence, and Irish intensity. She'd had cause to be on the receiving end of all that commanding intensity, and it hadn't been remotely romantic. Or, in most cases, even pleasant.

He leaned closer and tipped his head down slightly so that his lips hovered just above her ear. "I don't need experience, darling," he drawled smugly. "I need only to know how to fake it."

"Is that right, *Tupper*?" she said, using the nickname his fellow officers had bestowed. As far as she knew, strictly because he'd come from a family of sheep farmers. Her lips curved into a smirk at the irony of it all. "How dreadfully disappointing—and rather surprising, I have to admit." She raked her gaze assessingly over his solid frame, carefully combed dark hair, and smooth-shaven jaw. He must have stories. Maybe one day she'd prise them out of him, but that didn't help her right now. "If that's really your opinion, I daresay you're quite deserving of an earful from Mrs Battlesby and Mrs Pevensie."

She was gratified to see him stiffen, although she couldn't help but resent having to invoke the names of gossipy village ladies. "They're sure to want an explanation as to why you've been content to let your steady girl—the maid of honour, no less—prop up the wall at her best girlfriend's wedding," she said dryly, widening her smile.

Jamie's gaze darted round and finally settled on the pair, who were tucked cosily into a corner spot with a view of the entire hall. As she watched, two purple-veined hands shooed him toward the dance floor, whilst four twinkling eyes brooked no disagreement. Colour crested his ears.

"Clearly, I'm not the only one who thinks you're making a shoddy job of it," she said.

His lips compressed, and a little wrinkle appeared at the centre of his chin. Olive had been tempted to name that wrinkle—Horace seemed rather apropos.

"Come on," he said gruffly, laying his hand against her waist and nudging her forward onto the dance floor.

Just as Olive was finally being swept into his arms, she felt a finger tap against her elbow. Turning, she tipped her gaze down to the sunny, freckled face of Henrietta Gibbons. Inwardly, she sighed; outwardly, she merely smiled, bracing herself for whatever was coming.

"Hello, Hen," she said as Jamie dropped his hands. "I hope you're enjoying yourself." She'd narrowly avoided stressing the wrong word.

The girl beamed. "I've already had two slices of cake, and now I'm introducing Miss Featherington round."

Momentarily confused, Olive shifted her gaze to the woman hovering just beyond Hen, in a green-checked dress and pristine white cardigan. Rumour was she'd been teaching in London, at a girls' school that had shut down, and now she was staying with her sister-in-law, Betty Henry, while her brother was away with the Royal Navy. Her hands were neatly clasped, her smile was demure, and her complexion pure English rose beneath a set of perfect chestnut victory rolls. She was looking at Jamie, and one glance confirmed that he was looking right back. For once, Horace was nowhere in sight.

Olive waited for Hen to get on with the introductions.

"Miss Featherington is our new Brown Owl—our Guide leader." She added the clarification for Jamie's benefit. "She was lucky enough to take over just before our camping trip to Balls Wood next week."

That was one way of looking at it; another was that her predecessor, Miss Haverford, had made a timely escape to the nervy tedium of a munitions factory before she was forced to endure another tramp through the woods with a giddy group of Girl Guides, all of them eager to cook over a campfire, sleep in tents, and squat over a makeshift privy.

"That *is* lucky," Olive agreed, keeping her smile tightly in place.

"This is Olive Bright—just back from FANY training—and her fiancé, Captain Jameson Aldridge."

Olive reacted instantly, her coy "No-no-no" overlapping Jamie's startled and rather strident *"What?"*

"They both work over at Brickendonbury Manor," Hen went on, her body tilting conspiratorially toward Brown Owl. "Very hush-hush."

"We are *not*," Olive said, giving Hen a hard look, "engaged, as you well know." To Miss Featherington, she added, "We're just . . . enjoying each other's company." Olive smiled at Jamie, who looked as spooked as if he'd seen a cat—a quirk of his she'd yet to get to the bottom of—and forged on alone. "We're both busy with war work, and neither of us is thinking of marriage right now."

"I wouldn't have even known you were a couple," Miss Featherington admitted unhelpfully.

"Lucky we had this chat," Olive said, taking Jamie's arm in a firm, demonstrative grip. "Now, if you don't mind, I've finally convinced him to dance, and I'd just assume not lose my chance." She flashed a final smile before moving off. She really couldn't contend with Hen and Miss Featherington right now.

Looking rather confused, Jamie nodded and allowed himself to be led away. Thankfully, the record on the gramophone had been switched from a quickstep to the slower-paced "You Go to My Head," so she pressed close to him and stoppered her irritation.

After a few moments of moving round the floor, Jamie spoke. "Point to you."

Evidently, their little chat with Miss Featherington hadn't been a complete waste of time. She'd at least managed to convince Jamie of his less than loverlike attitude where Olive was concerned. Feeling too put upon to look at him, she murmured, "Lucky for you, I'm not keeping a tally." After a beat she added, "Was it really necessary to react as if I'm some sort of gorgon?"

"Well, aren't you?" he deadpanned.

She tensed in his arms, her head whipping round so that her face was mere inches from his. When she tipped her head back to meet his eyes, their grey-blue placidity riled her even further.

In the split second before her temper got the better of her, he tightened his grip and shifted slightly. "Steady on, Olive. I meant the good parts. Lesser mortals may not admire them," he continued offhandedly as they swayed to the plummy tones of Joe Loss, "but they've grown on me. More or less."

"You're not particularly good with compliments, are you?" she groused.

"That depends. Am I meant to be your commanding officer or your pretend lover?"

She leaned back in his arms, debating how awkward she was willing to let things become. At last, she said simply, "Never mind."

He shook her slightly. "You've got to admit, there are certain similarities. You're fiercely courageous—albeit at times to the point of stupidity." He hurried on as she tensed. "*And* rather eye-catching."

"I suppose you think you're clever," she said, trying not to smile.

He tipped his head in cocky acknowledgement, flashed his dimple, and shifted his hand against her lower back. A shiver ran through her, then quickly fizzled as she was struck yet again by her untenable situation: she was twenty-two years old, and romance was strictly off-limits. Her shoulders slumped.

"Is it all right if I lay my head on your shoulder? You won't bolt, will you?" she asked, hearing the quaver in her voice and quickly gulping it down.

"I think I can just manage to resist," he said wryly.

With a long sigh, she closed her eyes and imagined for a moment that she truly was dancing with her fiancé—or, at the very least, with someone who might be likely to kiss her properly at the end of the evening. But if a few fleeting moments in the strong arms of a handsome man were all she could get, it would have to be enough. The fabric of his jacket felt cool against her heated cheek, and his solid bulk was immensely comforting. This war business was rough, and for all intents and purposes, she was living it only vicariously. She could work her fingers to the bone as a pigeoneer and a FANY, sitting pretty in the English countryside, and while it was stressful and exhausting, and sometimes unbearably frustrating, she knew it was nothing compared to the conditions endured by the men and women living in the occupied zones on the Continent and beyond.

She felt his fingers shift and tighten at her waist and let herself relax. But too soon, the song was over, and she was pulling away, not wanting to meet Jamie's eyes, not wanting to admit that having him hold on to her for those few swaying moments felt uncomfortably comfortable.

"Ladies and gents," came a jaunty voice from the dais at the end of the room, "it's time to see the bride and groom off on their honeymoon."

Jamie took hold of her hand and tugged her through the milling crowds drifting toward the doors of the hall. Olive's father had loaned the couple his Hillman Minx and offered up a ration of petrol as a wedding gift. The couple was to spend two days in the Cotswolds before it was back to business.

Her friend was standing beside the car, her lavender dress almost glowing in the last remaining rays of late summer light. After clothes had been rationed at the beginning of June, the women of Pipley had stepped up to help outfit the bride. Olive had loaned her mother's pearls, Violet Darling had offered a glamourous silk shantung wrap the colour of ripe mulberries, and Lady Camilla had gifted Margaret with a pair of familiar marcasite hair combs, at which Olive couldn't help but look askance.

Even without a perfect, new white gown, Margaret looked radiant and impossibly happy, her complexion dewier than the prizewinning late-summer roses picked from Mrs Spencer's garden to be gathered into a lush bouquet. Her golden tresses had been released from the pinned arrangement of just moments ago and now hung in a rippling curtain to brush against her collarbones. She'd reapplied her lipstick and touched up her makeup, and it made Olive catch her breath just to look at her. Her new husband couldn't claim such cinema-star good looks, but Leo had plenty of other qualities to recommend him, and Margaret had eyes only for him. He looked quite distinguished in his formal suit, his pale hair slicked into place with pomade and catching fire in the setting sun—almost like a jazz musician or a continental playboy. She suspected he'd be quite flattered by the comparisons.

A few weeks prior, Leo had started work as the chaplain at nearby Merryweather House. It had been requisitioned as a hospital for some of the most tragically injured of HM Forces, and it was keeping him busy enough that a few of Pipley's occupants found themselves somewhat adrift. As a nearly minted vicar's wife, Margaret was the obvious substitute in his absence, but unfortunately, she wasn't quite ready yet to step into her new role. She'd recently confided to Olive that more than once she'd found herself lunging into shrubbery to spare herself the chatty confidences of one of her future flock.

Now she caught sight of Olive, hurried forward, and enveloped her in a tight hug. "It was all right, wasn't it?"

"It was perfect," Olive assured her. "And you looked perfectly lovely. Now, go off and enjoy yourselves."

Margaret rolled her eyes. "Thank heaven for these two days. I've barely seen Leo since he took the posting at Merryweather. Coming back will be so hard. But at least we'll be together—there's been no more talk of him joining up, thank the Lord."

Olive gripped her arms, squeezed. "Don't think about the war or Pipley or anything at all. Just be together."

"I promise." Beaming with happiness, Margaret glanced over Olive's shoulder to where Jamie was standing amidst the gathered crowd, then met her friend's eyes, a tiny wrinkle forming between her brows. "Everything all right with you two? You looked a little put out in the hall."

"We're figuring things out," Olive said, pasting on a smile. Not even Margaret knew that she and Jamie were only playing parts, and that her concern was entirely misplaced.

"I suspect you have him wrapped round your little finger," Margaret teased, her lips twisting with amusement as Leo tugged her gently back toward the car.

A few of the villagers had foraged in their gardens; others had sought out the wildflowers that grew rampant on the verge. All were now delightedly tossing a kaleidoscope of coloured petals into the air as the couple slipped into the auto. And in a moment, with a toot of the horn, they were off down the lane, with the cheers of the village ringing behind them.

Olive stared after them, shielding her eyes against the last flash of the setting sun as twilight began its dreamy descent. There'd been so many changes in the months since she'd ferreted out the murderer among them, and yet so much still remained the same. Like a child, she made a wish in the moment. A wish for something exciting, magical, and wonderful to happen to her. As it escaped into the ether, she felt a tug at her hand and turned, startled to remember that she was still playing a part, not yet free to relax.

"I'll walk you home," Jamie said, and to her surprise, he didn't let go.

As they reached the end of the high street and faced the open countryside, the sun nestled in among the trees, tucked in for the night by the encroaching velvet cover of gathering darkness. Their steps were slow and synchronised, and nary a word was spoken. After her ordeal with a murderer, there had been the weeks of recovery, and when she'd finally started work at Brickendonbury, they'd both been on tenterhooks. And after that, there'd been her training. She'd almost forgotten what it was like to spend time with Jamie. It required only a moment for Olive to conclude that being alone with him was very like being alone. As long as he refrained from chastising. And lecturing. And silent disapproval.

Olive stole a glance at him, relatively certain that the silent disapproval was simmering just below the surface. So long as it remained unvoiced, she was content. Unfortunately, the blissful silence lasted exactly three more steps.

"Did Lady Hailsham get you whipped into shape at Overthorpe Hall?" he inquired.

Olive rolled her eyes. Of course he wanted to talk about her FANY training. "It's more accurate to say that she tested our willingness to perform the most menial and revolting tasks. The better to prepare us for the demands of our commanding officers."

"A woman after my own heart," Jamie said.

Olive didn't bother with a reply, instead staring out over the late-summer fields. The long, hot days would soon give way to the crispness of fall, and still the war dragged on, seemingly interminable.

"I hope you're ready to get back to work," he said, an odd note in his voice. "You're to have an official assignment."

Her gaze swept round, her eyebrows dipping suspiciously. "More official than pigeoneer?" she asked dryly, plunging her hands into her pockets. "Does the Official Secrets Act cover it, or will I be required to sign in blood?"

"Very funny."

"Does the new assignment come with a new CO?" she asked casually. Her attention had been caught by the quick, darting movements of a little hedge sparrow, and she rattled off the words almost without thinking.

"I was under the impression," he said somewhat woodenly, "that we'd finally found a rhythm of sorts." She glanced over at him and noted the sudden hardness of his jaw and the whitened scar along its edge.

"We had," she allowed, stretching the words out, somewhat baffled by his defence of their partnership. "But that was mostly after matters had been resolved. Up to that point, our efforts at cooperation tended to resemble a mule cart."

"I presume in that analogy I'm meant to be the mule?"

Olive gestured, as if to say he'd drawn that conclusion on his own. But yes.

"How about I give you another analogy?" he said, sounding breathless with exasperation. "What about a grenade with a faulty pin that blows up in your kitbag before your mission's even begun?"

"I think that's a bit of an exaggeration," she said sharply. "If you're implying that I'm the pin, and faulty."

"You've not exactly been a model recruit. You're argumentative and insubordinate, careless and bloody reckless. In imagining yourself an amateur sleuth, you almost got yourself killed."

He hadn't said *deceitful*; that was something. Still, the dressing-down grated, and her emotions fizzed up like a firecracker. "Over these past few months, I've not *imagined* anything. I've *lived* every minute as pigeoneer, FANY, village pig keeper, amateur sleuth, dutiful daughter, and pretend girlfriend." She had turned and was toe-to-toe with him now, her gaze just barely tipped up to look him in the eye. "And quite frankly, my efforts on the last score justify adding 'bloody good actress' to the list."

The colour of his eyes seemed to lighten as she stared angrily into their depths. "You're right," he said, quickly sobering. "I've been too hard on you. My standards are high, and I expect as much of the men—and women—under my command as I expect of myself."

Olive's shoulders slumped slightly; the moral outrage had sputtered out, and she suddenly felt as if she'd let him down. By mutual consent, they started walking again, the sounds of a summer evening in the country steadily building.

After a moment, he went on. "You have had to contend with more than most. The others working at Station XVII are, for all intents and purposes, cut off from the outside world. They don't have to worry on a daily basis about keeping the secrets of their war work from friends and family members. None of them must contend with village affairs and gossip, not to mention the expected demonstrations of an . . . amorous nature."

Olive breathed a sigh of relief at having him understand—or at least profess to.

"As to the sleuthing . . ." he said heavily. One eyebrow winged up as he gave her a look of mild reproof. "You know my feelings on that," he added, slipping his hands into his pockets.

She did. And she didn't really give a fig. Inspired by the inestimable Hercule Poirot of her favourite mystery novels, she'd delved into the prospect of solving the murder of a local busybody with a zeal bordering on relish. Her efforts had proved successful, not only in outing a murderer, but also in uncovering a savvy black-market scheme, and they hadn't interfered with anything, except perhaps her own mortal coil. He had no business treating her like a recalcitrant child over the matter. Clearly, it fell to her to reestablish the nature of their relationship. And they were going to need a much better analogy.

With a heartfelt sigh, she began, "When you showed up at my pigeon loft, it was to request my services as a pigeoneer, reporting to you. In an effort to justify our spending time together, I invented a romance." She kicked at a stone and tamped down her still-fresh exasperation on the topic. "And when I asked to have a larger role in the efforts being undertaken for the war, I was told to sign on as a FANY. Working at Brickendonbury and, again, reporting to you."

She smiled blandly and waited for him to comment. He didn't.

"Obviously, you have a certain claim on my time and attention. You can take me for a drive, demand the use of a pair of pigeons, or put me to work filing papers or packing explosives. All completely within your purview. But some aspects of my life are not," she said emphatically. "That includes my family, my free time, and whatever hobbies strike my fancy. If I want to eat blackberries off the bramble or name a pig that will eventually be butchered or hunt for a murderer when the police have given up,

I don't need your permission, Jamie." She'd lowered her voice at the end and even slipped her arm through his, trying to smooth over the sting of her words. It wasn't an easy situation for either of them.

"Maybe not. But as your commanding officer, I'm going to give you a bit of advice." Stiffening, Olive detached her arm from his and shifted away a bit. He reached for her hand, and she let him take it. "Many aspects of war seem rather thrilling, and it's quite natural to view courage and heroism with starry-eyed urgency and excitement. But the price of failure is heavy. It's capture, incarceration, torture, even death."

"I know that," Olive protested, trying to shake her hand loose, but he held on stubbornly, so she gritted her teeth and looked up at the stars, little chinks in the armour of impending darkness.

"What I'm trying to say is that those things are also true when a person is fighting a war of their own. In the heat of the moment, wrapped up in discovery and justice and certitude, it's easy to forget things like caution and common sense." She frowned, not at all in the mood to be chastised. Again. His next words caught her completely off guard. "I don't know what I would have done if you'd been killed."

Her breath caught, just for a moment, and then he spoke again.

"Who would I have found to supply our pigeons?"

His grin flashed, proof he was teasing, but she shot him a withering stare, nonetheless, carefully extracting her hand.

"Seriously, though, Olive. Have a care. I can't stop you from poking your nose where it doesn't belong, but I can endeavour to keep you too distracted to allow it."

Her skin prickled, and her eyes widened. *What* did *he mean*? Was it possible he was experiencing the same restless feeling that plagued her? A need for connection and even, to a lesser degree, romance?

His manner changed abruptly from teasing humour to serious

intensity. "Olive . . . ," he said, his voice suddenly husky. Her heartbeat soared, and she felt her body instinctively leaning toward him.

Suddenly, he shied away, taking a step backwards and away. She froze, mortified and uncertain. And then the barest feather touch twitched against her calf. She reacted as if it were a live wire. Jerking her leg away, she whirled and found herself staring down at a shadow. As she blinked, the smudge of darkness materialised into a black cat with a white-tipped tail, poised to begin stropping itself against her.

Closing her eyes, she willed her temper to subside. It wasn't his fault that her frame of mind had almost had her . . . She didn't want to think about it.

"For heaven's sake," she scoffed, with a glance back at Jamie. "Let's hope the Germans don't send feral cats to invade us." She secretly relished that he had this little quirk. Jamie radiated command and control, but send a cat traipsing across his path, and the man was a pudding.

His gaze flicked to hers, and he tugged on the hem of his jacket, as if to restore a sense of decorum to the situation. He failed utterly. "It's not feral." His voice was tight. In response to her raised eyebrow, he nodded toward the break in the hedgerow behind her. A crushed gravel drive was pale in the milky glow of the rising waxing moon. "It surely came from in there."

Olive suddenly realised where they were standing. She peered round the hedge-fronted wall and stared down the drive to Peregrine Hall, Miss Husselbee's home until the recent tragedy. She could just make out a van in the forecourt, its doors being folded shut. Just beyond, a rigid and correct individual had turned to walk up the steps and into the darkened hall.

She heard a scuffle behind her on the path, followed by an oath, but didn't turn, her curiosity kindled by this new discovery. Between their housekeeper, Mrs Battlesby, and her stepmother, Olive was usually kept well apprised of village gossip, and someone new moving into Peregrine Hall was a juicy titbit indeed. Perhaps they'd just arrived.

With the slam of the driver's-side door, the truck roared to life. It crunched over the gravel and rumbled up the drive toward them, its slitted headlamps arcing through the darkness.

Jamie's breath hissed out, overlaying the grinding sound of shifting gears. Glancing back, Olive watched the cat dart into the hedgerow while Jamie stared after it with narrowed eyes. She hailed the driver.

"You need summat, Miss?" he demanded, staring down at her through the open window. His grizzled gaze shifted suspiciously to Jamie, who was suddenly looming tall and dark beside her.

"I was wondering," Olive said politely, flashing a smile, "if you could tell me who's living here now? This house used to belong to a family friend." A shiver swept over her.

"An older lady and her nephew. He was a patient at the hospital up the road in Little Biscombe. Horrible burns, he has." He cringed slightly and shook his head at the futility of it all.

"Well, I hope he's able to find some peace here," she said, prompting a nod from the driver before, with a shuddering heave, the van pulled out onto the road, leaving the pair of them in a swirl of dust.

"Miss Husselbee lived here," she told Jamie. "I wonder what the new occupants are like," she said consideringly, peering at the darkened silhouette of Peregrine Hall, the glow of an electric lamp illuminating a single, lonely window near the back of the house.

"It's a mystery," Jamie said lightly. "Perhaps it's the sort to satisfy your propensity for sleuthing."

Rather than retort, Olive instead set her mind to replaying Jamie's awkward little dance with the shadow cat. She suspected her smug smile looked like the Cheshire cat's, glowing in the moonlight.

* * *

There was always a kiss, on the off chance that someone was watching. They were, after all, playing a part. In the beginning they'd been unconvincingly chaste. It had required only a whispered reminder that he was a strapping young officer of HM Forces—and that she was ready and willing—for him to make some adjustments. Now their kisses were much more believable, at least as far as she could tell, and entirely acceptable—pleasant even. And if Olive held her breath in the moment and savoured the familiar flavour of liquorice once Jamie had gone, she wasn't prepared to examine her reasons too closely.

That evening, after he'd walked her home, he paused for a moment, his eyes scanning the darkened windows of Blackcap Lodge and the surrounding yard and drive. It was impossible to tell whether he was checking for an audience or an ambush, and she didn't ask. Her father viewed Jamie as he might any other young man seemingly intent on his daughter's affections, unaware that he was actually her commanding officer and was instrumental in a perpetrated deception that involved their pigeons and the Bright loft.

When she'd been informed that their loft had been passed over by the National Pigeon Service due to her father's uncompromising attitude, she'd agreed to put her birds to work for Baker Street, in secret. But with the pigeons out on regular training missions and their feed no longer dwindling, she'd known her father would require an explanation. So on a sunny afternoon in midsummer, a man purporting to be an NPS officer had shown up at Blackcap Lodge and vetted the Bright birds. In truth, he'd been an instructor of mechanical sabotage at Station XVII, one with a penchant for theatre, but to Rupert Bright, he'd been the real deal.

Olive could only imagine the outraged bluster that would ensue should her father discover it had all been a ruse. Her breath caught momentarily at the thought of it and then came shuddering out on a sigh. She wanted one single moment to relax and not think of what she mustn't say or do. She hated lying to him, but what choice did she have? She'd signed the Official Secrets Act; she was well and truly ensnared. One glance at Jamie, looking dangerous in the dark, and her thoughts shifted. Honestly, Rupert Bright would probably be only too happy that the man was interested in her pigeons and little else.

From the great hulking shadow of the dovecote, she could hear the birds cooing contentedly as the tension built inside her, leaving her quivering like a bowstring.

So when, after a long moment, he turned back to her, leaned in, and laid his mouth comfortably over hers, a touch of mania crept over her. Her arms snaked up, draped over his shoulders, and suddenly she was cupping the back of his head, holding him in place, the kiss extended. She skimmed her thumbs over his barely stubbled jaw, rocked forward onto the balls of her feet, and leaned into him. And she kissed him—*really kissed him*—with a thoroughness born of pent-up frustration. After a long moment she let go, brushed her hands briskly along the tops of his shoulders, settled back onto her heels, and nodded smartly.

"Goodnight," she said briskly, turning to go in. Let him think about *that* on the drive back to Brickendonbury. She'd explain later.

Startled—and rather impressed—at her own nerve, she was shocked out of her reverie the moment she stepped through the kitchen door.

"Where have you been?" her father demanded brusquely, his caterpillar brows scrunched together over a face pale with shock and worry. He was hovering over the kettle, seemingly bullying it to boil.

Olive warily approached. "With Jamie. We walked along the river and then doubled back. I didn't know anyone was waiting."

"We weren't," he said shortly. "But I could have used your help. Harriet had a fall."

Her stepmother had multiple sclerosis, and in recent months it had begun to limit her mobility significantly. She couldn't get round at all well without her cane, and often she needed the help of a willing arm, as well.

The distractions of a moment ago dissipated instantly, leaving a sickly void in the pit of her stomach.

"Where is she? It wasn't the stairs, was it?" she demanded, panic settling in. "Where's Jonathon?" He'd been living with them for only seven months—an evacuee from London—but to Olive, he was like a younger brother, standing in for the older one, who'd been away in Greece, working as a British liaison officer, for over a year and a half.

"I sent him to bed. He's a sensitive young fellow and was more worked up than Harriet." He stared at the teacups he'd arranged on a tray as he ran a rough hand over his jaw. "She's sprained her ankle and bruised up her arms. Dr Harrington is here and intends to give her something for the pain and to help her sleep—likely laudanum. I'm just waiting to bring up the tea."

"You go ahead," Olive told him. "I'll bring it up with the rest of this week's sugar ration, so she can get the medicine down. Shall I fetch the box?" Harriet's not-so-secret stash of cigarettes, used strictly when her condition got to be too much for her, was tucked away in a stylish jade enameled box on a piecrust table in the parlour. Olive suspected her stepmother was yearning for it even now.

"I'll get it on my way up," her father said heavily. His eyes looked bleak, and she couldn't blame him. Her injuries would make Harriet even more immobile and would leave her frustrated and fraught. And it would fall to the rest of them to make do.

On impulse, she leaned in to kiss his cheek. He smelled of carbolic soap and rosemary, as he had for as long as she could remember. He always kept a sprig of the woody-stemmed herb, tugged from the overgrown bush that grew outside his veterinary surgery, in his pocket and chewed it distractedly when there was a bit of hard thinking to do.

As he left the kitchen, Olive propped herself against the table and stared at the trio of china cups on the wooden tray. Jamie had smelled of bay rum and summer and had tasted, predictably, of liquorice. . . .

The kettle shrieked, making her start guiltily as she scrounged in the tea tin. Her thoughts were a sharp reprimand. No good could come of analysing those obligatory pecks of consenting lips—to say nothing of this evening's renegade effort. It was all just urgency and nerves and a fated recklessness. None of it meant anything. She just needed some excitement—some action. She was tired of waiting, hoping, and praying while others busily got on with doing the hard work.

She switched off the Aga and warmed the teapot. A sly smile curled her lips at the memory of Jamie's expression. She couldn't help it. He needed a bit of shaking up now and again—he was entirely too stodgy and set in his ways for a man in his midtwenties. But she'd worry about that later. Right now, her mind should be on Harriet. She had the tea tray in hand as her father filled the kitchen doorway.

"She's exhausted, poor darling, and almost asleep. She choked the laudanum down with a glass of water. Why don't you go up and check on Jonathon? I'll take the tray along to my study. Dr Harrington and I are going to have a quick chat," he said grimly, his hands gripping the tray a bit unsteadily. Olive had just time enough to remove Harriet's cup from the tray before he was gone.

Olive stood for a moment, staring after him. For the second time in less than a quarter of an hour, she felt helpless against the onslaught of her own emotions. She took a breath and focused on gathering the milk and what remained of the chocolate to make cocoa for herself and Jonathon. He'd fill her in on the latest heroic, but fictional, antics of James Bigglesworth, pilot and adventurer, and the world would begin to feel normal again.

As she stood in the kitchen, her thoughts buzzing with all the changes to come, she was rather startled to discover how much comfort it brought knowing that Jamie was exactly the same.

Chapter 2

"This can't really be roast beef, can it?" Olive said, staring down at the plate onto which she'd been served a thick, juicy slice of something that bore no resemblance to the tired, leathery portions that Mrs Battlesby managed with the weekly rations.

She directed her question to the man who had thus far proved to be Station XVII's most fascinating occupant: Tomás Harris. Born in Spain, he had finished school in London and was a widely known, gifted sculptor and owner of a prestigious art gallery. Olive still wasn't clear how he'd ended up as cook and glorified housekeeper at Brickendonbury, but his charms were obvious. With Mediterranean good looks, a cosmopolitan air, and a mischievous sense of humour, he would have offered a welcome diversion of the sort she'd lately been very much in the mood for. But it was not to be, as he was married, and Hilda Harris was equally charming, not to mention, in residence.

"As they say," came his ready response in the seductive tones of his native Spain, "if it walks like a cow and moos like a cow . . ." Tomás offered up a Gallic shrug, but his lips were quirked with amusement.

"I don't think that's exactly what they say," Olive said dryly.

"Oh, don't ask," begged Marie Wood. "I don't even want to know, particularly if it tastes good." Olive glanced at the wide blue eyes and full lips of the FANY who had started at Brickendonbury several months before she had. Marie was tidy and efficient to a fault, and she had a way of routing their shared frustrations with her wicked sense of humour.

"You're not the slightest bit curious as to what sort of sorcery is at work here?"

"Shove off, Olive," insisted Liz, the blond pixie behind her in line. "This is not the time for sleuthing. Load up on potatoes or beets if you want, but keep the mystery sacred."

The serving line had been set up along the far wall of the panelled dining room, but with tables scattered throughout, the space had the look of a makeshift canteen.

"Enjoy, Miss Bright," Tomás said with a wink. "If you decide you must know my secrets, you know where to find me."

Olive moved along in the line and let the ever-tolerant, fresh-faced Hilda fill her plate with a serving of vegetables before she followed Marie to the table where the new FANY recruit was already digging into her lunch. Kate Atherton was only seventeen and had the figure of a well-fed country girl with access to extra servings of butter and cream.

One bite was all it took for Olive to confirm that the mystery meat was the real deal. She forced her jaw to slow so that she could savour the nearly forgotten taste of a good cut of beef. She was perfectly content until Liz jostled her elbow.

"We've been run off our feet since you hared off for training. A whole new class of recruits has come in—Belgians this time— and they've all needed organising," Liz informed her, the words gushing out between bites.

"They're all ever so nice, though," Kate put in, her dark hair frizzing out of its pinned rolls.

"And utterly focused," Marie added distractedly, cutting her meat. "They're eager to finish up here and parachute back home again to have a hand in ridding their country of the hated Germans."

Olive smiled to herself, glad to be back. She'd missed the flurry of activity, and even Jamie's commanding intensity—just a bit. But mostly, she'd missed her quick, easy friendships with these women—on the clock and off. They'd taken advantage of the warm summer evenings, strolling barefoot over the manor grounds, dipping their bare feet in the river, and eating berries straight from the bush, each moment even more cherished now that so many of life's little pleasures had, of necessity, been stripped away. She hoped the weather would hold just a little longer. Although, she was rather looking forward to the picture Liz had painted of cosy autumn evenings at the manor: card games and dancing, shot through with liberal quantities of spirits, which never seemed to be in short supply at Station XVII.

"Is Miss Butterwick still at Overthorpe Hall, dispensing good sense and dire warnings?" Liz quipped. It had been more than a year since she herself had gone through the training.

Marie's lips twitched, but she didn't comment.

Kate's fork hovered in midair. "I quite liked Miss Butterwick," she said. "She had our best interests at heart."

"I think her interest was in ensuring that we'd uphold an antiquated model of British womanhood," Liz countered, before lowering her voice to add, "One devoid of any pesky sexuality."

Marie nearly spit out her sip of coffee. "You're exaggerating, Liz."

Liz instantly shifted her features to convey brusque disapproval, and when she spoke, her voice had taken on the nononsense tone of Miss Butterwick. "A certain amount of lipstick is perfectly acceptable in the interest of keeping up morale, but an excess can arouse feelings of a different sort."

Kate tipped her head down and focused on meticulously arranging her cutlery on her empty plate to a position of six o'clock on the dot.

In her own voice, Liz went on. "I only wish I'd had the nerve to question her experience on the matter. My only excuse is that I'd been brainwashed." Marie's lips curved coyly, but Liz forestalled any reply. "And lest you intend to inquire, not *that* brainwashed. I'd trade a week's worth of cigarettes for a man in a hayloft," she grumped.

Olive chimed in. "She kindly recommended I refrain from being quite so lippy on the job." She twirled the blood-red beet impaled on her fork. "Evidently, men don't like that quality in a girl."

"That depends entirely on what you're doing with them—lips *and* men," Marie said dryly. Liz snorted, and Marie added, "I've danced with quite a few who've seemed overly fond of mine."

"You must have been wearing an excess of lipstick," Olive said, grinning.

A rosy blush had risen to Kate's cheeks, but she had propped her chin in her hand and was biting her lip as her eyes darted between them. Olive wondered if the girl's mother was the Miss Butterwick sort.

"There was this one," Marie marvelled. "Every time I started talking, his lips would slide into a gorgeous but patronising smile and then settle over mine. I never did finish a sentence. Oh, that's not quite true. The words *insufferable clod* definitely left my lips unfettered."

Liz sighed and sliced violently into the remains of her roast beef. "My last dance partner was a conchie. He was handsome—bedroom eyes and built like a wrestler—but I much prefer a man in uniform."

Olive guiltily shifted her gaze. For reasons she didn't entirely understand, Liz fancied Jamie. And since she wasn't keen on testing the limits of their newfound friendship, Olive fully intended to keep mum about her own complicated liaison with the man.

With the other girls housed in Nissen huts on the manor grounds and warned to steer clear of the village, none of them had reason to find out. Particularly as their evenings out were farther afield, in the direction of RAF Hunsdon.

"You and every other girl hoping for a little romance," Marie quipped. "It *is* as if we've all been brainwashed, and our joint fascination with the RAF is worst of all." She tapped a fingernail against her china cup with a faraway look in her eye. "Is it the dashing blue uniform, those little wings on their caps, or the rakish demeanor and cocky attitude they all manage to cultivate within moments of signing up? Or is it simply knowing that they're willing to face the Luftwaffe thousands of feet in the air?"

Olive thought instantly of her best friend, George, away at flight school, and her stomach dropped.

"Whatever it is," Marie went on, "we're smitten. I spent an entire evening listening to one of them boast about his prowess." She slipped a bit of carrot into her mouth and chewed contemplatively before pointing with the tines of her fork. "He couldn't even land a satisfying kiss—after more tries than I care to admit—and him a bomber pilot bound for Berlin."

"Why did you give him more than one chance?" Kate blurted from behind her coffee cup. "To kiss you, I mean."

Liz snickered.

Olive blinked at the innocence of the question. Why did any of them let themselves be kissed by boorish, bumbling, boastful men? The same reason she had lunged for Jamie rather than settle for a chaste little peck. Over the past two years, something wild had grown up in them all. They were grasping greedily at life rather than chance having it snatched away from them untried.

Liz's tongue had slipped out, and it touched the corners of her mouth before running slowly along the front of her teeth, but she kept her thoughts to herself.

After a long moment, as if she, like Olive, had been grappling with something troubling to explain, Marie finally answered. "It

seemed the best way to get him to stop talking." Thankfully, that
broke the tension, sending them all into gales of laughter.

"Is it an inside joke, or is anyone allowed to hear it?" said a
voice behind Olive. Turning, she looked up into the friendly
gaze of Danny Tierney.

A favourite of Olive's and a good friend of Jamie's, he was the
instructor of self-defence at Station XVII. It was difficult to reconcile his copper-topped, boyish face and lilting Irish accent
with the man who could masterfully demonstrate at least ten
ways of killing a man without a weapon. But she'd seen a number of his scars and knew his history. He'd shipped out of Ireland with the merchant marine, then worked security for a
Chinese distributor of American guns, and eventually signed on
with the Shanghai Municipal Police, breaking up riots and street
fights. When war broke out, he returned to Britain and offered
his services to the War Office. Baker Street had been lucky to
get their hands on him.

"We're talking about kissing," Liz informed him, eyebrows
up. "Seeing as you're a willing member of the opposite sex, care
to offer any insights on the male perspective?"

With four pairs of eyes staring up at him, their gazes running
the gamut of innocence, amusement, and honest curiosity, Tierney was frozen in place, his lips parted uncertainly. "A willing
member?" he said hoarsely.

"She means willing to chat," Olive assured him.

"Right. Well, I don't know that I've anything to offer," he said
stiltedly.

"Come now, Lieutenant," Liz purred. "Don't sell yourself
short."

Tierney ran a hand through his hair, and a growl of frustration
emitted from deep in his throat.

"I think," Olive said, continuing in her role as translator, "he
meant to the conversation."

"Exactly. Whatever it is you're saying, I'm sure I agree," he added quickly, and as his gaze drifted to Marie, he began to back away. "And now I'm off, before it really gets awkward." His lips curved shyly, and then he turned, muttering in an aside to Olive, "That'll teach me to keep my mouth shut."

Marie's gaze trailed after him, but when she caught Olive's eye, she shifted her attention, carefully laying her own cutlery diagonally across her plate.

An audible crack jerked both their heads up and instantly stifled the low din of conversation. Its crockery-rattling aftershocks shimmied ominously across the dining room. And then the voice of Major Boom, the appropriately code-named commanding officer of Station XVII, roared through in their wake. "We've got to suss this fellow out!" Another crack resounded as he smacked the table a second time with the flat of his open palm.

Olive turned back to look curiously at her fellow FANYs. "What fellow? What's happened?"

Her eyes wide, Liz leaned in conspiratorially, and the others followed suit. "One of the storage buildings has been burgled, and some things are missing. Since not everything is inventoried, they're not sure what all was taken." She seemed uncharacteristically shaken.

"And they haven't any clues?" The hairs on the back of Olive's neck lifted, and a little curl of excitement whipped through her. Here was a mystery to be solved. It was just like Jamie not to mention it, while simultaneously urging her to keep her nose out of things.

"If they have any," Marie said calmly, "they haven't taken us into their confidence. They're not at all happy about it, though, and we've been asked to inventory the sheds." Her brows tipped up as she smiled blandly.

At this reminder, Kate said, "I suppose we'd best get back to work."

Liz rose, but before bussing her plate, she said crisply, "Don't forget your warpaint, ladies." She produced a shiny tube from her pocket. "I'm happy to share my Red Letter Red," she offered, glancing pointedly in Kate's direction.

"I wonder what Hilda will serve for tea," Kate said, clearly having very different priorities. "There are still a few wild strawberries on the vines," she added excitedly. "Perhaps it'll be scones. And clotted cream."

Olive rolled her eyes, certain that even Tomás Harris couldn't stretch to that.

"That's not your normal shade, is it?" Marie's eyebrows went up in question as she finished her coffee.

"It isn't," Liz said, pouting. "I seem to have misplaced my tube of Victory Red. Let me know if you find it, will you?"

"Miss Bright," asserted a familiar voice.

In a well-practiced movement, Liz shifted her shoulders back, accentuating her trim bust, tipped up her chin, and curved her lips just enough to round her cheekbones. It instantly confirmed Olive's suspicion: Captain Aldridge stood behind her.

Olive turned to face him, braced for an impending lecture on the detriments of an overly effusive kiss. Ready and willing to argue the point, she said, "Yes, Captain Aldridge?"

The barest furrow appeared between his brows, perhaps in the face of her subordinate smile. "If you can come with me, Major Boom will apprise you of your new assignment." He flicked a glance at her dishes, then across the table. "Can you handle these, Liz?" Not waiting for a reply, he gestured Olive to precede him.

Olive winced, shot Liz a look of apology, and turned, vividly imagining the daggers being shot from her friend's eyes straight into her back. Falling in step beside Jamie, she muttered, "You and I need to talk."

"If it's about Saturday night—" Jamie started, his voice barely loud enough to be heard over the bustle in the hall.

"It's not," she cut in sharply.

Was it her imagination, or did he seem relieved? "Go ahead, then," he said abruptly.

"I suspect you'd prefer somewhere more private," she said pointedly.

He shot her a baffled look but didn't press until they'd reached his office and he'd shut the door with a tap. When he turned to face her, Olive was already reaching into the glass jar poised on the edge of his desk to fish out one of the few remaining aniseed balls. Sweets were getting harder and harder to come by.

"Help yourself," he muttered, the rigid line of his shoulders relaxing slightly. "I assumed it was urgent," he said leadingly.

Olive unwrapped the candy, popped it into her mouth, and rolled it round on her tongue for a moment before answering. "Not life and death. More, bloody awkward."

"Olive," Jamie said warningly. She'd got very familiar with the full spectrum of his disapproving tones, and by the sound of things, she really was at risk of an impending lecture. She tucked the candy to the side and launched into a quick summary.

"It seems your gruff manner, and possibly the pleasant arrangement of your features," she conceded with a shrug, "are alluring enough that Liz has decided she fancies you." Ignoring the look of shock that had now transformed said features, she continued. "Given that, I think we should be extra careful in keeping our 'arrangement' a secret. And it would be best if you didn't show me any preferential treatment. That's all." Moving the aniseed ball back round, she stepped toward the door, eager to get on with things now that that was out of the way.

"The whole manor is aware of the pigeons," he said with some exasperation. "And I really don't see—"

Olive rolled her eyes, extracted the candy, and said slowly, "I'm referring to the arrangement that involves kissing."

Silence.

She raised her brows expectantly.

"You said this wasn't about that," he protested, running a rough hand across his jaw.

Olive sighed. It would have been preferable if Jamie had instinctively understood her lapse on Saturday evening, but clearly, she was going to have to enlighten him, if for no other reason than it might very well happen again. But she abjectly refused to explain the situation to *Captain* Aldridge while wearing her scratchy British khaki FANY uniform. Talk about ratcheting up the awkward.

"When we get a moment—somewhere private and less official—I will explain my own wayward ways, but right now, I'm more concerned about Liz. Shall I go over it again?" She kept her eyes locked on his until he shook his head with a single sharp jerk. "I think we're squared away, then," she said briskly. "Unless you have something else?"

Eyeing her rather ferociously, he yanked the door open. With a tiny amused smile, Olive popped the candy back into her mouth and matched his step down the hall.

Major Boom was mumbling incoherently to himself, fiddling with bits and pieces tumbled over his desk, but he waved the pair of them in, distractedly shuttling the project aside.

"Back from the fray, eh, Miss Bright?" A twinkle appeared behind his round spectacles, and his lips twitched beneath a short, bristly moustache. "I honestly don't know where we'd be without the FANY. Chasing our tails, no doubt." He nodded at the chairs arranged before his desk, and while Olive perched on the edge of one, Jamie remained standing. The CO settled his gaze on Olive. "Well, you've come back to us just in time. Captain Aldridge was quite insistent that you're the girl for this job, and I daresay he's right. This particular assignment should be right in line with your skill set."

Olive's momentary pleasure in Jamie's confidence was subverted by suspicion as to what he might consider her "skill set." Likely it involved nosy, reckless behaviour. Or pigs. Her shoulders slumped.

Major Boom clasped his hands together and leaned forward, glancing at a report open on his desk. "Naturally, this is all top secret." Olive's ready "Of course, sir" prompted an approving nod. "I'll let Captain Aldridge run through the details."

Jamie propped his shoulders just to the left of Alaska on the framed map on the wall, crossed his arms over his chest, and got straight to business.

"Perhaps you've heard of the Security Service and the Secret Intelligence Service, or MI5 and MI6, respectively? Some months ago, it was decided that German intelligence was important enough to warrant its own agency, prompting the creation of MI14. Intelligence of the sort they're collecting is extremely time sensitive, and in the current climate of war, months are passing before an agent can get word back to his handlers." He glanced at Major Boom. "Months we don't have," he said grimly, "particularly with the constant threat—real or imagined—of a German invasion." He paused a moment to let this all sink in before plunging on again. "Subsection MI14(d) was born of this ongoing frustration and has been tasked with using pigeons to solicit more up-to-date information from the Resistance networks in occupied Europe."

Olive's skin instantly puckered with gooseflesh as a shiver of pride ran through her. Little by little, pigeons were making a difference.

"Operation Columba," he said levelly, "was launched in April of this year."

"Clever," Olive murmured to herself.

"What's that, Miss Bright?" Major Boom's attention had swivelled instantly.

"Columba is the genus name for the common pigeon, so it's effectively been termed Operation Pigeon."

"Yes, I thought that might appeal to you," he said rather smugly. "They are, after all, the lynchpin of the entire operation. Carry on, Aldridge. Get to the meat of it."

"The pigeons," Jamie went on, as if there'd been no interruption, "are dropped individually by parachute, each with a questionnaire attached, requesting details on local troop movements, military installations, arms depots, and so on, as well as any information that might indicate an impending invasion." Olive took a breath, poised to ask a question, but he went on quellingly. "And before you ask, every pigeon is dropped with feed and instructions," he said with a wry twist of his lips.

Major Boom cleared his throat in preparation for taking back control of the narrative. "We understand they've had mixed results thus far. Being fully aware of these birds' potential to the war effort—in large part through the influence of Himmler himself—the Germans were quick to confiscate all pigeons in the countries they occupied." His hands lay fisted on his desk as he went on. "Columba is premised on the high-risk strategy of putting pigeons back into the hands of locals. What they decide to do with them will determine its success or failure. Some of the birds will be turned over to the Germans, and some will be killed or even eaten, poor devils. But with luck, a few will get back to us."

He paused for a moment, pulled off his glasses, and rubbed his eyes. Olive glanced at Jamie, saw that he was watching her, and looked away again.

His glasses replaced, Major Boom blinked twice. "Supplied by the NPS, MI14 is dropping pigeons from Denmark down into Southern France. As I mentioned, the response has been mixed, but they're cautiously optimistic. Particularly with the receipt of a recent message from"—he once again spared a glance at the report open before him—"a Leopold Vindictive in Belgium."

He sat back in his chair, which creaked volubly, and reached for a cup amid the detritus on his desk. Peering into it, he sniffed, then took a tentative sip, seeming to be tolerably accepting of the state of its contents. "The particulars haven't been shared, but suffice it to say, someone has managed to cram entire pages of apparently actionable intelligence onto two sheets of rice paper approximately three inches square. It could be the Germans—the blighters—trying to beat us at our own game, but we all want to believe it's legitimate, and that there's plenty more where that came from. Information, that is. Which is where the pair of you come in," he said brightly.

He settled back in his chair before bolting upright again to rummage about in the drawers of his desk. With an exclamation of delight, he produced a nearly empty packet of digestives, which he offered to the pair of them. As one, they declined. Undeterred, he selected one for himself, then crunched into it with gusto.

Distracted, Olive felt a twinge of worry grip her insides. Certainly, she understood the potential inherent in dropping vast numbers of pigeons on a fact-finding mission throughout occupied Europe, but she also knew it was likely that the majority of them would never make it home. That was arguably a risk worth taking, but her small loft population would be quickly depleted by this arrangement, and what then? She was suddenly aware that Jamie had started speaking again.

"As we have limited pigeons at our disposal, we're proceeding with a targeted approach. There is a group of Belgians among our latest recruits, midway through their training, who will shortly be reinserted to liaise with members of the Resistance and put their newfound skills of sabotage and subversion to work. With any luck, they'll manage to identify Leopold Vindictive, as well—the man's asked for more pigeons, and we are keen to supply them. Going forward, the birds will be dropped in agent-identified areas, which should prove much more timely and efficient than MI14(d)'s approach."

Olive's thoughts were in a whirl, but Jamie wasn't finished yet.

"Our hope is that, with the help of your pigeons, our agents and their network will pass on the sort of detailed intelligence that will allow us to better tailor our strategy and future supply drops. Maps and drawings defy the simplicity of Morse code but are bloody useful for the work we're doing." Jamie trained his expectant gaze on her.

"Operation Conjugal," Major Boom said portentously, if somewhat ridiculously.

Swivelling to look at him, Olive was certain she'd misheard, but she refused to glance in Jamie's direction as Major Boom went on.

"Captain Aldridge will coordinate on our end, and you'll report to him." He reached for his cup and took another swig of its contents.

Report to Jamie for Operation Conjugal? Good Lord. She said a quick prayer that her cheeks would resist pinking for the duration of the discussion and spoke up.

"Do I have other responsibilities in this operation, beyond supplying the pigeons, sir?"

"Quite," he said shortly. "Our intention is that communications with the agents in the field will be twofold—both pigeon and wireless transmitter. The transmissions will go through the Secret Intelligence Service, but they've agreed to send us copies of the transcripts, once decoded. Along with Captain Aldridge, you're to monitor those transcripts—and, of course, any messages carried back by the pigeons—track the whereabouts of the agents, and organise further drops of birds or supplies, as required. Particularly explosives." The last was added with a wink and followed by another sip from his cup.

Olive sat up straighter in her seat, thrilled to have been entrusted with such a task. "Yes, sir."

"Make an effort to get to know the chaps before they're off to Beaulieu for the remainder of their training," he suggested. "Better all round if there's a connection. Right, then," Major Boom said, setting his cup teetering down on a cluster of ball bearings, which began rolling in all directions and then shortly pinging off the floor. He stood up, ignoring the lot of them. "Once more unto the breach, eh, Miss Bright?"

Jamie pushed himself off the wall, and Olive rose, straightened her tunic, and smiled. "I look forward to it, sir." Secretly, she wondered if "Tupper" Aldridge had any insights into the naming of the operation. She fully intended to find out.

* * *

Olive zipped into Pipley on the Welbike she still had on loan from Station XVII. It had been proffered when her bicycle had been mangled in awkward circumstances, and quite simply, she'd never given it back. She adored the freedom it provided—and the exhilarating rush of speed. She would have liked to head home directly, but she'd promised Harriet she'd pop in at the library. The doctor had advised her stepmother to keep to her bed for a few days, to ensure the bones set properly, and already Harriet was going stir-crazy, her little phalanx of cigarettes dwindling, despite Dr Harrington's urgings to give them up.

After propping the motorbike out front, Olive pushed open the door to the library and slipped inside, marvelling at how easily the day's little irritations fell away amidst the velvet quiet of this cosy little corner of the village hall. Miss Swan, glancing up from her work behind the desk, offered a polite smile before instantly returning her concentration to what was in front of her. Olive turned and realised she wasn't the library's only visitor.

A man, who hadn't turned at the sound of the door, was perusing the bookcases on the far wall. He was tall and slim; his clothes—dark trousers and beige cashmere jumper, with the flash of a crisp white shirt collar circling his neck—were well tailored; and his hair was trimmed and neat. She didn't recognise him from this angle, and her curiosity had her casually moving closer, hoping he'd glance in her direction. Perhaps he was a newcomer to the village; perhaps her wish on the evening of Margaret's wedding had lured him here. Tucking back the smile conjured by this patent absurdity, she sidled even closer. After various sounds and movements didn't garner any attention, she tried another tactic.

"Hello?"

He turned abruptly, his brow above the black rims of his rounded spectacles distractedly furrowed. But as he focused his dark eyes on Olive, his lips curved into a shy smile.

Not a stranger, after all. He was, rather ironically, an instructor at Brickendonbury. It was no wonder she hadn't placed him. For the most part, the occupants of Station XVII were expected to keep to the manor house and steer clear of the village. She was the exception. And yet here he was.

She sighed over the loss, however much imagined, of a new man in the village, and her lips curved in response. "Oh, it's you, Lieutenant Beckett. Found anything promising?"

"Jules Verne," he said sheepishly, holding up a copy of *Twenty Thousand Leagues Under the Sea*. His face, narrow and rather pale, had clear-cut, handsome features, and she wondered suddenly how he might look without his glasses. He reminded her of a schoolboy, and his book selection seemed to encourage that impression.

"I'm more of a mystery buff myself," she admitted, "and I've developed rather a penchant for Agatha Christie. Her Poirot mysteries in particular." She nodded toward a shelf behind his shoulder, her eye instantly caught. "Ooh, this one's new," she said, reaching past him to retrieve it as she reread the title: *Five Little Pigs*.

Lieutenant Beckett was staring down at her. "I never could see the appeal. Everyone's a suspect with a dastardly secret, and at least one of them, a murderer."

"Everyone has secrets, Lieutenant Beckett," she said, her tone almost flirtatious. "As the saying goes, murder will out."

"Unfortunately, I'm afraid that's all too true," he admitted, gazing down at the book in his hands, his countenance grim. "I suppose I prefer my view of the world shaded by rose-coloured glasses."

Olive considered. He did seem the sort for ivory towers; he was probably a fan of King Arthur. Wanting to draw him out a bit, she asked, "Do you suppose my stepmother would enjoy Jules Verne?"

An eager grin rounded his cheeks and otherwise slightly pointed chin. "Absolutely. Particularly if she fancies herself an armchair adventuress."

"That's perfect," Olive said decisively, selecting from the novels on offer. After glancing over to confirm that Miss Swan was entirely distracted, she leaned closer and murmured, "I'm afraid I don't know what it is you teach at Brickendonbury."

"Machinery," he murmured conspiratorially. "The ins and outs, the weakest spots, the keys to effective demolition. And I understand you're our pigeoneer." Olive nodded, and he went on. "I've always been a little fascinated by pigeons and their unaccountable homing abilities."

"So you're not averse to all mysteries, then." Her smile hitched up, and he answered with one of his own.

"Touché, Miss Bright." He smiled. "I should be getting back, lest I be accused of consorting with the locals," he added with an amused smile.

Olive stared after him as he approached Miss Swan, who, with only a low murmur, managed to lure a chuckle out of him as she busied herself with library cards and rubber stamps. Olive quickly turned back to the shelves to choose another book for Harriet, then set the newest Poirot mystery on the top of her stack and carried the lot to the desk. Miss Swan didn't even bother murmuring, merely packed her on her way.

She was tucking the books into the basket strapped to the handles of the motorbike when she realised she should probably check in on her porcine charges.

One of countless schemes undertaken by the Pipley Women's Institute, the village pig club was unique in the sense that no one had clamoured to take on the running of it. Naturally, Harriet had volunteered Olive for the task, using the argument that her years of experience assisting her father in his veterinary surgery—not to mention her abbreviated stint at the Royal Veterinary College in London on the cusp of the war—made her the most experienced candidate for the messy job of raising healthy pigs to supplement the village rations. At the time she'd had few other responsibilities, whereas now she was nearly run off her feet.

A pen had been set up behind Forrester's Garage, and as Olive propped the motorbike against the fence railing, Finn trotted over, the black ring round his little piggy eye making him look like a character from a storybook, and in need of a top hat. He pushed his questing snout through an opening to sniff at Olive's skirt.

"I've nothing for you today, my good man, but I'll send Jonathon over with some odds and ends." This suggestion was met, Olive could only assume, by a grunt of approval before the pig trotted off to root about in the mud. Like his two sisters, Swilly and Eske, he'd been named by Jamie for rivers in County Donegal, Ireland, and Olive had developed quite a fondness for these easygoing, mildly affectionate beasts. After so many of the village children had taken a hand in petting and feeding them, she wouldn't be the only one saddened when it came time for butchering. With any luck, they'd have brand-new piglets to fawn over before that day came. As she gazed fondly at their corkscrew tails, peppery black spots, and whiskery noses, she couldn't help but wonder if Jamie might name those, too. How many rivers could he pull from his memories of home?

The creak of a cart rounding the corner drew her from her reverie, even as the three pigs trotted toward the commotion. Or perhaps it was the smell that drew them. Jonathon had dumped the contents of the village collection bin into his trek cart for delivery to the trough. His willingness to take on that odorous task had earned him Olive's appreciation and the undying adoration of the pigs.

"Our hero," Olive cheered, smiling at the tousle-haired boy. With his father away fighting in North Africa and his mother, a school chum of Harriet's, self-admitted to a sanatorium in Scotland, he'd been sent along to Pipley for the duration. The whole village adored him, and she didn't even want to think of his leaving one day. "How's Harriet?" she asked.

He looked pained as he let the cart roll to a stop behind him. "She's been trying to teach me to play bridge."

"Golly," Olive said, her face contorting into a grimace. Harriet despaired of her stepdaughter's dismal bridge skills, but Olive was too apathetic to improve. "You need an excuse," she urged.

"Already got one," he said coyly. "I'm building her a wheel-chair."

Olive's eyes widened. "*Are* you?" After a beat, she added, "That's rather ambitious—not that I don't have absolute confidence in your abilities, mind you."

Jonathon grinned. "Don't worry. I've lined up some help."

And with that mysterious statement, he slipped past her and round to the gate, his attention now reserved solely for the pigs. He was crooning something unintelligible when she wheeled the motorbike toward home.

Chapter 3

"What sort of things were taken when the shed was burgled?" Olive asked, trying for an offhand manner. She'd been summoned to Jamie's office, or rather the office of Captain Aldridge—it was frustrating to be always trying to switch between the two, one for work, one for play, so to speak.

"What?"

She was fiddling with the carefully arranged items on his desk while he pinned an enormous map of Belgium and Northern France onto the wall beside the door. He turned to look at her, frowned, and shifted his pencil cup out of reach before once again focusing on the map.

"After Major Boom's outburst at lunch yesterday, Liz mentioned that some things had been taken, and I understand the officers are on edge. Naturally, I'm curious as to what went missing."

"Naturally," he said dryly. After a moment he added, "It appears it was only a few smaller explosive devices."

"Have any suspects been identified?" she asked, glancing distractedly out the window.

Jamie turned and pinned her with his gaze. "You're not authorised to look into it, Olive. You have other responsibilities."

"I am perfectly capable—"

"And as your commanding officer," he said, his voice ringing with an edge of steel, "*I* am perfectly capable of reassigning you to the laundry. It's been quite muddy lately with all the rain."

"Yes, sir," Olive answered, the words bitten off. When he turned away, she couldn't resist sticking out her tongue.

"But don't worry," he said, pivoting quickly enough to catch her in the show of insubordination. He ignored it. "The matter is under investigation. And Major Boom has authorised a patrol rota to keep watch on the buildings round the grounds, with the order to ambush any intruders. So don't get any ideas."

"Very funny," Olive said, as he smoothed his hands over the map and meticulously shifted the thumbtacks until it was just so.

Jamie glanced at his watch. "They've a scheduled visit to an engineering plant this afternoon, so I've arranged for us to meet with the Belgians before that, in ten minutes' time." He looked over at her. "Giving the two of us time for a quick chat of our own." Crossing his arms, he propped himself on the edge of his desk.

Olive crossed her arms for good measure.

"How many pigeons are you managing right now?"

"Thirty-seven," she answered promptly. "But fewer than twenty are ready to fly the sort of distances you're expecting. The others are newly hatched or first- or second-year birds. They're not yet fully trained."

"How long?"

She sighed, having known ever since the day he'd stepped into her dovecote that she'd be pressed into compromise. "We don't typically let them fly farther than a hundred miles their first year, three hundred their second. After their third year of training, they are expected to go five hundred miles."

Jamie glanced at the map, a coloured scatterplot of Belgium's towns and cities, all linked by rivers and roads. She knew he was doing the math, trying to understand what would be necessary and girding himself to lay out the expectations.

She could have saved him the trouble, but she didn't.

Without turning, he said, "It may be necessary to shortcut your training regimen." He shifted slightly, slid his gaze in her direction. "And if you can encourage them all to think of England, we're going to need to increase their numbers a bit."

She smirked. "You may joke, but the process is a bit more nuanced than you imagine. The trick will be in knowing their limits and trying to manage the timing. Breeding interferes with flight training and will limit the number of viable birds for official missions."

"I'll just leave it to you, shall I?"

"As the man in charge of Operation Conjugal, I would have thought you'd want to be more involved," she countered.

He met her eyes. "There is that," he said, a twist of amusement marking his demeanour.

"I do want to be clear," Olive said, quite seriously. "You took a chance on me and the Bright loft because of our racing reputation, which was upheld by a particular standard of training. I'll do the best I can, but in these modified conditions, I can't promise the same level of performance."

"Olive, we trust you to do the best you can with the constraints you're given," he said, then cleared his throat to move on to other concerns. A curl of pride snaked warmly into her belly.

"We'll plan to send three birds on the initial flight out." Seeing Olive's nod of understanding, he swept on. "The next full moon is on fifth September—two and a half weeks from now. Conjugal will go then."

Olive nodded. "Once I've selected the birds, I'll arrange a few final training flights. It'll mean shirking a few responsibilities," she warned. "And some long days. The birds don't prefer to fly at night, but I've started to incorporate that requirement into their training."

"Good." He nodded. Then, extending his foot, he nudged the waste bin in line with the edge of his desk. "But even better, there'll be no time to spend on amateur detecting." He swung the door open rather jauntily. "Now we'd better get a move on."

The moment he was beyond the doorframe, Olive's foot shot out a tad too forcefully and sent the bin careening into a cardboard box before it toppled onto its side on the floor. Wincing, she darted out of the room, pulling the door closed behind her.

She quickly caught up to Jamie, and moments later, they slipped from the somewhat stuffy halls of the manor into the last lashings of summer sunshine. Olive shielded her eyes as they strode along the portico that ran the length of the rear of the house. Three men were standing, smoking, in the shade of the towering cedar just beyond it.

They turned as one as she and Jamie approached, and all of them gazed curiously at her. They looked simultaneously weary and poised for action. Their clothes were worn and wrinkled; their forearms, exposed beneath rolled-back sleeves, were scratched and bruised; and their fingernails, raw edged and blackened. Their eyes looked smudged and wary, but as Aldridge introduced her as their pigeoneer, every face split into a smile.

Before he could introduce them in turn, the tallest among them, a lanky, wavy-haired fellow with a pale scattering of freckles below his hazel eyes, spoke up.

"You're to supply the birds we will take back to Belgium?" he asked, his English overlaid with French flair.

"That's right," Olive said, prepared to argue her credentials if necessary.

"You have a big loft, Miss Bright?" asked the dark-haired fellow with the thin moustache and broad shoulders.

"Not very big—fewer than forty birds—but there's a bit of Belgian blood mixed in among them."

Eyebrows went up all round, at least among the agents. Jamie, standing off to one side, appeared amused by the exchange.

"Is true?" said Freckles expectantly.

Olive nodded. "My father visited Antwerp many years ago and returned with a champion racer, which has sired its share of prizewinning birds."

This prompted some delighted backslapping, and now the

third man stepped forward, extending his hand. "For now at least," he said wryly, "my name is Rémi." With a quirk of his lips, he gestured to the men beside him, first to Freckles, then Moustache. "That is Renauld, and this one, we call Weasel. When you get to know him, you will understand. He will be our operator."

Despite the latter's code name, Olive couldn't help but feel a sudden surge of admiration for the man. He would be the one entrusted with the transmitter, the one tasked with communicating the operation's progress and requirements. It was estimated that operators in occupied territory had an average life expectancy of two months. A chill came over her as Rémi went on.

"Before the war, we—each of us—raised pigeons to race. In Belgium this is very common, and lofts are passed from father to son." His head canted accommodatingly. "There is occasionally a daughter." His lips did not hold their curve as his jaw tightened, and the fingertips that held his cigarette turned white. "But when the Boche invaded, they cleared the lofts." He shook his head, emotion glossing his eyes. "All those birds, years of work, of companionship, destroyed." He took a calming breath. "But now your birds will come back with us, will be our allies in this fight. And one day soon, the pigeons will come back to Belgium."

This eloquent little speech thoroughly reassured Olive that training pigeons for the war effort, while seemingly insubstantial, was truly making a difference, not only for Britain, but also for all those unfortunate souls who were desperate for a little hope. A little link to the free world. Her chest tightened for just a moment, and as she took a breath, her eyes shifted to Jamie, and she had the uncanny feeling that he knew exactly what she was thinking.

Tugging on the hem of her tunic, she addressed Rémi. "I've yet to choose the birds that will accompany you—and there is still some training to do to prepare them. With racing postponed, petrol rationed, and every effort for the war underlined with urgency, they've got a bit softer than I would like." She smiled. "But don't worry. You couldn't have better birds with you on this mission."

Smiles broke out; then Weasel looked sly. "Perhaps you will choose a bird that is part Belgian."

"Perhaps," she allowed. She hadn't committed the pedigree of each bird to memory, but her father kept careful charts and documentation in his study. "But only if it is among the best candidates."

"Naturally," he conceded with a shrug. "But, of course, being Belgian, this is certain." This prompted wide smiles and a few hearty backslaps among the men.

Olive couldn't help but like them. Their undimmed patriotism and grim determination brought home the reality of what they were trying to accomplish so far from home, at a grand manor house tucked away in the centre of England.

For the better part of an hour, they pressed her, each in turn, about her birds. Within the first few minutes, Rémi began to pace, puffing on his cigarette with a fidgety intensity. As a concession to him, they embarked as a group on a leisurely stroll, gravitating toward the moat running along the back of the house, separated by a stretch of lawn. Jamie, Olive noted, followed along behind them, seemingly uninterested in the discussion, but his eyes were sharp, and she knew he missed nothing. It seemed the trio of Belgians wanted nothing more than to reconnect with the world of pigeon fancying, and they peppered her with questions on her breeding strategies, training methods, and her loft's racing credentials.

"All this you do on your own?" Renauld asked, then compressed his lips consideringly.

"It's technically my father's loft," Olive admitted, "but his work has kept him busy, and over the years, I took on more and more of the responsibilities." She paused to draw a deep breath. "And now," she continued, glancing at Jamie, "I do it all on my own. In secret." The last words felt raw and final. She thought of Jonathon then, unspeakably relieved to have him as a partner in crime.

Knowing glances were exchanged and heads bobbed in understanding as they stood beside the mirrored surface of the moat, its edges crowded with grasses and pale water lilies, the air dotted with damselflies.

Jamie cleared his throat, pulling their attention round to where he was leaning casually against a nearby tree, pointedly checking his watch. "You'd best get back, gentlemen. It's nearly time for your field trip."

Cigarettes were tossed to the ground and crushed into the grass, and the agents each stepped forward in turn to shake her hand and bestow a smile of true camaraderie.

"You need have no worry," Rémi said. "We will take good care of your birds. It will be our pleasure." This simple promise nearly brought tears to Olive's eyes as he went on. "And with any luck, they will take care of us." She squeezed his hand before, with a final nod, he turned away.

Weasel stepped forward. "After the war, when we have had time to rebuild our lofts, perhaps you will come to Belgium."

"That day cannot come soon enough," she told him earnestly.

Finally, it was Renauld's turn. He had a greasy-looking stain running along the length of one shirtsleeve. "We will see you again before we depart? You will bring the pigeons?"

"Yes," she assured him, smiling. "I'll be there." She looked up, fairly daring Jamie to countermand that statement, but he merely inclined his head in acknowledgement.

"Good. Then you can tell us their names," Renauld said before lifting her hand to his lips. "We are partners in this."

Olive was quite sure she must be blushing ferociously, but she took the gesture to heart. All her efforts in breeding and training her birds increased the Belgians' chances of undermining the Nazi war machine. Any message they carried home could be pivotal. These agents had placed their trust in her, and she was determined not to let them down.

Au revoirs were exchanged, hands lifted, and then they were hurrying back across the lawn, and she was left with Jamie.

"Why don't you take the rest of the afternoon for pigeon business?" he said as they trailed the agents slowly back across the lawn.

Olive nodded. "Once I've chosen the birds, Jonathon will help me get them ready. But I do need a bit of time to consider the best breeding strategy going forward."

"Of course," he said, somewhat brusquely. "I'd appreciate an update when you have it." He was being extraordinarily upright and correct, no doubt hoping she wouldn't choose this moment to chat about kissing. Poor man—he could avoid it only for so long.

As they parted ways, Olive resolved to find a way to get Jameson Aldridge to loosen up a bit. If nothing else, she would resort to whiskey—her dad had a forgotten bottle stashed in the surgery. It was entirely possible the result would be more interesting than the kiss, which, admittedly, hadn't been too shabby.

Having gathered her things, Olive was shortly back outside, climbing aboard the Welbike, when she caught sight of Lieutenant Beckett standing smoking under the porte-cochère, arguing with a wildly gesticulating Tomás Harris. Lieutenant Beckett had pulled a piece of cloth from his pocket and was running it distractedly through his fingers as he listened, unperturbed, to the cook's tirade. Her brow furrowed as she slipped on her helmet and tried not to stare. Despite the differences in personality, each man was easygoing and charming in his own way, and she couldn't imagine what might have prompted the disagreement, particularly as only a sporadic word or two carried to her ears.

Impossible . . . Can't be helped . . . Merde alors . . .

The latter, she'd quickly learned, was something of a battle cry for Station XVII. It translated as *shit then*, and Olive had had cause to adopt it on more than one occasion since finding herself in league with Baker Street.

As the motorbike engine roared to life, neither man glanced in her direction. Not surprising, given the deafening sounds that emanated from the Brickendonbury grounds on a daily basis. But just past them, coming up the drive, no doubt just back from an inventory of one of the sheds, Kate and Marie lifted their hands in a wave, which Olive jauntily returned. The men were still at it as she drove off down the drive, the wheels spitting gravel behind her.

Olive found Jonathon huddled in the shade of her father's surgery, a converted stable, where he occasionally worked on smaller animals. More often he was called out to area farms to minister to working animals, which made Olive's deception a little easier. The thirteen-year-old was dismantling what appeared to be a sodden pram, already surrounded by an organised array of bits and pieces.

"How goes the work?" she asked, unbuttoning her tunic. The air was hot and still, and Olive was desperate to shed the layer of serge.

Jonathon's head came up, and he flashed her a cheeky grin. "Better than expected. Tommy took his baby brother for a walk." He shrugged, leaving Olive to fill in the blanks.

Olive looked down at the mangled remains, suddenly worried. Tommy Prince was a bit of a daredevil, up for all manner of hijinks. "Is his brother all right?"

Jonathon nodded absently. "Tommy set him down in a patch of wildflowers before he gave the pram a mighty push and raced it down the hill." Jonathon glanced up at her. "He'd wanted to stage a daring rescue, but he tripped, and the pram made it to the river first and went sailing in." He shrugged.

She winced. "Oh, Tommy."

"Bad for Tommy, but good for me. Mrs Prince offered me the

wreckage, and it's perfect! I'm going to use the wheels and the metal supports for Harriet's chair."

"That's wonderful, Jonathon. She's going to be thrilled." That remained to be seen and would be entirely dependent on Harriet's state of mind during her recuperation. Olive wasn't entirely sure how her stepmother would feel about the restrictions inherent in a wheelchair. Then again, she may have no other choice.

She watched him for a moment as he continued tinkering, and then, glancing round to ensure no one might be eavesdropping, she said quietly, "We have a new mission to prepare for."

His head whipped up, his eyes rounding, and he scrambled up, his project momentarily forgotten. He moved closer and lowered his voice. "The autumn term doesn't start for a while yet, and this wheelchair won't take much longer. I want to help."

"I was counting on it." Smiling, she brushed the hair back from his forehead. "I'm going in to change, and then to the loft. Meet you in there?"

He gave her a mock salute and turned back to his project while she walked to the house.

In a matter of minutes, she was back outside in a cool, summery frock, sinking her teeth into a plum she'd plucked from the tree in the corner of the garden. She had peeked in on Harriet, who was cursing roundly, knitting a pair of socks with violent determination, and had thought it best to leave her be. Jonathon was waiting for her. He had unlocked the door to the dovecote and was standing guard against possible feline intruders.

After nudging him in before her and pulling the door mostly closed behind them, Olive bent to retrieve a broad-brimmed hat she kept stored in the bench seat on the near wall. She'd rarely been hit by droppings, but there was no sense in tempting fate. As usual, Jonathon decided to take his chances.

The dovecote was a divided space, with separate areas for the hens and cocks and, in breeding season, caged areas for the mated pairs. On her longer visits, Olive preferred to let them all mingle, but lately, she'd thought it best to manage their interactions. Now she crossed to the hen party, as she'd taken to calling it, unlatched the gate, and opened it wide. Little by little, the ladies would filter out from their nesting boxes to socialise, while she kept a close eye on the bachelors.

After filling the pans of water from a gardening can, Olive settled herself on the bench and ranged her eyes over the bustling little community before her. Jonathon sat quietly beside her, doing the same. Such was their ritual before getting down to business, whatever it might be. Amid the cooing and fluttering, strutting and preening, she tried to collect her thoughts and sort through everything she must do in the coming weeks. For the most part, her breeding pairs had produced strong, healthy birds who had taken to training and had thus far proved themselves over ever-growing distances. Now that her training regimen was effectively compromised, she would need to trust that further offspring from the mated pairs would perform similarly. Trying to experiment, mixing sires and dams, at this stage could prove disappointing—even disastrous. Besides, whenever possible, she much preferred to encourage a bird's devotion to a single mate.

That decision made things a bit easier, and she puffed out a quick sigh of relief as she thought ahead to the next round of breeding. There were younger birds and bachelors that needed pairing, and the birds' diet would need to be adjusted. The hens would need more grit to produce strong eggshells, and all the birds would benefit from extra vitamins and minerals, if she could get her hands on them. The difficulty was that the breeding process narrowed the field a bit, in terms of mission-ready pigeons. In the near term, Conjugal was going to be a bit short-staffed.

"What's so funny?" Jonathon said quizzically, jarring her out of her thoughts.

"Irony," she told him, smothering her amusement. She forestalled an explanation by launching into a quick summary of both

Columba and their participation in Conjugal. Jonathon was, as ever, committed to helping in any way possible.

"I met the Belgian agents," she told him, watching as Fritz, a blue-chequered cock and veteran of an earlier Baker Street mission, stepped into the pan of water, then showered droplets into the air as he dipped his breast in and shimmied through his bath. "They made a request." Olive turned to look at Jonathon, her hat brim drooping slightly. "They'd like at least one bird of Belgian descent to be included in the group. If possible."

Jonathon shifted his eyes away from her and let them dart round the dovecote, looking carefully at the pigeons perched up high and clustered down below, as if a few of their number might have hoisted that country's flag. "Do we have any of those?" he asked sceptically.

"We do," she said smartly. She'd taken a quick look through the breeding charts in the few moments she'd been inside. Pushing herself to a standing position, she tucked her hands in her pockets. "Robin Hood, for one," she said, moving toward the array of nesting boxes on the cock side, "was sired by a Belgian racer." His colouring was marvellous—a true blue bar, deep grey, with a throat of green iridescence shifting into a regal purple. His carriage was aristocratic, but he was a scrappy bird with plenty of personality. As she watched him strut about in his cubby, eyeing her curiously, Jonathon came up behind her.

"Do you think he'll do?"

"He did have that run-in with Pandora, but that was several months ago," she said, reaching for him, "and Dad has been quite happy with his recovery." She examined each wing in turn, looking for missing feathers, then shifted her hold and made as if to toss him into the air. Taking his cue, the bird extended its wings and beat them in powerful strokes as Olive watched assessingly. No sign of the injury inflicted by their most devious barn cat.

The activity round them suddenly increased, the pigeons flying to higher perches, strutting purposefully, and audibly expressing their outrage. Robin's wing strokes increased, becoming slightly frenzied, and Olive let him go.

"Speak of the little devil," Jonathon said, eyeing the door to the dovecote. Pandora had nudged it open and now scanned the enclosed space, deciding how best to proceed. She lived up to her namesake on a near-daily basis, but Olive forgave her everything whenever she deigned to cross Jamie's path. Watching him squirm had quickly become one of her favourite things.

"Out," Olive shooed. "We're working and don't have time for you."

Jonathon hurried over, spooking the feline into a quick departure, and pushed the door shut firmly behind her.

Olive searched the space for Robin, who was now perched strategically beyond her reach. "He's traditionally moulted late in season, after mating for a second time. With only one round of brooding so far this year and all feathers apparently intact, he's a fine choice." Olive spotted his mate, peering from the shadows of her box. "He and Queenie can celebrate when he comes home." If *he does*. She didn't utter the words, but they resonated through the dovecote, nonetheless. As she glanced among the birds, looking into one eye after another, it seemed as if they were all thinking it.

"What about Queenie, then?"

Olive considered the trim white bird. Jonathon had a point: her breeding was to be postponed, and she didn't appear to be moulting. But there were other considerations.

"I'm not sure I want to send a breeding pair out together. The psychological aspects might be detrimental. After single-mindedly racing home to reunite with its mate, how will the first-released bird react when the other isn't here?" She shook her head. "I wouldn't want to subject him or her to such a worrying situation."

Jonathon nodded, then bit his lip, considering. She suspected he wanted to be part of the selection process and decided to let him take the lead.

Cautious of the birds busy on the floor, he stepped slowly, his gaze pensive as he peered closely at each pigeon, weighing its suitability for the mission. His lips were moving, but he kept his thoughts to himself. Determined not to interrupt him, she took a broom from its hook by the door and began slowly sweeping up the debris littering the floor. Thankfully, the white-brown droppings all looked healthy, but judging by the feathers strewn about, a few of the birds were beginning their moult. She'd need to keep a close eye on the ones chosen for the mission and be prepared to substitute as necessary in the coming days. Missing feathers could significantly hamper a bird's flying ability over such distances, and this wasn't the time to be taking risks.

A moment later Jonathon stopped, his head canted as he looked up to where Aramis was perched, almost regally, on the ladder. Jonathon turned, caught her eye, and lifted his eyebrows. "He's proved himself once already," he reminded her.

It was true. Aramis had been dropped into France in May as part of her first mission as a pigeoneer. Relatively unproven over long distances, he had acquitted himself wonderfully, and Olive had kept him in practice as much as possible over the summer months.

Olive nodded once and smiled. "I'll need to examine him to say for sure, but if he looks good, then we'll give him another shot at it."

Jonathon flashed his teeth in a wide grin. "Just one more, then."

"Don't forget the spare," she said. "Just in case anything unexpected occurs—any health or training issues, any run-ins with the barn cats or other poachers," she added wryly.

"Are the hens all recovered from the last round of brooding?"

"I should think so," she said thoughtfully. "It's been well over a month since the squabs hatched, and they've been able to feed themselves for a little while, so the hens should be much back to normal. Then again, perhaps we should choose an untried younger bird. It seems that's the way we're headed." Her shoulders dropped, but she briskly carried on. "There's Alice. She's not yet three." Scanning the loft, she found the bird in question beside one of the dishes of feed. Her unique colouring triggered Olive's memory, and she said rather excitedly, "Now that I think of it, she's part Antwerp Smerle, which makes her a bit Belgian, as well."

Her father had been as enamoured with variety as he'd been with winning. He had traded birds regularly, across the country and beyond, and had been careful to avoid inbreeding. She'd done her best to improve on his efforts in the years since she'd taken over, but it couldn't hurt to look more carefully through the lineage charts. Now that she'd been tasked with expanding the loft, her strategies might need updating.

As Olive and Jonathon stepped closer, the hen inched away from them, round the edge of the dish, clearly wanting to be left to her supper.

Other than her toffee-coloured wing shields, Alice was precisely the shade of clotted cream, and her petite size and trim little beak put Olive in mind of a tony lady wrapped in a fur stole. She just needed a tiny strand of pearls.

"She's clocked some stellar times over long distances," she said consideringly, staring down at the bird in question and thinking hard. "I suppose it's time to test her mettle," she added, glancing at Jonathon.

His face shone with the pride of having contributed. Bestowing a cheeky wink, she said, "Now for the fourth musketeer." But before either of them could make a suggestion, a telltale jingle sounded on the drive. As one, they hurried out of the dovecote as the postman coasted up on his bicycle, his finger poised on the bell affixed to its handlebars.

"Hello, Miss Bright," he called. His nose was crooked—had likely been broken at some time or other—and seeing it, smack in the middle of two dark, friendly eyes, beneath a perfectly coiffed head of hair, always made her smile.

"Good afternoon, Henry," she said politely, clasping her hands in front of her.

He came to a stop before her, slipped his hand into his mailbag, pulled out a small stack of letters and, upon confirming the address one final time, handed it over, a twinkle in his eye. "It's a good mail day, I think."

Olive's brows went up, and she wondered, with a little quiver in her stomach, if there was a letter from George. But when she glanced down at the little stack, the quiver turned into a full-fledged plunge. There was a letter from her brother, Lewis.

Lewis had been stationed in Greece as a British liaison officer nearly since the start of the war, and they hadn't had a letter from him since February. She wanted to tear into it—to know where he was, what he was doing, and when he was coming home. Her palms itched with it. But the letter was addressed to her father, so the situation demanded restraint.

She looked up and beamed at Henry, then impulsively stepped forward to bestow a kiss on his sunburned cheek. "It's perfect," she assured him. "Thank you." His face got even pinker as he turned the cycle and coasted back down the drive, ringing his bell in salute.

"Is there one from George?" Jonathon asked, coming closer to peer at the letters clutched in her hand.

Olive was poised to correct him, but at that very moment, as she was shuffling through the rest of the envelopes, she found, to her great delight, that there was also a letter from George.

"Hot damn, but there's one from him, too!" she said excitedly.

"I suppose we have London to thank for your colourful vocabulary," growled her father, who appeared from the shadowed doorway of his surgery, wiping his hands on a raggedy towel. But there was amusement lurking in his eyes. Kíli, his black-and-white Welsh corgi, trotted along at his heels.

Eager to have him open her brother's letter, she blurted,

"There's a letter from Lewis," Hurrying toward him, her arm out-stretched, she added, "It's addressed to you, so I couldn't open it."

"Well, hot damn," her father shouted, dropping the towel so he could reach for the letter. "I rather prefer these Airgraphs. If the censors are going to nose into everything, there's no point in an envelope." He quickly unfolded the page, and Olive watched his gaze move over it like a typewriter platen under a flurry of keystrokes. She couldn't help but fidget, and Jonathon, unsure what to do, stood close beside her.

Finished reading, her father grunted in a manner she couldn't interpret.

"Dad," Olive said sharply. "What does he say?"

"Oh, yes. Sorry, my girl. Better to read it for yourself," he said, thrusting the page toward her. "Suffice it to say, all is well," he added in an aside to Jonathon.

As she snatched the paper and held it open against the gentle breeze, her father started dancing a little jig.

Delphi, 22 July 1941

Dear Dad,

I suppose I was lucky to have landed an assignment that al-lowed me to roam Parnassus and its environs for the past twelve months. Certainly, I've born witness to the harsh, ugly bits of this rough country, but the people and the air—and the lingering magic of the gods—have all been a daily reprieve. But it seems it's time to move on. The Germans have got too close for comfort, and we're pitifully outmanned and outgunned. For now at least, they're pulling us out. I'll soon be shaking the Hellenic dust from my feet to give the North African sand its fair turn.

I confess I long for summer in Pipley—lounging by the river, under the cool curtain of a willow, eating my fill of wild straw-berries. I'm just so tired . . . of all of it. But it's not over, not even close, so to come home now would be fruitless and bittersweet.

*Please give my love to Harriet and, of course, the incorrigible
Olive. I hope she's found a way to bring her mettle to bear on the
war effort. Otherwise, God pity you all.*

Until we're together again,

Lewis

By the time she finished, Rupert Bright had slipped his arm
through Jonathon's and was urging the boy into a jaunty turn as
he bellowed out a pub tune in his low baritone. Kíli, naturally,
had joined in, his squat little body circling the pair of them and
occasionally launching itself into the air.

Olive smiled, her heart lightened with these simple words
from the brother she missed so much. She glanced again at the
page, at the careful penmanship and the scrawl of his signature,
and she said a quiet, open-ended prayer to whatever gods were
listening that Lewis would be spared to come home whole again.

"I'd best show that to Harriet," her father said after clearing
his throat in an effort to resume respectability. He reached for the
letter. Knowing she still had a letter from George, Olive relin-
quished it, along with the other envelopes addressed to her stepmother. Rupert Bright was humming as he walked round to the
garden, accompanied by the dog.

Despite a deep inhale, Olive couldn't help but feel breathless.
Two letters in one day. It likely meant she'd have to wait an eternity for another, but at this moment, she didn't care. Grinning at
Jonathon, she quickly opened her second letter, careful not to rip
the paper.

My dear Holmes,

*Your last letter seemed disappointingly tame, all things consid-
ered. I was glad to hear the NPS finally came calling and that
Jonathon's victory garden kept you in prizewinning veg all summer, but while Lillian Crabbleton's disastrous elopement attempt
did make good reading, none of it was up to your usual standard*

of clamjamfry—a Scottish term I just picked up from the bloke assigned as my gunner, which means "various and sundry." But I suppose with FANY training and the poor, misguided Miss Butterwick behind you by now, you'll be ready to get back to it all. I fully expect you'll ferret out a bit of intrigue in your spare time, if only for my benefit.

No excitement here—training flights go on as expected, interspersed with guard duty and the occasional classroom work. When we do get a day off, it's off to the nearest village for a dance or a drink at the pub. We do occasionally have visits from Air Transport Auxiliary girls—the ones that ferry planes between airfields—so then they'll tag along. There's one in particular who reminds me of you, except nicer, if you know what I mean. Her name is Bridget, and she's smart and clever and efficient and marvellous with the aeroplanes. In fact, she's rather marvellous all round. More on that later, as duty calls.

Your devoted,
Watson

P.S. Gillian informs me you've been going out with a handsome captain for months?! Why on earth haven't you mentioned him?

P.P.S. Please tell me you've not got him wrapped round your little finger in the hope of some high-level assignment. God help him.

Olive bit her lip and folded the letter away, tucking it into her pocket. She thought of all the things she hadn't told him, some she could never reveal and others that would be better said in person. Who knew when that might be? Would the marvellous Bridget still be in the picture then? A swell of jealousy crowded out the nostalgia as she watched Jonathon dangle a dried bulrush just beyond the reach of Psyche's outstretched paw.

Bridget had precisely the sort of life Olive had yearned for before Jamie had shown up on her doorstep. A member of an auxiliary service, she was actively contributing to the war effort, living in a dormitory with other girls, and free to engage in romantic entanglements without risk of undermining an entire operation. It also sounded as if she was taken quite seriously, rather than being viewed as a disobedient ward (Jamie) or a nosy parker (George). Well, she was just going to have to do something about this. She'd have to give it some careful thought, but right now, she had work to do.

"Coming, Jonathon? Our birds are on pins and needles, hoping for the enviable designation of musketeer four."

Chapter 4

After a gruelling half hour spent at the breakfast table, listening to Harriet propose and eliminate fundraising schemes for the Pipley WI, Olive escaped with a sausage roll and a Thermos of cold tea, a petrol ration card, and the excuse that she needed to be off on NPS business. It was only partly a lie.

While she loved the exhilaration and freedom of driving the Welbike into the countryside on the excuse of training her pigeons, she did regret her time away from Brickendonbury. Her absences kept her frustratingly on the outside of interesting developments, not to mention gossip. How was she meant to discover who'd swiped the explosive devices if she wasn't on hand to do a bit sleuthing and subtle questioning? If she were, she could have volunteered to do some inventory work—she was actually rather curious to see what was stored in those sheds. But with Conjugal only two weeks away, the pigeons were her top priority.

Olive let out a whoop that morphed into a full belly laugh at that name. She was determined to quiz Jamie about it—making him twitch was one of her life's simple pleasures. But right now, she would enjoy the anaemic morning sunshine and go as far as she dared on the motorbike. Later, she'd ask round in the village to see if anyone was going farther afield for any reason and would be willing to tote a pigeon along for the journey.

She had just set off and was buzzing down Mangrove Lane, nearly to the drive which lead onto the Brickendonbury grounds, when a flash of movement to her left jerked her attention round and brought her foot up off the throttle. Suddenly, in a scrambling rush, the willowy figure of Henrietta Gibbons appeared near the edge of the road, barred from proceeding any farther by a tangle of nettles. Her auburn hair was pulling from its plaits, and her Guide uniform was somewhat the worse for wear. She stopped abruptly fifty feet on and stood with her hands on hips, breathing roughly.

Olive puttered closer and cut the engine. The pigeons cooed and fidgeted in their wicker carrier basket. "Guide camp not all it's cracked up to be?" she teased. It was entirely possible some sort of rodent was to blame. Or the damp or . . .

Hen tipped her head to the side, as if considering this. "Not in the way I thought, but it's definitely cracking." Before Olive could cautiously inquire what this meant, the girl was rushing on. "I was coming for help and heard the motorbike. I thought it might be you."

"What do you mean, you were coming for help?" Olive peered at the gatehouse just ahead amid the trees. "Don't tell me you were coming to the manor house?" Olive remembered, in some alarm, the dire results of her own impromptu visit to Brickendonbury several months ago and felt tremendously relieved that she'd happened to cross the girl's path first. She turned back to Hen and climbed quickly off the bike. "Where's Miss Featherington? What's happened?"

"She's sitting on a log, sniffling into her handkerchief," Hen said dismissively, before relenting. "Although I suppose I shouldn't blame her," she added in a rush. "I don't think she was expecting to come across a body."

Olive was momentarily startled. She stood very still, staring intently at Hen. "A human body? Is he . . . she . . . dead?" She could feel a humming urgency building inside her and hoped she hadn't sounded eager. Guilt suddenly reared up, demanding she clarify the matter in her own mind. It was that word *body* and her bedtime reading of Agatha Christie's *Five Little Pigs*. She simply wasn't thinking straight. Likely it was a vagrant who'd stumbled in among the trees and fallen asleep.

Hen, nodding solemnly, hadn't seemed to notice anything amiss. Her green eyes were large in her pale, freckled face. "It's a man. He's got a gash on his head, so a few of us who have our first aid badges took turns taking his pulse. None of us found one—not even a thready one." She took a breath. "He doesn't live in the village, but I've seen him there once or twice. I thought he might be from the manor . . ." Her voice trailed off as she glanced across the road in the direction of Brickendonbury.

Olive had a sudden, horrible thought. "What does he look like?" she demanded.

Hen thought, and Olive's nerves were suddenly so frayed, she almost lunged to give the girl a good shake. "He's handsome—dark hair and eyes—and neat. Clean shaven, with no hair in his nose or ears, either. At least not on display. There were spectacles on the ground beside him—they probably belong to him. His jumper is soft, with no darns or patches. Probably new." She shrugged. "He looks nice . . . like he *was* nice, I mean." Her eyes had gone glossy, but there were no tears.

Olive didn't want to believe it, but she worried that she knew exactly whose body it was. "Where's your camp?" she asked. "Near the pond, I assume?" Hen nodded, and Olive said, "Get on, then. I'll take you back on the bike, and then we'll decide where to get help, all right?" Hen nodded again. With something of a scramble and a tight squeeze, they both climbed on, and Hen clung to her as she started the engine and whipped the bike round to head back toward a navigable entrance into the wood.

With barely any time to think, they'd reached the camp to discover Miss Featherington had rallied and was overseeing the task of packing up. A little circle of tents had been set up in the sunny, wide-open space of the ride nearest the pond, and the air was dotted with the honey-coloured wings of gatekeeper butterflies and the iridescent sparkle of dragonflies. The girls turned as one to watch their fellow Guide ride up on the back of the Welbike with Olive. And while she knew they all wanted to hurry forward and share their own uncertainties and squeamish worries, Miss Featherington's calm assertiveness kept them back. Olive couldn't help but be a little impressed as the woman stepped briskly toward her, straightening her uniform on the way.

"You're not cancelling Guide camp?" Hen demanded.

"Henrietta, you were meant to be summoning someone in authority." She glanced dubiously at Olive. "I'm not sure Miss Bright is really equipped to handle a, uh—" She broke off, trying for decorum or courage and finding no recourse.

"I happened to be riding by as she burst out of the trees," Olive said, smiling tightly. "And I can assure you—" She was interrupted by Hen.

"Miss Bright was on the spot for our last body and single-handedly unmasked the murderer. Although she nearly died in doing it." Hen's voice faltered on the last bit, as if she had just remembered that part and was now second-guessing her decision.

Miss Featherington looked shocked, as well she might. "Good Lord. This wasn't a murder. It was a horrible accident." After a beat, she added, "But I suppose we might as well show her. And to answer your original question, Henrietta, we'll have to see what happens. It was quite a shock, finding him like that." She glanced round her nervously and rubbed her hands over her upper arms.

"Why don't I have Hen show me the spot, and then I'll go for help myself?" Olive suggested.

Miss Featherington glanced at the trees on the far side of the ride, nodded, and rubbed the back of her hand over her brow, which was glistening with nervous perspiration, before turning back to help the girls.

Olive left the bike leaning against the muscular-looking trunk of a hornbeam but unlatched the carrier basket to cart it along with her. Given the situation, it was probably best to release the birds, but Hen had already set off at a brisk pace. Olive followed, her pulse beating heavily in her throat. She desperately hoped she was wrong.

She wasn't. Even turned on his side and minus his glasses, the man was very obviously Lieutenant Jeremy Beckett.

Now tears glossed her own eyes, and she stood staring in utter dismay at the body of the man she'd bantered with only days ago. She'd let herself imagine for a fleeting moment that she was at liberty to flirt with him, that it might lead to a mutually acceptable conclusion in the middle of this horrible war. And now he lay dead, with a smudge of dirt on his face, his eyes wide and staring, and his perfect cashmere jumper—the one that had made her fingers twitch with a wanting to touch it—looking distressingly pathetic.

"You'll need to get closer," Hen informed her, "to see the gash and the blood."

Olive looked at her, blinked, and gathered herself. A shushing sound emanated from the carrier tugging at her arm, and then a lulling coo. Olive walked a bit farther in among the trees, searching the canopy for predators. Seeing none, she unlatched the basket and lifted the birds one by one to toss them into the air. Jonathon would wonder at their appearance so much earlier than expected, but she'd explain it later, when she understood what had happened.

Just as the third one—it was Alice—left her hands, rising into the air as she navigated the criss-cross of branches, Olive saw it. A long wire hung haphazardly from a lower bough of an elm tree near at hand. Stepping closer, Olive stared up at it, frowning. She then dropped her gaze and scanned the undergrowth as Hen marched over to peer up into the tree.

"Is it a clue?" she demanded.

Olive cut her eyes round at the girl. "What *do* you mean?"

"Well," she said primly, "if he's been coshed on the head, then that makes it murder." With raised brows, she invited Olive to draw the obvious conclusions.

A line of tension formed a ridge along her shoulders, but Olive forced herself to relax. Hen was being morbid. "There's no reason to think there was anyone involved at all. It was probably a ghastly accident—a heavy branch fell on him, or he tripped and struck his head against a rock."

"Hmm," the girl said.

They trooped back to Lieutenant Beckett, and Olive crouched beside him. Feeling helpless—and knowing it had already been done by countless efficient Girl Guides—she laid her fingers against the back of his wrist. On impulse, she leaned close, so that her cheek hovered just above his mouth. But there was no pulse and no breath. Girding herself, she clasped his shoulder and pulled him forward so that she could see the wound Hen had mentioned.

His brown hair looked incongruously neat but for the matted blood running from the crown of his head to his right ear. The cut was deep and had to have been made with something sharp, under considerable force.

"Do you see anything that might have caused this?" Olive demanded, her eyes scanning the vicinity. "Don't touch it if you do," she warned as Hen began a slow scan of the undergrowth. He'd fallen in a patch of true lover's knot, and his head was cradled amid their lush green leaves and the single dark berries that topped each quatrefoil. She rummaged through the leaves, jamming her finger on a stone in her urgency. She didn't bother to suppress the oath—it was for every bit of that horrible situation.

But when she realised the finger she was cradling was stained with blood, her breath caught, and she carefully looked again.

The stone was substantial, grey, and subtly sparkling, as if shot through with mica; it had a rough, jagged edge that came to a rather wicked point, now dyed red.

"It'll turn up," she said abruptly, reburying the stone beneath the leaves before getting to her feet, urgently wanting to keep her discovery from Hen. "I suppose I'd better go for help. You, my girl, should be trying to convince Miss Featherington not to cancel the remainder of the camp. This wood is plenty big, and this business doesn't touch any of you."

Hen nodded. She was striding away when she turned back to stare at Olive. "I thought you were going for help."

With a curse, Olive realised that at times Hen reminded her of herself, and it was damned inconvenient. She had stepped away from the body, back toward the tree with its unexpected appurtenance, and was peering into fallen logs and hidey-holes.

Hen hurried back. "What are you looking for? And what *is* that?" she said, indicating the wire that was swinging softly in the breeze.

Olive looked at her consideringly, carefully keeping her stained fingers tucked into a tight fist. "If I tell you, you're not to tell anyone else. Agreed?"

"Not even Jonathon?" she countered.

"He's an exception. But just the two of you. No one else." The girl nodded solemnly, and Olive said quietly, "It appears to be an aerial for a wireless transmitter, but I've looked, and there's no transmitter. It would be similar to a vanity case, but slightly larger and flatter. Have you seen anything like that—"

Her explanation was interrupted by a gasp from Henrietta. The girl shook her head vigorously before demanding, "Do you think he was a spy?"

"I don't think anything of the sort," Olive snapped. "It could belong to anyone—a spy or someone with a perfectly good reason to be sending messages in the woods." She frowned but quickly rallied, ready to be rid of Hen and her seemingly endless questions. "I'm sure there's a good explanation." She felt compelled to clarify. "For all of it." She'd intentionally included poor Lieutenant Beckett in that assessment, but that didn't stop her from being very worried indeed.

She went to Brickendonbury in lieu of the police. The dead man was one of their number, and the powers that be could telephone for the police more quickly and easily than she could motor into Pipley. After successfully skirting the booby traps ranged along the drive with well-practiced ease, she was soon hurrying into the manor, nearly tripping over Hamish, the Scottish terrier widely considered to be the mascot of Station XVII. She dashed down the hall, caught the jamb of Jamie's office door in a firm grip, swung herself round, and skidded to a stop just as he was coming through from the other side.

Their collision was violent, and she nearly knocked the pair of them off their feet, but he caught her, staggering, and by some miracle managed to keep them both from collapsing onto the floor. It would be some time later, in the dark of her bedroom, that Olive would relive that moment, focused on the muscles Jamie was clearly hiding under a bushel, or, more specifically, tatty jumpers and his captain's uniform.

He didn't even speak . . . or curse. He simply waited for her to explain her unorthodox methods while Horace the Wrinkle dug into his chin.

"I'm sorry," she said, distractedly straightening his lapel, "but this is important." With a shuddering breath, she raised her eyes to Jamie's and said, "Lieutenant Beckett is dead."

"What?" he said harshly, his grip on her upper arms tightening further, so that she winced. Instantly, he relaxed his hold and then dropped his hands. "Start at the beginning, but leave out anything irrelevant," he said calmly. "And do it quickly."

She nodded and in a rush told him how she had been flagged down by Hen, had followed the girl into Balls Wood, and had found the body. She swallowed then, her face slack with sadness. "There's no police as yet. I figured someone here would call them after . . . that is . . ."

He nodded and made to move past her out of the room, but she reached for his arm, noting with shock that her fingers were trembling. Jamie pulled round just as she snatched them back, tucking them into fists, which she dropped stiffly to her sides.

"There's something else," she said quietly. Normally, she would have said the words defiantly, but the situation had left her fraught with worry and uncertainty and a frightening sense of helplessness.

"Tell me," he said softly, as if sensing the fragility of her emotions.

Olive slipped her hand into the pocket of her tunic and pulled out a folded piece of paper. She stared down at it for the barest second before admitting, "I went through his pockets." It had been an afterthought, once Hen had left, but fruitful, nonetheless.

Horace dug in and was joined by a trio of wrinkles on his forehead. He huffed out an exasperated breath. "Don't tell me. This is my fault for telling you that once the police take over, you've lost your chance to get a good look at any potential evidence."

"Glad we understand each other," she quipped before adding softly, "It's a coded message." Without a word, he put out his hand, palm up, but she wasn't yet ready to relinquish the paper. "And there was a wireless antenna caught in a nearby tree."

He blinked and stared at her, his eyes vaguely hypnotic. It was the movement of his fingers gesturing for the confiscated message that finally distracted her. She handed it over and then walked to the chair that fronted his desk, and dropped into it.

Jamie stared down at her, then moved purposefully toward the jar sitting on the edge of his desk. From it, he retrieved one of the few remaining candies and handed it over. "The sugar will help. I'd offer to send for a cup of tea, but I'd like to go quickly, and I feel quite certain you won't agree to be left behind."

"There's always whiskey," she said.

"You're on duty," he said automatically, unfolding the note-paper.

Olive rolled her eyes. "You could make an exception—for medicinal purposes."

"I could," he allowed, frowning at the lines of jumbled charac-ters, "but you're enough of a loose cannon perfectly sober that I daren't risk it." He glanced down at her. "I assume you've not taken the time to decode this. Yes, well, we'll do that later. Com-ing, then?"

They took the Austin, a grim silence having settled between them. In a thousand heavy beats of her heart, they drove into the clearing. The Guides, who were clustered round a pair of trek carts full to bursting with tents and cookware and other camp paraphernalia, all turned to look as the tyres crunched and bumped over the ride. Their eyes were round with curiosity and tinged with fear, or, in the case of Henrietta, morbid fascination. Their new Brown Owl looked as if she'd like a whiskey, as well.

"What are they still doing here?" Jamie demanded.

"I'm sure they don't know what to do," Olive said. "Naturally, they don't want to continue to camp here, but Miss Feathering-ton probably didn't like to just march them off, leaving the b . . . leaving Lieutenant Beckett," she explained. "You look very competent and official, Captain Aldridge. Perhaps you could go over and reassure them that everything will be handled and they needn't worry—and shouldn't interfere." When he shifted his gaze round to look at her, she admitted, "That last bit is purely for Hen." Then she widened her eyes encouragingly until, with an exasperated sigh, he pushed the door open and stepped out of the motor car.

Olive followed suit.

"Where is he?"

Olive pointed, and he stood for a moment, staring in the indicated direction, before getting hold of himself.

They walked in opposite directions: Jamie toward the girls, Olive toward the body. She had crouched beside Lieutenant Beckett and was reaching out with quivering fingers to take his hand when she realised he was already holding something. Tucked partly under him, his hand lay pale against the loamy earth, black lines and letters caught in his palm. She was amazed and rather exasperated that she hadn't made the discovery earlier. Her probing fingers brushing his, she skimmed silk, then pulled it through his fingers like a magician. She held it up, let it fall open in front of her, and realised with a sense of foreboding that it was a map.

Just then she heard Jamie, evidently through with his errand and striding purposefully toward her. She stood and whirled to face him, the map wadded in her hands, shock likely writ clear on her face. His step faltered just barely before he came on the rest of the way.

"What is it?" he said sharply. He glanced down to stare at her fingers, which were crushing the silk.

"I've found something else."

He swore. "It isn't a scavenger hunt." The words were brusque to the point of rudeness, but she didn't take offense. As far as she was concerned, they both had a reprieve from good manners right now. His shoulders relaxed slightly, and he said more calmly, "What is it?"

Holding it by two corners, she let it unfold in a shimmery wave, so the map was lit by the sun and undulating in the breeze.

Jamie's brow unfurrowed, and he shot her a look of exasperation. "Put it back where you found it."

She shook the square of silk like a bullfighter, hoping to prompt a reaction. "In case it's not obvious to you, it's a map." She dropped her arms to her sides, the silk still stretched between them. "Of bloody Germany."

"Yes," he agreed mildly, brushing past her to where she'd crouched only a moment ago. "But as I'm quite certain it's one of ours, it's hardly important."

Olive stared down at him as her mind tumbled over that bombshell. Finally, she dropped down beside him, her hands now fisted with Germany. "What do you mean, it's one of ours?" When he didn't answer, she turned away from his steely profile to gaze down at the body of the dead man, the question, for the moment, unimportant.

He looked first at the wound—stared at it in silence—before making a thorough examination of the body. He patted down pockets, examined Lieutenant Beckett's shoes, and rolled him onto his side to look beneath him. Olive watched him steadily, silently. She suspected he wouldn't thank her for asking questions—or for pointing out what she'd already noticed herself. When he was finished, he stood, as she had, and scanned the area round the body. He saw the aerial—if it was one—and still said nothing. But as he stepped farther into the patch of true lover's knot, bent to search the undergrowth, the tension was vibrating through her, and she could no longer hold her tongue.

"It's there, just to the left of his right shoulder." She didn't clarify, but he clearly knew what she was referring to. He crouched down, spent a moment examining the stone, and then pivoted on the balls of his feet, searching for something else—something she hadn't found, let alone thought to look for.

She wanted him to confide in her of his own volition, but after several chest-tightening moments watching him rummage about, she was unable to wait any longer.

"Are you going to enlighten me?"

He'd stood and moved a bit away from her, but now he turned back to look at her. "It depends on what you want to know."

She had so many questions but took a breath and asked the one that was most important.

"Did you know him?" Certainly, he'd been acquainted with the man, but she wondered if they'd been friends.

Jamie looked back at Lieutenant Beckett, then at her. "Hardly at all. He was a nice chap, but he mostly kept to himself." He planted his foot on a rotten log, rocking it slightly, then leaned forward to fan his hand through the wispy fern fronds that surrounded it.

"What are you looking for?"

"The missing transmitter."

Olive felt a surge of satisfaction at having spotted, and identified, the antenna. "Do you think this was an accident?"

"I'm not an expert, but given the evidence, I'd say the most likely explanation is that he tripped over a root or stepped in a hole and had the bloody bad luck to hit his head on that rock when he fell."

Silently conceding that his explanation seemed logical enough given the evidence at hand, she chose to quiz him on other matters.

"What did you mean about the map being one of ours?"

"Those scarves are produced by MI9," he said shortly. "And I really shouldn't have even told you that," he added curtly.

"MI9?" Olive said, frowning. "What do they do?" She glanced down at the body. "Was Lieutenant Beckett working for them?"

Jamie glanced back. "No. Even if he did have the time or inclination, neither Baker Street nor MI9 would allow it. He may as well have been fraternising with the enemy."

"What do you mean?"

"Interdepartmental bickering is the stuff of legend. Every office has its own agenda, and no one's keen to trust anyone else."

"Then how did he come to be in possession of the scarf?"

"I didn't know the man, Olive. I can't possibly speak to the little things he has in his pockets, just as I'm sure that if I dropped dead suddenly, there would be no one to understand the significance of the items I've chosen to hold on to." No doubt seeing the pondering, quizzical look in her eyes, he barrelled on. "Maybe he was using it as a handkerchief—amusing himself in the knowledge that he was blowing snot all over Germany." Olive cringed, staring down at the scarf in her hand with sudden distaste. "Or perhaps he was simply using it as a map. For instructive purposes." Jamie shrugged. "It's frankly none of our business."

"It is if he was a spy," she insisted. She didn't want to think it, but how could she not? No matter how quick Jamie was to dismiss the idea, it was certainly possible that Lieutenant Beckett had kept himself to himself because he was hiding the fact that he was working for the Germans. She crossed her arms over her chest.

"Agreed. But I'd much rather assume he was a patriot, using his considerable insights to the benefit of the Allies. We do investigate prior to recruitment," he said in some exasperation. "And sometimes after the fact, as well." He deliberately shifted his gaze from her face and glanced sideways toward the swath of true lover's knot. Olive didn't need the reminder—he'd managed to unearth a truth about her own life that she hadn't known herself. "If there'd been anything in his history to indicate a tendency or a connection, it would have been investigated thoroughly, and if anything had come of it, he wouldn't be here now."

"I suppose you have an explanation for the aerial, as well?" she quizzed.

He frowned, staring up at the dangling wire.

"It could have been used at any time as part of a training exercise," he allowed. "If it got caught on a branch, they might not have been able to retrieve it." His lips curved wryly. "It would explain the missing transmitter."

"I suppose," she said, unconvinced. "That should be easy enough to verify."

"Olive . . . let it go," he warned. "We've too much else to worry about for you to be chasing shadows and following up imagined leads." He met her eyes, and it was as if he'd said the words aloud: *Don't be another Husselbee.*

"Fine," she said pettishly.

"Good. Stay with the body. I'll go back to phone the police and deal with everything else. When things finish up here, you can report in." With one last glance at Lieutenant Beckett, he turned and strode toward the car.

She suddenly remembered and called rather desperately after him. "What about the coded message?"

"I'll take care of it. We don't need your suspicions aroused any further than they already are." His jaw set, he climbed behind the wheel and shut the car door, drowning out her response. Good thing, too. He was the sort to take offense to that sort of thing.

Chapter 5

The following morning, Olive was leaning against the wall of the dovecote, fanning herself with her wide-brimmed hat, when a familiar car crawled up the drive. She'd been out early on the Welbike. The pigeons had resumed their training after the previous day's interruption and had been tossed into the sky at a spot far removed from Brickendonbury and Balls Wood and grim tragedy. And as she'd watched them wheeling over the land-scape, their wings moving in hypnotic, rhythmic beats, she'd thought of Lieutenant Beckett and felt, for a moment, a cathartic sense of peace.

She'd not told her father or stepmother about Lieutenant Beckett, but the village rumour mill had ground out a few titbits that had managed to reach Harriet's ears. With concern marring her smooth complexion, she'd quizzed Olive about his death, worried over a possible connection to the manor house. Olive had been quick to assure her that it had simply been a horrible acci-dent. But silently, her thoughts were frothing with suspicion, and she was more determined than ever to look into the mysterious circumstances surrounding his death.

By the time the police had finally finished with the body of

Lieutenant Jeremy Beckett, the sun had travelled a fair way across the sky, and she'd been tired and hungry and desperate for a bath. She'd been sad and disheartened and in no mood for company of any sort, so she hadn't gone back to the manor, as directed, and instead had come straight home.

And now here was Captain Jameson Aldridge to mete out her punishment. She groaned.

Both car doors opened simultaneously, and a ginger-topped head appeared on the passenger side. A smile crept over her face at the sight of Danny Tierney, but she tucked it away again as Jamie came into view. She stood waiting as they approached, refusing to give an inch.

"Hello, Olive," Tierney said, his dimple tucked neatly into his cheek. "I've business with Master Maddocks this morning."

"Oh?" she said curiously, deliberately not looking at Jamie. "Is he expecting you?"

"He is at that," he responded with a cheeky grin.

"Well, he's somewhere about. I'd try the garden if I were you," she told him, gesturing toward the side of the house. "Watch for cats," she called after him. "They're ferocious." She caught his incredulous look and merely smiled.

When she turned back to Jamie, a wry look in her eyes, she didn't expect him to be so very close. And she certainly didn't expect his lips on hers. It was only the usual token display, but it flustered her, nonetheless.

"Good morning," he said, his voice suspiciously jaunty. "I missed you yesterday, and I thought we could take a walk this morning."

"No one can hear you," she said flatly. "Dad's out on his rounds, and Harriet is having a one-sided conversation with a BBC radio programme that's evidently on her nerves. And being rather loud about it."

"The offer stands," he said in a voice edged with steel.

"Lovely," she agreed sourly, clapping the hat back on her head and turning with him to walk through the open gate.

He didn't chastise or press her in any way, and this was so un-expected that she finally broke under the pressure of their con-tinued silence.

"It was badly done of me," she admitted. "I know I was meant to go back to the manor, but it had been a very long day, and you'd been rather a b—"

"Yes, I know," he said shortly. "You said."

"Sorry."

He reached into his pocket and pulled out two folded sheets of paper. One of them looked familiar, and a shiver ran over her. He held them just out of reach. "I decoded the message you found in Lieutenant Beckett's pocket, and the result is here," he said, indicating one of the pages, "but if you'd prefer to translate it yourself, I've brought the original."

She eyed him wearily. As gestures went, it was thoughtful but utterly ridiculous. "You've missed the point entirely. It doesn't matter to me in the slightest that you did the decoding." She tipped her chin up. "I'm confident that I *could* have done it. That is, if I hadn't been shunted off to twiddle my thumbs as the po-lice did their work. They were precisely as pleased to have me looking over their shoulders as you are." Olive glanced at him as he walked beside her, his gaze trained on the ground and his hands tucked behind his back.

Now one hand came round and was extended toward her. It held a newer, crisper sheet of paper—the translation. She took it, and as she began to unfold it, he said, "Someone had to wait for the police, Olive, and someone had to notify the CO and Lieu-tenant Beckett's family and arrange for a funeral." Olive's fingers stilled on the page, and she felt ashamed. "We're not Holmes and Watson, puzzling out clues together. We have separate re-sponsibilities. Officially, we are not equals, and if I can't trust you to follow my orders, then this is not going to work."

She bit her lip, feeling the heat rise in her neck under the broad shadow of her hat. Her shock at the myriad discoveries had had her itching to make sense of it all, and she hadn't truly considered that there were other things that had needed to be addressed first. Very deliberately, she focused her attention on the paper and Jamie's careful printing. The original code had been written out, and below it, the translation.

> *Courage was mine, and I had mystery;*
> *Wisdom was mine, and I had mastery;*
> *To miss the march of this retreating world*
> *Into vain citadels that are not walled.*

She read it over twice. Feeling a bit gauche, she asked tentatively, "Does it mean anything to you?" As usual, their steps had led them down the river path, and she could hear the merry sounds of children through the trees as they splashed about in the shallows.

"If you mean, do I recognise it, no," he answered. "I have a pretty fair memory when it comes to poetry, but I'm quite certain I've not come across these lines before."

She blinked at him, startled to think of him as knowing anything about poetry, but met with his rueful smile and the disturbing feeling that he was reading her thoughts, she turned her attention to the words once again. "Do you think Lieutenant Beckett could have been the author?"

"It's possible. I'm beginning to think the man had hidden depths."

Olive couldn't help but think of her mother. Her skin prickled as she caught Jamie's eye, hoping he couldn't read her thoughts and wouldn't remember that afternoon, months ago, when he'd unearthed her mother's secret and confronted Olive with betrayal.

"Is it written in his handwriting?"

"That, I can't say. I've not gone to the trouble to compare it."

"Is it a clue, do you think?" They'd reached a drift of meadow buttercups, dazzlingly yellow bright, and she ran her hand over the tops before tugging a single bloom to twirl in her fingers. "That he was carrying these particular words with him, I mean."

"I'm prepared to give Lieutenant Beckett the benefit of the doubt. It could be that they reminded him of his role in this war. Then again, he might simply have appreciated the verse. I don't see that it hints at any nefarious purpose."

"Do *you* typically encode harmless notes to yourself?"

"I might if I wanted the practice. Or if I wanted to thwart someone snooping." He looked pointedly at her.

Olive rolled her eyes, exasperated. "Well, the police agree with you," she said with asperity. "They've concluded that, given the position of the body, the location of the stone, and the ground cover of the true lover's knot, camouflaging the terrain of that particular spot, such a fall was not unlikely." She sighed. "They've determined his death was an accident, not even suspicious enough to warrant an inquest. The coroner estimated time of death as being between nine o'clock Wednesday night and five o'clock yesterday morning." Olive had tried hard to keep her voice measured, but now she couldn't help herself and blurted, "The aerial was of no interest to them at all. There could have been a monkey sitting in the tree, and they would have given it only a cursory glance. But, of course, they didn't know about the scarf, or this." She had been folding up Jamie's translation with jerky, frustrated movements and now held it up before shoving it into her pocket.

"Both of which are likely to have innocent explanations." He paused and took a breath. "Well, I suppose that's that, then. All that's left is to give the man a proper send-off and get on with things. I suspect that's what he would have wanted, in any case." When Olive didn't immediately answer, he added, "I'd like that paper back, if you don't mind."

"What? Oh." She pulled it out again and handed it over before saying casually, "Perhaps I'll just pop into the library and ask Miss Swan for help in identifying the verse."

"Olive," he said warningly.

She stepped in front of him and spun round to face him so that he came to an abrupt halt. "I spoke to him in the village earlier this week, and now he's—" She stopped, took a breath, and started again. "There are too many things that just don't add up." She reached out to wrap her hands round his upper arms, willing him to really listen. "The encoded verse, the scarf with its damning map of Germany, the aerial, that argument with Mr Harris—"

"You and I can't talk for five minutes without falling into an argument," he objected. "That doesn't mean I'd murder you."

"Unfortunately, if I turn up dead, you'll probably be suspect number one," she said, grinning. With a commiserating squeeze, she released him and stepped back.

He rubbed his hand roughly over his temples and looked silently up at a blue sky that was slowly but surely giving way to a line of grey clouds.

"And then there's the fact that his hands were perfectly clean," she added. This fact had just occurred to her, but it was important, she knew.

Jamie frowned. "Why is that suspicious?"

"If he'd tripped, he would have reached out instinctively to catch himself. But I held his hand—there were no smears of dirt, no chlorophyll from the lover's knot, no scrapes from twigs or fallen logs. They were unmarked, one of them holding the map."

He shrugged. "I'm sure there's a good explanation."

"Treason is a bang-up explanation," she countered tartly, while privately conceding that in the imagined scenario, Lieutenant Beckett could just as well be the unwitting victim. But still, there was a mystery here.

Jamie turned to head back the way they'd come. "We'd best get back to work," he said.

Olive took his arm and leaned into him. "Please, Jamie. Just let me look into it a bit further. If it was an accident, there'll be nothing to find. And if it wasn't . . . Well, I promise I won't get myself killed. Deal?" she said brightly.

"You need to be focused on Conjugal, not to mention your strategy for supplying pigeons going forward. You don't have time to spare on amateur detecting."

This would have been the perfect time to quiz him on the choice of names for the mission, but Olive had other priorities. "I'll make sure it doesn't interfere with anything. I promise. And if I find anything at all, I'll come straight to you."

He didn't answer for a time, and the sound of machinery off in the distance was overlaid with the nearby sounds of birds in the hedgerow and a heavy, humid wind moving languorously through the trees.

They'd just come over the rise to see Blackcap Lodge in the distance, the dovecote thrusting up amid the trees beside it, when he finally spoke. "If you can keep up with your responsibilities and keep out of trouble, then I won't object." His jaw worked, as if he was having difficulty holding his reservations in check. "However," he added sharply when she let out a whoop of triumph, "I'll expect you to report to me with *any* progress. And if you haven't come up with anything that hints at foul play in one week, then that'll be an end to it. No exceptions." He turned to look at her, his eyebrow winged up. "Agreed?"

A surge of triumph shot through her, and she flashed an appreciative smile. "Agreed. And in return, I won't ask you to take me to bingo tonight in the village hall," she said with a laugh.

Back at the lodge, Tierney was waiting, overseeing Jonathon's work on the wheelchair. He stood, and after a quick word to the boy and a hand on his shoulder, he strode toward the pair of them. Jamie turned to walk toward the car.

"Aren't you forgetting something?" Tierney rocked back on his heels and slid amused eyes in Olive's direction. Jamie glanced back, and Tierney added encouragingly, "You're meant to be in love with her."

"He's already made certain . . . overtures," Olive reported, with a wink at Tierney.

"*Has* he, then?" Tierney said, grinning. "Well done, Captain

Aldridge. I suppose I should keep my mouth shut and leave the man to his work."

"Do that," Jamie said tightly before sliding into the car.

With a wave, Olive watched them go. One day soon, she and Jameson Aldridge were going to have a little chat. There were things she wanted to know, and things she felt compelled to tell him. She'd probably have to kidnap him.

The moment the thought popped into her mind, a grin suffused her face. She was whistling as she strode back to the dovecote.

None of the WI's various schemes had been more wholeheartedly embraced than the weekly game of chance. In fact, the only dissent among the ranks had stemmed from what to call it. Tombola had been out of the question, the word being of Italian origin, and bingo had been considered too flippantly American for an important wartime fundraiser. So, after much heated discussion, it had been decided that these events, to be held on Friday nights in the village hall, would be called the Lucky Lotto.

Olive hadn't won a single shilling after weeks of trying, but Margaret had yet to walk away empty-handed. Outwardly, the villagers had all responded good-naturedly to this stunning success by the vicar's wife-to-be, but Olive had sensed the grumblings.

With this, the first lottery since Leo and Margaret had returned from their honeymoon, the hall seemed positively atwitter with uncertainty.

Now, as Margaret carefully arranged her little stack of coloured wooden discs beside the black-and-white lottery card, Olive leaned over to speak to her.

"You know," she said casually, "it would smooth a few ruffled feathers if you let someone else win tonight."

Margaret's head swung round, her honey-gold hair glinting in the last rays of light streaming through the leaded diamond panes of the hall. Her eyebrows turned down, and her grey eyes darkened disapprovingly. "Don't be ridiculous! I don't want to set an example of being willing to set my own interests aside to the benefit of others."

Olive frowned. "Isn't that basically your purview, as the vicar's wife?"

Her friend's face softened for a moment, but the change was short lived. "When I said my vows, I committed myself fully to Leo, not to every soul in Pipley with a problem or complaint. I'll do my best, but I'll have to walk a fine line." She lifted her left hand, palm up. "Supportive and sociable . . ." The right hand rose to join it. "Reserved and firm." She shifted her hands up and down, as if juggling her options, and then promptly dropped the supportive hand while the firm hand reached for her drink.

Luckily, at that moment, Mrs Satterhorn bellowed into the room, "Is everyone ready? It's time to begin another fun evening of"—here her voice was drowned out by a raucous bellowing—"Lucky Lottery."

The hall was crowded, its round tables full of villagers willing to pay the entrance fee for a night of competitive camaraderie and a chance to win a little money. There was cake and punch and the occasional taunting jest shouted among friends. Olive tried to picture Jamie in this setting, but her thoughts filled instead with his intense storm-blue eyes. And Horace. Although she'd noticed that Horace always seemed to make himself scarce when she kissed him. . . .

"For heaven's sake, Olive, you've already missed one," Margaret said sharply, setting her finger on the fifty-seven square on Olive's lottery card. "You've no chance of winning if you're daydreaming about your captain."

"I wasn't—" Olive stopped speaking, sliding a disc onto the specified square. It was surely better if Margaret thought she had been. "You're right." She glanced round at the other occupants of their table. None of them appeared to be paying any attention.

She was glad to see the two newcomers to the village, Miss Featherington and Miss Swan, in attendance, sitting at a table with Mrs Spencer. When proffered an invitation, Violet Darling, lately returned to the village herself after many years away, had laughed uproariously and informed Olive that she'd rather kiss a frog, even with no expectation that anything would come of it. A list of other, equally appealing amphibious alternatives had punctuated Olive's retreat.

With a frown, she realised that Miss Swan was alternately dabbing her nose and eyes with a tissue she kept corralled in the sleeve of her cardigan. Olive wondered distractedly if it was hay fever or something more personal—she really needed to make an effort to get to know the woman. In contrast, Miss Featherington looked as perfectly turned out as if she were taking tea with royalty. Olive felt a stab of irritation with the woman.

Mrs Satterhorn turned the crank of the little red cage with gusto, the number tiles tumbling noisily about, until the next tile was pulled out and announced. "Twenty-three. The Lord is my shepherd," she said primly, smiling at Margaret, who was giddily—and obliviously—placing a marker on her card.

And it went on like that, with Olive dividing her focus between the game and the room. When Margaret finally called lotto in a clear, ringing voice, she had the full attention offered to the King during his wireless broadcasts.

Betty Henry bustled toward them, the list of called numbers clutched tight in her hand. Her tall, angular body bent over Margaret as she checked—and double-checked—every one. At last, she was forced to tip her head up and, amid the vacuum of bated breath, announce, "We have a winner."

Ignoring the grumbling that ensued as everyone began to crowd round the refreshments table, Margaret leaned close and confided happily, "I've signed up." Startled, Olive blinked at her, but before she could pepper her friend with questions, the answer came. "I've joined the Royal Observer Corps. I'm officially a spotter in training."

This news fairly boggled Olive's mind. Here was Margaret, a former London department store model, glamorous to a fault—even on the ration—and married less than a week, signed up to stand about in a makeshift hut, using a pair of binoculars to record the comings and goings of every single aeroplane sighted in the vicinity.

All Olive could manage was, "What prompted that?"

Her friend's lower lip jutted out stubbornly, but her eyes, when they met Olive's, looked vaguely hunted. "I admit it. I'm a little overwhelmed." Her fingers were worrying a cotton handkerchief bordered in precise pink embroidery. "I knew what life as a vicar's wife entailed—or thought I did—but it's all too much, too soon." Her eyes widened, almost imploringly. "They all need something, and someone is popping in at every moment of the day, wanting to visit or complain or commiserate or preen." Margaret clamped her hand over Olive's and squeezed. "Much more of this, and I'm liable to murder someone."

After a moment, her hand relaxed, and she seemed calm, but suddenly she sat forward again, in a fresh frenzy. "I really do need to stop using that word round you. Promise me you won't read anything into it if you happen to find another body," she implored. She must have felt Olive stiffen, because her eyebrows went up, and she leaned even closer. Dropping her voice to a whisper, she said, "I don't believe it. Don't tell me you were the one to find the body of that officer in Balls Wood."

Olive's own eyebrow lifted in answer.

"As you can imagine, I've heard all sorts of rumours—most of them ridiculous." Glancing at Olive, she added, "You didn't know him, did you?"

"Only a little, but I'm fine."

Now that everyone had indulged in consolatory cake and punch, Mrs Satterhorn resumed her position behind the table at the front of the hall and placed her hand on the crank of the tombola cage. "Are we all ready for another go?" she called jauntily, prompting a resounding response.

Margaret nudged Olive's elbow. "It's somewhat of an odd co-incidence, but I'm to be stationed at Balls Wood. At the end of one of the rides, there's a little hut. It's rather cosy, all things considered."

"Number eight," said Mrs Satterhorn, adding jovially, "the garden gate."

Olive and Margaret checked their cards. Neither of them could place a marker.

"Well, with any luck, you'll see nothing more exciting than a Guides camp tramping through the trees."

Margaret smiled, and Olive's thoughts ticked rapidly along, her impending investigation at the forefront of her mind.

"You're distracted today," her friend said with some exasperation. "You've missed another one." She leaned over to place a marker on Olive's thirteen square.

After another two numbers went down as misses on Olive's card and hits on Margaret's, Olive spoke up. "Do me a favour?"

"That depends," her friend said dryly. "You don't need me to put a hex on anyone, do you?"

There was a beat of silence, in which Olive missed another number called. She blinked. "Can you do that?"

Margaret's smile was sly. "It only matters what people *think* I can do."

"No hexes," Olive said briskly, but then followed her answer with an addendum and a cheeky grin. "For now, anyway. I just want you to keep your eyes open. The police have concluded the death was an accident, but I'm not entirely convinced." Seeing Margaret's reaction, she said quickly, "I'm just looking into a few things. But if you see anything suspicious—any odd comings and goings—just let me know, will you?"

Margaret nodded distractedly, placing a blue marker on square thirty-three. Glancing down, Olive was gratified to see the number on her own card and promptly covered it with a red marker.

"Sixty-two. Tickety-boo!"

Good-natured chuckling rumbled through the hall, but then a strident voice cut through the din. "Lotto!"

Everyone in the room swivelled and pivoted in their seats to see who'd been lucky this time. When the winner proved to be Lady Camilla, a resounding cheer went up. Margaret didn't notice, but likely wouldn't have cared, at any rate.

Olive glanced over at Lady Camilla, who was George's mother and the president of the Pipley WI. She'd been having a good run of luck these past weeks, as well, and Olive was glad to see it, fully aware of how she intended to use her winnings.

With confirmation from Betty Henry, another cheer went up, bringing a blush to the elegant woman's cheeks. As one, the occupants of the hall slid the markers from their cards, ready to go again.

The rest of the evening went much the same. And while Olive didn't claim any winnings, the discovery that Margaret would be on the spot with her binoculars was its own sort of triumph.

Chapter 6

On Sunday morning Olive dressed in a plain, rarely worn navy dress and went early to church with her family. But the jeweled fragments of sunlight streaming through the stained-glass windows set a jarring note, and Leo's well-intentioned sermon fell hollowly on her distracted ears. When it was over, she escaped into the heat of late summer, eager to ward off the chill in her bones.

Jamie was waiting for her beside the Austin, just beyond the lych-gate, and the pair of them set off in silence for the manor. Leo was going straight over from the church to preside at the service honouring Lieutenant Jeremy Beckett. His parents had come down on the afternoon train the day before to carry his body home and had inexplicably left his belongings behind.

So, as the men and women of Station XVII stood beside the moat to remember one of their own, the entire proceedings felt as somewhat of an afterthought. Leo said all the right things, but his words never altered the blank expressions of the onlookers.

It seemed as if no one had known the man enough to truly mourn him, and her sadness at this reality spread painfully through Olive's chest until it was choking her. She imagined she could hear the dull beating of her heart in low, mournful thuds, but as she placed a hand to her chest, she realised the rhythm was more sporadic. It almost sounded like fireworks going off, and with a pang, Olive imagined a very different moment, one in which they all stood round the moat, staring into a night sky lit with victory. But this was grim defeat.

The surface of the moat was scattered with delicate water lilies in pink and white and yellow, floating amid the round green pads. But as the sun beat down, the light delved deeper, drawing her gaze beneath the surface, past the tangle of stems that formed dark, twisted shapes underwater, the whole of it glossed with the oozing green of algae.

What if Lieutenant Beckett's death *hadn't* been an accident? What if he'd been murdered? Could one of these people gathered here to mourn him have done it? Her gaze darted among the familiar faces: Major Boom, Liz, Tomás, and dozens of others she saw on a near-daily basis, including the Belgian agents, whose training was nearly at an end. What did she really know about the lives of any of them? As she'd recently had cause to discover, some people were willing to kill to keep their secrets. A nervous panic suddenly welled up inside her as she remembered her own close encounter with such a person. But at that moment, her gaze settled on Jamie. He stood opposite her, across that watery divide, and she felt an immeasurable sense of relief to let herself be drawn in by his stormy blue gaze. Whether she understood him or not, she *knew* him. He had secrets—of that she was certain—but he would never let them consume or corrupt him.

She didn't want to look away. Leo's voice carried on, punctuated by her own measured breathing. And through it all, her eyes lingered on Jamie's. Until she'd contented herself that it had all been a ghastly accident, she was going to have to consider everyone at Station XVII a suspect. Except Jamie. Even Poirot had allowed himself the occasional exception.

She blinked and realised Jamie was watching her with a curious expression. There might have even been a touch of concern lurking behind it. She smiled, hoping to reassure him, but this only prompted a frown.

Olive sighed, and thankfully, at that moment, Leo said the final prayer. As everyone began to drift toward the house for a cold lunch and a toast to another life cut much too short, she waited, then fell into step with Jamie when he appeared at her side. He took her arm.

"Are you all right? You got very pale near the end, and I worried you'd fall face-first into the moat."

She cut her eyes round at him. "You worried, or you hoped?" she quipped.

His eyes were lighter now, mischievous. "It would have broken the ice, at the very least." She huffed, and after a few steps, he added, "I would have pulled you out."

"I might have pulled you in," she countered, with a wicked lift of her brow. "But I'm glad to have avoided the hassle and to have managed to stay dry. It'll be much easier to wander round and make subtle inquiries this way."

He pulled up short, his hold on her arm requiring that she did also. "Is this really the time for that?" he said harshly, looking about him at the trickling clusters of people.

"It's the *perfect* time," she insisted, turning to face him. "I didn't know him, and it'll seem the most natural thing in the world that I'm curious about the man." She laid a hand on his arm. "If it comes to that, I *am* curious about him. Don't worry—I'll be sensitive. And subtle."

A sound like a snort escaped him, and Olive frowned. The man needed to have a little faith in her abilities. She would channel the masterful Hercule Poirot, hovering innocently, waiting for the moment to insert a casual—but provocative—comment. She would watch reactions, listen carefully for the subtle nuances that might hint at pertinent information or reticence. She checked her optimistic outlook. In all likelihood, the result would be much the same as last time: a host of other guilty secrets would come glaringly to light and make for an awkward experience all round. But it couldn't be helped.

The clues—Olive was determined to term her curious discoveries as such—were all pointing to some little mystery. It may be nothing, or it may be very important indeed.

As they stepped into the shade of the portico at the rear of the house, Olive slid her gaze sideways and moved her eyes over the crisply curling waves of Jamie's blue-black hair, the narrow white line of the scar running along his jaw, and his impossibly long, dark lashes. Was he being entirely honest with her? Had he recognised the decoded verse and decided to keep the details to himself? He was certainly being disconcertingly amenable.

At that moment, he winced, drawing a hissing breath between his teeth, and pressed taut fingers to his temple.

Olive put a hand on his arm. "Are *you* all right?"

"Fine." But the word was bitten off. He must have sensed his reply was entirely unsatisfactory under the circumstances, because, with effort in his voice, he added, "It's just a headache."

Judging by the intensity and the speed at which it had come on, Olive could only assume it was the debilitating sort that had consigned him, after a near miss with explosive charges somewhere in Belgium, to a desk job for the course of the war. In the months since she'd known him, it was the first one she'd ever witnessed.

His steps got heavier as they moved inside, and his eyes slitted, as if even the light was unbearable. She tightened her grip on him. "Let's get help," she said urgently.

"It'll pass," he murmured. He detached her from his arm and said in a thready monotone, "I just need to lie down for a few moments. You work on being subtle and sentimental."

As he turned and walked stiffly up the stairs to his room, Olive couldn't help but stare worriedly after him. She'd never seen him so vulnerable. How often did these headaches come on, and how bad were they? Everything she learned about the man led only to more questions.

Everyone had milled into the dining room, only to ignore the lunch that had been set out in favour of the table crowded with an impressive array of spirits. Olive lurked just outside the door, staring after Jamie, thinking rapidly.

She didn't want to believe it, but she'd got the distinct impression that he was hiding something, and she couldn't help but wonder if it concerned the mysterious death of Lieutenant Beckett. Was he intent on undermining her plans to investigate? Her thoughts raced as she considered the singular opportunity that had presented itself: everyone was occupied with somber obligation and free-flowing spirits, except for Jamie, who, for the moment at least, was laid up with a debilitating headache. This was her chance to do a bit of sleuthing unobserved.

Yet she stood frozen, in a muddle of indecision. Should she go directly upstairs and pray she didn't encounter anyone as she crept along the halls, searching for Lieutenant Beckett's room? It was entirely possible that Jamie had already searched it, and quite possibly, he had discovered all manner of clues that shed light on the man and his death. If he had, he likely wouldn't have left them in situ, but rather would have moved them into his own office for further examination. She bit her lip, then heard a pair of voices on the stairs and made her decision.

A moment later, she was quietly tapping the door to Jamie's office closed behind her, waiting for her pulse to calm. Being alone in his private space felt both exhilarating and nerve racking. One thing out of place, and he would know someone had prowled. And he would—quite rightly—suspect her.

She glanced round her. The map on the wall was precisely aligned and stretched without a wrinkle. The waste bin, she noticed with a smirk, had been righted and set in its original spot. The candy jar, pens, and paper clips were precisely arranged on the desktop, and the wooden box, reserved for papers needing attention, sat empty on its front right corner, all its contents having already been dispatched.

There were only two places to hide something—the filing cabinet and the desk. Olive slid into the chair behind the desk and pulled open the top right-hand drawer with a sudden breathless feeling of déjà vu. She'd searched Miss Husselbee's desk to some success following her murder, but Jameson Aldridge was a cagey fellow.

What she found were folders, neatly stacked, most of them stamped CONFIDENTIAL, some even wrapped up with twine, a possible precaution against any secrets leaking out. She tugged the drawer out farther and reached into the recessed space to pull out a tarnished gold frame.

Jamie was easily identifiable in the photo, wearing a thick woolen jumper and muddy boots, standing beside a low stone wall, the hills behind him rolling gently to the sea. Beside him was a slender girl with long, dark hair, a narrow face, and a pointed chin. The likeness was obvious, and Olive realised this must be the sister he'd lost to the Luftwaffe. Feeling the guilt of intrusion, she carefully replaced the frame in precisely the same spot and slid the drawer shut.

On the left-hand side, the top drawer held letterhead paper, rubber stamps, and a Rolodex of names and numbers. And a quick search of both bottom drawers revealed file folders lined up with military precision. She was just closing the one on the right when her eye caught on a tab labelled PIGEONEER.

Olive debated with herself for a long moment but eventually pushed the drawer shut without even a peek. It might not even be about her, but if it was, she didn't need to look. As she was painfully aware, Jamie took his responsibilities very seriously indeed and wouldn't hesitate to let her know if he had a concern. And if she did read it and found something he'd failed to mention, she'd be unable to resist confronting him, thereby giving herself away. And that, almost assuredly, would go into the file. With a grim nod, she turned her attention elsewhere.

After her unsuccessful search of the desk, Olive was content to dismiss the filing cabinet—Jamie would never allow fraternisation between official war business and unsubstantiated clues. Perhaps he *wasn't* hiding clues from her. At that moment her gaze settled on the coat stand in the corner, whose curvaceous hooks put her in mind of an octopus. An olive-green jacket hung companionably beside a khaki overcoat, whose belt dangled down to skim the black umbrella corralled below.

On a hunch, she hurried round the desk and began rummaging through the overcoat's khaki folds. A faint whiff of liquorice scented the air, and she leaned in slightly, balancing on the balls of her feet. But despite nearly knocking the whole thing over, she found nothing even remotely suspicious. Feeling rather hopeless about the entire endeavour, she dutifully searched the jacket pockets. Nothing. She was tucking it neatly back into position beside the overcoat when she felt a hard shape near the lapel, and after pulling the jacket out again, she discovered an interior pocket. When she reached inside, her hand met with the crinkle of paper, the cool slide of silk, and the heft of a sturdy cylindrical shape. The first two items she'd seen on the body of the dead man: the page of coded verse and the scarf printed with a map of Germany. The third was a startling new discovery.

Olive stared down at it, an odd feeling in the pit of her stomach. She uncapped the tube and gave its barrel a twist until the well-used tip of red lipstick emerged. After a distracted moment, in which she thought carefully back over her thorough search of the body, she decided there was almost no chance she could have missed this. Which meant . . . what exactly? She blinked, feeling rather obtuse as a blush heated her cheeks. This was, after all, Jamie's private office, and he obviously had a private life, to which she wasn't a party. She stiffly twisted that familiar colour away again, slid the cap on with a click of grim finality, and dropped the lipstick back into the hidden pocket.

Determined not to consider the implications of that lipstick, she hurriedly spread the scarf over the surface of Jamie's desk. She checked the edges for a name or initials, then ran her hands over the luscious fabric, searching for anything that might give her a clue as to why Lieutenant Beckett might have had it in his possession. *Nothing.* Her urgent gaze darted across the map, from city to city, as she imagined RAF bombers dumping their payloads in retaliation for the brutal attacks on London, Manchester, Liverpool, and Southampton. And then she saw them, drawn in beside Berlin. Three tiny black crosses, the ink having bled into the fibres.

As she stared at those markings, which were almost invisible amid the busy print, her mind whirred. That this was a clue, she had no doubt. By all appearances, it was equally as cryptic and mysterious as the lines of verse Jamie had decoded. Words she wished she'd committed to memory, particularly as only the original, coded version had been tucked away in Jamie's jacket pocket. You were simply full of intrigue, Lieutenant Beckett, she thought. But there wasn't time to ponder that just now. She'd already been away too long, and every second that passed presented a greater risk of discovery. She stuffed the scarf back into its hiding place and put the coat stand to rights.

Her satisfaction in her success was tempered by exasperation with Jamie. The man was an officer in a top-secret intelligence organisation, and yet she'd ferreted out his hiding place faster than it took her to make a cup of tea. They really needed to have a talk. Then again . . . was it possible he'd been expecting her to snoop?

She froze. Had Jamie faked a debilitating headache to lure her into misbehaviour? Was he even now waiting just outside his office, arms crossed, for her to emerge? She stared at the door, unable to move. Would he be so duplicitous? Could he have anticipated her plans before she'd even made them? The door *had* been conveniently unlocked. Her eyes boggled at not knowing what he was capable of. Girding her courage, she walked to the door and, with a quick intake of breath, flung it open.

Finding herself staring at the wainscoted wall opposite, she peered round the jamb, confirmed that no one was lurking about, and let out a relieved sigh, eager for her heart rate to return to normal. With one final glance round the office, she slipped out, pulled the door closed behind her, and hurried back down the hall toward the sound of voices, hoping Jamie hadn't yet joined them.

He hadn't. She didn't even need to look, seeing as Liz accosted her the moment she was through the doorway. "Have you seen Captain Aldridge?" she asked, a telltale longing in her voice as she clutched her glass of gin. She was craning her head to look past Olive into the empty hall, and Olive couldn't help but admire the picture she made—every blond hair tucked neatly into place, her face powdered to an opalescent glow, her red lipstick worn like a badge of honour.

Remembering the tube of lipstick tucked away in Jamie's pocket—the very shade Liz had insisted had gone missing—Olive felt oddly flustered. "I'm sure he's somewhere about," she said, quickening her steps. She was suddenly starving and eager for a sandwich or two. A moment later, as she hovered near the picked-over trays of food and scanned the now-animated faces, trying to identify a starting point for her inquiries, Marie and Kate joined her. Liz followed in their wake.

"You look lovely, Olive," Marie said with a smile. "You put the rest of us to shame."

"I didn't even think to wear my uniform." Olive shook her head self-consciously. "I should have." Her words were abrupt, but she didn't want to try to explain her struggle to manage the various layers of her deception—particularly to Liz.

"It's so sad," Kate said dutifully. Her face looked blotchy, as if she'd been crying or been very close to it.

Olive agreed, and for a moment, she wavered. It seemed disloyal to question them, even casually. In the short time since she'd started at Brickendonbury, they'd all become fast friends. She could hear Poirot tsking in her ear and blurted, "Did any of you know Lieutenant Beckett?"

Kate's eyes looked as innocent as a doe's as she shook her head vigorously. "I collated some papers for him once, and he was very nice about it." She glanced round, then turned back. Lowering her voice, she said, "Some of the officers and instructors . . . I know they're very busy, but some of them are so brusque and dismissive." Her countenance crumpled a bit. "But not him—he always had a kind word. I sometimes saw him in the library, and I think he was a birdwatcher."

"He rarely joined in on the evenings that we stayed late, drinking and dancing, all of us determined to keep up our spirits and carry on." So saying, Liz swirled the ice in her glass with her index finger, looking rather forlorn.

"I'd spoken to him only a few times," Olive admitted. "I thought he was rather handsome."

"He was," Marie agreed. Then she added, "If you like the safe, professorial type." Her blue eyes and full mouth said quite clearly that she preferred a very different sort of man.

Olive countered, "Perhaps that was just for show. He had a nice smile—rather mischievous I thought."

"I love a cashmere jumper," Kate said dreamily, her fingers running distractedly over the rough fabric of her FANY tunic.

"He definitely had money," Marie allowed. Olive glanced at her quizzically, prompting her to go on. "You could tell. He had aristocratic manners and lily-white hands," she said, brows raised.

"He didn't fit in particularly well here," Liz admitted. Glancing up at their curious faces, she elaborated. "Don't get me wrong. He was very well respected, and I never heard a bad word said against him, but he was an outsider."

"A genius, more likely," Marie corrected. "The sort to avoid people and take refuge in his own intellect. No pesky frivolities or drama, no disappointments." She shrugged. "Sad, but true." The words were clipped and matter-of-fact, but Olive had the impression that she was truly affected. When they had a moment alone, she would broach the subject.

"I'd definitely seen him chatting with Mr Harris," Olive said, wondering if one of them might have overheard the argument.

"Maybe he had questions about the mystery meat," Liz said wryly.

Neither of the others could offer anything more useful, and when Danny Tierney strolled up to stand beside Marie, looking particularly rough round the edges, and not at all the safe sort, with his smudgy bruises and scraped knuckles, Olive made her excuses and slipped away.

She made the rounds, coyly quizzing both agents and officers on their impressions of Lieutenant Beckett. And as she watched for a telltale shift in expression, a stilted comment, or a fidgety movement, she kept her hand wrapped carefully round her glass and tipped back her gin without swallowing any of it.

Mostly, everyone was talking of other things—upcoming missions, explosive trials, and even the recent burglary. Olive was torn, wanting to listen, but feeling compelled to carry on, even though it had become distressingly clear that no one really knew Lieutenant Beckett or what he might be capable of. Then again, it was entirely possible that one of their number was a consummate liar and had had every reason to kill him.

She sidled close to Tomás Harris, then waited out his conversation with Major Boom and a man she didn't recognise, determined to eke out a bit of useful information after her thus far fruitless efforts. She had only to extricate herself from a chat with a subaltern whose cowlick was drooping like a flag at half-mast. . . . But suddenly a familiar voice spoke in her ear.

"I see you're taking the sleuthing very seriously."

Olive whirled round and found herself almost eye to eye with

Jamie. There was a pained wrinkle between his brows that closely resembled the typical disapproving wrinkle, and in the split second before she spoke, it was impossible to gauge what he knew. The subaltern scurried.

"I am, yes," she agreed. "Unfortunately, with very little success. But we can discuss that later. How are you feeling? Headache routed? Should you really be out of bed so quickly? Why not take a good long rest?" She was gabbling and now made to shoo him out of the room.

"You're really quite a bad liar," he told her. "Although I suppose in this particular case you're not so much lying as hiding something. But I can't bear to listen to any more just now, so carry on." He turned and walked slowly and carefully to the drinks table, where he poured himself a measure of whiskey. He didn't turn back.

Officially dismissed, Olive decided to worry about Jamie—and any possible consequences—later. Right now, she was determined to speak with Mr Harris. But when she turned to look for him, he'd disappeared.

Chapter 7

Olive had meant to spend the morning finalising new strategies for breeding and training that might meet the needs of Baker Street's current and future missions. But as she paged slowly through the loft's logbooks and lineage charts, her eyes running over the details of past training regimens, racing results, and breeding pairs, she couldn't keep her focus.

The difficulty might possibly have had something to do with her stepmother's decision to sit some ten feet away, her leg propped carefully on a cushion, a staggering collection of accoutrements arranged beside her. For a time, she focused quietly on her knitting, but as her frustrated outbursts became more frequent—and colourful——her fingers reached for the jade enameled box.

As one cigarette led to a second and then a third, Olive's eyes began to water. "Not keen to take Dr Harrington's advice, then?" she said lightly.

"About the cigarettes?" Harriet said, staring at the smoldering tip of the one caught between her fingers. "Oh, damn," she said viciously, stamping it out. "If giving them up will keep the MS at bay a little longer, I suppose I really should make an effort. Oh, but I will miss them." This last bit was said with great tragedy.

It was, quite possibly, Olive's smirk that galvanised Harriet into a new frame of mind. With a flourish reminiscent of her usual self, she snatched up pen and paper and began a comprehensive—and frustratingly audible—list of things that might be accomplished despite her injury. Naturally, she enlisted Olive's help with the task.

Sensing that her pigeon efforts would need to be shunted until Harriet was sufficiently distracted with an absorbing project, Olive pounced on an item from the list that held particular promise.

"I'd be happy to deliver a note of welcome to Peregrine Hall," she said, rising to tidy the books and papers strewn on her father's desk. "I'll take Jonathon with me, and a basket of fruit, as well." Before Harriet could countermand the suggestion, Olive fled, calling behind her, "I'll be back in ten minutes for the letter."

She went up to her room to squirrel away the notes she'd made and to check her appearance, which was surely dishevelled after hours spent trying to concentrate amid her stepmother's shared frustrations. One look in the mirror confirmed her suspicion: various curls required a ruthless re-pinning, and her cheeks and lips could definitely benefit from a bit of brightening. Given the war-ravaged state of one of the hall's new occupants, a slick of morale-boosting red lipstick was definitely in order. Olive wondered casually about the young pilot's thoughts on lippy women and grinned, very much looking forward to finding out.

Less than a quarter of an hour later, she and Jonathon had set out along the river path, with an eager Hen trailing along beside them. Olive had tucked Harriet's letter into her pocket, Hen swung a basket of nearly ripe plums in a jaunty manner, and Jonathon lugged the bulky pigeon carrier, which held a pair of first-season birds. At five months old, the pigeons' training was now beginning in earnest. A quick flight from Peregrine Hall would give them a chance to survey the landscape, particularly the track of the River Lea. But before that, they might also be a conversation starter.

Before her death that spring, Miss Husselbee had decided that the hall's wide, sloping lawns weren't doing anyone any good such as they were and so had asked the powers that be for the loan of a pair of Land Girls to transform them into a vast victory garden, whose produce could supplement the village ration as well as the WI's fundraising efforts. The girls had appeared as if by magic, had got on with their work, and had disappeared. Miss Husselbee would have nodded in brisk approval.

That August morning, as their little party approached the hall from the river path, it was clear that the long rows of vegetables were thriving, if slightly overgrown. The WI had devised the Husselbee Garden Scheme at the end of June in order to organise the work involved, and Jonathon was a regular helper. Olive hoped that the hall's new occupants would allow the scheme to continue.

No doubt hearing the chatter of Hen and Jonathon, a tall, plump lady in a white button-up blouse and loose buff trousers turned from an unruly hydrangea bush, secateurs in hand. She squinted at them, her broad-brimmed hat askew, and Olive put her hand up in a wave.

"We probably should have gone round to the front door," Olive murmured, "but a walk along the river is more pleasant than one along the road."

As they came closer, she smiled at them, looking genuinely pleased. Beside her, an oversize basket was filled with cuttings of blowsy white hydrangea blooms, and the scent of them was heavy in the air. "How wonderful to have visitors," she said, slipping the secateurs in her pocket. "I'm Lady Revell." She stepped forward to take each of their hands in turn, learn their names, and bestow a welcoming smile.

Olive proffered the letter from Harriet, and Hen, the plums, both of which were accepted with polite cordiality.

"What have you got in there?" Lady Revell asked Jonathon, indicating the carrier, which he'd been shifting from hand to hand.

"They're war pigeons," he said proudly, straightening his shoulders.

Lady Revell's eyes widened. "Really?"

Jonathon nodded and, with a glance at Olive, said, "We're supplying birds for the National Pigeon Service. And they'll send them on for use by His Majesty's Forces."

"Oh, I *see*," she said, with enough interest to gratify even Jonathon's pride in the birds. She glanced round, squinting again despite the overcast sky, and her smile wavered with uncertainty.

Olive followed her gaze to the terrace off the drawing room and saw the bowed head of a man sitting in solitude.

"Is that your son?" Olive asked quietly. "We'd be delighted to meet him. Jonathon would dearly love to show off his birds." She smiled, hoping Lady Revell wouldn't consider her overly intrusive.

The sparkle had gone from her eyes, but with perfect grace, she said, "I should think he'd love to see them."

So they all set off across the yard, chattering as they went. Olive kept her eye on the seated figure, wrapped in a deep blue dressing gown, his striped pajama legs stretched out before him. His hair was chestnut brown and considerably longer than the RAF allowed. It had presumably been grown out to shield his disfigurement from prying eyes. Better that than apathy. Olive felt a quiver in her stomach and impatiently quashed it.

As they approached the terrace, Jonathon spoke in a hushed whisper. "I wonder if he'd be mad if I asked him about his wheelchair."

Olive suggested, "Why don't we see how it goes, shall we?"

Lady Revell went round to stand on the far side of the wheelchair, leaving the three of them to line up opposite. With a tight smile and her hands twisting nervously, she said, "This is my nephew, the Honourable Maxwell Dunn. Or I suppose I should say Squadron Leader—"

"Leave off," the hunched figure said brusquely. "It's just Max. I don't feel very honourable, and I doubt I will again. And I'm certainly not in the mood to entertain guests." He stared out sullenly over the garden, clearly determined to be uncouth.

"Maxwell," Lady Revell said sharply. "Behave yourself." It seemed as if she wanted to say more, but instead, she let her lips settle into an apologetic smile.

"Hullo, Max," Hen said, no doubt appreciating his plain speaking. "I'm Henrietta Gibbons, Girl Guide. Call on me for any odd jobs. I've earned quite a number of badges, and my fee is quite reasonable."

Olive rolled her eyes, but when he didn't respond, she nudged Jonathon to speak up.

"I'm Jonathon Maddocks, sir." His voice wavered slightly, but as he glanced at the carrier, it firmed up nicely. "I'm rather busy helping out with pigeons and pigs, managing a garden, and now building a wheelchair, but you can call on me, as well, and I'll do my best."

Still nary a reaction, so with a dose of vinegar in her voice, Olive introduced herself. "And I'm Olive Bright, FANY, pig vet, and pigeoneer. You might as well look at me." Her tone was encouraging. "After all, I've donned red lipstick strictly with the thought of boosting your spirits. But barring that, I'm anxious to help you dispel the rumours clamouring through the village. They're ridiculous to the point of absurdity."

As his head came up, Olive plastered a wide smile on her face, setting Auxiliary Red to advantage. She desperately hoped her first glimpse of his puckered skin, bloodshot eyes, and slack jaw didn't cause it to slip.

He had been handsome: deep-set eyes, aristocratic nose, square jaw, and chiseled cheekbones. It was as if the burns had melted away all the sharp edges, blurring those features into obscurity. But he wasn't lost. The fire in his eyes and the hardening of his jaw as he fought to arrange his mouth into a wry smile gave some indication of the man he'd been. Someone he seemed to have cast off right along with his RAF uniform.

"What will you tell them now that you've seen the gruesome sight of me for yourself, Miss Bright?"

"I'm *hoping* I can tell them that we enjoyed a pleasant visit and you declared my birds quite impressive and up to the task before them."

It might have been her imagination, but it seemed as if the tight skin across his face relaxed a bit and the tension eased from his shoulders. "I suppose I better have a look at them, then, hadn't I?"

Worrying his lip, Jonathon knelt to open the carrier. He pulled out the blue-chequered cock and handed him carefully to Hen. Next came the hen, as stark white as a dove.

"That's Ernst," he said, pointing to the cock. "He's named after the middle son in *The Swiss Family Robinson*. And this one is Velvet, after the girl in *National Velvet*," he said shyly.

Max Dunn stared at the pigeons in silence, but after a moment, his eyes had shifted to become unfocused and disinterested, as if his thoughts had been drawn inward. Olive suspected he was remembering war-torn skies and his own tragedy.

"They'll do well enough," he said bitterly. "If they're hit, the end will come quickly. They'll not be caught in a metal trap that's going up in flames."

Lady Revell spoke up quickly. "Why don't I take the children into the kitchen? We'll prepare the tea while the two of you get better acquainted."

"We'll just release the pigeons first, shall we?" Olive suggested, already feeling a mild twist of discomfort at the thought of being left alone with Max Dunn.

With a single shared glance, Hen and Jonathon shifted their holds on the folded wings, and then, in tandem, they threw up their arms and released the birds into the summer sky. Their powerful wings beat vigorously, lifting them high into the air. High above the terrace, the pigeons panned in ever widening circles, with Velvet seeming almost to disappear into the pale, overcast sky. And then suddenly, they were heading north, toward home.

As Olive turned to gauge Max Dunn's reaction, she was disappointed to see him staring blankly out over the garden. She considered going with Lady Revell and the children as they set off but decided instead to dig in her heels. He might behave like a cad, but no doubt, he had good reason, and she could give as good as she got.

She settled into a nearby chair and let the silence run on for a moment.

"Please tell me you're not here out of pity. That would be so much worse than nosiness."

Olive glanced at him. "Certainly, I was curious—we all are. It may seem like the rankest busybodying to you, but there's such a thing as being kind and neighbourly. I do believe it's that sort of thing you—and all of us—are fighting for." He sat sullenly silent as she stared at his profile. Its ill-fitting flesh made her stomach curdle with thoughts of what he'd survived.

"My best friend joined the RAF," she said quietly. "He's been away at Secondary Flight Training School, but one day soon, he'll be up there in one of those metal cages, fighting for his life against the Luftwaffe." Her throat felt hot and tight, but no tears threatened. Yet. "I *hate* it—for him, for all of them. And that includes my birds." She watched a butterfly, flitting near the urns at the edge of the terrace. "I wish it was all over, that none of it— the rations, the blackouts, the secrets—was necessary. But it is, and it will be until it's truly over. And I'm afraid none of us is charmed. We're all afraid what this war will take from us." With a sniff and a deep, steadying breath, she said quietly, "I don't pity you, but I am sorry for you. Sorry that this war demanded such risks, such pain. I think you'll find that most people will feel the same. And they'll want to shake your hand, in appreciation of your sacrifice."

After her little speech, she sat quietly, letting the breeze cool her face, as she looked out over the trees and garden, its flowers heavy with bees, drenching the air in scent. As she lounged, her thoughts drifted. She thought of Lieutenant Beckett, who'd fought in his own intellectual, quiet way. He wasn't the picture of a hero, and for him, there'd be no glory. He hadn't been given the chance to brood in angry solitude or rail at the world. His death had been unremarkable and was, in fact, proving a confusing muddle.

"I'm told they only found me because of a pigeon," he said at last.

Olive's head swung round as he broke the silence, and his words registered the barest second later. Judging by his tone, he seemed to imply that this, in fact, had been the final, ignominious blow in the end of his pilot's career. She ignored that.

"Really? Was it to be your companion for the entire flight, or were you dropping it somewhere over Europe?"

He glanced askance at her, surprise in his eyes.

"I do know a little bit about how things work," she said. "Particularly as pertains to pigeons."

"He was our backup—in case our radios got damaged. We were on our way home, midway over the Channel, having dropped our payload onto the Hamburg docks, when our observer spotted the enemy aircraft. They'd scrambled some Messerschmitts and were dogging our tail. My gunners managed to light up a pair of them, but they were too agile, too quick. One of the bastards—" He glanced up at her, looking charmingly chagrined.

"Don't be sorry—they *are* bloody bastards," she confirmed.

He laughed, albeit somewhat harshly. Evidently, a bit of cursing was heartily curative. The unfamiliar shift of his facial muscles beneath those tight patches of new skin must have pained him a bit, as he winced before going on.

"Fair enough. One of the bastards strafed the left side of our

Vickers Wellington, shooting up my waist gunner in the process." His mouth was a thin line twisted into a grimace of memory. "When the engine caught fire, it burned quick, and it was all I could manage to keep the nose up, on the barest chance we didn't go straight into the water and die on impact." His hands gripped the arms of his wheelchair, and Olive noticed for the first time that they, too, were burned and blotchy in shades of pink. She stared at them as he went on. "I don't have any memory of anything more until I woke up in hospital, night having turned into the brightest white." He hung his head. "They told me what had happened."

"Your gunner?" she asked quietly, wanting to cover his hand with hers but worried that his wounds might still be painful.

"Johnny," he said quietly. "We had a crew of six, but our top gunner and navigator died in the crash, and the rest of us, all but Johnny, were badly burned. By some miracle, he managed to get the dinghy inflated and all of us dumped into it. Evidently, our transmitter was a goner, but Lord Byron—that was what we'd nicknamed our pigeon—was apparently fit enough to make it back home to let the ASR—that's the Air-Sea Rescue—know our location. One look at the group of us, and they likely wondered why they'd bothered. Johnny had bled out, and the rest of us were barely alive."

"I'm so sorry," Olive said, knowing the words were meaningless, but needing to say them, nonetheless. On impulse, she added, "Johnny was obviously the sort of person we all want by our side. The sort we hope we can be ourselves."

Max Dunn met her gaze, his eyes seeming shockingly dark in his pale face. "He was far better than I," he said flatly. After a moment, he snorted. "When it comes to that, so was Lord Byron."

"He does sound like a stellar bird," Olive agreed. "Was he a lady killer or merely prone to strutting about with a look of dissipation?"

"Because of his nickname, you mean? No, nothing like that."
He shrugged, suddenly looking rather shy. "It was just a bit of
absurdity. I read English literature at Cambridge and had a particular fondness for the Romantic poets."

"Oh, naturally," Olive said with a rueful smile. When his eyebrows shot up in confusion, she clarified, "A girlfriend of mine
suspects we're all under the spell of the RAF—all debonair flyboys with rakish charm and personality. You probably quote poetry rather indiscriminately, don't you?"

"*Indiscriminately* implies an utter lack of finesse, don't you
think?"

Olive grinned and suddenly had a wild thought. The memory
of Horace nearly chased it off but, in the end, was emphatically
ignored. With a deep breath, she reached into her pocket for the
paper onto which she'd copied down Lieutenant Beckett's lines
of verse from memory. Hopefully, they weren't too far off the
original. "Can you, by any chance, identify the author of this?"
she said, thrusting the paper in his direction. "I've recently come
across it—I can't tell you where—and it's rather important that I
find out."

He looked at her quizzically, but as his fingers closed over the
page, it seemed as if an understanding passed between them. A
moment later his gaze roved over the words.

"It's a bit of an odd coincidence, but I do recognise this. It's
very close, in any case." Seeing Olive's startled, gratified expression, he hurried on. "A friend from university joined up at the
same time—we went through training together. He was the sort
your friend was telling you about—tall and handsome, cheeky
grin, flair for the dramatic. He was fond of spouting these first
two lines at the drop of a hat."

Olive's heartbeat began to thrum in her veins as she waited for
him to go on. But at that moment, Lady Revell stepped onto the
terrace, carrying the tea tray, with Hen and Jonathon in her wake.
By silent agreement, the subject was temporarily dropped.

With Max having softened a bit toward visitors, he was immediately inundated with information about the village and its environs (Hen) and questions about his chair (Jonathon). They spent a pleasant hour chatting.

It wasn't until it was time to leave, when her companions had challenged each other to a race and Lady Revell had gone back to her hydrangeas, that Olive managed a few words alone with Max Dunn.

"Wilfred Owen," he said, without a word of prompting.

Her eyes widened, and the thrill of discovery swept over her. "I don't suppose you know the name of the poem?"

"I do, in fact, and it's rather apropos. It's called 'Strange Meeting.' Written about the Great War, if I remember right."

Olive's curious mind raced ahead, but she reined in her thoughts of Lieutenant Beckett's mysterious death to focus on her companion. They'd had a bit of a rocky start, but she rather thought things were shaping up nicely. Until he spoke again, thoroughly disabusing her.

"I'm afraid I don't know any more than that," he went on, "so don't expect any more help from me."

His voice was clipped, and she sensed she'd been dismissed.

"Thank you for your help. Believe it or not, it was a pleasure, Squadron Leader Dunn," she said.

"Max." The word was nearly a growl.

"I appreciate you telling me about Lord Byron. When you're stuck in a little country village, with the war barely touching you, it's nice to hear that the work you're doing is making an impact."

He didn't answer. His head had dipped down, and she wondered if he was in pain.

"Goodbye, Max. I hope our paths cross again soon."

As she walked away, her thoughts teemed with possibilities. Perhaps he could be her Watson now that George had gone off. Or barring that, a savvy Hastings. It didn't occur to her until she was nearly home that he might not want to see her again.

* * *

Harriet had relocated to the comfort of her chaise, and Olive devoted the better part of an hour to regaling her with the details of their visit to Peregrine Hall.

"You seem entirely fascinated with the man," her stepmother said, eyes shrewd.

Olive raised her brows. "He's new to the village."

"Have you had tea and a cosy chat with Miss Swan or Miss Featherington? Both came to Pipley some weeks ago." Harriet was baiting her now, and she knew it.

"Not yet. I went today only as a favour to you." She tapped her lip with her finger. "I suspect Jamie would like Max Dunn very much. I think I'll drag him along next time I have cause to visit." She stood. "Now, I'm afraid, it's back to work for me."

Certain that Harriet would ponder the topic of Max Dunn for the next hour at least, Olive slipped from the room, then closeted herself in the study.

He was, admittedly, on her mind, as well. She thought back over their conversation and his casual revelation of the poem's name and author. *"Strange Meeting."* It had been as if, after behaving like a grumpy hermit and then a tolerant uncle, he'd thrown off the mantle of self-pity to involve himself in her little mystery. But then the blue devils had taken over again, shutting her out.

Max Dunn was the first person in a very long time to have kindled a spark in her. Jamie obviously didn't count. And while she could certainly drag Jamie to Peregrine Hall, clinging to his arm and beaming up at him, it might fool Max, but it wouldn't change her own feelings of restlessness. It wasn't at all fair, but what could she do, even if she wanted to? Jamie wasn't going anywhere. Her mood now suitably glum, she turned her focus to the lines of verse.

A strange meeting could be arranged or unexpected. It could refer to common or cross purposes. It could be prompted by treason, but it might also be as innocent as the chance meeting of a pair of birdwatchers using the same blind on a predawn outing.

What on earth had it meant to Lieutenant Beckett?

She positively itched to get her hands on a copy of the entire poem and was pondering a visit to the library when her gaze ranged distractedly over the bookshelves lining the wall beside the fireplace. *It's just possible. . . .* She moved round the desk, eager to peruse her father's volumes.

Both of her parents had served in the Great War, and her mother had been a great fan of poetry. After a quarter of an hour, she conscripted Jonathon, who'd come in from the garden early for tea, into helping with the search. And together they finger-stepped their way over the volumes until Jonathon found an anthology of poetry written during the Great War. A quick scan of the contents had them crowing in triumph: "Strange Meeting" was among the works included.

"You are indispensable, my boy," Olive enthused, thrilled with their success.

Jonathon had been scanning the lines and now looked at her quizzically. "Why do you want to read this? It's very sad." After a pause he added, "It is, isn't it? Honestly, it's rather confusing."

"You're right," she agreed, thinking how he'd managed to sum up the entire situation. "It's both very sad and confusing." She lowered her voice. "There's a bit of mystery surrounding the man who died. I'm hoping this will help to solve it."

His face lit with understanding. "Is Captain Aldridge helping you?"

Olive suspected Jonathon idolised the man. "Sort of," she said noncommittally, then countered with a question of her own. "Is Lieutenant Tierney helping *you* with something other than the wheelchair?"

Jonathon tipped his head to stare at his shifting feet.

"You don't have to tell me," she said softly. "I suppose it's something I couldn't have helped with."

He glanced up then, the corner of his mouth curling like the tail of a possum. "He's teaching me to defend myself." Seeing Olive's raised brows, he added, "Just in case. A few of the older boys have taken to bullying some of the younger ones, and I want them to stop."

"Rightly so," she said, wrapping an arm round his thin shoulders.

He peered up at her through the tousle of his nut-brown hair. "I suspect your strategy would be the same as Hen's."

Olive bobbed her head consideringly. "I involve the testicles only if absolutely necessary. Best to stick with Lieutenant Tierney. And maybe share a few pointers with Hen."

He nodded and escaped to the kitchen, where Mrs Battlesby was spooning him a plate of beans on toast.

Olive hunkered down in her father's wingback chair with the poem, paying careful attention to the relevant stanza.

> *Courage was mine, and I had mystery;*
> *Wisdom was mine, and I had mastery;*
> *To miss the march of this retreating world*
> *Into vain citadels that are not walled.*

Her throat tightened as she read the other verses, which were full of the gruesome realities and brutal truths of the Great War, very likely foreshadowing the horrors of this one. Did the chosen words hint at an impending invasion—the march of Nazi fascism on the undefended shores of Britain? She thought back to that afternoon in the library, to Lieutenant Beckett talking wistfully of rose-coloured glasses. Had it all simply been an act? She'd imagined she was a better judge of character than that.

With fresh incentive, she pored over the poem, searching for any mentions that might hint at timing or location and for any other relevant references. Finally, with a hefty sigh, she fell back against the cushion and closed her eyes. Lieutenant Beckett's face took shape: his kind eyes behind dark-rimmed spectacles, his tentative smile with a couple of wonky teeth. She had trouble believing there was a nefarious bone in his body.

Even M Poirot had been known to dismiss a suspect based on character or disposition. And if he could do it, she needn't have any qualms on the matter. But she wasn't ready to take that step just yet. There were still too many unanswered questions.

Her lip jutted out as she stretched her toe over the Oriental rug laid before the fireplace. Lieutenant Beckett could have been the mastermind behind the recent burglary at the manor, with a plan to sell the goods on the black market. He could have been a double—or even a triple—agent. Or he could simply have been a man fond of poetry.

She'd been over those four lines so many times, they were running unchecked through her mind. Taken on their own, they weren't the least bit enlightening. Was it possible this was a dead end? Feeling frustratingly as if she'd been cast as the Hastings in this little mystery, Olive had a sudden thought. A thought she considered worthy of Poirot himself. It was entirely possible— and surely, quite likely—that the true message had been written in invisible ink.

Olive had been packing the belongings of an officer who was to be transferred to a facility nicknamed Churchill's Toyshop when she'd discovered a dog-eared, simply bound tome. Its cover had been printed with the unassuming words *Training Manual*. A quick rifle through the pages had sent shivers of excitement through her. It was Baker Street's regimen for its agents, covering everything from disguises to interrogation to secret inks. She'd begged Jamie, employing doe-like eyes and pouty lips, to let her borrow a copy, and after he'd given his temples and jaw a good going-over, he and Horace had grudgingly agreed. She kept it tucked amid her underthings and felt much like an agent herself when she pulled it out each night to read over another chapter. It had certainly got her thinking.

The moment she'd discovered that the paper pulled from the dead man's pocket was in code, she'd been eager to practice the deciphering techniques she'd learned. Jamie had thwarted that intention, but here, possibly, was another chance to demonstrate her newfound knowledge. Lieutenant Beckett would have been likely to have the skills, and access to the necessary supplies, to fashion invisible inks, and what better way to keep his hand in than using them for his private messages?

Olive shut the book, a sense of accomplishment having routed her dour mood. This revelation was going to go a long way toward diverting Jamie's attention from her unauthorised prowl through his office. If he'd even suspected it. There was, of course, a fly in the ointment: if a secret message *was* revealed via some sort of developer, it might not offer any additional insights. For the simple reason that no one seemed to know anything about the man. Still, it was worth a try.

As she slipped the little volume back into the bookcase, she resolved, once and for all, to search Lieutenant Beckett's room for further clues. And she would do it with or without Jamie's permission.

Chapter 8

After a nerve-racking morning and an afternoon spent mired in thoughts of death, Olive was ready for a drink—and a party. But first, she had to navigate dinner with her father and stepmother. The latter, whose vision had recently gone a bit blurry—Dr Harrington had diagnosed the condition as optic neuritis—was feeling rather fraught, particularly after her misdirected fork had sent her serving of peas rolling in all directions until she couldn't corral a single one. Olive had gamely tried to steer the conversation but had found she had rather a dearth of topics to choose from. She couldn't discuss the upcoming mission, her new strategy for the loft, her investigation into Lieutenant Beckett's death, or any of the day-to-day business at the manor, and really, what else was left?

"Margaret has joined the Royal Observer Corps," she finally blurted.

Her father's head came up. "Has she, now?"

"That's certainly unexpected," Harriet said, her voice cross as she spared one last exasperated look at her plate. "I shudder to think what the village will have to say about it. She won't be at their beck and call."

Her father snorted. "No doubt the desire to put herself out of reach informed her decision."

"She'll be close enough at Balls Wood," Olive replied automatically, forking up her last bite. As interest lit the eyes of both her father and stepmother, she could have kicked herself. Urgently desiring to change the subject, she swallowed too quickly and choked.

Jonathon piped up. "The Girl Guides were camping in Balls Wood when they found the body of that officer."

Olive winced, hoping her own role on that grim morning wouldn't be revealed.

"Margaret won't be there alone, will she?" Harriet said worriedly.

"Not likely." This from her father. "There'll be two of them on duty." He glanced round the table. "Good thing, too. It would be a mighty coincidence if a fit young man like that was felled by a rock. Foul play, on the other hand, is another matter entirely and needs investigating."

Oh, how Olive wanted to agree with him, to confide all the clues she'd collected and detail the time she'd spent investigating, all of it leading up to her latest suspicions. It would be wonderful to be able to *talk* about it all. But given that Lieutenant Beckett had worked for Baker Street, it was entirely possible that his death—if intentional—would fall under the Official Secrets Act. So she held her tongue and ignored Jonathon's darting glances.

"Fate is a monstrous companion," Harriet said bluntly, and quite bitterly.

Olive's father covered his wife's trembling hand with his own calloused paw. "You mustn't think that way, my dear."

"I can't bear the changes wrought by this war. Bombs and torpedoes, the horrible news of occupations and evacuations in Europe. Miss Husselbee, Lieutenant Beckett, and that poor damaged young pilot who's moved into Peregrine Hall, afflicted with those frightful burns. All those young men." Now her voice was trembling, and she was near to tears. This wasn't at all like Harriet, who could bear up better than anyone in the face of adversity—and come out better on the other side of it. All of them knew that her recent fall, likely prompted by her worsening condition, was to blame for her fretful state of mind, but it was no consolation.

Olive had no idea what to say to her, but she opened her mouth, hoping the words would come. Jonathon spoke up first.

"Good things have come of it, though—the war, I mean. All the schemes and fundraisers, everyone doing their bit, making do, rallying together for victory."

Her eyes twinkling with tears, Harriet beamed at him.

"And you, Jonathon, the best of all of them. Where would we be without you?" Olive said truthfully.

On that cheery note, she served the pudding—a berry tart with a dab of clotted cream—and vowed once again to find a project to occupy Harriet's time and mind.

"Where do you think you're going, my girl?" her father demanded as he and Kíli strolled out of the encroaching twilight to find her wheeling the Welbike from the shelter of the surgery.

"I've told you. I'm going to a party at the manor." She'd carefully avoided mentioning that it was a graduation party for a class of Belgian secret agents, the timing rather unfortunate.

"You did," he allowed, "and I assumed that Captain Aldridge would be in attendance."

"He will," she said brightly.

"Then it would be my expectation that he would fetch you."

Olive wanted to groan. If her father knew how she'd been spending her time lately, he wouldn't balk at her nipping up to Brickendonbury for a couple of hours in the dark. But he didn't, and so she must prevaricate.

"Jamie is—" she started, only to be interrupted by her father.

"Right on time."

And when she turned to see the dark Austin lumbering up the drive, as if conjured by her father's suspicions, she couldn't think of a single thing to say.

She heard the click as her father settled his pipe between his teeth and then the scuff of gravel as he moved off toward the dovecote. And without a word, she put away the motorbike and walked into the muted light of the headlamps, feeling only mildly self-conscious in her lemon-yellow summer frock as he stood just beyond the reach of light, waiting for her.

Full dark was her favourite setting for a conversation with Jamie. As she stared out at the shadowy road ahead, she could talk, blissfully oblivious to the inevitable frown lines, eye rolls, and tightened jaw. Admittedly, there were still copious sighs, but she could attribute them to the car or the hedgerow and carry on uninterrupted.

So as they bumped along the familiar path to the manor, she described the day's efforts, careful to emphasise the work she'd done with regard to the pigeons. She mentioned Max Dunn, her discovery of the relevant volume of poetry, and her suspicion that Lieutenant Beckett might have been using invisible ink. Jamie didn't argue or disagree—he didn't say a word. She was feeling quite confident when she broached the topic that was bound to rile him.

"We need more information to make sense of what we have. No one I've spoken to seems to know anything about the man. Beyond his good taste in jumpers and a preference for Jules Verne." As the headlights slashed an arc across the crisp white façade of the manor house, she concluded, "We need to search his room, and tonight we have the perfect opportunity."

Jamie cut the engine but didn't move to open the car door. He didn't look at her, and he didn't speak, and Olive found herself more nervous than she'd have been had he shouted at her. She sat very still, not at all certain how to proceed, as a cricket crescendo rose somewhere nearby. And then a bolt of fear shot through her, and she broke the silence.

"Something else has happened, hasn't it? What is it?" She jerked round to look at him, and he blinked at her, his face impassive.

"Nothing more alarming than your indiscriminate sleuthing," he said harshly, his left eyebrow having shot up so far, it had disappeared into shadow.

"Oh, *murder*," she muttered, her shoulders dropping. She should have predicted a lecture and scheduled this little chat accordingly. A glass of whiskey—or really any spirit at all—made Jamie heaps more tolerable, and his commanding intensity rather attractive. Although the glamour soon faded.

"I know you remember signing the Official Secrets Act, and I feel certain you understood its implications."

"Yes. And?"

"And yet you somehow considered it appropriate to share the details of evidence taken from the pockets of a now-dead officer of Station XVII."

"You said you thought his death was an accident." She realised her mistake instantly and hurried to backtrack. "And it wasn't the *actual* evidence—"

Jamie smacked his palm against the dashboard. "Don't be obtuse, Olive," he ground out. "Whether it was the actual slip of paper or not is immaterial. The relevance, if any, is likely in the words themselves."

"I wasn't aware you considered any of it relevant," she tossed back. "Surely you recall that I had to beg to be allowed to investigate."

"And I agreed." His voice was icy calm. "What does that tell you?"

Olive blinked. She'd thought it meant he was tired of arguing and couldn't see the harm. Did he actually agree with her that something was amiss? "I didn't reveal anything, and he didn't express any curiosity on the matter. He knows neither that I'm working at Brickendonbury nor that I'm investigating a suspicious death. He's been a recluse, much to the frustration of the village, and he has his own troubles." She'd share his pigeon story later.

"You're too spontaneous, too trusting, too bloody Machiavellian!" He propped his elbow on the window frame and rubbed a hand over his eyes. "If you were an agent, your handler would almost certainly have an ulcer. I daresay I'm doomed to one myself."

She couldn't think of anything productive to say.

"What if you put your trust in the very man that cryptic message was intended for—after Lieutenant Beckett had somehow managed to intercept it?"

Olive considered this theory far-fetched in the extreme. "You don't seriously think that?"

"No," he admitted grimly. "I was making a point."

"And here I was thinking you had no imagination." This admission prompted a disapproving frown. "Sorry," she muttered. "Allow me to counter. As a result of a casual conversation with a fallen RAF pilot, undertaken by yours truly, we now have a bit more insight into the verse Lieutenant Beckett was mysteriously carrying in his pocket."

He looked away from her. Shiftily.

"You already know which poem it is, don't you?" she accused. "You know, and you didn't tell me."

He huffed out a sigh. "That's not relevant at this moment. Right now, I need to impress upon you that there is a time and place for renegade behaviour. This. Isn't. It."

As she stewed in silence, envying the party-goers their drinks and laughter, she listened to the sound of Jamie's heavy sigh and then the unexpected words coming out of the darkness. "We'll search his room tonight. Together."

A thrill whipped through her at this unexpected pronouncement, but Olive was determined to rein in her reaction and treat the matter as if it were a fait accompli. Despite his underhanded tactics with the poem, his willingness to go along with her suggestion left her cautiously optimistic. Would he be a willing partner in crime going forward? If he wasn't keen to be cast as the Watson to her Sherlock, then perhaps she could allow him equal footing.

Jamie cut across her thoughts. "And I will explain exactly how it's going to work."

Naturally.

"While I'm not yet convinced that Lieutenant Beckett's death was anything more than an accident, I'd just assume not advertise the fact that we're investigating the matter. If it *was* foul play, then it's likely someone in the manor was involved."

Olive's fingers folded themselves into fists on her lap. The thought had occurred to her, as well.

"This is your chance to play at being an agent," he said wryly. "Your mission is to enter the room in the northwest corner of the first floor without being seen. I'll meet you there"—he checked his watch, tilting his wrist to catch the moonlight—"at a quarter to eleven. That's an hour and a half from now. The servants' staircase is located—"

"I know where it is," she said matter-of-factly.

If that surprised him, he didn't show it. "Neither of us has a reason for being up there—my own room is at the opposite end of the house—so it would be wise to have a ready excuse in case of company."

"Is that all?" she asked after a beat of silence.

"I suppose so."

"*Merde alors*, Captain Aldridge," she said, then slipped from the car with a grin on her face.

Chapter 9

25 August

Olive debated whether to drink a glass of gin. Was it better to have her senses ever so slightly muddled if it meant she'd be less likely to throttle Jamie? She thought so and proceeded accordingly. For an hour and a half, she danced with agents and officers, flirting harmlessly, and pretended that her single drink flowed into many. More than once she caught Jamie watching her, but she blithely ignored him, determined not to let him see that her nerves were rather frayed.

She suspected Jamie would view this entire endeavour as a test. Her ability to hold her liquor might even come into question. And she was determined to ace every bit of it.

By the time the clock chimed the half hour, Jamie had disappeared. Determined not to let it fluster her, she finished her swaying dance with Renauld, wished him luck in the final stage of his training at Beaulieu, then pretended to get her bracelet caught in her hair, making certain to tug a healthy hank from its pins. With a ready excuse to go in search of a mirror for a quick repair, she slipped from the room.

There was no one about. Either the manor's inhabitants were closeted in their offices, burning the midnight oil in a desperate attempt to turn the tide of the war, or else they were simply burnt out and engaged in the distraction of drink and dancing. And the FANYs, both expected and delighted to join in the festivities, wouldn't be ready to call it a night for at least another hour or two.

She hurried toward the back of the house, slipped through the baize door, and nipped up the servants' stair. Peering into the dimly lit corridor of the first floor, she wondered if Jamie was already in place. Treading carefully near the wall to avoid any telltale creaks of the floorboards, she hurried forward, stopping only to fix her hair in the reflection of a gilt-framed mirror. A moment later, she was tapping the door to Lieutenant Beckett's room shut behind her.

The room was dark as pitch, with barely enough light seeping in through the blackout curtains to hint at the bulky presence of bed, night table, desk, and wardrobe. She stood still for a moment, getting her bearings. A prickle rose over her skin, and suddenly Jamie materialised beside her, coming out of the dark like an ectoplasm.

"Better if we don't use the electric light." His voice was a mere vibration. "Someone might see it under the door—or at the edge of the curtain—and come to investigate."

She nodded, and he handed her a spare torch.

"You take the wardrobe," he said abruptly, having retreated to the desk.

"Gladly," she murmured before moving to the other side of the room. It took her less than a minute to decide that using one hand for the torch was going to seriously impede her search, so she clamped the end of it between her teeth and ignored the grimy taste of it on her tongue as she ran her hands over jacket linings, into pockets, and along the joins of the furniture itself.

Deep in the recesses of the wardrobe, a curtain of clothes

draped round her, Olive was struck by the strong scent of cloves. Obviously, Lieutenant Beckett was a fastidious fellow, eager to keep the moths from his tony jackets and cashmere jumpers. She extracted herself, straightened, and tipped her head up. There, on a narrow shelf, sat the neatly folded jumpers. She pulled them down, then stood on tiptoe and stretched as far as she could reach, and there, in the corner, her fingers closed over a lumpy little sachet, which surely held the source of the scent. Judging by the size of one lump in particular, it held something else, as well.

Her fingers fumbled with the drawstring, and a moment later cloves were tumbling into the palm of her hand. But then the torchlight winked on a curve of metal. That it was a signet ring was readily apparent—a gold Oxford cut with a reverse intaglio on the face of a dark stone. It felt weighty and important, and peering down at the detailed coat of arms, she couldn't help but wonder why it had been hidden away. Definitely a clue.

She pulled the torch from her mouth and turned, eager to show Jamie, but he was there, just behind her, startlingly close, and a shiver ran over her skin. "Skulking is not an attractive quality," she hissed.

"I beg to differ. In covert operations, skulking is inarguably appealing," he murmured.

Olive rolled her eyes. "I found something."

"You first, then," he said, raking the torchlight over her until the light landed on the discovery cradled in her palm. He picked up the ring and looked it over. "Perhaps it's something, perhaps not." Before she could retort, he waved a packet of envelopes clutched in his right hand. "As regards Lieutenant Beckett's death, these are probably more noteworthy."

Her pique momentarily forgotten, Olive put out her free hand. But Jamie pulled his discovery just out of reach. She glared at him, but he was impervious to her frustration.

"We're in a hurry. You can look later."

"What are they?" she demanded.

"Warning letters," he said soberly. "Someone clearly disapproved of something the lieutenant was doing."

"Was he threatened?" she asked eagerly.

"He was, but not very forcefully." He glanced again at her find. "Bring the ring. You can leave the cloves."

"Did you find the ingredients for invisible ink?"

"No," he said shortly. "Nor did I expect to."

"What about something written in his handwriting? For comparison purposes."

"There's an appointment book on his desk." He turned to retrieve it, and Olive quickly set the wardrobe to rights, tucking the little sachet, now empty of its secret, back on the top shelf.

They met at the door, where they tucked the spoils of the search into their pockets, and with a nod to her, he opened it, made a quick check of the corridor, and slipped out. She followed a few steps behind, her fingers tumbling the signet ring over in her pocket as the thoughts tumbled in her brain.

At the head of the stairs, she whispered, "Can we go to your office?"

His head whipped round, and his eyes blazed at the sight of her. "You were supposed to wait a moment, until I'd got downstairs."

She waved away his concerns. "I can assure you, no one cares a jot what we're doing. Not when there're drinks and dancing on offer."

They had slipped down the servants' stairs and had just come through the baize door when Liz appeared in the corridor just ahead of them, her hands tugging at her FANY tunic and her face newly made up. They froze, Jamie gripping her elbow tightly enough to make her wince, just as Liz glanced up, her eye caught by the furtive pair.

Olive had opened her mouth, but Jamie was quicker. "It seems you've caught us out."

Liz still hadn't moved—or blinked. Her eyes flashed between the two of them. To Olive's surprise, Jamie sighed before going on.

"It's been a hell of a week." Olive looked up at him, and he tipped his head down to look at her before glancing again at Liz. "But that's no excuse. It's just this bloody war, all frustrated urgency." He scoffed and ran a nervous hand through his hair as both women looked on, admiring his dark, sharp-edged features. Then he seemed to collect himself. "I hope you'll forget you saw us."

Olive stood there dumbly, parsing his words, wondering if they could possibly be more than lip service. But Liz simply shrugged her shoulders and said with a tight smile, "I don't know anything, do I?" As she turned quickly away, Olive didn't feel any relief—only the weight of Liz's disappointment in the face of this latest deception.

Olive groaned as Jamie closed the office door behind them. He turned to look at her, his eyes puzzled. "I thought that went as well as could be expected. Better, even."

"It would have been *better* if we'd been seen by someone other than Liz." Olive was pacing, rubbing a hand over her temples. "And what were you trying to do? Make her fall even harder with all your talk of frustrated lust?"

"What *are* you talking about?" he said, going round his desk to sit down.

Olive stared at him. "She fancies you," she reminded him.

"More fool her," he muttered. "Now, do you want to see the letters or not?"

Liz was promptly forgotten as the pages in question were pulled from their nondescript envelopes and splayed on the desk between them. Olive leaned over, read through them all, and then dropped into the chair across from Jamie, her lips pursed, her brow furrowed.

"*I know what you are—I've seen you. If I see you again, I'll tell,*" she quoted. All three letters were in the same vein. "What do you think they're implying? Possibly that Lieutenant Beckett was German . . . or a traitor?" She felt a hollowness in her chest even considering it.

"I wouldn't say so. As you know, he would have been scrutinised rather carefully. But anything's possible, particularly in war. Some men will go to diabolical lengths for a cause." He looked over at her. "Women are often worse, or so I've been told."

Olive shrugged, as if to say, *What did you expect?*

"It does look pretty damning," she said quietly. "The forgotten aerial, the scarf with its detailed map of Germany, and now these letters." Olive looked blankly at Jamie. "But why waste time with threatening letters? Why not inform on him outright? There's not even a blackmail demand."

Jamie crossed his arms over his chest, shrugging slightly. "Perhaps they were written by a friend or someone who imagined herself in love with him."

Olive considered this, her thoughts darting among her fellow FANYs. Had one of them secretly fancied Lieutenant Beckett? "If it was," she allowed, "that person isn't likely to have killed him."

"Hmm." He had a faraway expression, and Olive was more certain than ever that he was holding something back. Well, in fairness, she was, too, but that was the prerogative of the detective. Didn't Poirot always keep at least one little detail up his sleeve? But Jamie really had no excuse. Honestly, sleuth or not, she was sick to death of secrets.

Jamie held up the appointment book, forgotten until now, and Olive plucked it from his fingers to quickly rifle through its pages. Lieutenant Beckett's writing was neat and spare—not at all similar to the shaky alphabet that comprised the warning letters. The entries were few and far between, most of them numbers, likely denoting times, and there was nothing recorded for the week of his death. "May I see the page we found in his pocket? I'd like to compare it."

That snapped Jamie out of his private thoughts. "Later," he said brusquely. "We've been gone too long already."

"All right," she agreed calmly, wondering if Jamie's stalling truly had anything to do with appearances or if it was merely a part of his own secret agenda. She handed over the book and moved toward the door.

"What about the ring? Anything there?" He'd come up close beside her and placed his hand on the doorknob.

She'd been so distracted thinking of possible explanations for the letters that she'd forgotten it entirely. When she pulled it from her pocket, it was chased by a whiff of spicy clove.

She turned it in her fingers to discover an engraving on the band. *"Temet nosce,"* she said slowly. She didn't remember her Latin nearly as well as she should.

Jamie cut into her thoughts. "Know thyself."

His eyes met hers, and she wondered if they were both thinking the very same thing: that it was a fitting motto for the enigmatic Lieutenant Beckett. A consolation of sorts in a world of strangers.

"Taken as a whole," Jamie said consideringly, "your discoveries regarding Lieutenant Beckett are admittedly curious, and possibly even suspicious. But I think you'll agree that individually, there are innocent grounds for the existence of every single one of them."

She stared down at the ring in her palm, thinking helplessly of the dangling aerial; the three crosses inked on the scarf, on the edges of Berlin; and the mysterious coded verse pulled from "Strange Meeting," and she knew in her bones that together, they meant something. What it was exactly, she didn't know. Not yet.

" 'I know what you are,' " Olive quoted softly.

"The warning letters don't even hint at murder," he reminded her. "And I'll hold on to that." With a sigh, she handed it over, and he slid it into his pocket before pulling open the door and gesturing her into the corridor.

"But—"

He clearly wasn't interested in her opinion, for he continued, tiredly, "We didn't, any of us, know him well, and his death was a tragedy." He tapped the door shut behind them and was careful to lock it. "It's normal to want to lay blame, but we need to move on and focus on the mission ahead." Seeing Olive's mutinous expression, he went on. "As of right now, I'm no more convinced that Lieutenant Beckett was murdered than I was four days ago. And we both have other priorities." He raised his brows and started walking. She had no choice but to follow. "So, that's an end to it."

Olive didn't agree—with any of it. Her thoughts strayed to Max Dunn, the flash of white teeth and sharp, bright eyes showing through the blurring lines of new skin. She wondered what he'd make of it all, and rather thought he'd side with her. Although, with a guilty glance at Jamie, she realised she couldn't ask him. Or, at least, not directly. But surely there were ways round that. Perhaps she could tell him she was writing a mystery novel and quiz him on a hypothetical scenario.

She realised suddenly that Jamie was glancing quellingly in her direction as they neared the drawing room, no doubt expecting her to protest his cease-and-desist order. Unutterably frustrated, she considered reminding him that the week he'd allotted wasn't yet up, but then thought better of it.

"Yes, sir, Captain Aldridge," she said, her features arranged in a show of subordination.

He may have put an end to the Case of the Murdered Officer, but there was nothing stopping her from investigating the Case of the Dangling Aerial, and the two must surely overlap. The Case of the Red Lipstick, on the other hand, was one she wasn't particularly keen to solve. Although she was quite certain that if Liz was the culprit, this evening's run-in with the woman was going to make things very awkward indeed.

Chapter 10

As the date of dispatch for Operation Conjugal approached, Olive was almost entirely pigeon focused. In the interest of keeping up with Baker Street's demand going forward, she had kicked off a second round of breeding, encouraging a few romantically inclined cocks toward an equal number of receptive hens. The courtship rituals had always charmed her: the courtly bows of the cock, his neck feathers puffed importantly as he circled the hen. The drag of his tail feathers as he flirtatiously called, "*Coo roo-c'too-coo.*" And then the billing, a sort of kissing, where the hen placed her beak directly into the beak of the cock and much bobbing about ensued. The rest was all business, and when the deed was done, the exultant cock would fly up into the dovecote rafters, his wings meeting above his back with resounding claps, as if he were calling for applause.

They made it seem so simple, she thought wistfully. Then again, none of them had to contend with a pretend mate, a plethora of secrets, awkward jealousies, and all manner of confusing feelings. They simply got on with it, whereas she was simply stuck.

There was little time to bemoan the unfairness. This was to be the loft's second mission for Baker Street, and while she never would have admitted it—to Jamie or Jonathon—her nerves were frayed. But the process of prepping the birds for a long journey had always served to settle her mind, and now only a few hours remained until Robin Hood, Aramis, and Alice would be crated up and loaded into a Whitley to fly out over the Channel and be dropped into the darkness of occupied Belgium. They'd spent the morning with their mates, saying their final goodbyes, or so Olive liked to imagine.

Her father had never been a proponent of widowhood. Rather than separate a pair before a big race, he encouraged mated birds to spend their last hours together. He believed this strategy made the racer keener to get home again, flying amid the wind and rain and fog with single-minded determination, in a desperate hurry to be reunited. Olive, even more romantically inclined, had heartily approved of his tactics and had adopted them herself when she'd taken over the management of the loft.

As she pulled Robin Hood from the nesting box, where he was perched beside Queenie, she said stoutly, "I just need to confirm you're mission ready, my boy. Then I'll leave you two alone for a few more hours." She extended each of his wings in turn and examined them for missing flight feathers, a sign that he would need to be replaced.

Hen and Jonathon pushed through the door at that moment, with Hen, as ever, eager to chat. "Miss Featherington has been asking about you and Captain Aldridge," she blurted.

"Really." This irritated Olive more than she could say, but she carried on with her inspection, running a practiced gaze over the bird, loosening bits of mud from its feet before rubbing the bottoms with oil from a bottle she kept in her pocket. "I have no doubt you had some answers for her. Dare I ask what you told her?" She nudged Robin back beside Queenie, who was sitting on a pot egg to prevent the pair from mating before the mission, and turned, bracing herself for what was to come.

"I told her I'd never actually seen the two of you kiss." Seeing Olive's outraged expression, she hurried to add, "But I suggested a few villagers who might have."

"For your information," Olive said tightly, "we've kissed plenty of times. Not that it's any of anyone's business." A glance at Jonathon showed that he was trying hard not to snicker. She got hold of herself before continuing. "Honestly, Hen. What possessed you to say all that?"

Hen looked mildly sheepish. "She sort of tricked me."

Olive's eyebrow arched up.

"She invited me for tea and cake, and it all felt so grown up." Her shoulders slumped. "I'm sorry. I shouldn't have gossiped. It's just that her questions made me think. I've watched you with Captain Aldridge." Her brow furrowed. "And honestly, you don't seem at all like sweethearts."

Olive wanted to march Hen right up to Jamie and have her tell him the same, before adding, "This is what I've been saying!" When this satisfying, but quite imaginary little daydream was interrupted by the words *Miss Featherington*, Olive was quick to interrupt.

"She made her opinion quite clear at the wedding," she snapped. Rubbing the back of her hand over her perspiring brow, she resolved that she and Jamie would have to make some changes before their cover story was shot. Thoroughly exasperated now, she moved on to the nesting box being shared by Aramis and Roberta.

"She wanted to know all about him," Hen went on. "She asked so many questions. I'd say she plans to skulk about like a hyena, ready to swoop in once you've given up on each other. Then again, perhaps she's more like a lion, ruthlessly intent on its prey."

Olive cut her eyes round at the girl.

"We're doing a unit on Africa in school," Jonathon explained.

As if it wasn't bad enough to pretend infatuation with the dubious charms of Jameson Aldridge, now she was going to have to really sell it and, moreover, defend against interlopers. Miss Featherington was becoming quite a nuisance.

In the midst of her anger, Olive stilled. The woman had been camping in Balls Wood with the Girl Guides the day Lieutenant Beckett was killed. Could she have been involved? Was her interest in Jamie prompted by beguiling eyes and broad shoulders or something more sinister? Olive pictured the woman and thought the idea rather far-fetched, but M Poirot would have had her on his suspect list long before now, along with a whole passel of Guides. Not to mention the fact that Miss Featherington had every reason to be traipsing about the woods at odd hours in the guise of her role as Brown Owl—it really was the perfect cover for sending and receiving wireless transmissions. Thrilled to have a new line of inquiry, given that her investigation had stalled out in the interim, Olive spoke up briskly.

"Thanks for the heads-up, Hen. One way or another, I'll have to convince Miss Featherington not to get her hopes up," she said savagely. "And in the future, try to refrain from gossip—particularly about me and Captain Aldridge. Loose lips, you know."

"Yes. Sorry. Lesson learned," Hen said, with a smart little salute.

Olive had turned her attention back to Aramis but promptly heard whispers behind her. "Was there something else?" she asked, swivelling to look at them.

"Do you think you could arrange for us to visit Squadron Leader Dunn again soon? I'd like to get another look at his wheelchair."

Once again, Jonathon had proved himself a cracking partner in crime. She now had a perfect excuse for a pop-in visit to see Max Dunn. It would lend her own reasons for wanting to speak to him a defensible innocence.

"I'm rather busy right now," she said, "between jobs various and sundry, but why don't we plan on an afternoon visit the day after tomorrow? We can pick the last of the summer berries on the way." *And Operation Conjugal will be well and truly launched.*

"Do you suppose Miss Featherington might like to meet him?" Hen suggested, her wide eyes conveying her intentions quite clearly.

"I don't doubt it, but I refuse to be involved in your match-making schemes," she said dryly. "Now, if you're not busy, can you go collect some greens and seeds from the garden for the courageous birds who will shortly be setting off to do their bit?"

Hen knew the NPS story Olive had told her father, not the Baker Street reality, which was to be kept top secret. But the reality was the same either way: the pigeons would be coming and going, and Olive remained in charge of their breeding, care, and training. That particular cover story had been a stroke of genius. In one fell swoop, she'd stifled all manner of awkward questions. There was something to be said for a lie that closely resembled the truth.

Perhaps she'd finally hit on the reason her romantic liaison with Jamie was so fraught. They were utterly incompatible. But even inasmuch as it was all a charade, it needed to be believable. Today's admission from Hen was proof enough that they weren't making a very good job of it.

Olive decided, for the umpteenth time, that it was high time she had a chat with the man. And tonight was the night. There was plenty to discuss—namely, Miss Featherington, that ill-advised kiss, and if she could muster the gumption, perhaps even that tube of lipstick. Oh, yes, this was going to be awkward. But it would take her mind off the mission and her birds.

Shortly after supper and the washing-up, Olive slipped out of the house and hurried to the dovecote to ready the pigeons. Jamie would expect her to be ready and waiting when he pulled the Austin into the drive. Now that her father believed she was working for the NPS, she didn't need to skulk about quite as much, but any relief she might have felt was tempered by the knowledge that whereas before she was merely keeping secrets, now she was lying outright about his own loft and birds. It wasn't ideal. In fact, it was bloody difficult.

As if on cue, she heard a short, sharp whistle and the crunch of her father's boots on the gravel a little distance away. Kíli had probably been hunting rodents in the hedge, and her father had come out to fetch the little dog in. He'd surely see the glow of light in the dovecote and swing the door open, his curiosity piqued. Olive closed her eyes and took a breath. Fibbing had come to feel as quick and defensive as if she were pulling arrows from a quiver strapped to her back.

"Olive?" Her father's deep, gravelly voice rolled over her as she turned. "What are you doing out here at this hour? Nothing amiss, is there?" he asked, his eyes searching the loft.

"No. Not here, at any rate. I'm only getting a few more pigeons ready for the NPS."

"Now?"

Olive's stomach clenched, as it always did when she was forced to shirk the truth. "Yes. Mr Hickman rang earlier." Olive prayed that Harriet wouldn't contradict this. "He's had a puncture and asked if I could deliver the pigeons."

"Tonight?" Her father was clearly taken aback.

"They're in somewhat of a hurry to get them, and Jamie said he'd drive me. I'm expecting him any minute, as a matter of fact."

He growled, simultaneously expressing his resignation and disapproval, and moved farther into the loft. "Which are you sending along?"

There was no point in prevarication. Her father would quickly notice which birds were missing. "Robin Hood, Aramis, and Alice." Rather than look him in the face, she darted about, pulling the birds from perch and nest.

"Alice? She's not yet three years, is she?" Before Olive could answer, he added, with a scratch of his head, "Only three birds?"

As she carefully nudged the pigeon in question into the carrier and latched it closed, she said, "They're giving us time to adjust our breeding and training schedules." She smiled. "We'll soon be up and running full steam. But for now, I expect Alice will prove her mettle and show the NPS what the Bright birds can do."

Her father considered this, frowning. "And you're managing the extra work all right? If your duties at the manor are keeping you too busy, I could step in, help out a bit," he suggested.

A bolt of panic shot through her. Having her father underfoot in the loft, second-guessing her decisions and wondering at her choices, would be a disaster. "No-no," she said quickly. "I'm quite able to handle it. And Jonathon is happy to help out." She could see he had more to say on the matter, so she went on. "But I could always use help with the pigs, if you're offering."

The knock at the dovecote door drowned out her father's muttered reply, and Olive was laughing as Jamie's frame shouldered into the little room.

"Sorry to interrupt, sir," he said, nodding to her father. Then, turning his steely gaze on Olive, he added, "Ready, then?"

"I've got to go, Dad," she said quickly, before he could ask any questions or make any objection. She hoisted the carrier, crossed to kiss him swiftly on the cheek, and brushed past him, all but shoving Jamie out the door in front of her into the night.

When he was certain her father was in for the night, Jonathon would rig the bell wire that ran from the dovecote's window cage up to his room at the back of the house. They'd know the moment a musketeer returned, and the message it carried in the canister strapped to its leg would then be promptly relayed to Brickendonbury.

She and Jamie walked in silence through the pearly twilight amid a symphony of crickets. Neither spoke until they were bumping down the drive in the Austin, on the way to the airfield.

"I assume you have the situation under control?"

Well aware that he was referring to her father, she answered calmly, "Of course."

She'd decided to hold off on the other business until the drive home—no sense getting him worked up before the mission was officially underway. So they skimmed over the hills under a rising full moon, and even the pigeons didn't utter a sound.

The second time was much the same as the first, only a few short months ago. Different agents and different pigeons, excepting Aramis, but the same procedure, the same sense of urgency, the same nervous twist in her stomach as they stood on the airfield at RAF Stradishall.

The three Belgian agents who comprised Operation Conjugal circled round her as she pulled each pigeon from the carrier. One by one, she held them up for inspection, identifying each by name and notable characteristic, and then, just before she slipped the bird into its own cylindrical canister, she privately offered up her own words of luck and encouragement. First, Aramis, and then Robin and Alice, the two birds of Belgian blood. The words were always the same, every one uttered from a throat tight with pride and worry.

"You've trained for this, you're ready, and we're depending on you. Be careful, fly true, and I'll be waiting for your return. Godspeed."

When it was finished, Rémi said gravely, "Thank you for trusting us with your birds. You mustn't worry—we will take the utmost care with them and will send word of them if we can."

The Belgians themselves she sent off in the manner of both Baker Street and Hercule Poirot, shaking their hands and calling after them, *"Merde alors, mes amis!"* It garnered her a curious look from Jamie, but then, what didn't?

Eager to get her mind off the worry and tension that had built to a crescendo with the roar of the Whitley, its rapid clip down the runway, and its disappearance into the night sky, she started talking the moment the car doors had locked them in together for another long ride in the dark.

"I found the lipstick," she said abruptly. When he didn't answer after a long beat of silence, she elaborated, wondering punchily if it was possible he was in possession of more than one mysterious tube. "The one you're keeping in the interior pocket of your jacket. Which is hanging on the coat stand in your office." When her choppy confession didn't produce the response she'd expected, she decided to press on with a one-sided conversation. There were things that needed to be said, and she wasn't one for squeamishness.

"It's my fault, really. I could have come up with a better cover story when you first showed up at the loft, but Dad walked in, and the Daffodil Dance was on my mind, so here we are, three months later, floundering." She ran her hands over her trouser legs and watched through the windscreen as the Austin's dimmed headlamps ranged over the shadowed lane. "Honestly, we've got ourselves into a sticky wicket. It's not your fault you're struggling to fake a relationship that satisfies the village gossips. It has to be singularly difficult when you're secretly carrying on with someone else. Meanwhile, I am just *bloody frustrated* because I'm not carrying on with anyone at all." She darted a glance at him. "And that's my excuse really. For the kiss. If I'd known you were involved with someone, I wouldn't have been quite so—"

That did it. Jamie abruptly yanked the wheel over, pulling sharply off the road, and a field gate reared up in front of them as he slammed to a stop and killed the engine. He'd barely spoken ten words to her over the past couple of hours, and now she braced herself for the onslaught, her hackles already up.

"I don't even know where to start," he said roughly. "The fact that you searched my office? The absurd suggestion that I'm secretly carrying on with someone else? Or the supreme irony that *you're* bloody frustrated with *me*?" His voice had risen with each suggestion, and when he'd finally finished, the silence was vibrating between them.

"Start anywhere you like," Olive said primly.

He turned to face her, and she could see only the contours of his face and the barest glimmer of moonlight as it touched his eyes. He neither moved nor spoke, and an indefinable shiver crawled over her.

At long last, he broke the silence. "While I might not have had any say in your chosen cover story, I'm not so much of an idiot as to undermine it by carrying on, as you say, with someone else. There is no one else," he said carefully.

This admission had an immediate and buoyant effect on Olive's outlook. It was simple relief, nothing more: another person would complicate matters between them no end. Jamie must have registered her altered expression, but he was quick to bring her up short.

"As to the lipstick"—he ran a rough hand through his hair, and she watched the movement of his Adam's apple in the dark—"I don't owe you any explanation. In fact, I could have you brought up on charges for searching my office. But if you promise to behave appropriately going forward—and to come to me rather than engage in any further cloak-and-dagger activities—then I'll let it go."

"But you—"

He ruthlessly cut across her protestation. "*Promise* me." Almost as an afterthought, he added, "And let me see your hands—no crossed fingers, no tricks. Your word, Olive."

He rarely used her given name, and sitting parked somewhere along a lonely country lane in the dark, with her pale hands held up helplessly between them, she felt unguarded. "I promise," she said hoarsely.

"I'm tempted to prick our fingers to make it a blood oath," he said wryly, "but I'm going to trust you. Fair warning, though. You're running out of lives."

"So why *did* you have a lipstick in your pocket?" Despite what he'd said, she couldn't help but be curious. He must see that.

"You'd stashed it with the items I found on Lieutenant Beckett, but the lipstick was never there. If it was, I would have found it myself."

She could see the muscle flex in his jaw, even in the dark. "This is to go no further, understood?" She nodded, and he said grimly, "I found it in the waste bin in my office."

Olive frowned. "That's odd. That tube had plenty of wear left in it. And, really, who can afford to waste anything?"

"I don't think it was put there intentionally. I believe it's likely it dropped, muffled and hidden by the papers there, and the owner didn't realise. I only realised it myself because I needed to fish something out again."

He was being very cryptic. "Why didn't you just return it to the owner?"

"Because unless it's yours, I don't know who it belongs to. None of the other FANYs have had any reason to come into my office. If I need their help, I go directly to them."

"Well, it's certainly not mine. I would have turned your office inside out by now." She flashed him a teasing smile but quickly sobered. "It was probably just Liz."

"What do you mean, just Liz?"

Olive sighed heavily. "Love can do funny things to a girl's head. Perhaps she's been sneaking into your office merely for the chance to wrap your jacket round her shoulders. To smell your liquorice scent and daydream." She blinked, feeling suddenly self-conscious, but Jamie didn't seem to notice.

"Tell me you're kidding." The uninterrupted sound of crickets was answer enough for him to prop his elbow on the window frame and brace his head in his hands.

"Clearly, that's not what *you* thought had happened," she said pointedly.

"You're right. And I can't decide if that possibility is actually worse than my original assumption, which was that one of them had searched my office."

Olive huffed. "They wouldn't dare."

"You dared," he said flatly. Before she could respond, he went on. "Whoever it was might have been doing the same thing you were, but for different reasons entirely."

At first, she didn't follow, and realisation, when it came, stunned her. "You think one of them might have—" She didn't even want to say it; every one of those girls was a friend of hers. But she was quick to remind herself that this little detail hardly mattered. "Spying? They're certainly clever enough," she admitted, wondering disloyally if Kate might be the exception. "Not to mention resourceful. And if Lieutenant Beckett had discovered the truth . . ." A shiver rolled over her, and she said aloud, "If anyone could get away with murder, a FANY could."

"I don't doubt it," he agreed. "And yet, if the point of the search was to abscond with the evidence, whoever it was missed the mark. If, however, the point was to dig up information . . ." He exhaled a gusty breath. "It may have been a direct hit. The papers in my desk were rifled."

Olive pursed her lips and looked askance, really not wanting to have to drop any further in his good graces. A moment later she heard him sigh.

"It was you, wasn't it?"

"I'm afraid so," she said swiftly. "But I didn't read any of them. Not even the file you had on me. I was quite focused. And honestly, everything was tidy when I got there."

"For the love of—" He bit off the rest and shook his head, clearly wanting to forget all of it.

"Surely, then, the lipstick is justification to proceed with the investigation?"

He sat very still, his jaw tight, until he seemed to resign himself. "I think we owe it to Lieutenant Beckett. I also think that you're better suited to questioning our new pool of suspects—discreetly, of course."

"Of course. Although I'm sure Liz will tell you anything you want to know and more besides," Olive drawled. "Not to mention Miss Featherington, who I rather liked for the crime." She frowned.

"Miss Featherington?" Jamie looked blank. "The Guide leader?"

"The flirty Brown Owl, who's convinced, by the way, that we're not sweethearts."

"Perceptive of her."

Olive turned abruptly in her seat to level a hard stare at him. "It's clear we need to discuss the failings of our manufactured relationship."

"We really don't—"

"We do," she said firmly.

Jamie sat back in his seat, a man resigned.

She went on crisply. "We both know that there's nothing romantic going on between us, but there bloody well needs to be *something* if we're going to stave off suspicion. Not to mention the occasional reckless impulse."

"Are you suggesting that your recent behaviour stems from some sort of romantic shortcoming on my part?" he said incredulously.

"I admit, that kiss may have been a lapse in judgement, but your shortcomings are another issue entirely."

"Right," he said acidly.

Suddenly shy, she said quietly, "I'm having to hold myself so carefully. It's as if I'm a high-wire act, balancing all the secrets and deceptions, being ever mindful not to fall. And sometimes . . . sometimes I feel as if I'm losing my balance, and I need to grab hold of something. It's just that I know you're safe—you're in on all the secrets already—and you're the only one who is. So I suppose I just let myself go. I kissed you with all the fervour this war has built up in me. It was extraordinarily cathartic."

After a long moment he spoke. "It's all right. I understand."

Her heart thumped painfully. "Do you? Did you really mean what you said to Liz? The 'frustrated urgency' bit?"

"Yes." The word was nearly bitten off.

"And what did you do about it?"

"Nothing that satisfied."

"Hmm. Well, the kiss worked wonders for me. And given that it's a two birds, one stone sort of situation . . ."

"What are you saying, exactly?"

She deliberately didn't phrase her response as a question. "I think that for everyone's peace of mind, we should be a bit more . . . convincing when we do kiss." Jamie was back to rubbing his temples, so she pushed her luck. "And we should make a point of doing it—the kissing, that is—where we might be seen."

"Anything else?" he said dryly.

"No, I think that'll do nicely. And don't worry. I'm perfectly capable of kissing you quite thoroughly with no expectation that it will lead to anything further. Although I'll certainly raise no objection if you want to run your hands through my hair or over my—"

The suggestion was cut off by the car engine turning over and a smothered oath as Jamie got them quickly back onto the road again. Olive indulged herself in a mischievous little smile.

As they sailed over the hills and down the lanes on the way back to the lodge, Olive felt rather pleased with the evening's developments. In the long silence, however, her thoughts strayed to Squadron Leader Max Dunn.

But Jamie had clearly taken her words to heart, for when the car pulled to a stop beside the stable, he leaned toward her, snugged his arms round her, and dipped his head to hers. This time, it wasn't her hands and lips that went rogue, but his. And though she knew it wasn't real, she let herself glory in the fantasy just the same.

"Good enough?" he said when he eventually pulled back.

"Well done," she congratulated briskly before slipping from the car in somewhat of a daze and drifting toward the house with the pigeon carrier bumping unnoticed against her legs. She was struck by the feeling that it was getting harder and harder to distinguish between duplicity and the truth.

Chapter 11

6 September

Aramis had returned seven short hours after Olive had seen him off at the airfield, and it was likely four of them had been under his own steam. The Channel crossing would have taken less than two hours in the Whitley, but the drop, targeted at a field on the outskirts of Spontin, Belgium, could have left the agents and supplies scattered, requiring additional time to reconnoitre in the dark. With any luck, some of the local resistance had been on hand as a welcome party, thus making Conjugal's job easier, but time would tell. She'd deliver the message to Jamie the moment the sun was up.

Olive had been roused from a fitful sleep by the bell jangling at Jonathon's window across the hall and had hurried sleepily down to the dovecote with him close on her heels. The bird had seemed none the worse for wear, content only to be back home again and eager to see Roberta. Too fidgety to sleep, she'd spent the next couple of hours splitting her attention between *Five Little Pigs* and "Strange Meeting." But eager to be off before her father, she was motoring up Mangrove Lane, a scarf tied round her unruly curls, by the time the sun had poked its sleepy head over the horizon. Jamie, it seemed, had been up just as early and had gone out for a run.

She intercepted him on his way back to the manor but kept hold of the little brown canister she'd detached from Aramis's leg and followed him straight to his office. Olive was determined to wait while he decoded the message, and sat opposite him at his desk. In her sleepy state, she found herself quite hypnotised by Jamie's breathing pattern and the rise and fall of the muscles of his chest.

It was her name that roused her. "What does it say?" she demanded, sitting bolt upright.

"Read for yourself," he allowed, turning the page in her direction.

In his narrow, slanting print, the decoded message was a balm to her worried mind.

> *The drop went as planned. No serious injuries among us, and we've managed to collect all but one box of supplies. The last is caught in a tree, and it's unlikely we'll manage to retrieve it. The transmitter is intact, and the pigeons are resilient, their attitudes and appetites unaffected. Aramis is the most vocal and so must be sent home first. Tomorrow we will begin making inquiries regarding Leopold Vindictive and will send updates by wireless per the agreed-upon schedule. The pigeons we will hold as long as possible, in case of intelligence not easily transmitted. It is a risk to us all, but one, I believe, we are all willing to make, as Belgians and fanciers both.*
>
> *R.*

Olive let loose the breath she'd been holding. "Well, that's good news." She put a hand to her head, felt the scarf, and remembered she wasn't wearing her uniform. "I suppose I'd better go home and change."

"Why don't you get some rest"—he glanced at the open door of his office before leaning forward and lowering his voice—"and come up with a strategy for singling out the person who searched my office?" Before leaning back, he'd added, "Other than you, I mean."

She took a long nap, then got to work on a thorough cleaning of the loft, raking out the droppings, laying fresh gravel, and wiping down the boxes and nesting bowls. Her thoughts on her fellow FANYs ran the gamut.

Liz was missing a lipstick, a fact Olive had neglected to mention to Jamie.

It could, after all, be a coincidence.

Or the lipstick could have been left intentionally, by someone hoping to incriminate another.

All the girls wore red lipstick at least some of the time.

She didn't count Hilda in that. Tomás's wife wasn't a FANY, and as far as Olive could tell, she didn't wear any makeup at all.

Images flashed in her mind: her friends' faces, Lieutenant Beckett's sightless eyes, the scarf, the lipstick, the aerial, the coded message. She was forced to reexamine her conversation with Jamie the previous night—and how it ended—in order to break the cycle. And then it all began again.

At long last, having run through a spate of possibilities, Olive decided the least awkward and probably most productive option was to get them all together, tipsy and talking, so that they might relax enough to let something slip. Or perhaps, in the manner of M Poirot, she could merely observe the little details and inconsistencies that presented themselves, and hit on the truth that way. Either way, a night out was precisely what was needed.

While Jamie seemed rather set on the idea that the lipstick incriminated a FANY, Olive wasn't yet ready to eliminate all other suspects. She refused to cross Miss Featherington off the list, and she felt certain that Tomás Harris knew something. He had, after all, argued with Lieutenant Beckett shortly before he died. Perhaps the lipstick was merely a red herring.

After that, her thoughts took a rather fanciful turn. She imagined herself a famous detective, invited to a house party at Brickendonbury Manor. Naturally, a murder occurred, with everyone a suspect. After a few days' detective work, she gathered them all in the drawing room. She was extending her finger to identify the murderer . . . when Jonathon rushed in to tell her that two of the pigs were leaking out their back ends, villagers were panicking, and could she come quickly?

Merde alors! Literally.

8 September

Two days later, she was still dealing with the fallout from the pigs' bout with intestinal worms. The poor creatures were on the mend, but they'd been temporarily moved to a makeshift pen in the alley behind Mr Duerden's house so that their regular living space could be scoured for worms. Normally, Jonathon would have joined her in the muck, but she'd insisted that he stay behind at the lodge in case one of the pigeons returned.

In truth, the gossip had been more strenuous than the exertions. Villagers had fallen upon her in droves, either curious for news about the new occupants of Peregrine Hall or eager to share their thoughts on how Margaret was settling in to her role as vicar's wife. Olive had been much looking forward to the blissful silence of home.

Unfortunately, the kitchen was a bustle of activity. Harriet sat at the far end of the table in a straight-backed chair, her injured leg propped on a cushion-topped second. Baskets overflowing with soft plums and peaches sat before her on the table, and an enormous bag of sugar was slumped at the near end. Her stepmother was efficiently dicing the juicy fruit and sliding it into bowls, in preparation for the next step in the jam-making process. Wrapped in aprons, their necks damp with perspiration, Lady Camilla and Mrs Battlesby stirred huge pots simmering on the Aga, while Mrs Spencer pulled sterilised jam jars out of a steaming vat of water and placed them upside down on a drying rack.

Olive slid into a chair beside the sugar, exhausted and ready for tea.

"We've relocated our preservation centre," Mrs Battlesby trilled, "on account of Mrs Bright not being able to manage the hall."

"I don't suppose you're here to help," Harriet teased.

"I'm afraid not. I'm fresh off one of your other schemes as it is," Olive replied.

"I wouldn't say *fresh*, exactly," Harriet said, her nose twitching slightly. Olive had washed thoroughly as soon as she was able, but clearly, the scent of her afternoon activities still lingered.

"That's fair," she allowed, meeting the twinkling eyes of the other ladies with a twist of her lips as she hoisted herself up and filled the kettle. "I'm sorry to crowd in, but I'm desperate for a cup of tea."

When she turned back to the table, wondering if she dared pluck a plum from the pile, she was startled to see Miss Featherington coming through from the hall. The pretty brunette smiled tightly and, with a proprietary air, moved to stand beside the sugar, where she resumed the task of measuring out cups in readiness for future batches of jam.

Olive wanted to laugh at the little idiot, whose empty jealousy was so transparent, but she chose instead to ignore it. Biting her lip, pondering how she might broach the subject of Lieutenant Beckett, she missed her chance.

"Harriet said you've met our village recluse," Mrs Spencer said coyly, her hair having frizzed itself into a halo round her face.

For a shocked moment, Olive thought she might be referring to the dead man, but realisation quickly dawned. "Squadron Leader Dunn, do you mean?"

She nodded. "Poor man. I understand he's quite badly off.

Leo told me they've done all they can for him at the hospital, and now it's just a matter of recovery."

"Resigning himself to his condition and the changes in store will be the most difficult." Harriet spoke from bitter experience.

Mrs Spencer pressed on. "What was your impression of him, Olive?" She was peering critically at a spoonful of thickening syrup that seemed to hold every juicy red tone of summer. "Not quite yet," she murmured to herself.

At that moment, the kitchen door was flung open, and Violet Darling stood in the doorway, holding a bushel basket of stone fruit. Her face was shaded by a wide-brimmed hat, but her lips were clearly visible, deep cherry red, a cigarette caught between them. Olive smiled to see her. Violet had come back to the village after nearly ten years away and had, until recently, been disinclined to involve herself in village affairs. But here she was, dipping her toe into the Pipley Jamboree.

Settling the basket on the table beside Harriet, she said, "I convinced Henrietta Gibbons and that sweet boy she has wrapped round her little finger that it all needed to be harvested and would be a very good deed indeed." She shrugged. "They scrambled up to the very top—far enough that I thought the branches wouldn't hold. Miracles *do* occur," she said with wide-eyed mischief. "Afterwards, I was obliged to remind *her* that some good deeds do, in fact, go unrewarded. Brown Owl material, I am not." She pulled out a chair and sank into it.

Harriet chuckled and lifted a shaking hand to her mouth.

At that moment, the kettle went off, diverting everyone's attention. Filling the teapot, Olive went on, as if she'd not been interrupted. "I'd say the recluse was none too pleased to have company, but eventually, he came round, and we had quite a nice chat."

Violet's brows rose sardonically. "Which curmudgeon is this?"

"Squadron Leader Dunn," Miss Featherington said fiercely before Olive could answer.

"The pilot who's moved into Peregrine Hall." Violet's perfectly groomed eyebrows rose with interest. "Yes, do go on," she said in a seductive drawl.

"There's nothing really to say," Olive admitted. "He seemed understandably bitter, and I couldn't look at him without thinking of George." She exchanged a glance with Lady Camilla before going on. "In the end, we talked of poetry—he evidently has a fondness for the Romantics." Olive wondered suddenly if Lady Camilla had heard anything about the ATA girl who'd piqued her son's interest.

"Sounds as if you had a cosy chat," Miss Featherington said frostily.

"It wasn't like that at all," Olive snapped. "It was awkward for both of us—me, not knowing what to say or where to look, and him, striving for patience as I struggled."

Mrs Battlesby had fished her handkerchief out of her apron pocket and was dabbing at her eyes. "Those poor boys, so young . . . what this war is doing to them all." Lady Camilla wrapped a comforting arm round her shoulder.

Harriet added, "His aunt said his burns are significant enough that she barely recognised him when he came home. And certainly, his disposition is indelibly altered. In some ways, it must be like living with a stranger."

Violet had taken up a knife and was neatly paring a plum. "He'll come round—he just needs to be pulled out of himself. He needs a hobby or a project. And the motivation to see it through." Olive turned to look at her and wondered if that was what she'd needed when her life had seemed quite desperate. "He's certainly better off than the other one," she said, her face slack of emotion.

"What other one?" Miss Featherington demanded. Olive suspected the woman was keeping a close tally of all eligible men in the vicinity.

"I suspect she's referring to Lieutenant Beckett," Olive said, glad to have been given an entrée into the matter. "Had you met him?" she asked Brown Owl.

Refusing to meet Olive's gaze, the woman answered, "Only in passing. He wasn't really my type." She smoothed the front of her apron, which remained pristine.

"What she means," Violet said knowingly, tossing a plum stone into a bowl of scraps reserved for the pigs, "is that *she* wasn't *his* type." Before Miss Featherington could protest with more than an outraged huff, Violet went on. "It's impossible to keep a secret in this village. Close quarters, curious ears."

"Were you eavesdropping?" Miss Featherington hissed, the flush in her cheeks from the heated kitchen deepening to an un-flattering feverish shade.

Violet shot her a look from beneath lowered lids. "It wasn't nearly interesting enough for that."

Miss Featherington wrung her hands angrily. "It was a misun-derstanding."

Olive tamped down a snort even as she considered this morsel of gossip. So, Miss Featherington had been rebuffed by Lieu-tenant Beckett. But why? In her experience, the woman was ex-actly the sort of female who appealed to the opposite sex: pretty, petite, and willing. Olive tucked the information away for later.

The older ladies had kept silent through this disclosure, each quelling the curve of her lips.

"That poor man," sniffed Mrs Battlesby. "And him working at the manor on secret war business . . . to have died from such an accident."

"Wasn't it you who found him?" Violet asked innocently, pointing with her knife, seemingly oblivious to the deep red plum juice dripping from her wrist as she looked curiously at Miss Featherington.

Violet Darling was going great guns, asking questions, spout-ing hypotheses. Olive couldn't help but wonder if she might be another amateur sleuth in the making. She poured herself a cup of tea and settled in to watch.

Miss Featherington coloured slightly and cleared her throat. "Well, I was there but not alone. There were lots of us—it was Guide camp."

"Did you see him or speak to him before he died?" asked Violet.

"What? No. Of course not! How could I? Why would I?"

"The lady doth protest too much," Violet muttered dryly. "Perhaps he stumbled into your camp, and you asked him to help pitch your tent—or invited him to join you for toad in the hole round the fire. Maybe you wanted to give him another chance . . ."

"I tell you, I didn't," Miss Featherington exclaimed, near to tears now. Very real ones, if Olive was any judge. "And if you don't believe me, you've only to ask Henrietta Gibbons. She spent the entire time by my side, peppering me with questions." She took a breath. "I didn't see him until he was already dead, lying in the dirt, wide eyed and so very pale." She bit down hard on her lower lip, and still it quivered.

Olive poured her a cup of tea and handed it across. This detective business wasn't for the faint of heart. Although Violet Darling, who was now contemplatively sucking on a plum stone, seemed to be taking it in her stride. Thanks to Hen, it appeared she could eliminate Miss Featherington as a suspect.

"We mustn't dwell on the poor man's death, God rest his soul," Lady Camilla said briskly as she transferred her pot of bubbling thickened jam to the trivet on the table so that Mrs Spencer could ladle it into jars. "We need to focus our energies on finding ways to carry us through this war and help those poor souls we can."

Mrs Spencer, having got straight to work, agreed. "There must be something we can do for Squadron Leader Dunn."

"You mustn't feel sorry for him," Violet said knowledgeably, talking round the stone. "He'll resent you and go on feeling sorry for himself."

"Well, then, what do you suggest?" Miss Featherington said cattily.

Violet shrugged. "Treat him as you would anyone else."

"It will be difficult," Harriet said consideringly. "But that would probably be the best thing for him. He may not be up to certain jobs that we would ask of him—at least not yet—but he's a man and would no doubt appreciate being asked his opinion."

"That's opening a can of worms," quipped Mrs Spencer.

In a moment they were all laughing.

"We *do* need ideas for the Spitfire Fund," said Mrs Battlesby, stirring the requisite sugar into several pounds of diced fruit. "Between us, we've not come up with any new fundraising schemes."

"He won't want to be involved in any schemes," Violet asserted.

"Perhaps not." This from Harriet. "But we might at least try to pique his interest. Any volunteers to broach the topic with him?" She was looking at Miss Featherington, who was deliberately avoiding her gaze. No doubt she'd stare at the poor man's burns and make a ninny of herself. Not wanting to subject him to such an ordeal, Olive volunteered.

"No promises, but I'll do my best." Once again, she found Violet's unreadable gaze on her, but she hadn't time to interpret it, as at that moment she heard the faint jangle of a bell.

Another of the pigeons was back!

She stood, nudging the chair with the back of her knees, and moved toward the door.

"You don't have to do it right now," Harriet said, somewhat startled.

"I'm not," she gabbled. "I think I might have forgotten to latch the door to the loft. Rather critical," she said with an apologetic smile before darting out the door.

Robin Hood stood perched in the return cage when Olive burst into the loft. At first glance, he looked rather rough round the edges, and as she stepped closer, the relieved smile fell from her face. An examination revealed that several of his tail feathers were missing, and there was a nasty gouge along his back. By all appearances, he'd had a run-in with a hawk and had narrowly escaped. Her father was dosing the sheep at a neighbouring farm with antibiotics but should be back soon. He'd want to be involved in tending the injuries. Very carefully, she unclipped the canister from Robin's leg and left the bird in the comforting presence of his mate. She raced back across the yard, slipped into the house, and tiptoed through the hall, dragging the telephone as far as possible from the kitchen door. For once it was a relief that the ladies of the Pipley WI were arguing.

She placed the call to Brickendonbury, and it was only a moment before she was connected with Jamie. Crossing her fingers for luck, she made her whispered request, which stunned him into silence. It took so long for him to answer, she prompted, "Can I? *Please?*"

Finally, he relented. "All right. You have a quarter of an hour. If you haven't finished by then, I'll have to take it with me." And then he hung up.

Olive returned the phone to its cradle and took the stairs two at a time. She was so excited, she was shaking with it. All agents were instructed to select a poem on which to base the cipher they'd use to encode their messages. Weasel had selected a British nursery rhyme, "Lavender's Blue," and Olive had copied the verses down days ago and had been keeping the page tucked deep in her pocket.

Now, as she settled herself on her bed, she pulled the curl of rice paper from its canister and quickly got to work, carefully transposing the letters using the grid form she'd learned at FANY training. She made a couple of mistakes and was glad not to have Jamie looking over her shoulder, but in the end, she finished with two minutes to spare and, with a satisfied exhalation, sat back to read over her efforts.

Have made contact with the local resistance. They are a dedi-
cated group and have done some good work but are desperate for
supplies and assistance to proceed with bigger targets. There is a
fuel depot nearby and an aerodrome. I have attempted to draw out
a map. We are in need of explosives—limpet mines in particu-
lar—money, and more agents to best capitalise on all targets.
French-speaking is best. Have located a secure safe house and will
begin transmitting soon.

She frowned, lost in thought, and turned the page over to
glance at the map on the back. It highlighted the targets mentioned, along with the landmarks of the Bocq River, Château de
Spontin, and the Ardennes.

She heard the motor car in the drive and glanced at the clock
on her bureau; it had been precisely fifteen minutes. Olive flew
out of the house to meet him. The moment Jamie was out of the
car, she took his hand and tugged him toward the river path.
Sheltered in the confines of a willow tree, she handed him the
canister and the decoded message.

She waited while he read over her translation and then carefully extracted and unfurled the original rice paper to look over
the map.

"The message seems off," she finally said.

"What do you mean?" he demanded, glancing at it more
closely.

She shrugged. "It doesn't sound like the men I met—any of
them."

"It likely wouldn't. They're under tremendous pressure over
there," he reminded her.

Her shoulders dropped. "Yes, perhaps that's it. It's only that
they were so invested in the pigeons. I would have thought
they'd at least have mentioned them. They did in the first message."

"I'm sure they're doing the best they can, Olive. But you must remember, nothing ever goes exactly as planned. At times it's an utter cock-up, and they've got to improvise. And we have to adjust our expectations accordingly—it's part of the job." He looked at her pointedly, brows raised. "So don't worry?"

She nodded and let Jamie walk her back to the lodge.

"This map," he said consideringly, "is very useful indeed, so three cheers for Robin Hood." So saying, he tucked everything into his pocket and set off for Brickendonbury.

But as Olive stared after him, she couldn't help but wonder and worry.

Chapter 12

11 September

Olive's responsibilities as pigeoneer and self-appointed sleuth for Station XVII kept her mind busy—and rather fraught—over the following week.

She pondered the curious items found on Lieutenant Beckett's body and the ones later discovered in his room, trying to reconcile them with the man she barely knew.

She thought of Rémi, Renauld, and Weasel, and the two messages they'd sent back with her pigeons, and she wondered how Alice was bearing up almost a week since she'd left home. Robin had been stitched up, with her father looking on, and was recuperating nicely, pampered by Jonathon.

She forced herself to think objectively in her consideration of the FANYs, resigned that one of them—Liz, Marie, or Kate—might be a traitor and a murderer. Going forward, that possibility would, of necessity, focus her efforts. As much as she wanted to find Lieutenant Beckett's killer, she was just as eager to clear them all of suspicion.

Before she left for the day, she corralled the three under the porte-cochère. A fine mist had settled in the air, and Olive's hands and neck felt clammy. Liz and Marie lit cigarettes, holding them between long, pale fingers and leaving red rings where their lips pressed the paper.

Olive flashed a look at each of them, her eyes widened encouragingly, and said, "Who's up for a night out?"

"Definitely me," said Liz, blowing out a stream of smoke. "Presuming there'll be available men." Her eyes met Olive's, and she raised her brows ever so slightly, her lips forming a tight smile.

"I'm fed up with Pipley at the moment," Olive said. "I thought we could drive over to Little Appington and have a drink or two at the Golden Goose."

"I'm fed up with all sorts of things, but do you have a car—and a petrol ration?" Marie asked sweetly. "Because I'd just assume not pile onto a couple of Welbikes for the journey."

Before Olive could answer, Kate chimed in. "I can get us a car." The other three swivelled their heads to stare at her, momentarily silenced. Kate pursed her lips, her cheeks rounding as she smiled, suddenly self-conscious. Olive noticed that her lips were a pretty, natural pink. "Well, I can."

"Are you going to tell us how?" Liz said encouragingly.

"Harold Ennis and I are friends," she said simply.

Olive pictured the short, stocky mechanic who managed to keep every engine on the estate running smoothly, and looked at Kate with fresh eyes.

"The sort of friends that do things in motor cars?" Liz asked slyly.

Swatting at her, Marie stifled a laugh.

"Occasionally," Kate admitted. "Although not the sort you're imagining—not quite."

A pregnant pause and then they were all laughing, Kate included.

"Will he still let you have the car if he doesn't come with it?" Olive asked seriously.

Kate shrugged. "I'll find a way to convince him."

The manor door was yanked open at that moment, and a pair of officers, both scowling ferociously, met the snapping eyes of four capable FANYs. Dipping their heads and murmuring apologies, they hurried past the cluster of women and off across the lawn, hunching their shoulders against the mist.

"Jolly good, then," Olive said. "Shall we meet back here at eight?"

Marie and Liz took the final puffs from their cigarettes and stamped them underfoot.

"Shall we wear our uniforms or get dolled up?" Marie asked.

"Not uniforms," Kate pleaded. "I think I'm getting a rash." She twisted her jacket round her middle, wearing a moue of distaste.

"The works, then," said Liz. "Full glam."

Olive grinned and added, "Wear your lipstick, Kate, and don't let Harold distract you. We're counting on you. Now, I'm off to see to the pigeons, but I'll be back on time." She tossed them a wave before dashing off to retrieve the Welbike.

She hadn't realised it, but her heart was racing. There hadn't been anything devious or underhanded in her suggestion—in truth, she was gasping for a night out—but she felt like an imposter, a spy. Because whether she suspected them or not, the whole point of inviting them out was to trip them up, draw them out, identify a suspect, and catch a murderous traitor. Poirot would think nothing of the deception, but she felt almost sick with it. As the mist needled at her face and the wind chilled in its wake, she forced herself to breathe deeply.

The worst of it was that there was no one to confide in. Jamie, she'd decided, was hopeless. And anyone else would be too curious, too probing, too risky.

Almost without thinking, she passed the turn for the lodge and buzzed farther along the lane until she was turning in at the gates of Peregrine Hall, wanting to speak to Max Dunn. If he had thoughts about the Spitfire Fund, so much the better.

Lady Revell greeted her unexpected guest graciously and pointed the way to the terrace, where her nephew was sitting much as Olive had left him on her first visit. He was wearing the same striped pajamas, this time topped with a navy jumper. The sky was still overcast, but the mist had let up, and a few feeble rays of sun were streaming through the gaps, warming the air deliciously.

"Let me guess," he said savagely, raking her up and down. "You were a Girl Guide once upon a time, and I'm your good deed for the day."

Olive really wasn't in the mood for his fractiousness. "It will be entirely up to you whether this visit becomes one or not," she retorted.

His eyes assessed her, and she thought one eyebrow hitched up a bit. "How many of you are they planning to send?"

"How many of whom? FANYs?"

He ignored her and went spouting on. "Don't tell me you're coming of your own free will? I might be RAF, but not the sort beautiful women hope to scrape an acquaintance with—at least not anymore," he said ruefully.

"With that attitude, I suspect not," she said tartly, pulling a chair over to sit beside him. She'd inadvertently chosen the side of him mostly unmarred by burns, and his profile gave her a glimpse of what he must have looked like at the beginning of the summer. The thought of what he'd lost caught in her throat, and she was ashamed.

His lips moved awkwardly, and it seemed as if he might be trying to whistle. After a moment, he gave up and blew out a breath. "Lucky me. You're as much of a spitfire as she was."

Utterly exasperated, Olive demanded, "You might as well tell me. Who else has visited you?"

"Her name was Violet Darling—or so she said."

"That's her real name," Olive said automatically, more than a little surprised. No one would ever accuse Violet of Guide behaviour. She did precisely what she wanted and made no bones about it. *What is she up to?*

"Did she ask you about the Spitfire Fund?"

"Is that why you're here? How apropos. I wonder if the aircraft was named for women like you."

Olive didn't answer.

"No, she didn't ask," he said flatly. "We played cards. She's rather a shark."

"Would you feel less suspicious if I offered to play cards with you?"

"Why are you here?" he said abruptly. His tone was more matter-of-fact than outright rude.

"I need someone to talk to."

The admission brought him up short. "I assume you're not referring to fundraising."

"No," Olive said simply. And before she could stop herself, she blurted, "What would you do if you suspected a friend of treason?"

He turned sharply to look at her, and she met his eyes, careful not to let her own track the burned skin across his face. Neither of them spoke for a long moment. "I'd like to say I'd turn him in without a second thought, and if it happened today, I probably would. But before . . . I don't know. I would have thought it an impossible situation."

"It is," she agreed, the guilt once again welling up inside her. She shouldn't be talking about it, even in this nebulous fashion, but she couldn't help it. "I wish I could risk going the easy route."

"Confrontation?" Olive nodded, and his eyes locked on hers. "If you're wrong, the consequences would be bad enough, but if you're right, you'd be taking a very great risk."

Olive had been chewing on her bottom lip, and now a shiver ran over her. "You're saying the best way forward is simply to find proof."

He didn't bother to answer; he didn't need to.

"But how should I go about it?"

"Find out what the person doesn't want to talk about and force them to talk about it," he said. "One way or another, that will give you your answer."

"I don't suppose that's going to be easy."

He shrugged. "People hold tight to secrets—especially damning ones."

The clouds scudded across the sky as they sat in silence, and Olive wondered fleetingly if she was, even now, walking a treasonous line herself. Jamie would likely say yes, but she was confident that Max Dunn had no clue whom or what she was talking about. She'd merely asked for advice. In fairness, identifying a treasonous friend was really something that should be covered by the BBC or, at the very least, addressed by a guest speaker at a WI meeting.

Max cut into her thoughts. "Have you convinced yourself yet?"

Startled, Olive cut her eyes round at him. *"What?"*

"Your lips were moving, and you were tipping your head back and forth. I assumed you were engaged in an internal debate of some sort."

"I was," she admitted. "And I have." She was glad to have asked his advice.

"Be careful," he said soberly.

She smiled, feeling somewhat better about the whole business, and narrowed her eyes consideringly. "Are you, by any chance, a fan of mysteries?"

"I haven't any idea."

"I'll bring one next time I come, and you can let me know. But now I really need to get your thoughts on the Spitfire Fund. The ladies of the WI are anxious to hug you to the bosom of the village. So to speak."

The corner of his mouth chased his eyebrow up the side of his face. "Now I'm intrigued."

*   *   *

Margaret had flagged her down at the gates to the lodge, looking quite smart in her Royal Observer Corps uniform: cinched-waist coveralls in blue-grey serge, bearing the ROC white eagle badge, and jaunty beret. "I'm fresh off duty and not in the mood to go back to the vicarage just yet, so I thought I'd see if you might want to hide for a bit under the willow at Pipley Pool."

Olive's lips quirked. "Haven't quite settled into the role of vicar's wife, I see."

Her friend made a face. "I don't want to talk about it." The far-off thuds of explosives had them both stilling. Then Margaret tipped her head up, her eyes scanning the sky in all directions. Seeing nothing, she said, "The good news is, it doesn't sound like bombs."

Olive merely murmured her agreement. The goings-on at Brickendonbury were strictly top secret, but the sound wasn't coming from the direction of the manor. It was coming from across the fields, from somewhere beyond the trees lining the lane. She'd heard that sound before—at the service held for Lieutenant Beckett. If she'd been alone, she'd have gone in search of the source of it, but not with Margaret trailing along. For the time being, it would remain yet another mystery she hadn't solved. She hadn't mentioned it to Jamie, but then again, he might already know what it was. That possibility only frustrated her further.

"I only have time for a quick chat. Will that suffice?"

"I suppose it'll have to. Can you give me a ride on that thing?"

"Hop on," Olive said, restarting the engine. Margaret straddled the bike, laid her head gently against Olive's back, and wrapped her arms snugly round her middle. "Tired?" Olive called over the rumbling motor.

Margaret nodded.

"Well, try not to fall off. I'll have a devil of a time explaining that."

Minutes later they were lounging on the island in Pipley Pool, closeted together behind the fringed curtain of its grand weeping willow.

"Where were you coming from just now? Pigeon training?" Margaret was lying on her back in the grass with eyes closed.

"Peregrine Hall." Olive winced, knowing what was coming.

Margaret bolted up and wrapped her arms round her knees. "Who did you see?"

"Both Lady Revell and Squadron Leader Dunn, but mostly the latter."

"Ooh, very formal. And?"

Olive shrugged. "And what? I was sent to speak to him by the ladies of the WI. You really should be more involved, you know. Even Violet Darling was there."

"Well, bully for her," she said dismissively. "What did you think of him?"

"Have you met him?"

"Several times," she said, her face softening. "I met him at Merryweather House. I've gone with Leo and had tea with some of the men." She sighed, and when Olive glanced at her, her eyes were far away. "They've come back so damaged." A shiver overtook her friend.

"At least they came back."

"They don't all share your perspective."

"I hope that's only temporary. Time and distraction might be all they need to start again." She already had plans for Max Dunn.

"What sort of distraction?" When Olive turned, Margaret was looking at her with pointed interest. "And where does Captain Aldridge fit into all this?"

"Not that sort of distraction, Mrs Truscott," Olive said quellingly. "It was just a friendly call, made at the behest of the WI."

She snorted. "That's rather boring. If your captain doesn't work out, you might consider the possibility. I quite liked Max

Dunn." She lay back, and they lapsed into silence, each brooding her own thoughts.

A moment later, Olive was startled to hear the sounds of Margaret crying. She levered herself onto her elbow to look down at her. "What is it?" Her friend had harboured a painful secret all alone until recently. Olive hoped a new one wasn't troubling her.

"Leo's been requested as the new chaplain on a submarine," she said, sniffing. Before Olive could think what to say, Margaret blurted, "I don't want him to go. What if he ends up like one of those poor men at Merryweather House? That makes me sound horrid, I know, but honestly, I don't care how he looks. What if he were to sink into self-pity, and I couldn't pull him out of it? What if he never came back to me?" By the end of her speech, she was clutching Olive's hands tightly.

She didn't seem to expect an answer, which was lucky, because nothing Olive could have said would have been a comfort. So, she simply let her friend go on.

"If he didn't want to go, I would do anything—*anything*—to get him out of it. But he *does*. Why would he want to go? We've just got married." She let go of Olive's hands and pressed her own against her face. "I'm a shameful coward. I know I am. When Leo railed against the security of his positions in Pipley and at Merryweather House, after seeing all those men who'd faced down the enemy, I joined up so that the pair of us—together—could be doing more. I sit in that dank little hut for hours and hours, with my eyes buried inside binoculars, straining for the first glimpse of enemy aircraft, to give us all the greatest possible warning." She pulled a handkerchief from her pocket and pressed it against her cheeks, clearly not finished. "It's not a courageous posting by any means, but it's important, nevertheless. Leo's job is equally so—bringing peace and comfort to those who are injured, worried, or fearful, those who have lost their faith, given in to despair, forfeited hope." She sniffed loudly.

"Of course they're important," Olive said urgently. Only recently had she managed to resolve her own feelings on the matter, giving up the chance to be an Ack-Ack girl and aim the anti-aircraft guns in order to be a pigeoneer. "But some people can't stomach the thought of staying behind when others are risking so much more."

Margaret stilled. "You're one of those people, aren't you?"

"I was," Olive admitted. "I've come round a bit," she added, smiling.

"Maybe you should talk to Leo . . ."

"You know I can't do that. And it wouldn't make any difference." Olive sat up. "But I think what you're doing is marvellous."

Margaret smiled. "It is actually rather interesting. I'm getting quite adept at identifying aircraft—both British and German—at a fair distance."

"Well done, you," Olive said.

"Next Sunday I'm to take a master test at the cinema in Hertford. I'll need to identify the aircraft flashed on the screen with ninety-five percent accuracy. I'm not at all certain I'm ready for that."

"You'll be fine."

"I'd almost forgotten," she said suddenly. "You know how you'd asked me to be on the lookout for anything suspicious in Balls Wood?" She had sat up again and was re-pinning her hair distractedly.

A frisson of awareness slipped along Olive's spine. "Did you see something?"

"Well, I saw *someone*."

Olive braced herself, anxious to hear Margaret's description. The FANYs under suspicion all looked sufficiently different, although perhaps not at a distance or through the trees.

"I've actually seen him twice now, skulking about," Margaret clarified. "Two Saturdays in a row. I forgot to tell you, but it's entirely possible he'll be back again this week."

But Olive's brows had knit together the moment Margaret had started talking. *Him?*

"He looks very shifty," she went on, "glancing about, walking quickly. He's certainly not out for a nature walk."

"What does he look like?"

"Well, he's certainly not *my* type." Catching Olive's eye, she tried again. "Light hair—sort of ash brown, I suppose. Hawklike nose, pocked skin, bristly chin. Wearing work clothes and boots."

"You aimed the binoculars at him?"

"Well, you asked me to keep a look out," she insisted.

"It was good thinking and may be very helpful." Except that Olive could think of no one bearing that description. A mysterious stranger, and new suspect, presumably not linked to the lipstick in Jamie's office. "Have you ever seen him before this?"

She shrugged. "Not that I know of."

"I don't suppose you could see what he was doing?" She imagined an oily, sneering individual pulling a wireless transmitter from under a log and tapping out treasonous messages that could endanger everyone at Brickendonbury.

Margaret shook her head. "But he was in the same place both times, at the other end of the ride from the hut. Right about where the body was found. Henrietta Gibbons gave me the full report." The last bit was said with a quirk of her lips.

Olive bit her lip, considering. After a moment she shot a glance at Margaret. "What time did you see him?"

"Round about the gloaming."

Her favourite time of day, unless it was damp and overcast. And now she had a reason for an evening walk. She'd have to drag Jamie with her; otherwise she was bound to get into trouble. At least she'd have company, and his, she'd discovered, wasn't always quite so objectionable as she'd originally thought.

The sun had dipped down behind the houses whose back gardens looked out over the river. She needed to get home for supper, and then she'd be heading out again to meet the girls for a drink. She would have liked to invite Margaret, but she had a job to do, and her friend was liable to ask some awkward questions. So she stood, dusting bits of grass from her uniform.

"Try not to worry too much about Leo. He has to make the choice for himself. And I suspect the corps will keep you plenty busy and thoroughly distracted. Pipley is just going to have to bear up without constant comfort and chatty afternoon teas at the vicarage. With any luck, it will all be over soon."

It was odd, but she had trouble imagining her life after the war, without Jamie.

Precisely at eight o'clock, Olive slid into the back of the promised motor car with Marie. Liz had insisted on driving, despite Kate's protestations.

"Harold's been teaching me all sorts of things," she'd insisted.

"No need to brag, sweetie," Liz had said, punctuating the statement with a wink.

With a small smile, Kate had shifted over. She was, Olive noted, wearing lipstick, but it was a shade of pink that made her cheeks look flushed and dewy in the electric lights of the manor.

They'd all peeled off their FANY uniforms in favour of dresses with full skirts, nipped-in waists and, in the case of Liz and Marie, flashes of cleavage. The pair of them had also slicked their lips with sharp red lipstick. They were fillies let off the lead. Gone were the quiet, efficient, obedient assistants of Station XVII; tonight they railed against daily injustices, gossiped about every last occupant of the manor, and eagerly embraced their night of freedom. Olive bided her time.

The Golden Goose was overrun with servicemen from the local base, and the four of them, being female and dressed to raise flagging morale, were kept busy chatting and flirting until quite late, at which point Olive hustled them out into the night air.

"Why did we have to leave?" Liz moaned.

"Because we all have to be up at dawn tomorrow," Olive insisted, "working our tails off for the officers you were complaining about not five minutes ago."

"You've nothing to complain about," Liz snapped, spearing Olive with a fierce look, which she seemed to regret instantly, wrapping her arm snugly about Olive's waist for the dark walk to the car.

They switched things up for the ride back: Olive drove, with Marie beside her, and Liz and Kate, their heads tipped close together, rode in the back. Kate hummed distractedly, but with a lovely, even pitch, as Olive navigated the dark lanes with little help from the car's shuttered headlamps. Soon Liz joined in, adding the words to the familiar tune "Oranges and Lemons," and then Olive, with more exuberance than musicality. Despite the air of camaraderie, Marie remained silent, although her fingers, pale in the moonlight, tapped along to the tune.

"Come on. Join in," Olive pressed.

Marie shook her head, and the song abruptly fizzled out.

The silence was short-lived, however. Before Olive could decide how to proceed with her questioning, Kate made the first conversational sally.

"Liz told us about you and Captain Aldridge, Olive. I suppose you have to keep it a secret? I remember Miss Butterwick warning us not to fraternise with the officers . . ."

"That was code for another verb entirely," Liz said with a snort.

"What do you mean?" Kate said.

"Don't tease her, Liz," Marie said, glancing into the backseat before levelling her gaze on Olive. Judging by the silence, they were all waiting for her to elaborate.

Evidently, the inquisition would start with her. So be it: perhaps it would prompt a slew of confidences now that alcohol had loosened their tongues and inhibitions a bit.

"You're right. It is a secret. Liz shouldn't have even told you," she said sharply. "I know it's utterly inappropriate, but it just happened—a consequence of too much time spent in each other's company. And too much pent-up frustration. And gin." Her lips curved into a smile. "And I know I'm not the only one who's given in to temptation. Harold had to be convinced somehow." The idea of Kate and Harold fairly boggled her mind.

Kate didn't answer, and Olive assumed she was blushing to the roots of her hair. Liz, however, had plenty to say, all of which Olive had been dreading.

"You waltzed in—snuck in, more like—like an Amazon, but with pigeons, for God's sake, and you stole the dishiest one of the lot. Why couldn't you have been assigned to Haverty, with his unruly sideburns and cabbagey breath? This war is really testing my patience." She huffed out a piteous sigh.

"She's not really mad at you," Marie said.

Kate added, "Major Haverty has been particularly smelly lately. It's as if it's coming out of his pores."

"Yes, don't worry," Liz said, rallying. "I'm involved with a certain groundskeeper. *He's* not off-limits, and he knows every hidey-hole on the manor grounds, and a few other things, besides . . ." Her voice trailed off suggestively. Olive's thoughts buzzed with curiosity. Could this mystery man have had something to do with the burglary, or worse? Was Liz shielding him or even possibly involved? Surely not.

"I suppose that leaves only Marie," Kate said. "And honestly, she could have her pick. You would not believe how often I come across men fumbling for the words to speak to her or staring after her as she walks off."

Liz leaned forward confidentially. "Lieutenant Tierney, in particular, is quite smitten."

Marie didn't rise to the bait.

"I've dressed the man's wounds," Liz said pointedly. "He looks very capable of all manner of things, if you know what I mean."

"We're friends, that's all," Marie said quellingly.

Now Kate's head jutted forward over the seat back. Her voice was quiet, girlish when she said, "Is there someone else? Someone you're waiting for?"

"No," Marie said hurriedly. "Nothing like that. I don't want the distraction—worrying about another person is too hard . . ." Her voice trailed off as abruptly as if a door had shut between them.

"That's a shame, because I suspect Lieutenant Tierney is *very* good at distraction," Liz drawled, leaning back. "But if you're not interested, perhaps I could lure him away."

"Suit yourself," Marie said, her voice clipped, just as Kate protested, "What about your groundskeeper?"

As the pair in the backseat hashed it out between them, Olive glanced at Marie. She'd turned to stare out the window, her chin tipped slightly up. Olive's thoughts rolled back to Max Dunn's quiet advice. Was she really prepared to force Marie to talk about something that could very well be nothing?

"We may not be in the thick of it, but this war has been hard on all of us," she said quietly. "It's stressful and exhausting and heartbreaking, and we all need a little reminder now and then that there are other things—lovely, wonderful things—in the world. There's no shame in indulging in a little bit of hope."

Marie didn't answer.

"I haven't seen my brother, Lewis, in almost two years. He joined up right at the start of the war and has been stationed in Greece. We've just had a letter that he's being transferred to North Africa. I worry about him every day." Now the whole car had gone silent. "Do you have brothers?" she asked, once again glancing at Marie.

"No."

"Sisters?" Olive pressed.

"No," Marie asserted, no longer quite so emphatic.

"Then who are you worried about?"

"What?" Marie turned to look at her, her heart-shaped face shadowed like a crescent moon, her one visible eye wide.

"You said worrying about another person is too hard. Who is it?" she said softly. Olive held her breath and wondered if this might be her breakthrough.

"I really have to pee," Liz whined, and Olive could have throttled her.

The window for confidences had firmly closed, and Olive was left to listen to grumblings about their living accommodations compared to the men's. Rather than allow her to pin down a single suspect, her fellow FANYs had managed to make her suspicious of each of them in turn. She was struck by how much she really didn't know about them—or what they might be capable of. A vision of Lieutenant Beckett's body, lying in the loamy earth of Balls Wood, shot a shiver up her spine.

But outwardly, she carried on as they did, her own secrets tucked carefully away.

Chapter 13

Jamie's desk was covered over with various maps of Belgium and intelligence reports, which tried to keep pace with the ever-changing landscape of an occupied country. Factories were commandeered, infrastructure was repurposed, and troops and vehicles moved like so many pieces on a game board. Olive would never have admitted it, but she was slightly giddy to be engaged in a strategy session focused on pinpointing sabotage targets and organising the supplies necessary to wreak such havoc.

They'd been at it for hours, and Olive was getting a crick in her neck and was desperate for a cup of tea, when there was a knock at the door.

"Come in," Jamie said without looking up.

Marie swung the door open, caught Olive's eye, and said briskly, "This just came through on the teleprinter, Captain Aldridge."

His head came up, and he reached for the paper.

The hairs on Olive's arms bristled to attention. This could be the transcript of Conjugal's first wireless transmission, decoded by the Secret Intelligence Service before being forwarded on to Station XVII.

Without another word, Marie slipped from the room, and Olive looked after her in bemusement.

No questions, no curiosity, no insubordination. Straight to the point and all business. Jamie probably loves her.

She stood up and came round the desk to read over his shoulder. To his credit, he didn't say a word, even when she blurted, "There's something wrong. This proves it." It was her follow-up demand, "Well, doesn't it?" that finally prompted a response.

"I hadn't finished reading it yet," he said irritably. "But what I assume you're referring to isn't proof of anything, merely an indicator."

She leaned over him and traced the words with her index finger as she read aloud from the page. *"Transmission came in on schedule, using accurate key code. Leading and trailing security codes missing. Transcript. Proceeding with plans for sabotage—several areas targeted. But we are in great need of supplies and money—we have had to bribe a number of officials. Additional agents requested. Please convey when we can expect a drop. Our efforts depend on your continued support."*

"Yes, thank you," Jamie said icily.

"They didn't use their security codes. Isn't the whole point of those codes to offer a measure of assurance that the operator is who we think he is? If they're missing, shouldn't we assume he's compromised?"

"In theory, yes. In practice, they're often left off transmissions. The operator is working under extreme duress, trying to transmit critical information while staying one step ahead of the Germans and their radio direction finders."

Olive's shoulders dropped in exasperation. "But their absence *could* indicate a problem," she pressed.

"Yes," he agreed, sitting back in his chair with one final glance at the page. The wrinkle had settled comfortably into his chin, and for once, Olive was relieved to see it. Ever since Robin had returned, she hadn't been able to shake the feeling that something was off with Operation Conjugal.

"Are we going to do anything about it?"

He rubbed his hand roughly over his jaw, shielding Horace

from view, but he didn't meet her eyes. "I'll call Leo Marks over at Signals and ask his opinion on Weasel, using his real name, of course. It'll be in his file." He reached for the telephone at the edge of his desk. "I've heard Marks has an uncanny memory of these fellows, down to what mistakes they made in their coding and transmissions when they went through training. Perhaps he can tell us if Weasel was error prone."

As he dialed and the call was transferred, Olive paced, her gaze flicking to the map on the wall and the part of Belgium where Operation Conjugal was trying to get a foothold. Soon Jamie was speaking, and over the course of the entire conversation, his face gave nothing away. She pounced the moment he pulled the phone from his ear.

"Well?"

"He wasn't infallible. According to Marks, he was prone to the occasional error both in his coding and his technique. And yet he described Weasel as an impressive operator, calm under pressure."

"That's all he said?"

Jamie was silent for a moment, his lips compressed and his forehead creased with lines. When he spoke, it was reluctantly. "He cautioned me not to dismiss the importance of missing security codes."

Olive nodded smugly. "I did, as well."

"We can't make an accurate assessment based on one transmission, particularly his first. He may just be getting his bearings."

"Not just the one transmission. I told you I thought the message I translated—the one carried home by Robin Hood—was off somehow."

"You barely know these men," he insisted, his voice rising with exasperation. "And it might not even have been Weasel who wrote that message. It could have been any one of them. You have a hunch," Jamie said firmly. "That's not actionable."

"An instinct," she countered tartly. "The sort that quite likely drives all manner of decisions in this war."

Jamie sighed. "You have very little experience with this business, Olive."

"But I have loads of experience with pigeons, and even other fanciers," she said tightly. "And something is off."

"It's possible," he allowed, staring down at the papers covering his desk.

"So, what do we do now?"

"We wait," Jamie said flatly.

"Until when? For what, exactly?"

"For the next scheduled transmission. It'll give us a better impression of Weasel's performance in the field."

"What about the requested supplies? If Conjugal is compromised, we could be dropping them—and, worse still, *agents*—right into German hands."

"We could be," he agreed heavily. "But everything comes with some level of risk. For now, we proceed with our plans for another drop in three weeks' time. With any luck, Weasel will have settled in by then and be sending regular transmissions with his security codes intact."

When she made to protest, he held up his hand. "This is the way it is, Olive. We're doing the best we can."

She bit her lip. The refrain was the same across all of Britain, but the worry was that it simply wouldn't be enough.

13 September

Hercule Poirot was fond of making little lists. And careful analysis of these curious incidents, unexplained objects, and suspicious behaviours always led him to the truth. With her thoughts in a jumble, Olive was game to try anything, so with a scrap of paper foraged from the waste bin, she came up with a list of her own.

1. *Wireless aerial*
2. *Coded lines of verse*
3. *Silk scarf*
4. *Signet ring*
5. *Warning letters*
6. *Lipstick*
7. *Burglary*
8. *Stranger*
9. *Argument*

Olive scanned the list, struck by the possibility that some of the items they'd found on Lieutenant Beckett's body and in his room were not his own. Perhaps he, too, had been collecting clues, suspecting a traitor was operating at Brickendonbury.

Then again, was it possible that each item on the list was part and parcel of a distinct secret, thoroughly unrelated to the others? Her first effort as an amateur sleuth had led to just such a discovery. The villagers of Pipley had been harbouring a startling number of sordid secrets. Were the occupants of Station XVII guilty of the same?

With a groan of frustration, Olive set down her pencil and set herself back to work. She was meant to be typing up a progress report Jamie had written on the status of Operation Conjugal, and a list of requests for the upcoming drop. But her typing skills were atrocious, and rather than riddle the page with mistakes, she was pecking out the letters one by one. Staring at the half-finished page emerging from the typewriter, she resolved to buckle down and then reward herself with a visit to the kitchen. If she had to stake out Balls Wood with Jamie in tow, she might as well bring a few goodies along. And it would give her a chance to quiz Tomás Harris about the argument he'd had with Lieutenant Beckett shortly before he died. The only words she'd overheard were *impossible*, *can't be helped*, and *merde alors*, and in her suspicious mind, they'd taken on an ominous meaning.

An agonising quarter of an hour later, she pulled the sheet of paper from the platen and stood, then smoothed her skirt and straightened her tunic, determined to look accomplished after her pitiful efforts. She slipped out from behind her assigned desk amid the cluster allotted to the FANY, smiled at Kate, who was busily typing away with both hands, and headed for the kitchen.

Hilda was at the wide table, chopping vegetables, while Tomás bent over the Aga, pulling loaves of freshly baked bread from the oven. Hamish was in the corner, his pointy black ears twitching as he slavered over a meaty bone.

"If it isn't Olive Bright," Tomás said, straightening. "Here to ferret out my secrets, are you?"

Olive blinked, rather disconcerted that he'd been expecting her.

"You never did trust my roast beef, did you?" he added.

Her smile was one of relief. "It was too good to be true," she admitted. "Pure sorcery." She leaned in conspiratorially. "Precisely why I came to see you."

Tomás raised a single eyebrow and crossed his arms, amusement slipping through the cracks of his aloof demeanour. "Is that right?" he said, his words accented by his Spanish heritage. Hilda's cheeks rounded as she tucked back an indulgent, pale-lipped smile.

"Captain Aldridge and I have some business in Balls Wood this evening, and I wondered if you had anything for a picnic basket."

The eyebrow rose even higher. "Business, is it?"

Olive felt a sudden warmth in her cheeks, but she said coolly, "It is."

Tomás's grin spread across his face. "If you say so. If I rummage, I can probably find a few things for you."

Olive beamed at him, her brain darting about for a way to broach the subject of the argument with the small talk thus dispatched.

"I'll tuck a stem of rosemary into the basket," he said soberly. He had shifted to stand at the table beside his wife and was turning bread dough out onto the wooden surface. This dough looked nothing like the grey, anaemic substance that Mrs Battlesby fussed over at the lodge. It was as pale as cotton, springy as a baby's cheek, and smelling deliciously of yeast. "For remembrance."

Olive blinked. It seemed she wouldn't need to broach the subject of Lieutenant Beckett, after all.

"Was he a friend of yours?" It would settle her mind to know that there was one person at least who had known him and truly mourned him.

Tomás shrugged. "We were friendly. We had an arrangement."

"Oh," she said casually, tripping her fingers over the neat clusters of summer vegetables awaiting the knife. "What sort of arrangement?"

"Mutually beneficial. He liked to take walks in the woods"—here he paused, his eyebrows rose, and his face expressed a general acceptance—"and I like to cook with interesting ingredients."

Olive frowned. This was not at all what she'd been expecting. "I don't understand."

"He'd rummage through the hedgerows and forage over the forest floor to find all manner of foods you cannot find at the grocer or on the ration. Herbs, berries, mushrooms, greens. It was a beautiful collaboration."

"Then why were you arguing with him?" she blurted, feeling instantly gauche.

Hilda glanced at her husband. "He's a slave to his temper, this one. It is quite something to behold."

His voice a low purr, Tomás answered his wife in Spanish, and her cheeks coloured rosily. To Olive he said, "You heard that?" A shrug. "He'd not brought me the mushrooms he'd promised. He said he'd found something more interesting than mushrooms."

Tomás scoffed at the suggestion. "But he was careful to add that it was nothing I could use in my cooking."

Olive felt a flutter of excitement. "What was it?" she breathed. It occurred to her in the seconds before he responded that Hercule Poirot would have already known the answer, and for him, this admission would merely be confirmation. *She* hadn't the slightest idea, but decided that this moment of discovery was quite good enough.

"He didn't say."

Olive reined in her frustration. Yet another dead end. Almost without realising it, she pulled out a chair at the table and dropped into it, then splayed her hands over the smooth, oiled wood.

Without a word, Tomás took up a knife and cut into a cooled loaf of bread. He expertly smeared the slice with a thin layer of butter and topped it with a dollop of jam before sliding it across to her on a chipped china plate. "Not what you wanted to hear, it seems."

Olive didn't answer, merely sank her teeth into that thick slice that smelled of yeast, sweet cream, and sun-drenched summer berries. She closed her eyes and let her thoughts stream back to the halcyon days before the war.

Before long, reality came roaring back, but Olive couldn't help but savour the comforting moments in the manor kitchen.

"The WI has just put up jam, as well," she said, swiping a finger through the berry-red slick. "I hope to goodness that it's as good as this." The bread was a revelation. She hadn't a clue how Tomás managed it, but she was delighted to enjoy his efforts.

"Ah, yes, the famous WI. Those women are a force to be reckoned with."

"Agreed. They roped me into heading their pig scheme at the beginning of the summer—quite against my will." Olive shook her head and took another bite, the corners of her mouth already sticky with jam. "Just recently they've turned their collective attention to raising money for the Spitfire Fund." She licked her lips. "And, of course," she added wryly, "a newcomer to the village. A downed pilot recuperating from painful and disfiguring burns. He has no idea the sort of dedicated rehabilitation he's in for, poor man."

"Was he at Merryweather House?" Hilda asked, her face drawn with sympathy. "There are many of them there, aren't there? Mostly RAF?"

Olive nodded soberly.

"Why not bring together the bastions of Britain," Tomás suggested. "The WI and the RAF?"

"What do you mean?"

Tomás shrugged again, looking every bit a cosmopolitan gentleman, but for the flour coating his hands and apron. "The pilots, they are present among us, stationed on local bases, defending us from above. They are clean-cut and official in their blue uniforms, and they are appealing with their confident—dare I say, cocksure—attitudes. Men do not understand the appeal, but women?" He snorted. "Women, they swoon." He looked askance at his wife. "Not Hilda. She is quite happy with a messy cook who argues about mushrooms."

"*Mi amor*," Hilda said dutifully, batting her lashes at him while her knife continued its measured progress down the length of a carrot.

Marie, too, had remarked on the effect RAF men had on women, but Olive was having trouble imagining that the women of the WI were similarly affected. Would a charming smile and a sharp uniform ruffle Harriet's brisk demeanour, Lady Camilla's elegant calm, Mrs Spencer's no-nonsense manner, or Violet Darling's blasé attitude? And even if they did, what then?

Clearly exasperated by the dubious frown on her face, Tomás propped his hands on his hips. "Host a fête and charge women for the chance to mingle and dance and enjoy the company of those flyboys. I guarantee you it will work."

"From where would you suggest I recruit these handsome, charming servicemen?" Olive said tartly.

"Merryweather House, of course."

Olive was pondering whether the WI could make a success of Tomás's rather ingenious suggestion when she returned to her desk, replete with fresh bread and answers. Every bit of satisfaction she'd felt drained away when she noticed her list lying beside her typewriter in full view.

She snatched it up and quickly shoved it into her pocket. With her heart suddenly pounding like the hooves of a racehorse coming down the home stretch, she glanced round. None of the FANYs were currently at their desks. They'd likely taken a tea and smoke break, but any one of them could have seen it. Which meant she no longer had the advantage. If any one of the clues was relevant, the list would surely indicate she was investigating the murder—and would even hint at her progress. Olive pressed a hand to her forehead, relieved that she hadn't been inclined to jot down her suspicions with regard to each of her friends.

She dropped into her chair, trying to look on the bright side. It was, after all, entirely possible that no one had seen the list. And she dreaded having to confess her carelessness to Jamie. Perhaps it was best if she bided her time and tried to deduce who—if anyone—was now privy to the progress of the investigation.

"*Murder*," she muttered fiercely to herself.

The sky was clear and a lovely shade of violet when Olive set down the picnic basket the Harrises had packed. Just above her hung the forgotten aerial that dogged her thoughts, and for a moment, she stared up at it with fresh curiosity.

"It's still here," she marvelled.

Jamie followed her gaze and admitted, "Because I haven't made arrangements to have it taken down. I'm afraid I've been working under the wildly optimistic view that it might produce a lead." He glanced wryly at her. "The imagined traitor returns with the transmitter to get on with her nefarious deeds . . . or she returns to get rid of the evidence." He shrugged, then added grimly, "Until then, it's serving as a marker for where his body was found."

Olive nodded, glancing sadly at the rotten log a few feet away from where she'd crouched beside the body of Lieutenant Beckett. She placed the sprig of rosemary on the ground beside it, feeling a renewed determination to find the man's killer. With a guilty glance at Jamie, who'd settled himself on the log, she reached into the basket, pulled out a pair of sandwiches, handed one over, and unwrapped her own. Then she sat beside him.

"I'm not entirely sure what we're doing here," he said, eyeing her warily, "but I hope you haven't lured me here for one of your little talks."

"Well, at least here no one can hear you scream," she quipped with some irritation.

Olive chewed thoughtfully. In truth, she had been dreading this moment and now braced herself for the awkward bit.

"Remember how you told me I wasn't to court danger or confront murderers on my own?"

He blinked at her as his jaw stilled in mid-chew. The gnashing of teeth soon followed, and Olive couldn't help but stare, wide eyed, as he finished his bite of sandwich. "Olive," he ground out warningly.

"Don't get excited. Neither of those is likely."

"But they're possible?" he demanded, glancing quickly round him.

She laid a hand on his arm. "Let me explain."

"You couldn't have gone over this while we were walking?"

"Of course not. You mightn't have come."

"And that's the truth," he said dryly.

"Margaret's joined the Royal Observer Corps and is training as a spotter. She's currently stationed at the edge of Balls Wood."

Jamie's face was impassive, his ire carefully banked. His ability to hide what he was really thinking was one of the things she most admired about him. Now probably wasn't the time to tell him.

"Well," she went on, "I asked her to keep an eye out for anything suspicious." Olive widened her eyes to convey that the important bit was coming. "She told me there'd been a man skulking about."

The remains of Jamie's sandwich hung forgotten in his hand. "That's why we're here?" he demanded in disbelief before huffing out a sigh. "This isn't one of your mystery novels, where everyone's a suspect and behaviour you don't understand is a cause for further investigation. This is a country wood." He enunciated every word carefully. "All sorts of people wander through here, for all manner of reasons. Some, I'm sure, even skulk, and that's their prerogative. We're a country at war, and none of us are privy to every secret. All of us are hiding something—"

Olive saw a flash of movement near the other end of the ride. She laid a hand on Jamie's arm, shushing him, and whispered, "Someone's coming this way."

Jamie was suddenly alert, peering through the trees in the direction she'd indicated. "I know you told me to stop investigating, but let's just see, shall we? We're already here, enjoying our picnic." When he didn't object, she tugged him up off the log to pull him deeper under the trees, his arm rigid under her hand.

"You do realise you left the picnic basket in full view," he said sourly.

Olive cursed. There was nothing for it but to hope the stranger didn't notice.

The waiting seemed an eternity, but at long last, the man, having walked nearly the full length of the ride, stopped level with the spot where Lieutenant Beckett had been found. He had an efficient, catlike grace but was utterly nondescript in a bulky bush jacket, worn work boots, and a flat cap pulled low over his face, all of it shaded a muddy brown.

She looked at Jamie.

He leaned toward her and spoke in her ear. "Let me guess. You suspect he might be the murderer and want to ambush him."

Keeping her voice to the barest whisper, Olive said, "You needn't sound so lord of the manor. I have a bit more experience with this sort of thing than you do."

"Murderers, do you mean? Certainly, as a victim you do. I've never managed to irritate anyone quite so thoroughly as you." He was so close, she could smell the liquorice on his breath.

"Don't bet on it," she snapped. She didn't like to be reminded of that dreadful day in late spring when she'd thought her life was coming to an end. "I'm going to speak to him. You're welcome to come, but only with an open mind." She looked him over. "I don't suppose you've taken lessons from Lieutenant Tierney?"

"I'll do my best," he said dryly.

Thankfully, the emerging night sounds of the wood had muffled their whispered conversation, and as the violet sky began its quiet fade to navy, the pair inched forward. Their quarry was crouched beside the log and busy at some mysterious task, and Olive did her best to move stealthily. The skulker, no doubt hearing the sounds of their approach, shot to his feet and spun to face them. He moved instinctively to shield what he'd been doing.

"Hello," Olive said cheerily.

"Evenin'." His voice was wary and distinctly unfriendly.

She slipped her arm cosily through Jamie's and gabbled, "We're out for an evening picnic and a stroll through the wood. Isn't it romantic?" She glanced doe eyed at Jamie, who responded with a stiffened arm and utter silence.

"I s'pose."

"Do you come often at twilight?" She couldn't make out his features with any certainty. She had the impression of hooded dark eyes, a squashy nose, and thin lips in a sea of dark stubble, but much of that could be owed to shadow. And while he clearly wanted to be left alone, she was determined to be as tenacious as M Poirot.

"Sometimes."

This was getting them nowhere, and Olive decided to go straight to the point. "Did you happen to know Lieutenant Jeremy Beckett?"

Silence.

"He was a friend of ours, and we were quite saddened by his sudden death," she said.

"Sorry to hear that," he muttered. "I should be off—"

Olive peered round him to stare at the ground at his feet. "You knew him. That's why you're here, isn't it?" She released Jamie's arm, her heart beating a furious tattoo, and moved closer to stare into the stranger's eyes. Jamie tried to draw her back, but she pulled free of his grasp.

Even in the growing dark, she'd seen the circle of wild mushrooms at the base of the hornbeam tree, and the tiny wooden cross among them. Near it lay a careful arrangement—a seedpod, a feather, an oyster shell, and a fragile piece of a hornet's nest. She thought of Lieutenant Beckett—and the senseless loss of such a life—and wanted to crouch down and run her finger over each item in turn.

"How did you know him?" she asked.

"Olive," Jamie said warningly from just behind her, and it struck her at that moment that he spent a fair bit of time saying her name in precisely that tone.

"I've known him for years. We met . . ." His voice trailed off as he looked away through the trees. "A long time ago."

She spoke tentatively. *"Temet nosce?"* They were the words engraved on the signet ring. *Know thyself.*

The stranger's body jerked and then seemed to hunch in on itself, and then the words began to pour out of him, drawn by grief and the obscurity of darkness. "Yes. I gave him that ring as a talisman against an unkind world. We weren't ashamed," he said fiercely, "but for obvious reasons, we met in secret, doing our best to hide that part of ourselves. We were lucky to be stationed near each other but couldn't often meet. When we could, we came here." He glanced bleakly round him. "Jeremy took regular walks so as not to arouse suspicion—and because he loved it. He was like a magpie, always discovering things and squirrelling them away. He was a private person and kept himself to himself, but out here, he *belonged*."

Olive thought suddenly of her list of clues, the tangible items they'd discovered, and wondered how many of them were utterly insignificant to her investigation and instead merely the collection of a wandering, curious soul.

"I'm sorry," she said, reaching to take his hand. "I didn't know him well, but I wish I had."

He briefly tightened his calloused fingers over hers and then let go and stepped back. He nodded to Jamie, and then, with a final glance back at the little shrine, he turned away and walked determinedly out of the trees.

Jamie let out a long breath.

"Not the killer, after all," Olive said jauntily, "and that's one clue explained, at the very least."

Jamie stared at her for a long moment, wearing a long-suffering expression. When he finally spoke, his voice was tight. "Possibly two. Partly, at least."

Olive ran through the list in her mind and gasped. "The letters?" She considered this. "You think someone saw them together?"

He shrugged. "It isn't illegal unless they were engaged in certain behaviour," he said gruffly. "But if their secret got out, it could make things awkward and uncomfortable. Possibly even dangerous."

"And yet," she said, stepping carefully, "there was no demand for money. As blackmail letters, they were pretty tame."

"Agreed."

Olive stared up at the silvery glow of the half-moon and the scatter of stars across the sky, some of them caught in the gossamer netting of drifting clouds. "Although, honestly, it's exactly the sort of letter Miss Husselbee would have sent. No, scratch that. She would have confronted him in person and expected nothing less than his complete capitulation."

"Yes, well, I think we can safely eliminate her as a suspect."

Despite his mocking words, Olive's lips slid into a smug smile. Slowly but surely, she was homing in on the murderer. To celebrate, she pulled Jamie down with her onto the log—the irony of the pair of them picnicking amid the true lover's knot not lost on her—and dug into the basket. Hilda's wild strawberry scones would be a delicious reward.

Chapter 14

Her optimism was short lived. When days went by without any leads or inspiration, Olive couldn't help but feel disheartened. Her mood was exacerbated by her certainty that Operation Conjugal had somehow gone awry. Alice had still not returned, and the communications they had received hinted that matters were not quite what they seemed. Worse still, she couldn't get those bleak lines of verse out of her head.

> *Courage was mine, and I had mystery;*
> *Wisdom was mine, and I had mastery;*
> *To miss the march of this retreating world*
> *Into vain citadels that are not walled.*

She'd compared the handwriting on the slip of paper found in Lieutenant Beckett's pocket with the notations in his appointment book and couldn't be certain whether he'd written the coded verse or not.

Why *those* words? Why had they been encoded, and by whom? *For* whom?

An idea was taking shape at the back of her mind, and she'd

retreated to the peaceful quiet of the dovecote to ponder it further. Unfortunately, her father managed to scare her up, having worked himself into a full bluster.

"Let's have the truth, my girl," he said, beetling his brows formidably and filling the doorway so that he looked like a charging bull who'd seen red.

Olive stilled, caught neatly in the trap. She hadn't a clue how he'd caught her out or on which of her myriad lies. She blinked, willing a suitable response to land fully formed on her tongue.

Perhaps sensing her anxiety, Fritz flew down from his lookout in one of the dovecote's roofline pigeonholes and, with a vigorous flapping of wings, landed on her head.

"Bugger off, Fritz," her father said. "You're not involved in this. At least, not directly." The bird allowed himself to be removed, and Olive set him on the bench beside her.

Her father's gaze flicked between the pair of them before he stated baldly, "I telephoned the National Pigeon Service this morning, and the bloody fool who took the call denied having ever vetted our loft. The bastard was still laughing when I hung up the phone." Rupert Bright was clearly still fuming, but he quickly got control of himself. "I know I've given you free rein with these birds, but don't think for a minute that I'm not expecting to be kept apprised." He glanced at the tray of food, circled round with pigeons. "I know you're training them for someone. Our replenished feed supply is proof of that. So, out with it. Who is it?"

What could she say without giving away the truth? Her thoughts pinged frantically, while her pulse, beating squarely at the base of her throat, nearly choked her. And then she had it. Jamie had passed on what he'd found to be a highly amusing bit of intelligence, and it was the perfect diversion from the loft's top-secret efforts. With a sigh of relief, which she hoped her father would read as resignation, she began to talk.

Apparently, Britons, already worried over the infiltration of

German agents and an impending invasion, now also suspected pigeons of being in on the conspiracy. It was thought that these Nazi pigeons were flying home with crucial details about British defences. Even talking to a pigeon on a park bench was considered highly suspicious. In keeping with the War Office's purview to thwart German spies of any sort, they'd arranged for a crack team of British pigeons—the Bright birds—to be based along the coast for the sole purpose of subversion.

Her father, who'd been pacing the dovecote as she relayed the "truth," his frown sinking ever farther into his forehead, now turned to look at her. She met his gaze unflinchingly.

"So, our birds are the last line of defence, eh?" He scratched his bristly cheek, thinking. "What's the idea, then? They'll be a Pigeon Observer Corps to watch for suspicious birds flying in the wrong direction out over the Channel?"

"Exactly," Olive replied, extemporising. For, in reality, she had no idea how it was meant to work—Jamie's interest had only been minimal. "With any luck, our birds will lure their German counterparts back here, thereby undermining the delivery of critical intelligence."

"These German blighters might show up in our loft?" he boomed. His perspective shifted instantly from outraged Briton to worldly pigeon fancier. "I'd certainly like to get a look at them," he muttered. "Perhaps we could even snip the leg rings from one or two of them and let them defect. German pigeons are sturdy stock, Olive."

"Possibly," Olive allowed.

Putting that eventuality aside, Rupert Bright glared at his daughter once again. "Why was I—the owner of this loft, mind—kept in the dark about this?"

Determined to keep her lies to the absolute minimum, she answered truthfully. "I was instructed not to tell you—to lie if I had to—if only to make certain that you'd cooperate." After a pause, she added, "You have something of a reputation."

"A damn fine one," her father answered explosively.

"As far as pigeons go, yes," Olive agreed. "Your work with humans is not quite so impeccable."

"That's because they're all idiots."

She cleared her throat pointedly, brows raised.

Her father snorted and then, rather surprisingly, chuckled. "Touché." He frowned again. "Who was that man, purportedly from the NPS, who came to the lodge to speak to me?"

Olive shrugged. "A friend from the manor. I knew you'd never be content to let our birds do their bit without your say-so."

Her father looked at her askance; Olive smiled innocently. "That's quite diabolical, my girl."

"Not really," she demurred. "We're all just doing what we can, trying to win this war." Her words might have been nonchalant, but her thoughts warred between chagrin and smug satisfaction. "What made you call the NPS?"

"They were being rather stingy in pulling from our loft—a couple birds here and there. I was going to suggest we ramp up our breeding process to provide a bigger pool of birds."

"Yes, well, this will be much the same—only a few birds needed at a time. Of course, that could change depending on how the War Office believes the best birds should be used." She was reaching the limits of her prevarication skills, hoping to mollify her father's disappointment at having been passed over, while doing her best to hint subtly that he should leave matters to the men in charge. And her.

"All right, then. Carry on, and I will endeavour not to poke about too much." He made to leave but then turned back. "Never hesitate to come to me, Olive. I trust you absolutely, but sometimes men are incorrigible when it comes to women."

"I understand," she said.

As he turned, glancing round the dovecote, she heard his gleeful muttering. "We'll outsmart those bloody Germans yet."

The moment the door slammed shut behind him, she turned to Fritz. "Your timing is spot on, my boy," she said with a wink. "If only your skills could stretch to detective work."

She tried to settle back into the work of her little grey cells, but it wasn't to be. Jonathon burst in moments later.

"Captain Aldridge wants you at the manor," he said, breathing hard with the effort of running. "And he says to hurry."

The weather had turned, the warmth of summer having given way to brisk winds and the chilly damp of early autumn. Treks on the Welbike, Olive realised, were not going to be nearly as pleasant in the coming months. As she hurried along the corridor to Captain Aldridge's office, tucking frizzy bits of hair back into their pins and wiping the moisture from her face, her heart kicked nervously, and her thoughts buzzed with curiosity. With a perfunctory knock, she swung open the door and stepped in. He was sitting behind his desk, his dark hair carefully combed, his uniform pristine.

"What is it that you couldn't tell me on the telephone?" she said. "Do you know who the murderer is? Is there a new message from Conjugal?"

"No, on both counts," he said, his words bitten off. "Close the door."

Olive pushed it closed behind her and moved to sit down, then promptly propped her elbows on his desk.

"The scarf is gone."

She glanced at the jacket hanging innocently on the curved arm of the coat stand. "Someone else discovered your hiding place?"

"Unless it was you who took it?" The question she'd imagined as rhetorical clearly wasn't. Jamie was staring at her, his eyebrow raised in query.

"Of course not," she answered quickly, a tinge of outrage in her voice. Then she remembered her unsanctioned search of his office and tried to cover with an upturned chin and a brisk manner.

"Right," he said grimly.

"You probably should start locking your office door."

"You don't say," he said sourly. "After your little foray, I have been. It appears someone picked the lock. Which means that scarf is important." Olive sat up straighter. She had, in fact, tried to convince him of it from the very beginning, but now wasn't the time to mention it. "And the fact that it was found on Lieutenant Beckett's body is rather incriminating."

"It could be unrelated. Remember Signet Ring said he collected found objects."

"Signet Ring?"

"The man in Balls Wood who—"

"I know who you mean." He ignored her huff of exasperation. "The difficulty with that hypothesis is that no one, other than you and the CO, knew it had been found on the body, let alone that it was here in my office. It seems likely now that he was murdered."

In other circumstances, Olive would have relished the concession, but her own carelessness had undermined it. She felt a prickle at the back of her neck and realised she was going to have to confess.

Oblivious to her discomfort, Jamie tapped the end of a pencil rhythmically on his desk. "What I don't understand is why the murderer didn't just take it off the body."

"Maybe he'd just found it—maybe it didn't even belong to the murderer." She was talking too fast, pressing her fingers to her temple.

"I just explained how—" Jamie stopped and narrowed his gaze, searching her face. "You did something, didn't you? What is it?"

After a beat of silence, she said, "It wasn't deliberate. It was pure carelessness, and it won't happen again."

"What is it?" he repeated, each word punctuated full stop.

Not wanting to see the disappointment, exasperation, or anger swimming in his gaze, she closed her eyes and confessed. "I'd written a list of all the clues I considered possibly relevant to the murder, and I"—she swallowed painfully and screwed up her features for the rest—"left it out on my desk in the FANY carrel for a few minutes." Olive didn't say any more, merely waited.

Jamie didn't say a word, and eventually, she opened her eyes, expecting him to have pulled an explosive device out of his desk to set in front of her. It wouldn't be the first time such a thing had happened.

He met her gaze. "When was this?"

"The day we went to Balls Wood."

"So, long after the lipstick was left behind," he said, Horace hunkering down for a comfortable stay. "Can I see this list?" he asked, one eyebrow winged up.

With a heavy sense of responsibility pressing on her chest, she pulled the list from her pocket and handed it over. She'd already drawn a line through *Signet ring*, *Stranger*, and *Argument*, leaving six clues left to resolve.

He read it over quickly.

"Several of these are new to me, but I assume you're planning to enlighten me should they lead to any actionable intelligence."

"Of course."

"Quite," he said dryly. He glanced again at the list before adding, "It's an unfortunate setback, and yet it may have prompted the murderer to act, thereby providing us with another clue." As he folded the page and handed it back, he went on. "At the very least it seems to have corroborated the suspicion that one of the FANYs is guilty of either murder or treason. Possibly both. Otherwise, why not simply come to me and ask for the return of the scarf?" He glanced at the maps on the wall beside them. "I wonder if the scarf was only incidental—perhaps she returned for something else entirely."

Olive followed his gaze, her eyes skimming over the country map of Belgium and then the overlay that Jamie had requested from MI9, its scale blown up in the area where Conjugal was based. Her heart rate settled into a slow, torpid beat. "You think she might somehow be undermining the operation? Using the aerial and the missing transmitter?" Suddenly her stomach dropped.

"I just don't know," Jamie said, running a frustrated hand through his hair. "There was something, you said, that seemed suspect about each of them. Tell me."

So she did, and he didn't even rein her in when she lapsed into amateur psychology and baseless hunches. First was Liz, who seemed mad at the world and rather desperate to be noticed and appreciated. Jamie's blank stare seemed a good indicator that he'd forgotten the aforementioned crush, and Olive really didn't want to have to go into it again. She moved on to Marie, who, she suspected, was hiding something to do with her family. The fact that she was resisting the sweetly flirtatious Lieutenant Tierney when she was clearly smitten was equally suspicious. Whereas Olive was determined to get to the bottom of that little curiosity, Jamie indicated by a roll of his eyes that he wasn't interested in that aspect of things. Olive moved on.

"I can't quite put my finger on it, but Kate is by far the dodgiest of the three. She looks so young and innocent, with her apple cheeks and innocent brown eyes, but some of it has to be put on. For one thing, she's a lot smarter than she seems—possibly a behaviour drilled into her by her mother." Her fingernail was tapping irritably on his desk. "Not to mention Miss Butterwick. When she thinks no one is looking, she's efficient and organised. And I've caught her in the library, reading scientific texts. But if you ask her a direct question, it's all wide eyes and measured words. She's hiding something, all right, but it might just be her brain." She frowned. "And then there's Harold."

"Harold Ennis? What about him?" He'd begun tapping his

pencil again, in time with her fingernail, but now he stopped abruptly.

"They're engaged in the sort of thing that everyone imagines we are," she said pointedly. "But as far as I know, *they're* not faking it."

Jamie swore, and Olive stared at him. "What is it?"

He glanced at her from under his lids. "This is, of course, confidential." Her nod prompted him to go on. "Harold Ennis is a bit of a dark horse. Before the war, he was engaged in some questionable . . . some criminal activities," he said, correcting himself. "He was given the choice of prison or coming to work at Station XVII. The man is brilliant with his hands."

"I'm beginning to see the appeal," Olive said, with a twist of her lips. Jamie rolled his eyes. "Taken all together, it appears Kate is a bit of a dark horse herself. She may not be wearing red lipstick, but perhaps she's savvy enough to have planted a tube of it, knowing she wouldn't be suspected."

"This is all very nebulous, but it does give us a bit more to go on, and a few things to think about. Do what you can to encourage confidences without arousing suspicion. Your list—if it was seen—could have spooked any one of our suspects into further action. Be careful, Olive," he said soberly.

"Of course," she said distractedly.

After a moment lost in thought, she realised the room had been silent for some time, and she glanced up to see Jamie watching her.

"You already have a plan," he realised resignedly.

"Only the barest idea." She was behaving just like Poirot at his most irritating, but she couldn't help it. Sometimes it was best to keep one's little ideas to oneself, particularly if there was a chance they were misguided. When a few more details slotted into place, it would be her pleasure to impress him with her insights.

Jamie cut into this pleasant thought. "I suppose the best I can hope for is that you stick to our agreement."

She flashed him an appreciative smile that had him blinking. She'd have him trained yet.

Having sung the verses of "Jerusalem" with their customary gusto, the ladies of the WI had settled comfortably into the chairs arranged in rows to face the little dais at the far end of the village hall. As always at this point in the meetings, there was a sense of bonhomie and, of course, delighted anticipation at the promise of tea and cake. It was typically during the business portion that things tended to get a bit more colourful.

Her father had used a bit of precious petrol to get Harriet to the meeting, so that she might participate fully in the fundraising discussion, which was to kick off with Olive's report on her recent exploratory visit to Peregrine Hall. Olive intended to follow it up with Tomás Harris's idea of a collaboration between the WI and the RAF and hoped the ladies would take the idea to heart.

Lady Camilla stepped onto the dais, her hands clasped, her blond chignon tucked neatly at the base of her neck. She smiled benignly at the assembled group of women—a good turnout.

"Most of you have been working hard in the preservation centres, putting up jam with the summer fruit from our gardens, orchards, and hedgerows. We were split this year, the official Pipley centre here at the hall and a smaller, secondary centre at Blackcap Lodge, which allowed Mrs Bright to take an active part. I'm delighted to tell you all that between the two, we managed three hundred jars of jam." The women, almost all of whom had worked in close quarters, slicing, stirring, and sterilising for hours on end, applauded their efforts, the shine of pride in their eyes.

"As previously agreed, some of the funds from the sale of the jam will be donated to the Spitfire Fund," Lady Camilla went on. "However, as I'm sure you'll all agree, we can do better." Her gaze ranged over them. "Among ourselves, we've not yet managed to decide on a new scheme for this purpose, but in an effort to include the newest arrivals to the village, Olive volunteered to call in at Peregrine Hall." Her eyes darted about and finally settled on Olive. "If you'd like to come up, dear, you can fill us in."

Olive walked to the front, sparing an interested glance for the table of refreshments on her way. On the dais, looking out at the sea of curious faces, she noticed that Violet Darling was studying her with a cool appraisal that felt oddly disconcerting.

She began, "Lady Revell is utterly charming and eager to take part. She's come up from London, where she was a regular volunteer with the Red Cross." This titbit prompted a few murmurs of approval. "When her house was requisitioned by the War Office and her nephew, Squadron Leader Dunn, was sent to Merryweather House, she decided to relocate here to Pipley." Olive paused. "Now that he's been released, she's been focused on assisting with his recuperation."

"How is the poor man?" Mrs Spencer spoke up, asking the question that had been hovering on all their lips. The unspoken question being, "Are his burns horrible?"

Olive glanced at Violet, whose expression gave her no help. She said awkwardly, "A good bit of his face was burned, and his hands, as well." As dozens of eyes bored into her, she felt compelled to add, "Of course, I can't speak to the full extent of the damage."

Faces looked pained, grim.

Olive soldiered on. "The flesh is healing, though. It's his thoughts and memories, I believe, that pain him the most. I think he simply needs to start again. He won't fly again, and the reality must be rather excruciating in the middle of this bitter war. We all need to feel as if we're making a difference."

There were nods all round.

"Poor boy. But he's not alone in his suffering," Harriet said, her hand absently massaging her own slowly atrophying leg muscles. "Far too many brave souls have ended up at Merryweather

House. Perhaps we could think of a way to help them find a new purpose."

"We should ask the vicar," said Mrs Crabbleton.

"If we can catch him," Miss Danes replied with some asperity. "He barely has time for the likes of us."

Olive glanced nervously at Lady Camilla, who'd reached up to touch the clip holding her chignon. Catching Olive's eye, she lowered her hand and smiled blandly.

"Perhaps because he knows there are others who need his attention more than we do," Harriet said sensibly.

"We should do whatever we can for our boys," Mrs Satterhorn said stoutly. She was the no-nonsense wife of a farmer, with two sons of her own in HM Forces. "But we'll still need an idea for the Spitfire Fund."

"Did Lady Revell or Squadron Leader Dunn offer any suggestions?" Lady Camilla inquired hopefully.

"They did not," Olive admitted, having noticed that Violet's mouth was now curved in a secretive smile. Olive was tempted to call her up to the dais to help field the group's questions but decided not to give her away. She obviously had a reason for keeping her visit to Peregrine Hall a secret. When the chatter eventually subsided into a dispirited silence, she went on. "But someone else did."

"Who?" came the inevitable calls from the assembled group.

"Top secret, I'm afraid. But I have permission to share his idea."

This, naturally, had a buoyant effect—intrigue was always appreciated. Harriet raised her brows in a nod to Olive's tactics.

"It was suggested to me that if the two bastions of Britain should join forces, the results would be tremendous." She paused for the barest second before going on. "I'm referring, of course, to the WI and the RAF." Titters rolled through the hall. "We are in an ideal position—if we are up to the task—to combine two schemes into one. Merryweather House is full of injured RAF pilots and crew. They need a purpose. Meanwhile, every one of us knows the role the RAF played in the Battle of Britain and is still playing against the Luftwaffe. They've captured our hearts and imaginations." She raised her brows, hoping to draw them along with her. "What if we held a fête? Attendees could mingle and chat with the RAF guests of honour. I suspect a great many people would be willing to donate money to the Spitfire Fund at such an event."

For several seconds, the occupants of the hall seemed stunned into silence. Faces stared back at her with wide, questioning eyes, slack expressions, and wrinkled brows. Then, all at once, there was an eruption of sound, questions being fired from every quarter, at an ever-increasing volume.

Lady Camilla clapped her hands lightly. "Clearly, we all have our opinions, but if George were to be injured in the line of duty"—her voice quavered with emotion—"I would hope he'd not be forgotten. I'd want him to be reminded that his sacrifice had not been in vain and encouraged to see that his injuries need not define him."

Miss Swan's hand went nervously up. When George's mother nodded at her to proceed, the women stuttered into silence. Flushing to the roots of her hair, she swallowed and asked, "Have all of them been burned?"

"Not all, I believe," Lady Camilla answered. "Some have other injuries, but all of them are quite debilitating."

"Yes, quite," Miss Swan said with a nod. "I just think we'd have to be extraordinarily careful to ensure that the event is carried off with a sense of appreciation and renewal." Her voice dropped uncomfortably as she forced herself to utter the final words. "We certainly wouldn't want it to be seen as exploitative."

The cacophony of reaction this suggestion produced was surely enough to have the poor woman regretting she'd mustered the gumption to speak up. Her hands curled into each other in her lap, and her shoulders hunched forward as voices clamoured round her.

"Surely, no one would think such a thing."

"Well, of course, it would all be arranged with the utmost discretion and taste."

"What *sort* of other injuries?"

"How would those poor men manage the festivities?"

"Marcellus can guide us," Miss Danes informed them portentously. Olive could sense the suppressed groan of the assembled group. Thus far, nothing—including a string of wildly inaccurate predictions—had managed to assail Miss Danes's confidence in the newspaper astrologist's abilities. The women of the WI considered him a particularly irritating thorn in their collective side.

"I think it's a marvellous idea," Harriet chimed in with authority, "but it's certainly a delicate matter and needs to be handled as such. I would suggest we discuss it with Leo to see how he thinks the men would respond to such a request. If they're willing to give it a go, then we shouldn't quibble." She turned back to her stepdaughter. "Well done, Olive. You've given us an opportunity to really do some good with this effort."

"Would the fête be held at Merryweather House?" The question came from Miss Featherington, who was wide eyed at the possibility.

Violet Darling spoke up. "Perhaps we could convince Lady Revell and Squadron Leader Dunn to hold it at Peregrine Hall?" Her cheeks had pinked with the suggestion, a hint that her interest in the injured pilot was personal.

Even as a cold feeling of isolation swept over Olive, she warmed to the idea of the pair. "That's perfect," she agreed.

"Oh, yes," Mrs Crabbleton enthused, "a perfect way for them to get involved and introduced round in the village."

"What if I ask Margaret to speak to Leo?" Olive suggested. She cynically wondered if her friend had arranged her shifts with the ROC to coincide with the regularly scheduled meetings of the WI.

"Perfect. It's all settled, then," Lady Camilla said with equanimity.

The women all clapped with the sense of a job well done, and Miss Danes stood to lead them in "Rule, Britannia!" Clearly, it was time for cake.

Olive met Violet's eyes, the truth of the situation clear between them. The little matter of a fête, held by the WI for the RAF, the latter being represented by a damaged and despondent few, was far from being settled.

Chapter 15

Despite her sense of gratification that she was, little by little, getting to the bottom of the curious mysteries of Station XVII, Olive was struck by the reality that her amateur sleuthing was creating more and more questions. Nothing seemed straightforward, and her thoughts frothed with suspicion. When the postman delivered the latest letter from George, she imagined it would be a perfect respite. Instead, it muddled her thoughts even further.

> *Olive,*
>
> *I confess I'm not at all surprised that you've stumbled over another body. I'll count my reprieve from this latest hobby of yours a solid benefit of having joined up for this bloody war. And, believe it or not, it's not the only one. I've logged enough hours and sat through enough classes to have earned my sergeant's stripes and RAF wings, and I've already flown a few sorties out over the Channel. I know I should be terrified up there—those German pilots are fearless and their gunners quite ruthless—but the nerves don't come till after. In the moment, it's not a matter of life and death. It's a game of strategy—and chicken. And honestly, I like my*

chances up there better than when I'm facing you across a chess-board.

Bridget—I wrote to you about her, the ATA pilot—has been a real brick. When I've come back to Earth, and when the full measure of what we're really doing up there, and what's at stake, really hits me, she's content to hold my hand. It's impossible for her to truly understand, but it almost seems as if she does. She lets me win at darts and snooker, and she even convinced me to enter a couple of dance-offs. By the end of them, we were pressed together, holding each other up, and honestly, that was my favourite part.

I can only assume you have the men stationed at the manor under your thumb, but I rather hope there's at least one who can claim the sort of steely fortitude that won't let itself be railroaded by your lovable brashness of manner. (Although if there is, he's probably cheerfully murdered you by now.)

Take care, my girl. I miss you more than I can say.

Your devoted Watson

P.S. Have you met the new occupants of Peregrine Hall? Tell all. I wonder if Miss Husselbee is already haunting them with the ominous taps of her umbrella.

There were tears in her eyes by the end and an uncomfortable lump in her throat. But neither stopped Olive from reading the letter through again. George was so dear to her, but now he felt so unutterably out of reach. Not only was he facing up against the guns of the Luftwaffe, but he was also, slowly but surely, replacing her with the incomparable Bridget.

Her best friend was easing his way into romance, while for her, it would remain an impossibility indefinitely. To think of Captain Aldridge under her thumb was laughable. A cheerful murder, on the other hand, was likely something he considered daily. She sniffed, smiling to herself, and reread the postscript.

If Lady Revell agreed to host the fête at Peregrine Hall, might they lure a greater crowd by suggesting the house was haunted by the infamous Miss Husselbee? She'd drop the idea in Harriet's ear and let her decide. The ladies of the Pipley WI were quite Machiavellian when it came to fundraising and good works.

Olive glanced over the letter again, struck by the thought that she was engaged in her own game of strategy and chicken. As much as she hated to think of it, she and another FANY—a close friend of hers, no less—were working at cross purposes, one clinging to a secret, the other determined to reveal it. The outcome was likely to be explosive.

She'd need to confront each of them individually, probing gently, steering the conversation, parsing their innocence or guilt. There was no room for sentiment, only cold-blooded logic.

She'd start with Kate.

Olive found her first suspect sitting on a crate in one of the outbuildings, making notes on a clipboard, her dark head bent over her work. Behind her, the metal shelves were stocked with a myriad of explosive devices designed to sabotage anything from railroad lines to aircraft factories to power stations. The remaining space was crowded with various and sundry items. Pigeon canisters were stacked alongside neatly folded silk parachutes, and first-aid supplies shared space with colourful spools of insulated wire. There was even a corner crowded with the sort of dummies Danny Tierney used during combat fighting instruction, as if they were patiently awaiting their turn against his knife. Every one of the FANYs had spent time logging the various inventory after the recent burglary, and it seemed Kate had been assigned to check the counts.

"Need any help?" Olive inquired, inspecting a nearby crate for potential splinters before settling down beside her friend.

Kate's eyes were as rich and dark as a cup of pre-war cocoa and at the moment looked rather cagey. "Everything is still shipshape in here. I suppose we have our burglar to thank for that."

She looked down at her clipboard. "Their best guess is that several small explosive devices were taken"—she cleared her throat— "along with an entire box of condoms."

Shortly after Olive had started at Station XVII, Jamie had informed her that condoms had been appropriated as an effective waterproofing mechanism for one of the explosive devices. It was impossible to guess whether Kate was aware of this official use for the prophylactic, and Olive wasn't about to go into it. She rather suspected the thief wanted them for their originally intended use.

"I was under the thumb of Miss Butterwick at the time of the break-in," Olive said. "I'd only just learned of it when Lieutenant Beckett was killed." Olive paused slightly before voicing the final word. The girl had surely believed, like everyone else at Station XVII, that his death had been a terrible accident. But Kate's bland expression and raised brows surprised her. Olive went on. "It's an uncomfortable feeling knowing that two crimes have been committed in such close proximity to the manor, and that both remain unsolved."

There was a moment's pause, and then Kate seemed to come to a decision. With it, all her gentle curves seemed, almost imperceptibly, to disappear. The lines of her spine and shoulders straightened; her chin tipped up and suddenly looked rather pointed; and, most noticeable of all, her eyes sharpened and her nostrils flared. Olive felt a flicker of uncertainty.

"I suppose you thought to shock me?" Kate chirped. She seemed amused at the possibility. "If you meant your investigation into Lieutenant Beckett's murder to be a secret, you shouldn't have left your list of clues out on your desk." She tsked. "You'd never make it as a secret agent with that sort of careless behaviour." She smiled gently, taking the sting from her words, but Olive cringed nonetheless, having not yet forgiven herself the lapse.

"What makes you think I'd want to be an agent?" she said irritably.

"Why wouldn't you?" Olive opened her mouth, but Kate clearly wasn't interested in an answer. "Oh, I know it's beastly hard work and desperately dangerous, but imagine the treachery one could wreak while remaining essentially above suspicion. Men are quick to underestimate. They want to believe we're all helpless innocents. And for that, they deserve every comeuppance."

Olive blinked at the sweet-faced young woman with the perpetually rosy cheeks, who was clearly capable of living a double life. In all likelihood, she would make a stellar spy. Could she, in fact, be the one Olive was looking for? It seemed impossible, or at least it *had*, but she was no longer quite so certain. With this opening salvo, it was as if Kate had just declared, "Check," and Olive was now forced to reassess the board in front of her.

"So, who do you think murdered him?" Kate pressed, hugging the clipboard to her chest. "And why?"

The conversation was spinning wildly away from her, and Olive wanted to groan in frustration. Moreover, for a few fleeting moments, she wanted the quiet, malleable Kate back, not this grand master of worldliness, bent on confrontation.

"I don't know who murdered him," she snapped. "I'm working on it."

Kate gasped. "Wait a moment. Am I under suspicion?" She grinned broadly, and it transformed her face from youthful prettiness to striking magnetism. Olive was utterly bemused by the feeling that she was seeing her friend for the first time. "I didn't do it, you know. I wouldn't've. There wasn't a mean bone in his body. We both liked words—books and poetry and crossword puzzles and ciphers. We'd both end up in the library late some evenings, and occasionally, we'd have a chat."

Olive frowned. Was this all an act? Could she believe any of it? *For heaven's sake, speak up, before she starts off again!*

"Did you confide in him your aspirations to be an agent?"

She shook her head. "It wouldn't have done me any good. Lieutenant Beckett was very good with machines, but not so much with people. Perhaps because he had a rather scandalous secret of his own," she said coyly.

"What sort of secret?" Olive asked carefully, wondering if this was a fresh clue or the one she and Jamie had unearthed on their foray into Balls Wood.

"You'll not get it from me."

"Right," Olive said, suddenly a bit fed up with this new Kate. "Do you have any information on the burglary—namely, who might have done it?"

"If you mean Harold, you might as well ask outright."

Olive took a breath. "Did Harold admit to the crime? To either of them?"

"Of course he didn't," Kate said harshly. "He wouldn't murder anyone, and he's signed the Official Secrets Act like the rest of us. He may have been a thief once upon a time, but he's not dishonourable."

It wasn't the time to quibble with the details. She had other questions to ask.

But Kate, it seemed, had plenty more to say.

"Do you know why I like Harold?"

Olive shook her head. Harold's charms had thus far remained a mystery.

"He doesn't try to protect me. In fact, quite the opposite. He says I need to know how to take care of myself. And I want to—I do. I don't want to depend on a man to make the decisions and get things done. I'm not the shrinking violet my mother seems to think I am."

"That's been made startlingly clear," Olive said dryly. After a moment of fidgety silence, she said, "What has Harold told you about himself?"

Kate levelled her with a look of disgust. "*Et tu*, Olive?"

"I just meant—"

"You want to know whether he's told me about his life before the war." She lifted an eyebrow and stared, immovable, until

Olive resigned herself to nodding feebly. "Do you know what we do when we're alone in the car together? When it's parked in the dark quiet of the barn?"

Olive's eyes flared, her cheeks surely flushed, and she laid a hand on Kate's narrow wrist, hoping to forestall any further confidences.

"We talk," the girl said flatly. "I tell him about home, about my brothers—all of them off fighting—and about my mother and father wanting to lock me away like a canary in a cage."

Olive hadn't known she had brothers and strongly felt her own lapse as a friend. But there was no time at the moment to address it—Kate was confiding the rest.

"He talks about losing his father to the Great War, picking pockets so his family could eat, and little by little graduating to bigger and better things until he was fleecing fancy gentlemen of valuables they didn't even miss." The flash in her eyes seemed to be daring Olive to denounce him or, at the very least, to discourage their association. When she didn't, Kate continued in a scathing tone. "Don't misunderstand. I'm under no rose-tinged illusions. He's no Robin Hood and certainly not a gentleman. But he's a survivor, and he refuses to make excuses for himself or anyone else. I admire that."

Kate stood, laid her clipboard on a nearby shelf, and yanked at the hem of her tunic. Then she crossed her arms over her chest and stared down her nose at Olive.

"What I don't understand," Olive said, her skirt catching on a rough edge of the crate as she stood, "is why you felt the need to deceive us all into thinking you're a timid rule follower."

Kate laughed harshly. "The better to prove myself. When I finally request to be considered as an agent, I'll have demonstrated my aptitude for the task. I'll have collected all sorts of information not strictly for my ears, because men are easily fooled by a vacant expression and an innocent smile."

Was it more likely, Olive wondered as she stared at the young

FANY, that the officers in charge would balk at the deception, utterly nonplussed by such a strategy? She'd had every expectation of dismissing Kate as a suspect, but after their little chat, she simply couldn't do it. As far as she was concerned, the girl was a wild card.

"I hope it works out," she said truthfully. "See you at tea, then?" Without waiting for an answer, Olive slipped between the shelves and out into the paltry sunshine, to walk briskly back to the house, her mind in a jumble.

A single distracting thought cut through it all: *Do I have the calibre of an agent? Could I handle the pressure and uncertainty, to say nothing of the desperate fear and the horrors of getting caught?* Now wasn't the time to pursue that line of thinking, but she was determined not to dismiss it entirely. She smiled to think what Captain Aldridge would say of the idea.

It was the following morning before Olive managed to steal a few private moments with Marie. Olive was passing the nursing station with an armful of filing when she caught sight of Danny Tierney's copper hair. He was perched on one of the cots, a sticking plaster affixed just beneath his left ear and a soppy grin splayed over his face, as he stared at Marie, hovering just beside him.

Olive moved closer. "Don't tell me you're letting your guard down intentionally so you can come for regular visits?" she teased, tucking back a smile as the pair shifted awkwardly apart. Tierney was colouring up like a beet, his hair clashing splendidly, and Marie's eyes were downcast, a shy smile playing at her lips.

"Come find me when you've an hour off, Miss Bright. If you're up to it," Tierney said, the customary twinkle already back in his eye as he stood to leave. "I'll wager I can teach you a thing or two."

"Challenge accepted, Lieutenant Tierney."

He grinned then. "Sure, an' I expected it." With one last longing glance at Marie, he sauntered into the corridor and disappeared.

"He reminds me of my best friend, George," Olive said fondly. It was an outright lie—the pair couldn't be more different—but Marie had already made it clear that she didn't want to discuss Lieutenant Tierney, and Olive needed an in. "I got a letter from him yesterday. He just got his wings." She added the last almost as an afterthought.

"So, he's in the club," Marie said, smiling ruefully. "I suppose he's tall, dark, and handsome, and charming to boot. It really is uncanny." She was returning the bottle of alcohol and the tin of sticking plasters to the supply cart.

"He is, so I really shouldn't be surprised," Olive said as she slumped down onto a cot and propped her shoulder against the wall. She was being overly dramatic, she knew, but it wasn't entirely an act. "He's met a girl."

Marie turned to look at her. "Ah," she said, a world of understanding in that one little syllable.

"I should be happy for him, but instead I'm feeling sorry for myself. I know it's beastly of me."

"It's understandable."

"Is it really?" Olive pressed. "Because it feels utterly wrong."

Marie sat down beside her and took Olive's hand in hers. "The two of you have a history, and this new girl will, unavoidably, change its course. Things won't be the same between you. Loyalties will be tested. And inevitably, some of what you cherished will be lost."

Olive blinked, feeling considerably worse than she had a moment ago. At the same time, she had a sense that her friend's words stemmed from personal experience, and she was determined to glean a bit more.

"Surely, it's not as fraught as all that," she said wistfully.

"I hope it isn't . . . for you."

"I don't want to pry"—an utter lie—"but how did you manage?"

Marie hopped up and moved away from the cot. "I didn't mean me. It was someone I knew," she said. "But it really wasn't the same situation at all."

"What happened to her?"

"Nothing irreparable. There was a boy she loved, and in the end, it didn't work out." Her shoulders lifted in matter-of-fact acceptance.

"Was he . . . German?" Olive suspected that Marie was leading her down the garden path, and she was content to follow, but she was going to do her damnedest to find a bit of truth nestled among the shrubbery. Someone had gone to considerable risk to get that scarf back, very likely the same someone who had marked it with three tiny crosses.

"What? Why would you ask that?" she demanded irritably. "Of course he wasn't German. He was just"—she struggled to find a fitting word amidst her anger—"a namby-pamby."

"And your friend? Has she quite recovered? Found someone new to make her forget her feckless young man?"

Marie sighed. "Not yet. But it'll happen eventually."

Olive scoffed. "The word *eventually* seems almost like a death knell these days. I find myself feeling quite desperate at times." She caught herself before bemoaning her lonely state and said instead, "I think that's what happened between me and Captain Aldridge. It's nothing really—both of us are merely grasping at a feeling, at a desire for something lovely and normal in a world that's draining the life out of us. Look at poor Lieutenant Beckett," she urged, her words having conjured her true feelings and a gloss of tears.

"It was an accident," Marie said consolingly. "It was horrible, of course, but you mustn't dwell on it."

"I don't know how you do it." Olive sniffed.

Marie blinked. "Do what?"

"Keep your head above water with such cheeriness. Nothing seems to faze you."

"Oh, I wouldn't say that."

"Tell me one thing, then," Olive insisted. "One thing that frustrates you enough to want to murder someone." Seeing Marie's start of surprise, she added, "Hypothetically, of course."

Marie didn't immediately answer, so, ever helpful, Olive prompted. "Your mother? Father? Weak tea? Darned stockings? Cakes made with veg? Handsy men? Sanctimonious old ladies? Nosy friends? Namby-pambies?" She said the last word with a grin.

Marie's face was placid. "I'd never want to murder anyone. Too messy," she said, the twist of her lips more smirk than smile. "I'd rather devise an exquisite revenge. So much more satisfying, I'd imagine, to watch as your nemesis realises what you've done."

Olive blinked. First Kate and now Marie. Both with unplumbed depths that made Olive think she was the tamest of the bunch. Perhaps she needed to work on that. If she wasn't careful, these interrogations were going to prompt a reinvention of herself.

"And do you have a nemesis?" Olive said, leaning in conspiratorially. She tracked the infinitesimal movements of Marie's blue eyes, noticed for the first time the striations of pale and dark, as her friend considered whether to answer the question.

"He's a family friend," she said tightly. "An utter clod with delusions of grandeur. Nothing too dire."

"Oh, one of those," Olive commiserated, secretly thrilled to have gleaned even this tiny bit of information. "Surely, you don't have to see him very often."

"Thank heavens, no. But he has a long reach." She added the last bit rather grimly. Olive didn't bother to press her; she knew Marie had closed the subject even as she turned away. "I'd better get on with it. I need to log Lieutenant Tierney's injury, and I'm certain you have plenty to do. If you want to chat anymore, you'll have to fake an injury," she said with a wink.

Olive collected her folders and stood. "If I let Lieutenant Tierney teach me a few things, one of us is bound to end up back here for a bit of first aid. I wonder which you'd prefer," she said teasingly. "See you later."

She made a beeline for Jamie's office, but he was out somewhere. She'd thought of a way to involve him in the investigation, but it seemed it would have to wait.

After skulking round the manor house, searching for Liz, between various assigned tasks, Olive finally queried an adjutant with blotchy skin and soulful eyes. He was quick to report that she had driven Major Boom to The Firs in Whitchurch and would likely be out for the entire day.

Thanking him, Olive sighed, both frustrated and relieved to have such a reprieve. While she was anxious to question Liz, she was also dreading the ordeal. Justified or not, Jamie had come between them. The whole business was bound to be awkward.

By the end of the day, the pair had still not returned, but rather than going home, Olive went in search of Danny Tierney, more than a little curious about how she'd fare against the instructor.

"I knew the truth of it—you're keen to prove yourself," he said. He was lounging in the chair at the front of his classroom, his booted feet up on the desk. He was reading from a brown leather volume, which she shortly discovered was *Middlemarch*. "Ready, then?"

Olive looked down at her trim tunic and knee-length skirt. "Can I manage in this?"

Tierney levelled her with a look. "If someone attacks you while you're in uniform, will you simply give over because you'd rather be wearing trousers?"

"You're really going to stand there in trousers with that attitude?" she retorted. "Why don't you give me the lessons, and then you can go put on a skirt, and we'll see how well you manage."

"You've made your point," he conceded, leading her into the gymnasium, which she remembered from her Stratton Park School days.

After they'd removed their shoes, Tierney having informed her, "We'll get to footwear later," he faced her on the mats laid across the floor. With the late-afternoon sun streaming in through the high windows, his face was awash with the palest freckles. She'd never realised he had quite so many. But the thought went straight out of her head as he started the lesson.

"I'll tell you what I tell all my students," he said seriously. "When engaged in hand-to-hand combat, always assume you're fighting for your life. And if your opponent is a man, always follow up with a knee to the testicles."

"Happy to do it," Olive said smartly.

Tierney, who'd been about to go on, shot her a wary glance. "Right, then." He lifted his right hand in front of him, fingers together, thumb extended. "The edge of the hand is an efficient, effective weapon if used correctly. When you strike," he said, meeting her eyes as he tilted his hand, "do it with the outside edge of your hand and connect with your target at the midpoint between your first knuckle and wrist."

Olive raised her hand, positioned it accordingly, and tried to envision striking someone with it. "This won't break my hand, will it?"

"Not if you do it right," he assured her. "You'll need to draw your arm in at the elbow and pull your forearm back like a spring before releasing it with a short, sharp stroke."

"What do I aim for?" she said, trying out the motion he'd demonstrated.

"If your assailant has grabbed you, aim for their wrist, forearm, or bicep to break the hold. If you're free to attack at will, strike the side or back of the neck, or just below the Adam's apple. You're quite tall, so that's to your advantage."

Olive nodded smartly. "Ready, then."

"You want to try it on me?"

"Isn't that sort of the point?"

"The point is for you to learn, not for me to take an unnecessary beating. We'll use a dummy. And then, when you're ready to defend as well as attack, we'll spar as opponents."

"All right," Olive agreed. And for the next few moments, she used the side of her hand to pummel the dummy's arms, neck, and torso. "Got it," she said briskly. "I think I'm ready for the next lesson."

He taught her the chin jab and the thumb hold and how to break the single- and double-handed throat and wrist holds. "I think that's enough for one day." He eyed her thoughtfully. "Still think you're up to sparring?"

Olive shrugged. "Why not?" With a quick inhale, she positioned herself to face him, and suddenly he moved, and she reacted on instinct, feinting out of reach. He came at her again, caught her wrist in a brutal grip. She struck out at his arm, using the edge of her hand, and felt a tingle along the nerve running up her arm even as she threw up her knee. Tierney dodged it but released her. She spun away from him, breathing quickly, focused and intent. She met his eyes and tried to predict his next move, even as she planned hers.

He lunged for her, going for her throat, but in a completely inelegant flurry of hands and another lift of her knee, she had him in momentary retreat.

"I've never had a student with such a hair-trigger knee."

Suspecting that the chatty comment was intended to break her focus, she didn't answer but kept her hands ready, waiting for the perfect moment to attack.

Olive feinted as if she intended to force his chin up, and he reacted by turning away, exposing his neck. She swung the edge of her hand round, aiming for his throat, but he dodged the full force of it, pulling back. In what was apparently her signature move, her knee came up quickly, targeting the all-important testicles. He twisted his body away just in time, slipping on the mat and going down on one knee.

Staring down at him, her chest heaving with adrenaline and effort, she huffed out a satisfied breath. "Good save. You might need those later." She paused for breath. "Particularly," she added, straightening her skirt, "if you can convince Marie you're worth the effort."

Running a hand through his hair, Tierney sat back on his haunches, sighed, and said, rather appropriately, "Bollocks. I don't know what else to do. Sometimes I think I might be winning her over, and others . . ." He shrugged. "I don't suppose you have any suggestions?"

"I have a hunch that there was someone in her past that broke her trust. Probably she's just being cautious." Olive reached out to give his shoulder a squeeze, and he flinched away from her.

"Sorry, but you seem the sort who likes the element of surprise." His eyebrows shot up as a thought occurred to him. "You could be my ticket back onto a cot, the focus of Marie's full attention."

"Do you really want her treating your bruised testicles? What? It could happen," she insisted, hoping to dissuade him from the idea. "Why don't you ask her for a drink or a walk? Much less painful and embarrassing."

As far as Olive was concerned, Marie owed her a debt.

"Does Jamie know how to fight like this?" she asked curiously.

"More or less. He'd had a bit of experience before we met, so he does things a bit differently. And he's not quite so ardent as you, one way in particular."

"Understandable," Olive said musingly, freshly curious about the man. As far as she was concerned, Jamie was still an unknown quantity, a full-blown mystery. And what better practice for an amateur sleuth. She wouldn't mind sparring with him, either— the physical aspect was bound to be tremendously satisfying. Although a knee to the groin might alter their relationship. She'd have a think on it.

Chapter 16

Olive was ashamed to admit it, even to herself, but if one of the FANYs had indeed killed Lieutenant Beckett, she had a preference.

When Olive had trespassed on the Brickendonbury grounds the previous May, eager to involve herself more thoroughly in the war effort, Liz had efficiently patched up her wounds. Olive had liked her at once, and while it had been clear from the first that Liz was infatuated with Captain Aldridge, it had seemed a harmless, if misguided, crush. But Liz had started to resent Olive's connection with him, and while that was mildly uncomfortable, things had gotten vastly more awkward when Liz had discovered the pair of them returning from Lieutenant Beckett's room. Jamie's excuse had sealed them all together in an imaginary, and rather pathetic, love triangle, from which Olive quite desperately wished to escape.

Liz's tipsy confession with regard to a certain groundskeeper had left Olive cautiously optimistic. While it was unlikely that Jamie's replacement had the same dark hair and fiercely grey-blue eyes, the same square jaw and hard, muscled frame, with a little practice, he could surely frown and bark and bluster just as well. But on the chance that Liz might still be harbouring a crush on Jamie—and resenting *her* for its remaining unrequited—Olive had left the task of questioning Liz till last. But she couldn't delay any longer. So, when she caught sight of Liz going into the tiny powder room set aside for the FANYs at the end of the hall, Olive took her chance, darting away from an approaching officer. A moment later, she'd slipped into the room behind Liz and closed the door. She propped herself against it to ensure a few moments private conversation.

The room was crowded with furniture deemed too feminine, fragile, or trivial to be used elsewhere in the manor, and Liz was sitting on a tufted ottoman in the centre of the room, adjusting her stockings. "Oh, it's you." The words weren't exactly polite, but the tone, at least, was neutral.

"Yes. I was hoping we could chat a moment."

"Damn. I did snag them," she said with fierce exasperation. Her shoulders dropped dramatically. "What is it?"

"Tell me about your groundskeeper."

"Why should I?" And then, "You don't have a cigarette, do you? No, of course you don't." She stared sullenly at Olive.

"Because I want to know what the two of you are doing together."

Liz's eyes flashed in amusement, and a smile spread slowly across her face, making her pointed incisors look a touch vampiric. She scoffed. "Do you really?"

"Yes," Olive said flatly, "but you can skip any lurid details. I'm not interested in the sex."

Suddenly Liz was laughing. "I'm almost sorry for Captain Aldridge."

"Don't be." Olive's voice was clipped. "Is there more to it than that?"

"Why?" she demanded. "What do you care?"

"I want to know who killed Lieutenant Beckett," Olive said harshly, her patience at an end.

Liz's bravado crumpled in confusion. "Killed him? But it was an accident," she insisted.

So, she hadn't seen Olive's list of clues—or else she was lying. Doubtful. She seemed genuinely shocked and confused.

"It wasn't an accident," Olive said simply. "Someone murdered him."

"Well, it wasn't William," Liz insisted, her fingers tangling up in each other, her gaze, always so direct, now shifty.

Olive narrowed her eyes. "You know something."

"I don't. I'm sure I don't." She was shaking her head and now pinched her lips together nervously.

On a hunch, Olive said, "Is it to do with the burglary?"

Liz's head snapped up to look at her, her chest rising and falling with nervous breaths, her eyes showing white.

Eager to press her advantage, Olive moved farther into the room, dropped into a narrow straight-backed chair, and leaned forward confidingly. "Tell me, Liz," she urged. "Is William involved? Are you?"

"No," she said tearfully, shaking her head. "No, I would never intentionally do a thing like that. It would be like sabotage. Treason, almost. Unforgivable. And William, he wasn't . . . He didn't—" She shook her head violently.

She was almost babbling now, and Olive snatched at the one revelatory word. "Not intentionally. Of course not. You made a mistake, didn't you? Everyone does that," she said gently.

Liz's breath hitched as she tried to get hold of herself. With her lips twisted, as if to hold back further emotion—or a confession—she nodded. "I was feeling a bit lonely and a little reckless," she began, her eyes shiny with tears. A knife of guilt twisted through Olive, but she smiled encouragingly. "I hitched a ride to the pub. No one I knew was there, and a couple of local men asked if I'd have a drink with them. I don't suppose you have a handkerchief? I never seem to have one when I need it."

Wordlessly, Olive shook her head, prompting Liz to press her hands to her face to wipe away the tears. With a choking swallow and smeared lipstick, she went on.

"They were sweet and wanted to buy me drinks, and I was flattered." She shook her head at the memory before glancing at Olive. "We played twenty questions, but I only ever said yes or no. I thought I was being so clever, and when I realised I wasn't—that I could get in real trouble—it was too late. And then the next morning, the burglary was discovered."

Olive straightened and let out a long breath. By her account, Liz hadn't been a direct participant in the crime, but it was impossible to say whether that little detail would be enough to save her from punishment. She'd violated the Official Secrets Act, to criminal effect.

"And you didn't tell anyone, because you were scared. And no one found out." It wasn't a question, but Olive wanted confirmation, nonetheless.

Liz stiffened. "No one knew—I'm sure of it. Certainly not Lieutenant Beckett, if that's what you're implying." She must have seen something in Olive's face, because she added, "You don't believe me?"

"I didn't say that." Olive honestly didn't know what she believed. She'd become fast friends with the three FANYs stationed at the manor, but it was now clear that there was artifice in all three. Not one was exactly what she seemed. And despite having lured startling bits of information from each of them, Olive hadn't managed to eliminate a single one as a suspect in the murder.

"Had you ever come across Lieutenant Beckett walking in Balls Wood?"

"What? No. If I'm going for a walk, it's with a man or to find one. Lieutenant Beckett wasn't my type." She raised a brow. "And I'm quite certain I wasn't his." Her remorse was fading quickly, self-possession settling back into place. Olive hurried on, desperate to come away with something useful.

"Did you happen to get the names of those men in the pub?"

"Only their given names. Reggie and Jack. It was them, wasn't it?" she said, picking at a snag in the fabric of her skirt, her voice resigned.

"It does seem rather likely—"

"What if they admit my part in it?" she said worriedly. "If I'm kicked out of the FANY, I don't know what I'll do. My father will be mortified and will probably insist that I go to work as a Land Girl." She shuddered and looked to Olive with panicked appeal. "I can't do it. I just can't. I loathe dirt. And bugs and worms and all of it. I don't even like potatoes, because they remind me of dirt. And it would be all over me." Her head rocked back and forth, her eyes looked troubled, and her mouth was twisted in disgust.

Olive struggled to keep a straight face. "Why don't you leave it with me? I can't make any promises, but perhaps a little distance will help smooth things over," she said, hoping Liz could read between the lines. The girl really didn't need Jamie, the oblivious object of her misguided crush, roaring at her about responsibility and carelessness. She'd likely fall to pieces, giving him yet another reason to get rid of her. Olive thought she might deserve a second chance.

"I'm glad he chose you, Olive," she said quietly. "I never would have lived up to Captain Aldridge's rigid standards. But William and I . . . He's good for me. It's true what I said before. He knows all the hidey-holes, the quiet spots where no one goes. We sit and imagine there's not a war going on. He's so true and kind. I wouldn't have thought I wanted that, but I do."

While Olive forced her lips to curve in an understanding smile, her thoughts weren't nearly so encouraging. All she could think was that one of the FANYs was a murderer and quite possibly a traitor. And whoever it was had thus far managed to outsmart her. Her jaw tightening and her gaze levelling on Liz's teary pixie face, she silently sent up her battle cry. *Merde alors!*

* * *

"Anything to report?" Jamie said as she slipped into his office with barely a knock.

"This whole investigation has gone utterly pear shaped," she grumped, pacing the tidy little room. She ignored his smirk of amusement. "But," she added, lingering over the word, "my little idea may be enough to get at the truth." Eventually.

"I'd have thought you'd have a big idea by now," he said dryly.

She rolled her eyes. If he didn't read the Hercule Poirot mysteries, that was his affair. She certainly wasn't going to enlighten him that a "little idea," as referred to by the detective, could actually be a rather complex strategy. Not that hers resembled anything of the sort.

"Perhaps it can wait until we review the latest transmission from Conjugal," he suggested.

Conjugal was scheduled to transmit on Mondays and Thursdays, at six o'clock Greenwich Mean Time. There'd been plenty of time for the message to be received by SIS, decoded, and sent over via teleprinter.

"You haven't looked at it?" she said, glancing at him.

He nodded at the brown folder on the edge of his desk marked CONFIDENTIAL. "I thought it would be less traumatic to wait for you," he said dryly.

Olive beamed at him approvingly. "I'll have you trained yet," she said teasingly.

"Would you like to do the honours?" With his brow quirked in some private amusement, he sat back in his chair, prepared to wait patiently.

Poised to open the folder, she suddenly stilled to stare at him. Her shoulders dropped. "You've read it, haven't you? And this is merely your idea of a grand gesture."

"It was a gesture of trust and cooperation, which you've now undermined with your suspicious nature." His voice was clipped and exasperated. "Now, are you going to open it or not?" He prodded the corner of his calendar until he was satisfied it was perfectly aligned with the edge of the desk.

Olive quickly slipped the relevant page from the folder, rounded the desk, and laid it in front of Jamie. She leaned over his shoulder, and they read it together. Olive was first to finish. It read:

> *Transmission came in on schedule, using accurate key code. Leading and trailing security codes verified.*
>
> *Transcript:*
>
> *We are eagerly anticipating the scheduled drop of equipment, money, and agents on the next full moon. Pigeons not needed at this time. The drop zone used before is preferable—there are no German guards stationed for some distance in any direction. We will have men waiting and will flash our torches to guide the plane's approach. Hoping you will soon dispatch another operator, as I am sometimes needed to transmit messages for others, and the pressure is great. God save the Kings of Belgium and Britain!*

Olive felt a prickle of unease crawl along her arms and up her neck.

"I don't believe these messages are coming from Weasel," she said emphatically. "And if they are, then he's being told exactly what to say."

Jamie sighed. "I assume you noticed that this transmission included the correct security codes, both leading and trailing?"

"Yes," she said dismissively, but if he's been threatened with torture—" She stopped, not wanting to think of it.

Jamie said softly, "Why are you so certain that Conjugal is compromised?"

For a moment she could only stare at him and wonder how he could say these things with a straight face. But as his eyebrows shot up expectantly, she answered, "Do you remember when you introduced me to the Belgians as the girl with the pigeons? They were eager to talk to me, to hear about the birds that would go with them, and to tell me about the ones they'd raised back in Belgium. They promised me they'd take care of my birds."

It probably wasn't the most prudent decision to lay a hand across the mouth of one's commanding officer, but once done, Olive figured she might as well take advantage—the consequences would come either way. Ignoring the tickle of his hot breath against the palm of her hand, she went on. "And don't tell me that they're under pressure and distracted. I know they are! But those men are fanciers. Birds were their daily companions before the war, and the Nazis have destroyed the ones that belonged to them. Whether Alice is dead or alive, they would have mentioned her." Her lips were now set in a mutinous line, and she was in fighting form.

Jamie detached her hand.

"They requested a bird with Belgian blood," she reminded him, propping her hands on her hips. "They were rooting for her before the mission even began."

"Hmm," he conceded, and she was gratified to see that Horace had officially made an appearance.

"Don't you see? They admired the birds and understood what made them individual and special. They couldn't have just forgotten about her—they wouldn't," she insisted.

When he didn't answer, she persisted. "I'm worried about them."

"Well, if they *are* compromised and we cancel the drop, then it could very well put them in danger."

"What'll we do, then?"

"Let me think on it."

"What if we ask a question only Weasel can answer in our return message? That would be proof enough, wouldn't it? One way or another."

"It might work," Jamie said consideringly. "The question would have to be phrased with care. If the Germans have control of the wireless, we don't want to tip them off to our suspicions," he told her.

Olive nodded, determined to come up with something.

Jamie tucked the transcript back into the folder and laid his hands, fingers linked, on top of it. Olive went back to pacing.

"Now, would you like to tell me your little idea? Presumably, it has something to do with Lieutenant Beckett's murder."

"It does."

"And?"

Unfortunately, she couldn't really discuss it. Jamie wouldn't be at all impressed by her convoluted explanations.

"I'd rather keep it to myself for a little longer," she said, stalling.

He sighed. "So you have no new information?"

"Oh, I have all sorts of information." She widened her eyes to carry the point across. "You really wouldn't believe." Seeing that he was about to object, she went on. "Not to worry. I don't intend to keep anything from you. I just need a bit more time to muddle through the details."

"Why can't we muddle together?"

The words, coming from the mouth of Captain Aldridge, adjutant of the CO of Station XVII, had the effect of stopping her in midstride. Since when was he a muddler? And why did he now want to muddle with her? She frowned and distractedly brushed her finger against the front of her chin to determine whether she had a wrinkle of her own. She could call it Husselbee.

"You're not speaking," Jamie said, stating the obvious. "It's so out of character, it's got me expecting the worst."

She said shortly, "Very funny." When she'd decided to investigate Miss Husselbee's sudden, unexpected death, she'd wanted a partner in crime, but he'd not been the slightest bit interested. Now, suddenly, he wanted to muddle? Was he really meant to be the Hastings to her Poirot? Could she tolerate such a lack of imagination? Gazing at him critically, she realised there was something she'd been meaning to ask him, but it eluded her.

"I'm happy to muddle with you," she finally said, "but not yet. And not here."

"When, then? And where?"

"Balls Wood. Tomorrow evening." She nodded, sealing the deal. She'd surely have her thoughts in order by then. Or better still, they'd catch the traitor red-handed.

He seemed amused. "Still gathering clues?"

"I'll stop looking for clues when the murderer is apprehended," she retorted.

"Fair enough."

Olive gathered a stack of folders from the out-box on her desk and, clutching them to her chest, walked briskly down the corridor. When it was obvious that no one was paying her any attention, she slipped into the library and swung the door closed behind her.

Kate's passing comment that Lieutenant Beckett had spent time in the manor's library had made her wonder. And so, after setting down the folders, she walked slowly along the edges of the room, scanning the spines standing at attention on the shelves. Thankfully, they were arranged by subject. Her eyes ranged over the spines of books on mythology, archaeology, history, and ornithology. Everyone, it seemed, was keen to write a treatise.

Finally, on a low shelf near the fireplace, she found a small collection of poetry. Her pulse began a race of eager anticipation as her fingers tripped over tooled leather volumes graced with names like Bacon, Yeats, and Tennyson. And there it was. A thin, rather nondescript book of verse by Wilfred Owen, crowded among its distinguished fellows. A frisson of satisfaction coursed through her, making her fingers tingle even as she reached for it.

It fell open where she'd known it must, and a slip of paper

fluttered to the floor at her feet. As she crouched to pick it up, she felt certain this was the clue she'd been searching for—the secret that had led to the murder of Lieutenant Beckett.

The moment was short-lived and rather excruciatingly disappointing. The paper was blank. Not even an inkblot or an impression. Utterly blank.

Olive's shoulders slumped in defeat. As she slotted the bookmark back into place, coincidentally marking the poem "Strange Meeting," she noticed a few fine pencil notations. The familiar verses were underscored, and beside them, "Huzzah!" had been written in the margin. Other lines, too, were marked, including, *The hopelessness. Whatever hope is yours, / Was my life also; I went hunting wild / After the wildest beauty in the world.*

She read through the poem again, wondering at the significance of it all. And what of the underscored verses, particularly the ones she'd found tucked into the pocket of the dead man? Had they anything at all to do with his murder? She thought of the little shrine in the wood and the stranger's words. Lieutenant Beckett had been a collector of bits and bobs and a very private human being. The world, Olive imagined, must have felt extraordinarily unwelcoming. Perhaps these words were, like the Latin engraving on the signet ring, just another reminder to live nobly, regardless of prejudice. Perhaps they were simply a tribute to his own partner in crime, so to speak.

At that moment, Olive felt unutterably sad. Lieutenant Beckett had lived his life in secret, and he'd died violently and unknown.

It was going to be a great pleasure to unmask his murderer, no matter who it might be. Unfortunately, despite all that she'd discovered, she felt more uncertain than ever.

The door to the library snicked open, and Olive turned to see Kate in the doorway.

"I'd wondered where you'd got to." She smiled a cat-and-canary smile. "Still sleuthing, are you?"

Olive slipped the book of Wilfred Owen's poetry back onto the shelf and cut her eyes round at the newest FANY. "Closing in, rather," she said as she walked to the door.

Kate's eyes narrowed. "I don't believe you. I suppose it's just as well you don't intend to become an agent, after all."

Feeling very much put upon, Olive marched past her out of the room.

Chapter 17

B y the next morning, Olive had decided that her frazzled mind needed a mini break, so she telephoned Jamie and told him not to expect her before their afternoon date.

"But it's not a—"

She rang off before he could finish, and popped into the parlour to see Harriet. Her stepmother was reading a book, which she promptly set aside.

"Hello, darling," she said tiredly. Her dark hair had been silvered for some time, but a shock of white was beginning to appear near her right temple. Olive thought it suited her stepmother very well. "Have you managed a chat with Margaret yet? The ladies and I have been diligently plotting a marvellous fête, but we're anxious to hear Leo's thoughts on the matter."

"Yes, right. I'm going to speak to her today." Assuming her friend wasn't holed up, plane spotting in Balls Wood. In truth, Olive had forgotten, or more accurately, the matter had been shunted aside in favour of more important efforts. "But going forward," she said regretfully, "I'd prefer if Violet Darling could fill my role in this particular scheme."

Her stepmother glanced at her in surprise.

"Between my responsibilities at the manor, with the pigeons, and with the pigs, I've been run off my feet," she admitted. To say nothing of her efforts to track down a murderer.

"I quite understand, and I'd love for Violet to be more involved. Do you imagine she'll be amenable?"

Olive remembered the way the woman's cheeks had pinked when Max Dunn had become the topic of conversation. "I really haven't any doubt."

"Well, that's fine, then. I'll invite her to tea, and we can work things out between us." She adjusted the knitted afghan carefully over her legs.

Olive felt a twinge of guilt. She'd barely been of any use to her stepmother since the accident. Thank heaven for Jonathon. "How's the leg coming along?"

"Well enough." Harriet had the stiffest of upper lips when it came to her own comfort. "And you needn't worry," she added intuitively. "I've all the help I need." She turned to the little piecrust table at her elbow and retrieved a little brass bell, which she held up. It shivered with the barest hint of sound as Harriet's hand shook slightly. "Jonathon left it for me. He declared himself at my service for as long as needed." She looked fondly at the tarnished little bell, cradling it in her hands. "He's such a sweet boy." A frown marred her brow, and Olive imagined she was thinking of his home life, so fraught with uncertainty. Quickly coming back to herself, Harriet said, "Would Margaret come to tea? We could hash everything out over a nice cuppa."

"I've plans to go down to the vicarage later. We're meant to be writing letters to the Friendless Serving Men. Two birds with one stone," Olive said brightly.

"Well, the invitation stands, if the pair of you change your minds."

Olive slipped into the quiet cool of the dovecote, clapped a hat on her head, then crawled onto the bench. She propped herself against the wall and hugged her knees to her chest. She was meant to be assessing the birds, selecting which would be seconded to Conjugal for the upcoming drop, but her heart—to say nothing of her mind—wasn't in it.

Instead, every pigeon that came into her line of sight became a character in an imagined Agatha Christie mystery. The portly, strutting colonel, a throwback to the early days of the Raj; the svelte lady all in white; the fluttery dandy with his air of cocksure confidence; the two twittering old spinsters, gossiping to each other in the corner; and even the shy, pretty female receiving dark-eyed glances from the black sheep of the family. A true gathering of suspects—except that none of the group represented any of the actual people under suspicion.

Jamie had narrowed the field to three with the discovery of the lipstick—and the subsequent removal of the scarf—but she'd been unable to narrow it further, despite several new and very interesting discoveries. Thus far, there was nothing to suggest that any of them had a connection to Germany, and she rather suspected that was the key. Perhaps Jamie could reexamine the background information collected by the War Office on each of her fellow FANYs. It was worth a try.

Olive shook her head, trying to clear the images of a pigeon murder mystery, but the alternative was bleak. She felt certain that the agents of Conjugal were compromised, so the thought of sending additional pigeons was troubling, to say the least. But she was no longer in charge of her birds; she was expected simply to follow orders. It rankled.

But then again, her hands weren't completely tied. . . .

It took only a moment to make the decision. Rather than send her best birds, she chose three younger birds that hadn't yet finished their training regimens. It was a calculated risk—if dispatched with a message from Belgium, they might not make it home. But she'd never been one for half measures. She could only hope that Jamie could convince Major Boom that they were flying headlong into a trap and thereby spare her the sacrifice of three promising pigeons. Otherwise, they were all buggered.

The chatter of conversation broke into her morbid thoughts, and a moment later, Hen and Jonathon burst into the dovecote and hurriedly shut the door behind them.

"Is school out already?" Olive demanded. Had she been so absorbed in thoughts of martyrdom and murder that she'd lost all track of time?

"How long have you been in here?" Hen demanded. "At least two pigeons have pooed on your hat."

"It could have been one really industrious one," Jonathon mused, a twinkle in his sharp brown eyes.

"Much too long," Olive admitted, sweeping off the deeply brimmed hat to send its latest decorations onto the floor. She glanced at her watch. "I've got to pop into the village for a quick visit with Margaret and then get back to the manor to meet Captain Aldridge on top-secret business." She winked to let them know she was laying it on a bit grand. "What are you two up to?"

"We're going to take the wheelchair on a test run," Jonathon told her.

Olive's eyebrows rose in mild concern. "Well, steer clear of hills. And ponds. And Tommy Prince," she said pointedly.

Hen had crouched beside Wendy and was reaching for the bird, her hands hovering uncertainly just above it.

"She won't bite, you know," Olive teased. "None of the birds mind being handled, as long as you're gentle. Just scoop her up, watching that you keep her feathers tucked down and her feet free." A quick learner, Hen scooped up her quarry in one graceful movement and beamed at the bird.

"Well done," said Jonathon before peeking into the nesting boxes to check on the hens.

"I suppose the pair of you know that the WI is scheming to raise money for the Spitfire Fund?"

"I heard you're hoping Lady Revell will host a fête at Peregrine Hall," Hen promptly replied.

"We're lucky you're on our side, Hen. If the Germans ever got hold of you, we'd be done for." The girl preened. "Well, I think I've come up with a way to make things a bit more interesting." Olive paused to consider before adding, "Which has yet to be approved." Jonathon nodded as Hen stroked a gentle finger over Wendy's grey head. Olive went on. "If we were to put it about that Miss Husselbee still roams the house, thumping her umbrella and generally expressing her disapproval, would the pair of you be willing to spearhead the haunting?" It was a risky request; the pair did nothing by halves.

"Absolutely," Hen said with great enthusiasm.

Jonathon was tentative in his response. "You don't suppose anyone would consider it disrespectful, do you? She *was* murdered, after all."

"I thought this would be a nice way for the village to remember her, and I think she'd be rather tickled with the idea that one more chance glimpse of her had people pulling out their purses for the RAF."

"Right, then. We're in. Two ghosts, at your service," he said stoutly.

Margaret was ushering a petite woman out the door of the vicarage as Olive came up the walk.

"I will convey your concerns, Mrs Bailey. You can be sure of that," she said, carefully patting the moth-eaten cardigan covering the woman's shoulder.

Mrs Bailey's eyes lit with interest as she caught sight of Olive. "Morning, dear," she said sweetly, her papery skin looking almost translucent in the afternoon light. She kept a pair of ceramic ducks in her garden and dressed them with sewing scraps. On occasion, all three of them could be found wearing matching dresses and hats.

"Hello, Mrs Bailey. How are you?" Olive said politely.

"Very well, dear. Although I've been telling Mrs Truscott"—
she gave a glance back at Margaret, who was the picture of virtu-
ous concern—"someone's been in my garden, and I suspect it
was one of the Jerries."

Olive flicked her gaze to her friend, who was now rolling her
eyes heavenward. "What makes you think that?" she asked, ignoring the wild waving of her friend's hands.

Mrs Bailey extended her neck, and Olive obligingly leaned
closer. "Because my English roses are blighted, dear." Her eyes
widened, willing her audience to grasp this incontrovertible
piece of evidence.

"The bloody bastards," Olive exclaimed, secretly amused by
the shock on Mrs Bailey's face. "I'm sorry. It's just that I'm so fed
up with this war and those diabolical Germans. Leave it to me,
Mrs Bailey. I know just what to do." And with a reassuring wink,
she swept by her into the vicarage.

She was draping her own cardigan on the hall tree as Margaret
shut the door.

"You shouldn't have done that," she said tetchily. "Who do
you think she's going to come to when nothing comes of your
empty promise?"

"What makes you think it's an empty promise?" Olive demanded with feigned affrontery.

Margaret crossed her arms and winged up one beautifully
groomed eyebrow.

The corner of Olive's lips hitched. "I intend to send Jonathon
over to take care of it. If anyone can revive her English roses, it's
him. You're welcome," she said haughtily.

Margaret's lips twitched as she shook her head. "Well, we'll see."

"I was hoping you could do me a favour in return," Olive said
expectantly.

"Oh, naturally. What is it? Or are you, too, going to require tea
and a plate of carrot biscuits before you'll come out with it?"

Olive made a face and pulled her friend down beside her on the well-worn sofa, then briefly outlined the WI's latest scheme. "What do you think?" she asked. "Do you suppose Leo will support it?"

Margaret's brow had wrinkled as she considered the idea. "Certainly, if he thinks it will be good for the men, but you don't need his approval. You'd have to speak to the doctor in charge."

"I was sort of hoping he might do that," Olive admitted.

"Oh, I see," her friend said wryly. "It's to be a favour from me *and* a favour from Leo. Not to mention a good word from the doctor—"

"So, you'll talk to Leo and do whatever's necessary to convince him?"

"I'll certainly make a concerted effort," she promised. They grinned at each other.

Olive glanced at her watch. "Good. I've got time for a cup of tea and a letter, and then I've got to get back to the manor." She ran a hand along her calf, checking her stockings for runs. "I'm going for a walk with Jamie," she said, her eyes suggestive of a much more pleasant outing than was intended, "in Balls Wood."

Margaret gave her a look of reproach. "Most people find that dead bodies dim their romantic ardour." Olive's guilty expression had her exclaiming, "Don't tell me you're involving Jamie in your amateur sleuthing. What will he say when he's finally got you all to himself and you're more interested in hunting for clues?"

The precise words that came to Olive's mind were not the ones Margaret would want to hear, so she said instead, "He really doesn't mind."

Her friend simply rolled her eyes and led the way to the kitchen to put the kettle on.

She suddenly whirled to face Olive. "I'd forgotten to tell you—I've got my ROC first class certificate!"

"That's wonderful, Margaret!"

"All that studying and sitting in the dark cinema to watch footage of different aircraft has paid off, and now I'm rather good at spotting. I can tell the fighters from the bombers, and the British planes from the German."

They got out paper and pens and laid out the tea things, Margaret jabbering all the while. "There really is quite a variety, all of them heading different places with their own particular jobs to do," she said, pouring out the tea. "We were taken up to Hunsdon to have a look at the aircraft and even to climb inside a couple, so that was a bit thrilling. They've got Douglas A-20 Havocs and Hawker Hurricanes, which are mostly used to intercept bombing raids and on patrols over the Channel." She stopped suddenly and stared at Olive. "Here I am blathering on and on. You should have shut me right up."

"It's better than listening to you moan about the clothing ration," Olive quipped just before scalding her tongue on the first sip of tea.

"Fair enough," Margaret said. "Shall we turn our attentions to the Friendless Serving Men?" she said.

"Yes, let's."

For a few moments, Olive couldn't think what to write. Everything interesting was hush-hush and thus off-limits. As a result, some poor man was going to open a letter from home that chronicled the somewhat sordid lives of three village pigs. She signed the letter, *Your friends, Olive, Eske, Swilly, and Finn.*

The prospect of good news had Olive eager to get back to Brickendonbury, but one look at Jamie's face dashed her hopes.

"Bad news." He didn't seem at all enthused with the prospect of revealing it.

Olive groaned. "Just tell me."

"Major Boom doesn't believe we have reason enough to call off the second drop."

Olive's eyes flared in disbelief. "You told him about the agents—about their history and interest in the pigeons? About Alice, who remains unaccounted for? About the missing security codes in the first transmission?"

"I told him," Jamie said quietly.

"What more does he want?"

"What he wants and what he's likely to get are two very different things. He's going ahead because the reasons to abort are not compelling enough. The missing codes could have been an oversight. Alice could have been lost or forgotten. The best intentions might have been shot to hell by German patrols, radio direction–finding vans, or exhaustion and fear."

"But—"

Ruthlessly, he cut her off. "Don't argue. You made your case, and your commanding officer assessed the information and decided to proceed with the original plan unchanged. Keep in mind that he has considerably more experience than you do in such matters, not to mention the jurisdiction to make the decisions. It's done," he told her flatly.

Olive hung her head, resigned. He was right, even if Major Boom was wrong. Her birds would be sacrificed to the cause.

"Understood," she said tightly.

"Why don't we go for that walk?" he suggested.

They set off across the broad, sweeping lawn of Brickendon-bury Manor, in the direction of Balls Wood. It was a lovely afternoon, the glorious scent of summer having given way to the rich, warm colour of autumn. The leaves were shades of ochre, russet, and copper, and the hedgerows were busy with birds collecting for winter. Olive sighed with pleasure, wishing she could enjoy the moment with no distractions. But it wasn't to be.

Her mind worked busily, worrying over a mission fraught with uncertainty, a murderer not yet brought to justice and, quite possibly, a traitor working among them. They'd barely crossed into the wood when the whirl of thoughts finally coalesced into a firm idea, a strategy. She just needed a bit more time to finesse it before she'd be ready to share it.

Newly optimistic, she tucked her hand into the crook of his arm and gave it a squeeze, saying, "Let me catch you up on our suspects."

He glanced at her suspiciously. "You rallied quickly."

She merely shrugged, then threw herself into the narrative, trying to imagine him as a more insightful Hastings. Like Poirot, she kept back a few bits of information that could very well be irrelevant but, nonetheless, formed the basis of her hunch. "And now that I've done the dirty work," she went on, "it's your turn." She only narrowly resisted tacking on a *mon ami*. "You have access to their records." She knew this from personal experience.

"What exactly is it that you think I can find out?" He'd been livid that Liz's loose lips had led to the break-in, and downright shocked by Kate's deceitful strategising in a bid to become an agent. Marie's close-lipped secrecy didn't faze him in the slightest—probably because he was similarly inclined. But Olive was suspicious of all three FANYs.

She scuffed her feet over the fallen leaves. "I want to know if one of them has ties to Germany." They should have pursued that line of inquiry days ago, but it simply hadn't occurred to Olive to ask him. "It won't be obvious, or it would have likely been flagged already, but surely there's some hint or clue from the past—something that would lead one of them to this. I know only what they've told me, and obviously, none of them have any qualms about lying. But I feel certain that the scarf is the key."

"I'll see what I can dig up," he said, not sounding at all optimistic. "But it's likely there's nothing there to find. People change loyalties, fall in and out of love, and are otherwise unpredictable. And some are very good at keeping secrets."

As they strolled along the tree line, Olive watched the swooping flights of warblers and tits as they nipped in and out of shadow. "Did you ask the instructors if they've held any demonstrations or training exercises in these woods?"

"There've been none," he said flatly. "The special training schools tend to be rather compartmentalised. While we deal in sabotage, Arisaig House in Scotland devises more comprehensive practice missions as part of its commando-style training."

"Right. Then we can assume that the aerial was being used for some nefarious purpose—most likely treason. Which brings us round to Germany again."

"It seems likely, but we never found the transmitter. The aerial is innocent enough without it."

"Why didn't we ever find the transmitter?" Olive grouched, talking mostly to herself. She hadn't bothered to tell Jamie that she'd asked Hen to don her Guides uniform and scrounge through the wood in search of that missing clue. The girl hadn't managed to find it, or anything else that seemed to incriminate any of the FANYs. Olive thought of Liz's groundskeeper and his penchant for hidey-holes, of Marie's determined reticence, and Kate's seemingly unfettered access to the manor's cars. "What if it's being used right under our noses?" The very idea made Olive twitch with impotent fury.

She pulled a crumpled page from her pocket: her list of clues, some of them now struck through.

1. *Wireless aerial*
2. ~~*Coded lines of verse*~~
3. *Silk scarf*
4. ~~*Signet ring*~~

> 5. *Warning letters*
> 6. *Lipstick*
> 7. *Burglary*
> 8. ~~*Stranger*~~
> 9. ~~*Argument*~~

Jamie, reading over it with her, pointed at number seven, his voice hard. "I thought we'd put that down to Liz's poor judgement and a couple of delinquents who will shortly be apprehended."

"I wanted confirmation that it had nothing to do with the murder," she said wistfully, "although I suppose the verses can't be strictly eliminated, either."

"Whoever it is we're looking for has gone to great lengths to keep her identity secret," Jamie said. "We're being outmanoeuvered." He frowned.

The pair was quiet for the next few moments, caught up in private thoughts.

Olive decided to reveal her fledgling strategy. "What if we set a trap?"

Jamie sighed. "We included your pigeon question in the last transmission. It went unanswered. I doubt a second one will prove more useful."

"I was thinking of something a little more immediate." She smiled grimly. "An ambush in Balls Wood."

He looked down at her, his left brow raised in judgement. "We're not gamekeepers, Olive. And these people—Lieutenant Beckett's killer and whoever you believe might be sending wireless messages under the guise of Conjugal—aren't pesky voles. In all likelihood, they're spies who've not yet been caught, which means they're smart and careful and not likely to be taken in by a slapdash effort to draw them out."

"Naturally," Olive said sweetly, nudging him round for the

walk back to the manor, "we'll just have to be smarter and more careful." He looked down at her, and Horace settled in disapprovingly. Olive had a strong desire to run her finger over the front of his chin, smoothing things over. She chose instead to say, "That is, if you're up to it."

"That remains to be seen," he said dryly.

Chapter 18

28 September

Miles from Pipley, Olive stared out over mud-brown fields, tracking the path of her first-season pigeons as they made their eager way home. She wasn't in the mood to follow them. Unmoved by reason and cajolery, Jamie had balked at setting an outright trap for the fugitive FANY. It was Olive's frustration that had driven her to do what she did. That was no excuse, but it was done, and now she would need to confess.

He wasn't going to take it well, and she wasn't quite ready to deal with the fallout yet. Which was probably why she shortly found herself turning her motorbike—she'd decided she wasn't ever giving it back—into the drive of Peregrine Hall.

Margaret had spoken to Leo, and Leo, in turn, had broached the subject of the fête with the commandant of Merryweather House. The idea was deemed quite acceptable, and Violet Darling had been given the task of approaching Lady Revell and Max Dunn to solicit the use of Peregrine Hall. For the time being, at least, Olive had no further responsibilities in the matter, but she found herself wanting to speak to Max.

He was, as expected, on the terrace, sitting much the same as always, staring out over the grounds, his gaze set on nothing she could see.

"Hello, Max," she said briskly, determined to look him full in the face, with no shifty-eyed shirking.

He glanced at her with mild interest. "Don't tell me that was your motorbike I heard?"

Before she could answer, Olive's gaze settled on the little table pulled up beside his chair. There was a glass of something sitting there—some sort of spirit, judging by the colour—and a pair of books. One was an Agatha Christie mystery.

"I see you've decided to try a mystery, then," she said, dropping into the chair beside him.

He flicked a glance at it and picked up his glass. "I didn't have anything to do with it. The Girl Guide has been by a few times, proffering all manner of good deeds."

"Hen," Olive said automatically.

He canted his head slightly before going on. "And since there's nothing to read in this house but improving texts and tomes on local history, I sent her to the library for a book of poetry. She brought it and that mystery novel, as well." He took a careful sip of his drink, his mouth gaping somewhat round the rim of the glass, before setting it back on the table. "I've read a few pages, but the detective is the sort who gets under my skin."

Fully aware, from the title of the book, that he was referring to Hercule Poirot, Olive smiled. "I rather like the old fellow," she said. "He's clever and methodical and confident."

"Confident is fine until it veers into cocky."

"As an RAF pilot, I'd have thought that'd be your stock in trade," Olive said glibly. "Perhaps a sweet village spinster sleuth would be more in your line."

"You mock, but I have a rather good rapport with little old ladies."

"You don't say."

He shrugged and pulled a packet of cigarettes and a lighter from his pocket. "Do you mind?"

She shook her head and watched him as he carefully shook one out, fumbled a bit setting it aflame, and finally took a long drag.

"Has Violet Darling visited on behalf of the WI?" she asked carefully.

"She has," he said, the corners of his mouth forming the barest smile as he stared at the burning tip of his cigarette, "but she didn't leave with the answer she'd hoped for." He looked up at her, glared. "None of us chaps want to be put on display, Miss Bright. If we shy away from the mirror, imagine how well we'll do with a bunch of curious onlookers, feeling as if they've paid for a glimpse of oddities at the circus."

"You can't remain locked away, imagining you're a beast in a castle, forever. Otherwise, the village will be agog for even the barest glimpse of you. If, however, you and the other airmen agree to be guests of honour at the fête"—she shrugged—"you'll squelch the mystery and gossip and ease yourselves back into everyday life in a single afternoon. You will, of course, lose the aura of mystique you've cultivated. I'm afraid you'll be as boring as the rest of us."

"Oh, I expect I'll be able to capitalise on the heroic story of my disfigurement for quite some time," he drawled before putting the cigarette to his lips.

"I daresay," she agreed. "Which is exactly the reason the WI has approached you." She leaned closer, her eyes quickly skimming over the damaged flesh of his cheek and temple before locking onto his fierce dark eyes. "Those little old ladies you mentioned would adore the opportunity to spend an afternoon with the charming, resilient heroes of the RAF." She lowered her voice. "They won't be the slightest bit put off by your injuries— you'll have them all in the palm of your hand. And when you do tell your story, be sure not to leave out the part about the pigeon. To be saved by Lord Byron!" Olive fluttered her lashes and sighed dramatically.

He snorted but didn't comment.

They sat in silence for some minutes as he smoked. Olive imagined he was considering the idea, and she wasn't keen to interrupt him. Instead, she relished the cerulean blue of the empty skies. No clouds and, for the moment, no planes.

"You've made quite an argument," he said wryly. "I can't speak for the others, but I'll consider it. Perhaps you could send Miss Darling back for my answer in a couple of days?"

She lifted her eyebrows and said around a conspiratorial grin, "I can probably manage that."

"Then we might have a deal, Miss Bright," he said, stabbing the tail of the cigarette into the ashtray at his elbow.

"Olive," she corrected. "In that case, perhaps you can help me with something else?"

He was instantly suspicious.

"Nothing to do with you—or the hall," she said quickly.

"Go on." He'd leaned forward in his chair, his tumbled hair shielding his eyes and a portion of the burns on his face, waiting for her to go on.

"Were you issued a scarf before you began flying sorties across the Channel?"

For a moment, he didn't move, but then he turned to look at her and sat back interestedly. "I assume you don't mean the white ones intended to keep the leather from chafing. And let me guess, you can't answer any questions or give me any details." Seeing the truth of it on her face, he eyed her evenly. In that moment she got a glimpse of the officer he'd been before the tragedy. With a sigh, he answered her. "Any crew flying missions over enemy territory is issued silk scarves, each of them screen printed with a map of relevant countries and their frontiers. It's a precaution, in case the worst should happen. Knowledge of geographical landmarks and border crossings is critical to finding a way back to Britain."

So, any pilot crossing the Channel might have a scarf. But only a select few would have one emblazoned with a map of Germany.

Olive bit her lip, wondering if she dared broach the topic. The look in his eyes seemed to be challenging her to do so. Eventually, she gave in. "Are there many maps of Germany being issued?"

"Did you, by any chance, find one of these scarves?" When Olive didn't answer, his eyes raked her up and down, as if noticing for the first time that she was in uniform. His carefully cultivated ennui gave way to wary curiosity, and he said, "You're a FANY. Right, I remember now. Working for whom? Surely you can tell me that."

"I'm at Brickendonbury Manor, working as a secretary."

"You're not a very good liar," he said matter-of-factly.

"I bloody well am," she countered, rather stupidly, all things considered.

Thankfully, he ignored that. "I came across a history of the place amid the books here. An old school requisitioned for the war effort. Now you have me curious."

"I really can't say anything—"

"I understand," he said in some distraction. "And I think the information you're wanting is rather common knowledge to the men keeping track over in Germany, so it can't hurt to fill you in. To be honest, any cocksure flyboy you'd meet at an airfield dance would be liable to tell you. You wouldn't even need to ask."

Squadron Leader Dunn rubbed a finger over his eyebrow, pulling at the already stretched skin at the edge of his face. Olive watched him and waited, trying to hold still. A new lead always got her blood fizzing. She desperately hoped this might be one.

"As you've probably guessed, only the crews of bombers flying over Germany would be issued that particular scarf. That narrows things considerably, because only a select group of planes has the range to go that far, and carries enough fuel to make the return flight. The Bristol Blenheim and the Vickers Wellington are two in particular."

Olive's thoughts flashed to Margaret, chatting about her visit to the airfield. "I don't suppose you know if any are flying out of RAF Hunsdon?" Station XVII used RAF Stradishall, but none of its agents were being dropped into Germany. Hunsdon was the closest airfield to the manor and could possibly provide a clue as to where the scarf had come from.

"As you can imagine, I've not been kept apprised of the goings-on in RAF Bomber Command, so naturally, the situation could have changed. But I don't believe so. They're flying Havocs and Hurricanes out of Hunsdon, mostly as night fighters. I wouldn't imagine any of their crews would have need for a scarf of the sort you referring to."

Olive remembered suddenly what he'd told her of his final flight, of bombing the docks in Hamburg. "But you were issued one, weren't you?"

He nodded slowly, reaching once again for his packet of cigarettes. "I wondered if you'd remember that."

"Do you still have it?" She didn't suspect him, but it was curious—and perhaps more than a mere coincidence.

"I suppose you're going to want to see it—to have actual proof that I'm not a suspect in this little mystery."

Olive lifted her chin, determined not to let his teasing affect her. "If you wouldn't mind."

He smiled then, but it transformed only half of his face. Both eyes, however, lightened in amusement. He shifted in his wheelchair, tossing the packet of cigarettes onto the table. Olive stood, wondering if he needed help getting back to the house. She'd taken a tentative step toward him when he held up his left hand, palm out, then closed it in a sweep of fingers and, with a flourish, used finger and thumb of the opposite hand to delve into his curled fist. A second later, a swath of silk was emerging from that carefully gripped hand as she stared, her mouth agape. Pearl-white silk criss-crossed in black and red and green ink. It looked identical to the one she'd found clutched in Lieutenant Beckett's cold hand.

Their eyes locked. "How did you . . . ?" she started.

"An eccentric old uncle taught me a few magic tricks when I was a boy, and when I realised they were a surefire way to impress girls, I became quite skilled."

"You're full of surprises," Olive said truthfully. "May I see it?"

He handed it over, and she spread it over her lap. Her eyes scanned the map, in search of Berlin and three little inked crosses. Just to be sure. As expected, they weren't there.

"Have I been granted a reprieve, then? You're satisfied this isn't the scarf that's caused the trouble you're in?"

"I'm not in trouble."

"If you say so."

He was sitting in his pajamas and dressing gown, as composed as if he were wearing his full dress uniform and was facing her down across his desk. "Do you always have this with you?" she asked, peering down at the scarf. When he didn't answer, she added, "I'm only curious."

A nod was the only answer he gave, and she thought perhaps she understood. Wasn't she carrying round the letters from George and Lewis, trying to keep them close? Looking at him, with his proud jaw and lost eyes, she decided to confide in him, and before she could second-guess the matter, she blurted, "The scarf I found had three little black crosses marked on it, ringed round Berlin."

His eyes flicked toward her, startled and cautiously curious. "Should you be telling me that?"

"Probably not," she admitted. "But can you honestly say you've puzzled anything out from what I've told you?"

He ran a hand over the sleeve of his deep blue velvet dressing gown, worrying the nap of it, as he considered the situation. Finally, he took a deep breath and said, "All right, I'm game. Your very own mystery, is it? With you playing detective?"

"Something like that," she said stiffly.

With a sigh, he said, "The crosses would be in remembrance of three souls—either dead or left behind." He spoke without a trace of uncertainty.

"That's what I thought, as well. But as clues go, it's not been enough. Whomever the scarf belongs to is hiding their connection to Germany very well. But you've given me one more clue— it wouldn't have been easy to come across this particular style of scarf round here."

"Stradishall was probably the closest. The No. 214 Squadron was flying Wellingtons, but they'd intended to retire them and replace them with Whitley bombers. Perhaps they've not got round to it yet."

Olive stared at him. Ever since becoming Station XVII's pigeoneer, she'd been accompanying her mission-ready birds to Stradishall, but before her, someone must have been delivering explosives and other supplies to be dropped with the agents. It had almost certainly been a FANY. Whoever it was would have likely come into contact with the pilots and crew of various Wellingtons, many of them carrying identical maps of Germany.

"Was it something I said?" Max said drolly. "Your face has just lit up like you've found a stash of Cadbury at the back of the larder."

"Better," Olive admitted. She was one step closer. "And thanks for that."

"That's lucky, as I'm not sure what else I could tell you on the matter." He was running the silk through his fingers, over the burns that marred his hands.

"You've been a great help—more than you know. I really wish I could tell you all about it." Impulsively, she leaned forward, gently pressed her hand to his, conscious of the sleek new skin alongside the roughness of the old. "I'd like to bring my CO round to speak to you, maybe convince you to do your bit on the ground this time."

His hand tensed under hers, but he didn't pull away. He looked at her, and while he didn't move, Olive imagined she could see his bearing transform from that of a listless invalid to that of an upright military officer, eager to throw himself into the fray all over again.

"I suppose that means I'd have to start getting dressed, then."

Olive grinned. "I'm not sure the RAF uniform has the same effect on men, but it certainly couldn't hurt. Now, I better go," she said, rising. Staring down at the fallen officer, the scarf fluttering in his lap, she couldn't help but marvel at the vagaries of fate. He'd gone down over the Channel, his map useless. But thanks to a pigeon, he'd managed to get safely back home again. Now his insights could very well help identify a traitor in their midst.

"Welcome to Pipley, Squadron Leader Dunn. I suspect you're going to fit in quite nicely. Let me know if you'd like a turn taking care of the pigs, and I'll send Violet round for your final word on the fête."

She offered up a wave and strode round the side of the house toward the gravel drive, her hand skimming giddily over the hydrangea bushes and then, distractedly, the prickly holly. "Damn," she muttered, sucking at the bead of blood on her finger, as she climbed back onto the Welbike.

She was buzzing up the lane on her way back to Brickendonbury, determined to share this new information with Jamie, no matter the consequences, when she rounded the corner to see another motorbike roaring toward her. Its driver raised a hand in greeting, and Olive realised it was Danny Tierney, with Marie riding pillion on the back.

Grinning broadly, she slowed the bike, and as she came abreast of them, she called out over the noise of the motors. "Where are you two off to?"

"Out for a ride and a picnic," he said. The smile was ready on his lips, but his eyes, not quite meeting hers, were mildly troubled. Olive was well aware she and Jamie were to blame, she considerably more than he. She'd taken Tierney into their confidence, soliciting his help with the investigation, and it was obvious he wasn't enthused.

Marie, her face framed by a pale-pink scarf whose tail was even now whipping in the wind, said, "We will *not* be practicing self-defence."

Tierney's face split into a grin. "Well, that's very gratifying," he said, with a cheeky glance back at her.

Marie shoved him gently. "That's not at all what I meant, Danny Tierney. I suspect I could show you a thing or two."

"I look forward to it," he said politely, his rounded cheeks belying his amusement, even as he tried to maintain a straight face.

"He's hopeless," Marie confided, her eyes lit with shy delight at the man.

Oh, they've got it bad, all right.

"Well, enjoy yourselves. I'm back to the manor for a bit more work."

Tierney flicked a glance at the basket strapped to the back of her bike. "On pigeon duty this morning?"

"Every morning," she quipped. Even when she wasn't ferrying the birds about on missions of their own, she kept the basket in place as cover for whatever else she might be doing. Deception, she'd discovered, had many layers. "You'd best be off, then," she said, glancing up at the sky, which, for the time being at least, seemed amenable to a burgeoning romance.

With a sober nod from Tierney and a wave from Marie, the engine was gunned, and off they went, bumping along the lane, her arms wrapped tightly round his waist.

As Olive stared after them, her stomach lurched with uncertainty. But the matter was out of her hands; she'd simply have to wait and see how it played out. Poised to set off again, she heard a familiar low rumbling in the distance, but it wasn't coming from the direction of the manor. It sounded very like the mysterious sound she'd heard in the days since the burglary. Armed with the new information gleaned from her conversation with Liz, she wondered if she was hearing the sounds of stolen explosives being detonated for some mysterious purpose.

Feeling rather desperate to solve one mystery, Olive set off on the bike, determined to follow the sound to its source.

It took a bit of backtracking, but eventually she tracked down the perpetrators.

She left the bike propped against the gate of a neatly tilled field that was already showing the first green leaves of spinach and cool-weather lettuces. Only moments ago, the crack of an explosion had sounded through the trees just beyond the farmland. Thankful to be wearing trousers and boots, Olive manoeuvred carefully, avoiding the mud and working her way along the edge of the field, stepping on rocks, tufts of wild grasses, and the dying stems of summer wildflowers wherever possible. In a moment she reached the trees and could hear voices.

"This is working a treat," said one man, his voice nasal and gruff. "That was a grand idea you had, chatting up that FANY."

There was a grunt in reply, then the sound of effort in the second voice. "Don't know what they're thinkin', letting girls in for jobs important to the war effort. I don't suppose half of them have a lick of sense." Olive heard the suck of breath and a sharp curse, prompting the corner of her mouth to edge up in a smirk.

"Poor thing didn't have the slightest idea what she was telling us. Suppose a Jerry had come along asking questions. She would have told 'im whatever he wanted to know, and the rest of us be damned."

"Do you suppose we should make an anonymous report to those chaps in charge over at the manor? Loose lips sink ships, you know—or, in our case, roust out the rabbits." Some loud, guffawing laughter followed as Olive crept closer, trying to peer through the trees without being seen.

"As well as this is working," said the gruff individual, "we may want to stock up as a precaution against these vermin. They had plenty of the stuff stashed in that shed and not a guard in sight. As I see it, we've as much right to it as anyone." Dressed in muddy coveralls, his hair thinning on top, he was leaning against a shovel that was standing straight up out of the ground. "Aren't we slaving over these fields, working our fingers to the bone trying to harvest enough to feed the whole bloody countryside?"

"Heroes on the home front, we are—the last line of defence against the Jerries," said his wiry companion with smug complacency. "I expect His Majesty would tell us the same if he popped down from the palace for a visit."

"I ask you, what would the wife say to that?"

Olive couldn't be bothered to listen to their jocular speculation on the matter. It was quite obvious that the pair—no doubt Reggie and Jack—had burgled the storage shed at Station XVII in order to get their hands on some low-grade explosives. Thankfully, their target was no more nefarious than an infestation of rabbits, but it was still barbaric, and she had to force herself not to burst out of the trees and confront them. Instead, she pivoted on her heel and quietly retraced her steps, having decided to leave the pair to Jamie. Perhaps he could unleash his fierce intensity on someone other than her and get it right out of his system.

As she climbed onto the Welbike and set off toward Brickendonbury, dreading the impending confession, her thoughts were buoyed by the knowledge that the puzzle of clues was slotting into place, and she was, at long last, closing in on the murderer.

Chapter 19

Jamie had been closeted with Major Boom for the remainder of the day, and so Olive was granted a reprieve until the following morning. But worry over his reaction to various admissions on her part had resulted in a sleepless night and a punishing headache. It wasn't that she felt guilty—she didn't. She hadn't disobeyed a direct order—not technically—and the only bits she'd confided to Max Dunn were anonymous, with no identifying context. It was simply that she didn't like being at odds with Jamie. And she was feeling quite desperate to unmask the culprit.

Facing him across the tidy inches of his desk, she led with the "rabbit rousters" and basked in the glow of his praise for a cool thirty seconds. He lauded her quick thinking in running the burglars to ground and her restraint in choosing to report the incident rather than confront the men on her own. So encouraged, she cautiously disclosed her visit to Peregrine Hall and her conversation with Squadron Leader Max Dunn. She put particular emphasis on the information he'd been able to provide but stopped short of any defence of her actions.

"As ever where you're concerned," Jamie said tightly, "I don't know whether to be impressed or incensed." He rubbed a hand over his forehead, working to smooth out the wrinkles. Horace was still very much in evidence. "You're walking a very thin line here, Olive. If you continue to go rogue, I can't guarantee I'll have the authority to protect you."

"Yes, sir," she said obediently. She didn't need to tell him what was at stake; he knew as well as she did. And while he didn't have all the answers, he expected her loyalty, and she owed him that. Which made what she still had to confess even worse. But as she met his stormy gaze, her lips clamped shut. What was done was done. It would either succeed or fail. But until it did, she would hold her tongue. There would be plenty of time for punishment later.

As his shoulders dropped and he looked away from her, she wondered if he'd managed to read her thoughts. But he said nothing as he distractedly straightened the three folders—one for each FANY—on his desk. Finally, he sighed. "Liz and Marie have taken it in turns, ferrying equipment to Stradishall. I've not yet sent Kate, as I couldn't decide if she could manage the trip." He rolled his eyes at the realisation of how thoroughly he'd been duped.

"I'd say it's likely one or the other of those two," Olive said. "In fairness, Kate's a bit of a wild card, but by the sound of things, she's entirely intent on becoming a spy. She has three brothers off fighting the Germans and even carries a picture of them in her pocket. It seems unlikely she'd be working for the enemy. And Lieutenant Beckett was a friend of hers. If he'd known her secret aspirations, it's unlikely he would have told. Judging by the coded verse, the warning letters, and his clandestine walks in the wood, he was a great proponent of secrets."

"Agreed," he said flatly, tossing Kate's dossier into the out-box on his desk and arranging the other two side by side.

Olive stared at them, a lump in her throat. "Have you managed to uncover any new information framing up one over the other?" The idea that one of her fellow FANYs had acted with such perfidy was quite horrible, but she couldn't help but be torn. She suddenly wanted to be far away from Brickendonbury, to forget the duplicity with a cup of tea dark enough to drown in.

"It's a wash. Liz was raised in Coventry, daughter of a factory foreman, no siblings. Hard worker, good scores on her FANY exams, a candidate for the cipher school but for a tendency toward lippy impertinence." Jamie glanced up at her. "Seems we've no shortage of that hereabouts." Olive shot him a look of asperity, and he went on. "They didn't want to have to manage it in an environment already fraught with tension. There's also a few complaints that she was rather too hung up on men." He cleared his throat awkwardly. "But no mention of anyone in particular."

"So," Olive said, tucking back a smile at his discomfiture, "it seems she has the necessary skills to use a transmitter."

Jamie inclined his head, as hesitant as she was to condemn either of the two.

"What about Marie?"

He opened her folder, scanned the page. "Parents died in a train accident in France when she was young, raised by her great-aunt, the Countess of Aviemore, in Scotland." His eyebrows rose significantly. "Signed up for FANY training near the start of the war. Excellent marks, a couple of commendations. Seemed to have the aptitude for cipher school, but her scores indicated she didn't quite have the knack for it."

"Siblings?"

He glanced down again. "None."

"Lovers?"

His chair creaked as he shifted position, refusing to meet her eyes.

"This isn't a gossip, Jamie," she said patiently. "It's a murder investigation."

Looking pained, he said, "A university student with more showmanship than sense and a soldier who died at Dunkirk." With a grim sense of finality, he closed the folder. He ran a rough hand over his face before pushing back from the desk to pace, frustrated, about the room.

Olive frowned. Something was niggling at her, but her mind couldn't catch hold of it, particularly with Jamie too fidgety to keep still.

"I don't like this." He whirled on her. "Morgan didn't find anything when he searched their Nissen hut. Not the scarf, the missing transmitter, or any hint that either of them had reason to kill Lieutenant Beckett. I could have them followed, but I'm not at all certain it's worth the man hours. We could have it all wrong. Maybe Liz really has been sitting in my office, mooning over my things, and the lipstick is a dead end," he said harshly. "Do we really believe that either of them—any of the three, for that matter—could have murdered a man in cold blood?"

"I don't want to believe that of anyone, but someone *did*, and I think we've narrowed it down to the two most likely suspects. Don't forget the scarf was stolen after I'd left the clue list on my desk in the FANY carrel."

"What if there's an innocent explanation?" He was staring out the window, where the trees were bucking in the autumn wind and the sky looked poised to open up. Her gaze followed the lines of his uniform, stretched taut across his broad shoulders, and the dark waves of his neatly trimmed hair. "What if Lieutenant Beckett wasn't murdered? What if you're too intent on playing detective, and we've overstepped?"

Olive had the impression that he was wavering in his support of a continued investigation and thought it best to come clean. She braced for an unpleasant scene. "About that . . ." she said tentatively. He turned to face her, his eyes wary and incredulous, and Olive kept her gaze locked on the scar running like a white seam along the edge of his jaw. She took an unsteady breath. "Don't get mad."

He made a sound very like a growl. "I'm afraid it's too late for that. I suggest you come clean quickly and hope I don't throttle you."

Olive's stomach dropped, and her teeth tugged worryingly at her bottom lip. Only for a moment, though. She quickly rallied, determined not to let him bully her, no matter that he might possibly have the right of things.

"Honestly, the reason I don't want to let you in on things is that, invariably, you behave like a curmudgeon. I'm not even sure *you* agree with all your fusty edicts and decrees." He took a warning step toward her, and she hurried on. "It's barely any change to the original plan. I spoke to Lieutenant Tierney, as agreed. I explained that we'd been investigating Lieutenant Beckett's death, having been unsatisfied with the official verdict of accident. I told him we suspected he might have been murdered—by a FANY."

Jamie waited silently for her to go on.

"He couldn't credit it and was, in fact, so insistent on proving Marie's innocence that he worked up the nerve to ask her for a proper day out. The perfect opportunity for him to assist with our inquiries." She cleared her throat nervously.

Jamie frowned. "But let me guess. Rather than ask him simply to keep his eyes and ears open, as instructed, you decided to take a different tact."

"I set the trap." Her pulse hammered at her throat.

"You acted counter to my express wishes." The careful measure of his words had gooseflesh cropping up on her arms.

"You weren't comfortable going ahead, and with the drop looming, there was too much at stake." Her fingernails bit into her palms. "And you never expressly forbade it," she blurted, forestalling the condemning words that were surely on his tongue.

Olive desperately wished these confessions weren't necessary. It was like being hauled up before the headmaster, made to feel as if you had done something horrible and needed to be taught a lesson. Deep down, she did feel mildly guilty about keeping secrets from Jamie, but she was also unutterably frustrated. She'd done almost every scrap of work in this investigation, and they were so close to catching the culprit. Why were her instincts so readily ignored? Simply because she was a woman and a FANY in a war where men in uniform made all the decisions?

She met Jamie's eye unapologetically and, with a bitter sigh, told him the rest.

"In the interest of ruling Marie out, I asked him to casually convey that you'd convinced Major Boom that Conjugal was compromised. That the drop previously scheduled for the fifth of October would instead be miles from its original target, its supplies reallocated to another mission." She swallowed nervously, waiting for his reaction, braced for the consequences.

"I see. Is that all?" he inquired politely.

She nodded, tension stiffening every inch of her body.

"And did he do it? Did he tell her all that, and nothing else besides?"

"He said he did, and I believe him. I spoke to him this morning. He didn't like doing it, but he went along with it, knowing it might make a difference."

"You could learn something from that," Jamie said sharply, before adding, "I assume you plan to keep a close eye on her?" When she nodded, he went on. "Where is she now?"

"She's typing Sergeant Flaherty's lecture notes, and judging by the stack of pages covered in his illegible scrawl, she'll be trapped behind her typewriter for the foreseeable future."

He frowned. "We'll come back to that. First things first. If we assume there *is* a traitor and that Kate can be eliminated, what's your plan for Liz? To conscript her groundskeeper to feed her the same lies?"

"I don't think it'll be necessary." When she didn't elaborate, Jamie narrowed his eyes, glaring at her, as if he could prompt her confession by sheer force of will.

And he would have managed it, but for his impatience.

"If you'd prefer to outline your insubordinate strategy to Major Boom directly, by all means." He gestured grandly to the door. "Otherwise, get on with it," he ground out.

"If Marie is innocent, she will almost certainly confide in the other FANY. And then the real traitor will act."

He eyed her shrewdly, comprehension dawning. "You're not interested in ruling Marie out. You've already made up your mind that she's the one: traitor and killer." He dropped into his chair and ran a hand over his jaw, not even bothering to wait for confirmation. "Why her? What else have you been keeping from me?"

"I can't tell you."

"I don't see that you have much choice in the m—"

"I can't tell you," she said archly, "because it's nothing specific. It's a hunch, a guess, an instinct. A little idea. And I know that's nowhere near good enough for you." She tipped her head down, not wanting him to see how frustrated she was with herself. "But I thought maybe we could catch her out."

"I'll remind you again that we have no proof that Conjugal is compromised, let alone that one of our own either murdered Lieutenant Beckett, or was engaged in the further perfidy of betraying Baker Street agents in occupied territory."

"Not a shred, but I think we both believe all of it to be true," she countered.

He sighed. "I can't deny that instinct plays as big a part as verified intelligence in strategic planning, and I admire your determination in chasing up every lead, but"—he looked away from her, his finger tapping out a silent tattoo on his desk—"I think you're reaching." His voice softened. "I want this matter resolved as much as you do. But I'd just as soon not alienate the women who keep this place running smoothly. Does this plan of yours have you staking out Balls Wood every evening at quitting time for the foreseeable future?"

"Something like that."

His eyebrow went up. "I thought I told you no more solitary escapades. Defy me even once, and I'll sack you. Who were you going to get to go with you, and how were you going to explain your absences to Mr and Mrs Bright?"

"I assumed it would have to be you," she said tartly, "and I can't think why I didn't ask you from the very beginning." Her lip curled, his smile flashed, and the tension eased ever so slightly. "It won't be as difficult as you think. Marie works in the manor all day and shares the hut with Kate and Liz at night. There are only so many opportunities for a treacherous individual to sneak out in order to transmit clandestine messages."

"If I didn't know better, I'd think you were writing for the sensational press."

"Very funny." After a pause, she added, "Given that Lieutenant Tierney kept Marie out all evening yesterday, and escorted her directly back to her room, tonight would be her first opportunity, *if* she plans to act on the false information." Seeing his intent to object, she added, "I had a chat with Kate this morning, and she confirmed that Marie was the last one out of bed and, in fact, had to hurry to be on time."

Jamie nodded. "It'll be a tricky business. We don't know where she might have hidden the transmitter, and following her from the manor across acres of open land might give the game away before it's even begun."

Olive smiled winningly, much relieved not to have been on the receiving end of a stern lecture and gratified that Jamie was taking her seriously. "I'll have Mr Harris pack us another picnic, and we'll make the best of the whole situation. We can play twenty questions," she said, thinking of poor Liz.

"Not a chance."

Thus far, Jamie had remained unconvinced.

"What about five questions?" she asked.

"No."

"One, then."

He glanced at her long enough to respond in the emphatic negative, then turned back toward the ride. They were concealed among the trees at the opposite end from the ROC station, where Margaret was currently on duty.

With a flash of inspiration, Olive had asked her friend to keep an eye out for anyone entering the wood.

"Do you happen to know any birdcalls?" Olive had asked her dubiously.

Margaret had flicked her eyes at Jamie, clearly wondering if her friend was serious. His answer had been a helpless shrug and a shake of his head. He was already a bit put out to be carrying a picnic basket.

"I'm afraid that isn't one of my skills," Margaret said.

"Can you manage a fox's bark?"

"Not without feeling a fool."

"Just do it," Olive insisted. "Please. I'll owe you one."

That prompted a rather mischievous smile, but it was quickly shunted in favour of a brisk manner. "I'll do my best, but you do realise I'm meant to be watching the skies, not the woods." She indicated her binoculars and glanced up, only to frown at the thick layer of cloud cover obscuring the view. "Not that I'll manage to spot anything."

Olive nodded. "Understood. If you do bark, make it loud. We'll be at the other end of the ride."

Margaret held out a torch and lifted an eyebrow. "The better to find her in the dark, without the need for barking," she said dryly. "And I expect that returned at the end of the evening."

Pocketing the torch, Olive rolled her eyes. "This doesn't get you off the hook."

They'd left Margaret at the station hut and walked through the darkening twilight, accompanied by the scurries and calls of nighttime. Neither had spoken, and Olive's eyes had darted eagerly through the shadows. A dragonfly had hovered beside her, a winged escort for the journey, but the moment they had stepped off the open ride, it had departed, leaving them to the watch.

That had been a quarter of an hour ago, and Olive was getting fidgety, her nerves jangling with anticipation and inactivity. Not so much as a hedgehog had crossed the ride in all that time. And while the company was determinedly disagreeable, the deepening colours and sharp smells of autumn were something of an antidote.

"Why not even one question?" she demanded. "Why are you so determined that I not know anything about you? If nothing else, you could at least offer up a few anecdotes I might use for casual chats in the village. It's been months! If we're meant to be even a bit serious about each other, I should know *something*." She glanced quickly at the scar running along his jaw. Its origin was one of two bits of his past that he'd shared—and she'd had to bully it out of him.

He didn't turn from his surveillance, merely said, "If anyone can concoct an imaginary history, it's you. I suspect you're already quite far along as it is."

She didn't bother telling him the amorous details she'd conjured out of precious little for the sake of Margaret's curiosity. "Perhaps I should. In fact, I suppose it's as good a time as any." So, as the light faded and she peered intently through the brush for any telltale movements, she began the tale.

"Some twenty-odd years ago, in the deep green vales of County

Donegal, a boy was born with coal-black hair, stormy grey-blue eyes, and a temper that could set the world on edge."

"What rubbish," Jamie said with feeling.

"As he grew up along the banks of the Rivers Eske, Finn, and Swilly"—Olive found she was quite enjoying herself, tucking the little bits and pieces Jamie had confided neatly into her story— "tending his family's sheep, he learned discipline and patience. And for the times that both virtues failed him, he learned how to fight."

His muttered curse had her tucking back a smile, but then she stilled, squinting hard through the branches at . . . nothing, after all. A trick of the wind. She moved, winced, and countered his curse with one of her own. "I think our picnic spot is in the middle of something prickly."

"Pipe down," he said with no heat. He turned to look at her. "You're really not cut out for this sort of work. Can you hand me a sandwich?" Flipping open the basket, she did as he asked. "Your expectations are much too high. Did you imagine we were going to sit here for a quarter of an hour and your quarry was going to stroll past, toting the transmitter and singing 'Die Fahne hoch'?"

"It could happen," she said, with a twist of her lips. Put like that, it sounded utterly ridiculous.

"Of course it could. But it's just as likely that she won't come at all, or that it'll be someone else entirely—someone we didn't suspect, following his own schedule. Only think of the blow to your pride," he teased.

"It doesn't hurt to be optimistic," she said primly, taking up the binoculars as he sat there, lecturing her round his sandwich. She'd show him how well she could manage.

"No," he agreed. "It doesn't. Unless that attitude is responsible for giving you a rose-tinted view of everything. Then it can be dangerous."

Olive could see nothing through the binoculars, no matter

which way she trained them, and, for once, she didn't want to argue with Jamie, because she very much feared he was right. She turned to look at him. "Perhaps I should go to the other side or move farther down the ride. We'd have a better chance—"

"We're staying right here—*both* of us. You're not going off on your own with a murderer possibly on the loose. That sort of behaviour hasn't worked particularly well for you in the past," he said pointedly.

Olive rolled her eyes and smothered a growl of irritation. It was getting darker by the minute, and she worried that momentarily they'd not be able to discern a skulker from a shadow unless it was fewer than twenty feet away.

"What if she slips past Margaret and her rendezvous is somewhere at that end? We'll never see her."

"Her rendezvous?" Jamie dug into the picnic basket, found an apple, and took a rather violent bite. "Don't tell me you're now expecting someone else, as well."

"I was referring to the transmitter and her counterpart on the other end of it," Olive said defensively, a low drone buzzing in her head.

He raised his binoculars and raked the woods that surrounded them. "Too many unknowns. Which is why this operation of yours is almost certainly doomed to failure. Let me think a moment."

Determined to put a little distance between them, Olive stood and moved a little away, skirting a fallen log and ducking when a low branch would have brained her. While he thought, she would prepare the next chapter of her story, in which Jameson Aldridge got a bracing comeuppance—and maybe fell face-first into a cowpat.

Olive was staring blindly through the binoculars, imagining just such an episode in full Technicolor, when a movement brought her tumbling back to reality. A shadow had detached itself from the dark tower of trees midway down the ride. It was as if an electric shock bolted through her, jarring her thoughts and tingling through her fingers, as she watched, waiting and wondering if this, at last, was to be the end of it.

After another moment, she was sure: there was just enough light from the rising moon to distinguish the shape and movements of a woman. Lithe and blonde, clad in trousers and a dark jumper, it could have been either Marie or Liz. As she watched her, Olive's thoughts began to scroll back through recent memories—lunch at the manor, the night out at the pub, those little private chats. And the one she'd had with Max Dunn. Like a flashbulb going off in her brain, she knew for certain who was lurking farther along the ride.

From the distant ROC station hut, a high-pitched bleat of "Incoming!" reached her ears.

Olive winced, keeping her eyes trained on the figure as it moved through the gathering darkness. "If that doesn't give the game away," she muttered. "We agreed she'd bark like a fox if someone—"

"Olive," came the sharp reprimand just behind her. She ignored it, peering out of hiding amid the roaring of urgency and excitement in her ears.

"Get down," Jamie shouted, just before a growl came alive in the sky and a siren rent the air. But he didn't wait for her reaction. He had closed the distance between them and now gave her arm a sharp tug, so she tripped over the log. He caught her hard against him as they tumbled to the leaf-strewn earth.

For a long moment, she lay still, her head against his solid chest, the air having been knocked clean out of her. Only then did she manage to understand. They were no longer predators but prey.

As the siren cried on, her eyes locked with Jamie's, and the buzzing, roaring, droning of the planes began to rattle her bones. "Don't fight me," he said brusquely, just as his arms banded round her and he began to roll.

She barely felt the discomfort of every little twig and root and stone, the urgency so consumed her. The tumbling whirl of flush torsos and tangled limbs seemed to go on forever, but it could have lasted only a second or two. They were tucked beneath a rotting log, her hip lodged in a puddle, and only a breath of space between them, when they heard the terrifying, high, keening whistles.

Bombs were raining down.

Chapter 20

29 September

Jamie's arms tightened round her, and she curled into his embrace, her breath caught in her lungs. Olive closed her eyes and prayed the bombs would fall in empty fields and no one would be hurt. She'd wanted so desperately to be a part of the war effort, but she didn't want this—this wild, helpless, frantic uncertainty.

And then the crack of an explosion rent the night, sent tremors through the earth beneath them, shook a skittish flurry of leaves crumpling over them. They pressed even closer as a second one, nearer still, jolted Olive enough that she smacked her head against the log and blurted a string of furious curses at the Luftwaffe pilots, the Nazis, and Hitler, in particular.

The bomb tore open the ride a hundred yards from their shelter, with an inferno of sound and fury. The shock wave rocked through them, and on the heels of it came a hailstorm of earth, the panicked frenzy of forest dwellers, and a swell of heat rolling out from the crater.

Several long, stunned moments later came the deafening silence.

The German planes had moved off, but as Olive stared up at

the sky, she could see the silhouettes of what surely must be the RAF, scrambled out of Hunsdon, skimming through the clouds, bearing down on the enemy, ready to shoot them out of the sky.

She glanced at the dark head nestled at her shoulder. He hadn't looked up. Olive felt a lurch in her stomach, felt panic ready to overtake her. But with a rumbling groan, he lifted his head and looked down at her. His face was a rictus of pain, which he seemed determined to ruthlessly set aside.

"You're hurt," Olive said, gripping his shoulders, trying to sit up. "Let me have a look." Her voice sounded far off and distorted, as if it were filtering through a London fog.

The muscles of his arms were like bands of steel holding him above her as he tried to tell her something she couldn't hear. Staring at his lips, she guessed at the words *leg* and *broken*, and her eyes flared. Olive scrambled out from under him, conscious of the wetness now spanning the seat of her trousers, and stared in considerable dismay at the hornbeam branch lying across the back of his right leg. It hadn't been a shock wave she'd felt, but the force of the branch dropping down on them. And she'd felt only a bit of it, because he'd cushioned the blow.

She crouched beside him and, pantomiming wildly, tried to convey that she would try to lift the weight off him and he should roll out from under. His exasperation was more evident than ever, and as she took in the perspiration on his brow, and the deep, pained wrinkles in his face, Olive winced with regret at having dragged him back to the wood. After gripping the broad branch, she hoisted it a scant inch, then another, her muscles straining as the bark chafed her palms. She groaned with the effort, trying to marshal her strength, as Jamie fought to drag himself clear.

Finally, they'd done it, and she dropped down beside him in the dirt as, with considerable effort, he twisted himself round to lie on his back. One look at his leg had her biting back a curse. He wouldn't be able to walk on it, and he was likely going to need more help than she could provide. The picnic basket wasn't equipped for first aid. She bit her lip, glancing out over the tumult of the ride. She was certain she'd spotted the traitor before the Luftwaffe had blitzed through her plan, and if the bombs had spooked her quarry—entirely understandable—they might have a better chance at catching her. With another look at Jamie's injury, Olive realised that, for the time being at least, *they* had dwindled simply to *her*. And she came to a decision: she'd hunt down the murderer first and fetch the doctor as soon as it was done.

Her intentions must have been clear on her face, because his hand shot out and gripped hers. She met his stern gaze with equanimity. As his lips began to move, she read them, hearing their echo in her head. "Do *not* go prowling through these woods alone. Go back to the manor and bring the car—and Danny, if you can find him."

If she followed his orders, her quarry would almost certainly elude her. And then this whole evening would have been a bloody waste.

She shook her head, pointed to her ear, and mouthed, "I can't hear a word." Then she pulled away to stand and waited until she was a step away before saying, "I'll fetch someone, and it won't take a moment. I'll ask Margaret to call ahead." She prayed the ROC station had fared better than they had, and with her fists clenched, she went on. "But she's here, Jamie. I saw her just before the explosion. I need to try to find her." His arm reached for her ankle, but she nimbly dodged it. "Stay still, and I'll be back in no time at all."

Then she turned and ran as best she could, stumbling through the trees. She was gratified to realise that her hearing was coming back. Even at a little distance she distinctly heard Jamie's voice trailing her. "Olive! Come back here!" She spared a single stunned moment for the tremendous crater left behind by the nearest bomb, only a prayer away from their hiding place. After that, she didn't look back and instead turned her focus to the search.

She would need to be extra careful, as her hearing had not yet fully recovered. The thought of prowling about in the dark in her current state was a bit terrifying. Olive couldn't help the worried breath that shuddered through her, its evidence visible in the chilly night air. Her heartbeat thudded dully, felt keenly in her throat and temples, as she neared the spot where she had seen her quarry slip amidst the trees.

She heard muffled voices—one male and one female—coming from the direction of the ROC station hut and felt relief sweep through her. Margaret and the portly fellow who rounded out the duty rota seemed to have weathered the night's raid but were clearly frazzled with the job at hand. A call to the doctor would be low priority right now, but she'd fetch one herself just as soon as she found her quarry.

She slipped through the trees. The path was criss-crossed with dark branches and strewn with roots and fallen logs. She narrowed her eyes, knowing she had the advantage. She'd grown up in these woods, and with any luck, her quarry didn't know she was coming. Unless, of course, someone had given the game away.

She stepped softly, carefully, then paused to listen, with the desperate hope that her ears would cooperate. As her darting gaze swept over the landscape, checking at any possible hiding place, her heart kept up its urgent thrum. Her quarry was here. Somewhere.

Jamie, bless him, had realised the need for stealth and had stopped calling the moment it became evident Olive wasn't coming back, and now there was little more than the sound of her own breathing vibrating in her ears.

Thus far, there wasn't a clue to indicate that anyone had been here or was still lurking. No clicks or snaps that might indicate a transmitter case being opened or shut; no rhythmic taps, long and short, in little bursts, that would hint at a message being sent. No sounds of leaves crackling or twigs snapping underfoot. Nothing but the far-off spiraling thrum of the air-raid sirens and the distant drone of planes, which she desperately hoped were RAF.

It went on like that for several heart-pounding, breath-catching, ear-straining moments. Olive moved as if in slow motion. She was rather adept at tracking, as a result of time spent hunting and in the Guides, but the limitations of sight and sound rather levelled the playing field. With any luck, she'd come upon her quarry with sufficient stealth so as to allow a bit of eavesdropping. And then she'd move to ambush.

Unfortunately, someone was ready and waiting for her.

Olive had only a moment's warning. A little sound just behind her. She stilled, balanced on the balls of her feet, and spun round in time to see an arm poised above her, ready to strike. She lunged to the side and likely saved herself a concussion, or worse, but the stone didn't miss entirely, and a sharp pain burst in her shoulder. She cried out, her right arm now hanging limp at her side, as she faced down her opponent.

"I wouldn't have pegged you as the type for blunt force," she said lightly, her mind whirring ahead to the outcome. "It's too unreliable for murder." She'd optimistically envisioned a red-handed Marie, consumed with guilt, allowing herself to be led away with little more than a condemning hand on her shoulder. But judging from her first foray, Marie was not about to come quietly. And given the current state of her shoulder, Olive didn't much like her chances at hand-to-hand combat, even if Marie sportingly dropped the stone. As Marie stepped closer, Olive stumbled back, blurting, "Now, poison or a gun or even a good shove. Onto railroad tracks or in front of a bus—"

"Shut up, Olive," Marie said harshly. "Lieutenant Beckett was an unfortunate casualty. He found out what I was doing— what I am. So, I had to kill him. But now I've done it. I've crossed a line, and there's no crossing back. So this time"—her eyes glittered as they stared remorselessly into Olive's—"I came prepared." Dropping the stone, she crouched to fumble at her boot, and a moment later, Olive was staring wide eyed as the moonlight trailed along the blade of a wickedly sharp knife.

"Or a knife," Olive said, referring back to her murderous list. She hoped her voice didn't sound as wobbly as she felt.

"A gift from Lieutenant Tierney," Marie said, a sad little smile playing at her lips as she stared down at it. "You probably shouldn't have encouraged our friendship." She sighed deeply. "Oh, Olive. When you came tiptoeing through the trees just now, I really hoped it was coincidence, that I could get by with simply knocking you out. But you made it quite clear that you'd found me out." She raised her brow in a wry reminder. "And after being reprimanded for lippy tendencies by the old battle-ax herself."

"Fair enough," said Olive, who was on tenterhooks now that a knife was in play.

Marie took a step forward, the knife point aimed at Olive. "I've always disliked vapid girls who thought of nothing else but how to catch a man and what to do with him after. I wanted clever friends who didn't shy away from expressing their own opinions, no matter that they were unpopular or even forbidden."

Another step, and a shift of the knife from the right hand to the left, prompted Olive to retreat a matching step, her shoulder throbbing.

Marie went on. "But you've taught me the error of my ways. You and Liz. Kate is sweet but rather a fool. Everything would have been so much easier if the pair of you had been more like her."

"If you only knew," Olive muttered.

"But the pair of you are too curious, badgering and spying, refusing to be content with your own lives. You *had* to know every little detail—what I was up to, where I came from, who I'd left behind. But I couldn't tell you any of that."

"Because you're German," Olive said, finishing for her.

Marie seemed to shrink a bit before her eyes, and for a long moment, she stared up through the leaf-stripped trees at the half-moon that hung above them. Then her grip tightened on the knife. "You knew. Then why did you follow me all alone? Let me guess. I was to be another feather in your cap. You fully intended to go marching back to the manor in triumph, having confronted the traitor and solved Lieutenant Beckett's murder."

"It does sound quite nice," Olive admitted. "But really I just wanted it all to stop. I couldn't bear the thought of our agents being imprisoned—or killed—because I hadn't tried hard enough to find you."

"How very noble," Marie said archly.

Olive frowned at her. "How could you do it? Working ferociously long hours, at the officers' beck and call, responsible for every imaginable detail, all of it to support these agents and their missions, only to undermine them once they're out of reach."

"It's not all of them," she said tetchily. "Only the ones being sent to Belgium. I didn't want to do it—not any of it." She seemed suddenly flustered. "What gave me away?" she asked, almost petulantly, shifting the knife again, closing the distance between them.

This time when Olive stepped back, she pretended to lose her footing on a bit of uneven ground and took the opportunity to subtly shift the direction of her retreat.

"It wasn't easy," Olive admitted. "While there were plenty of clues, I had a devil of a time trying to ascertain which of them were relevant and how they all fit together." She was speaking offhand, as if over coffee in the canteen, but she was hyperaware of every shifting shadow, every flicker of expression, and every tip and tilt of the knife. And all the while, she was trying to devise a strategy. She didn't like her chances against a knife, particularly with a bruised shoulder. And while she could call for help, it was likely no one would come. Margaret surely had her hands full, urgently searching the sky for enemy aircraft, and Jamie was immobilised with a broken leg at the other end of the ride. She'd handle it; she just needed a few moments to think. Which meant she'd need to stall. "Honestly, we were floundering a bit until we found the lipstick."

"What lipstick?" Marie's head swivelled as she casually searched the surrounding trees. "And don't bother pretending you're not here on your own."

"Captain Aldridge will be along in a moment," Olive told her. "He's been searching the other end of the ride."

"Then we'd better hurry this along, hadn't we?" Marie said, her brows knitting as her grip tightened on the knife.

Olive whirled to put the trunk of a hornbeam between them. "Just wait a minute," she insisted, her heart pounding. "I thought you were curious." She crouched to run her hands over the ground, hoping they'd close over a rock, a heavy branch, or a fry pan left behind by an errant Guide. But there was *nothing*.

"It doesn't matter," Marie said dismissively as the knife flashed yet again. "I may have made mistakes, but I fully intend to remedy that. *Arduis invictus*."

The FANY motto: "In difficulty, undaunted."

Olive had to admit, it was a fair point. If one of them should be daunted by the current situation, it wasn't Marie.

"Humour me, then," she insisted, feeling only slightly desperate. "You're planning to kill me, anyway. Why not give me this last hurrah?" Olive pushed away from the hornbeam and darted behind the trunk of another, confident that Marie wouldn't throw the knife unless she was absolutely sure of herself.

Marie laughed. It was a strange, disembodied sound. "We are very alike, you and I. I think you could have made a very good spy, but for your misguided sense of trust. I realised some time ago that no one can be trusted." She didn't speak for a moment, and Olive tensed, waiting, but then Marie said brightly, "Go on, then, if you must, although I can't guarantee your lecture won't be cut short."

Olive peered carefully round the trunk of the hornbeam to watch Marie move cautiously closer. She tentatively rolled her shoulder and winced at the ache in it. Suddenly she spied a pale, round stone glowing in a shaft of moonlight, and she lurched toward it, relief surging through her. But the feeling was fleeting— the beastly thing ripped apart in her hand, nearly sending her sprawling. She wanted to bellow in frustration at having found no better weapon than a *mushroom*.

"You're testing the patience of a murderer, Olive. Remember that."

The words were more chilling than the misty drizzle that had started to fall, and they brought Olive up short. Marie was not only offering her a chance to stall, but also to expound—at abbreviated length—on her amateur detective work. There would be no gathering of curious and nervous suspects, no great unmasking. But beggars couldn't very well be choosers. Channelling the great Hercule Poirot, Olive began.

"While the police were convinced that Lieutenant Beckett's death was an accident, there were several clues that convinced me that it was murder." Olive quick stepped from the protection of one tree to the shelter of another a few yards nearer the ride. With any luck, she could lure Marie to follow, cat and mouse, and eventually position the pair of them within reach of anyone coming to investigate the crater. Poised to carry on, she tipped her head back against the tree at the very moment that something hit the other side with a deafening crack. She sprang away from it.

"A little reminder not to drag this out."

Where is she getting these bloody rocks?

Olive's eyes flared angrily in the dark. How could she be expected to expound on the methods she'd employed in the hunt for a murderer while she was being actively hunted by the killer herself?

"Very well," she said archly. "I'll be brief, but it's not ideal." She eyed a beech tree nearby and wondered if its narrow trunk would leave her too exposed. "It was a lot of things . . . the lipstick, as I mentioned, the scarf, a coded message. But the biggest clue was the aerial left hanging from a tree near Lieutenant Beckett's body." So saying, Olive launched herself from her hiding place and moved at a zigzagging run as she darted toward the shelter of a wild service tree.

No crack accompanied her progress, prompting Olive to peer nervously back the way she'd come. She scanned the open spaces between the trees, light amid the shadows, and saw nothing. Her heartbeat pummelled at her veins as she stared out at the empty stretch of wood. She urgently rolled her shoulder, steeling herself against the dull ache of it, wondering if it would hold up in a fight.

"Perhaps it's easier like this," came the disembodied voice of Marie. "More like the commando training the agents get. Creeping up on the enemy, pouncing in the shadows. Dead without ever having to look anyone in the eye." Her voice sounded hollow, almost regretful.

"I felt quite certain it all signified a traitor," Olive said crisply, determined to shutter the talk of another murder. "And that, in turn, hinted at further treachery. So it became more important than ever to ferret out the culprit." She paused. "But none of those clues pointed to you specifically."

"Go on, then," Marie said, sounding amused. "When did I become suspect number one?"

"It started with your knife and fork, actually." Hoping Marie was sufficiently distracted, Olive darted for the cover of a split-trunk hornbeam a few yards closer to the ride. "I'd seen someone else lay their cutlery across their plate in the same manner you did—with the tips arranged carefully in the ten o'clock position." She was peering into the darkness, looking for any movement, hoping Marie hadn't somehow come round behind her. "For the longest time, I couldn't think who it was, but then I remembered. It was a friend of my father's—a German who'd stumbled into his field hospital during the Great War, missing a hand. They'd struck up a friendship over a mutual love of pigeons, and he visited us occasionally over the years."

"A coincidence," she said, her brevity rather irritating, as it gave Olive very little time to pinpoint her location, let alone consider her next move.

"Perhaps, but when I started to suspect you, it was just one more clue. There was also the singalong on the way back from the pub. 'Oranges and Lemons' is a common English nursery rhyme, but you knew neither the words nor the tune."

"I could have forgotten. Or never learned the gruesome little song." Marie's tone was careful, and her voice sounded closer than it had only a moment ago.

"True. But, again, it was curious." Olive groped on the ground beside her, found a hollow length of branch, and chucked it toward that cold, calculating voice. Then she moved, glancing round as she did so, and imagined she caught a glimpse of Marie's golden hair a little distance away, in the shelter of a recently abandoned hornbeam.

She resumed her narrative, determined to keep her voice level. "The real investigation circled round the lipstick and the scarf." She walked carefully backwards, her eyes scanning the darkness, then ducked behind an elder bush to peer out from among the berries. "The discovery of a lipstick in the waste bin of Captain Aldridge's office pointed to a FANY but provided no clues as to what she might have been doing there. Then, rather conveniently, the scarf we'd found clutched in Lieutenant Beckett's hand went missing from the office. A scarf printed with a map of Germany, marked with three inked crosses near the city of Berlin," she said portentously. "Someone was clearly very attached to it and quite keen to keep it a secret, making it a clue of paramount importance." Olive paused to let her words sink in and realised she might have been a bit overzealous in her channelling of M Poirot.

She went on. "I met a RAF pilot recently who explained that only crewmen flying sorties over Germany would have been issued such a scarf. RAF Hunsdon doesn't have any aircraft that can make the trip there and back, but Stradishall scrambles Wellington bombers. Both you and Liz had been running supplies and equipment up to the airfield on drop days. Either of you could have chatted up a pilot or other airman going on runs into Germany. And it wasn't until Captain Aldridge and I were hunkered down, waiting for you to walk into our trap, that I remembered you had admitted as much."

The mist hung in the air, stifling all sound, and Olive shivered at the unpredictability of the situation. Very likely startled at the idea of being outmanoeuvred, Marie didn't answer, and Olive went on.

"I suspect the missing scarf once belonged to the pitiful pilot who never did manage to land a satisfying kiss."

Once again, she waited for a reaction that didn't come. Not a word, not a breath, not a step. A prickle of unease crept up her spine. If Marie was feeling desperate, her actions would be unpredictable. Olive quickly scanned her surroundings, not wanting to be caught unawares. She needed to move.

Her choices were a pair of spindly-looking beeches hunched together just beyond a rotted log or a sturdy-trunked wild service a bit farther off. She moved quickly, in an ungraceful flurry of limbs; got tangled in an elder bush, judging by its scent; swatted herself free; and finally dodged into the shelter of a fat beech twenty feet on. A skittering rush to her left sent panic clawing up her spine, but as she whipped her head round, the graceful lope of a hare darting out of sight had her sighing with relief. Until another sound, just behind her, brought her rearing round again.

This time, it was the enemy.

The knife flashed, and in dodging away from it, Olive fell back and acted without thinking, kicking out, aiming for a pair of testicles that weren't there.

Naturally, she didn't connect with any important bits, but she managed instead to catch Marie's knife hand. The force of the blow loosened her grip, so that the knife was knocked away. It arced through the dark to land with a thump a little ways off. It required only a second for Marie to decide she'd never find it and to turn on Olive with single-minded intent.

"Why couldn't you just mind your own business?" Marie ground out, cradling her injured hand. Her jaw compressed, as if she was fighting down a surge of temper. "Well, you're right. I suppose that's what you wanted to hear. I *did* take the scarf from that beastly pilot. To him it was a backup plan, in the event his plane went down in enemy territory. To me, it was a flimsy tether to a happier life. I was devastated when I managed to lose it on a walk in the woods. I went back, looked for it, but found nothing. Then I saw Lieutenant Beckett at the manor, flaunting its existence, and I was desperate. I thought he might have seen me with the transmitter. I had to make certain he wouldn't . . . *couldn't* betray me." She stopped, and her breath sounded harsh in the silence.

She shook her head angrily and started again. "Once he was dead, I searched his room and couldn't find it. I didn't know what to do." Olive wondered if she'd regretted her decision to do murder. "But some days later, I saw the little list you'd left beside your typewriter, and realised the scarf was likely now in the possession of Captain Aldridge and a clue to your amateur investigation. The very idea enraged me." She looked hard at Olive.

Olive scrabbled to her feet. Needing to understand what had driven her friend to such lengths, she said gently, "Why was the scarf so important?"

Marie's face, half in shadow, wet with mist, was a mask of anger and sorrow. "I have been so careful. I've kept nothing of my family or my life in Germany. I am a ghost without a past, tethered to a cause I don't even believe in, at the mercy of loyalties that are not my own." Her head dipped, and with a deep sigh, she said, "My parents and younger sister died when the Allies bombed Berlin almost two years ago. I'd escaped Germany some months before, when it became too dangerous to speak out against the influence of the Nazi Party."

Olive blinked at her. Jamie's information had been utterly wrong. Fabricated. Somehow Marie had managed—no doubt with help—to thoroughly conceal her true identity.

"But I only *thought* I'd escaped. It was no coincidence that my stepbrother found me." *Not just a sister, but a stepbrother, as well.* "As it happens, he is an agent for the Abwehr in Roeselare," she said bitterly.

Olive remembered the name of the city from the map that covered Jamie's office wall. "Is that how you ended up working for Baker Street, alongside agents being dropped into Belgium?"

"He arranged it all. You would be surprised how many fifth columnists have infiltrated the upper echelons of the British war machine." She paused, seemingly on the verge of a momentous revelation, and Olive was torn. Given Marie's distracted state of mind, it was a prime moment to jump her, but at the same time, Olive was rampantly curious as to what might be divulged. Curiosity won out, and they stood ten feet apart under a canopy of trees and a lovely half-pearl moon while Marie mustered the words.

"I was training as an agent when I was accosted by a man claiming a family connection."

"You were training as a Baker Street agent?" Olive said, incredulous. *Is everyone training to be an agent but me?*

Marie nodded. "I'd changed my name, concocted a story about my parents' death years ago in Paris, and was careful to emphasise my connection to Scottish aristocracy."

Olive gestured impatiently for her to go on.

"I was nearly done at Arisaig and headed for finishing at Beaulieu. And then, quite suddenly, it all fell apart." She paused and seemed to be remembering those pivotal days. "The man who found me was carrying a letter from my stepbrother. He'd had people searching for me, worried that I'd be seen as an enemy alien and face internment on the Isle of Man." She looked away and, with crossed arms, rubbed her hands roughly over the sleeves of her jumper. "He compelled my loyalty, reminding me that it had been the Allies and their bombs that had killed Papa and Mama and Hannah." Her voice wavered slightly, but she quickly got control of herself.

She continued. "He knew about Baker Street—the special training schools, the protocol, all of it. And I knew there must be a mole at the highest levels. But I didn't know what to do about it, and he wasn't asking for much—only a little information. He confessed that he didn't support Hitler's rampageous ego or shocking brutality, but insisted that if the local resistance in Belgium started an uprising with support from the British, he'd surely be demoted, only to be replaced by someone more committed to party methods." Her lips twisted. "I was trapped," she insisted. Her raised hands were pale in the moonlight, a gesture of her untenable situation.

Olive refused to feel sympathy and said fiercely, "What of the agents you betrayed?" She hadn't admitted it to anyone, but she still searched the skies, watching for Alice's return, despite her certainty that the young bird was lost to her—another casualty of

this war. "And what of Lieutenant Tierney? He refused to believe you were the one—because how could he be falling in love
with a murderer?"

"Yes, well," she said swiftly, tipping up her chin, even as Olive
registered the hint of sadness in her eyes. "He really didn't know
me very well. None of you do." Her lips quivered, and her eyes
turned angry. "I have as much reason to hate the Nazis as you do.
They brainwashed the man I intended to marry."

Olive felt a little flicker of sympathy but quickly quashed it as
Marie went on.

"Luca was the perfect ideal of Hitler's master race—blond
hair, blue eyes, muscular physique, and an impeccable lineage.
He was smart and shy and sensitive, with few friends, but they
all joined the SS and spoke of patriotism and camaraderie. They
lured him further and further away from me, finally urging him to
put himself at the disposal of the Lebensborn programme, to
couple with racially pure women in order to populate a new
Aryan nation." She spoke bitterly but stared bleakly through the
dark as Olive shuddered at the horror of it and tried to think of
what to say.

Marie sprung at her with no warning, and even as Olive tried
to dodge her, she managed to get her hands round Olive's throat
to press her thumbs uncomfortably against her windpipe.

Olive felt a sharp moment of panic as she struggled for breath,
scrabbling at Marie's brutal grip, listening to the metronome
rhythm of her heart and the dizzying roar in her ears. It seemed
impossible that matters had come to this. George would be
aghast, and Jamie, she felt quite certain, would be furious. After
her last run-in with a murderer, she really should have taken the
business more seriously. Instead, here she was, staring blankly
into her opponent's eyes while her body struggled for air.

Despite the darkness, Olive could clearly read the desperation
in Marie's gaze. Determined that her enemy would not have the

same satisfaction, Olive closed her eyes and willed herself to think as her lungs slowly emptied. While her own training had barely progressed past breaking holds and targeting testicles, there'd been many occasions when she'd deliberately detoured past the gymnasium or the lawn, where Lieutenant Tierney alternately held classes, in order to watch the men sparring. She must have learned something she could use.

Her eyes flashed open, and with the last of her breath, she stomped hard on Marie's left foot and swept her arms sharply upward with enough force to break the hold round her throat. She made a grab for Marie's wrist, ready to twist it round and force it up behind her back, but Marie had completed a full course in hand-to-hand combat at one of Baker Street's special training schools and broke the hold easily.

Marie spun away from her, a triumphant glint in her eyes. "You're here alone, aren't you? Captain Aldridge refused to play along with your little detective game." Her eyes widened as realisation struck. "The information on the parachute drop was fabricated, wasn't it? A trap, set by you? The drop is to go ahead, after all." She tsked. "Well, no matter. When I'm done with you, I'll simply transmit the correction."

She's already transmitted the false information. The plan worked! Now I simply need to not *get murdered in order to prevent its being undone.*

Ignoring the rasp of pain in her throat, Olive gulped in the cool, damp air, frantically trying to remember the throws and holds she'd seen demonstrated, wondering which of them she might successfully manage to perform on Marie. "You can't possibly think you could kill me and not be suspected. A second death would prompt a thorough investigation." She clutched her shoulder, hoping to convince Marie that the motion required to break the hold had done her in. But all the while, she was plotting.

"Unfortunately, you will simply be another accident—concussed by the bomb blast. It'll be easy enough to arrange. Once I've dispatched you, I'll knock you on the head with a tree branch and let the police draw the obvious and simplest conclusion."

Olive lunged for her like a berserker, raising her right arm to shoulder height like a call to battle. As Marie reared back, Olive connected with the side of her neck in a sharp, chopping motion and stunned her enemy into momentary submission. Moving quickly, Olive wrapped her arm tightly round Marie's neck and pulled her down, forcing her to bend at the waist, as she tightened her grip and locked her opponent's arm into position with the opposite hand.

Heaving a sigh of relief, Olive looked round her and realised that her situation was only mildly improved. She was still alone in the wood with a murderer, an injured shoulder, and no real recourse. She very much doubted she could keep control of Marie long enough to march her out of the trees and call for help. She began to feel fresh flickerings of panic.

After an agonising minute, in which Marie made several grabs for various parts of Olive's anatomy, forcing a continually tightened grip, Olive's shoulder was an aching throb, and she was no better off. And then she remembered Margaret's torch, tucked away in her pocket. One little conk on the head wouldn't hurt Marie, and with luck, it would knock her clean out. And honestly, she deserved it.

Olive realised she'd have to adjust her hold in order to reach the torch, and with the girl clawing at her, she might not stand a chance, but as it was, Olive couldn't hold on much longer. She'd have to risk it. She took a deep breath and tightened her right arm, wincing against the thudding pain in her shoulder. Fumbling at her pocket with her left, she wrenched the torch out even as her right arm was beginning to give way. With the weapon poised above Marie's head, Olive closed her eyes, willing herself to get on with it.

"I think you've done enough," said a voice some ten feet away.

Both women stilled, and Olive's head jerked up to take in the very solid form and shadowed face of Jameson Aldridge, who, while balancing precariously on one leg, nonetheless looked extraordinarily dangerous.

And that was before she noticed the gun he held in his hand.

Chapter 21

4 October

Olive sat on the gate, staring up at the sky. The practice had been force of habit in the years before the war, as she searched the sky for her pigeons, whether amid the peaceful monotony of training runs or the giddy excitement of race days. But since the start of the war, that wide vista had changed dramatically. It was regularly streaked with fighters and bombers, clouded with smoke, or clamouring with the sound of air-raid sirens bouncing off the clouds. Now it was where she looked to remember what she'd lost, to reaffirm what they were all fighting for, and to envision a victorious future.

She still thought of that evening in Balls Wood, now nearly a week past, when she'd cheated death twice in the space of an hour. And she remembered Lieutenant Beckett and Alice, neither of whom had been so lucky. Marie Wald, her name Anglicanised to Wood as part of her grand deception, had seen to it that Operation Conjugal was compromised, its mission a failure. The fate of its agents had yet to be discovered. Marie had lost her love and her family, and while she'd faced an intolerable situation, Olive would never believe it justified her actions.

She couldn't help but feel horribly sad that Lieutenant Beckett had managed to get caught in Marie's tidy web of deceit, whether by accident or design. He'd visited Balls Wood frequently for reasons of his own, and while it was entirely possible he'd witnessed her treachery, it was equally conceivable that he'd known nothing at all.

It was she who'd written the warning letters, hoping the risk of exposure would encourage him to find another rendezvous. But he'd ignored them, and shortly after Marie's scarf went missing, she'd seen it in his possession. Perhaps she hadn't known about MI9—or how common such maps truly were. Or perhaps she was simply a woman stretched to the breaking point, and the loss of that scarf, with its marks for her dead family, had tipped the scales. She had felt fraught and exposed, had been convinced that Lieutenant Beckett was a danger to her, and she'd resolved to get rid of him.

She'd had every intention of dispatching Olive, as well, and she might have prevailed if Jamie hadn't appeared in the nick of time.

He'd kept his anger tamped down until Marie had been safely delivered into the hands of Major Boom, and even while he'd allowed his leg to be set and bandaged. All of it had been accomplished in a matter of a few hours, and it had been late. But he'd instructed her, in no uncertain terms, to wait.

So she had, not really wanting to go home, in any case. She had sat in the library, by the light of a single lamp, and had drunk cup after cup of tea, pondering the things people were capable of when pushed to the brink of desperation.

He'd stumped in at some point in her musings, leaning heavily on a wooden crutch, crossed to the sofa in silence, and collapsed beside her on the cushions. Neither of them had spoken for some time, but she had darted occasional glances at his injured leg, and he at her bruised throat.

She could hear him even now, days later, in the golden light of a new autumn day, and it made the corners of her mouth hitch just to think of it. "I distinctly told you not to go off on your own with murderers." His words had been utterly polite, but Olive had known he was boiling mad.

Unable to help herself, she'd snapped. "Well, I wouldn't have thought it needed to be said, but it's unwise to ramble about on a broken leg. You can't always do things by the book, Captain Aldridge, or there'll never be a new story." They'd both seethed then, until she'd passed him the plate of sandwiches Hilda had plied her with and said quietly, "I'm glad you found us. I really didn't want to hit her."

His face was pale, and the tumult in his eyes made him look simultaneously unapproachable and extraordinarily appealing. If left to her own devices in the dark, after the ordeal she'd had, she wouldn't have balked for a single second at kissing him. But in a quiet room of Brickendonbury Manor, with a murderer being questioned just down the hall, such an action might have been considered unseemly. Even so, her heart beat a little erratically. He looked utterly composed, and she wanted, more than anything at that moment, to unravel him.

"You knew it was her all along, didn't you? That was your little idea?" he said.

Olive nodded. "I suspected her for lots of little reasons that could be easily explained away. It wasn't until I remembered a certain pilot's kisses that I knew for certain."

Jamie's eyebrows went up, and his cheeks flushed with a bit of much-needed colour. "I'll let Major Boom sort that out."

She turned to face him. "Did you know that she was training to be an agent?"

"I did."

"And you didn't think that was useful information to share?" Rather than unravel the man, she now wanted to truss him up and dunk him in the moat.

He sighed, but a look at his face made her wonder if the sound was an involuntary reaction to the pain in his leg. He spoke before she could. "The number of applicants that undergo the rigours of Baker Street training is not inconsiderable. A large percentage of them are eliminated from consideration as agents at one step or another in the process but are placed in other parts of the organisation. Marie failed her final objective at Arisaig and never made it to Beaulieu to get her assignment and identity. She ended up at Brickendonbury." He shrugged and, meeting Olive's eyes, added, "They're going to need to find the mole that allowed her to slip through the cracks."

Olive nodded and said cagily, "I wonder if I would make a good agent."

"You wouldn't," he said flatly. "And I don't want to go into it right now," he added, seeing her face. "Suffice it to say, you don't follow orders, and you've nearly been killed twice in the English countryside. I rather think your chances in occupied Europe would be bleak indeed."

Olive's mouth flattened in irritation now as she remembered *those* words. As chilly gusts scented with windfall apples lifted her hair and filtered through her jumper, she mulled over the successes and failures of recent months, quite proud of her record. It wasn't at all inconceivable that she could succeed as a Baker Street agent. Of course, she'd need more training if she decided to pursue the matter, but she'd already made a good start all on her own. She was pondering how best to raise her defence with Jamie when a tiny movement caught her eye. A single bird, high above her, winging its lonely way across a patch of empty blue sky.

As she watched, it swooped lower, and Olive frowned. It was quite clearly a pigeon, but she didn't think it was one of her own. When not on training flights, the birds tended to go off in groups, swooping leisurely over meadows or foraging in the hedgerow, rarely going farther afield than the village, preferring the comforts of home.

But this bird was approaching with extraordinary speed, its

wings beating furiously, their efforts further assisted by a brisk tailwind. In a moment it had circled close enough that Olive's heart was racing with excitement. *It can't be.*

She jumped from the gate and took off at a run, tracking the bird's progress as it flew unerringly and slipped in through the cupola on the roof of the dovecote. After pushing open the door to the loft, Olive watched as Alice hovered for a moment on spread wings before dropping to the floor to pad quickly to the pan of water.

Alice, who'd been dropped by parachute into Belgium over a month ago, who Olive had assumed was long dead, was standing before her, looking none the worse for her extended trip abroad. She caught the bird up, vowing to scrounge a few green titbits from the garden in celebration of her return, and fingers fumbling, detached the canister strapped to her leg. Set back down in the same spot, Alice took a long drink before beginning her bath.

Desperate to know if it held news of the agents, Olive debated skipping the phone call to Brickendonbury and decoding the message herself. So tempted was she that she pulled the rice paper from its Bakelite container and unfurled it between her fingers and thumbs.

It wasn't encoded. It was in French, and there were rudimentary drawings, marked with words she still recognised from lessons learned long ago: *aérodrome, pont, dépôt.*

Her eyes scanned the page, squinting to make out the small script, and there, at the bottom, was a name she didn't recognise: *Elise.*

She didn't understand how it was possible, and decided to wait for Jamie to translate the message and explain. For now, she chose to be optimistic, hoping that Rémi, Renauld, and Weasel had managed to disappear of their own volition, and that she would see them again.

She replaced the paper in its canister and cast a fond glance at the young bird, her heart lightened.

"Olive?" The voice was Jonathon's, but she suspected he was on an errand for her stepmother.

"In the dovecote," she called. "You won't believe it, but Alice is just back."

Naturally, in the excitement, it was several moments before he managed to convey his message. "Harriet wants to know if you can go into the village and check on the progress of the committees for the fête."

"Of course. I'll just need to call Captain Aldridge with the news about Alice."

"Well, don't worry about Hen and me. The ghost of Miss Husselbee will be in fine form, nosing into everyone's business," he said cheekily, "and doing its level best to scare up donations."

"I trust you implicitly," Olive said stoutly. She then flashed a conspiratorial smile and added, "I only wish I wasn't in on the secret."

5 October

Olive stood on the terrace under a grizzled sky, looking out over the wide lawn and the carefully tended gardens of Peregrine Hall. The ladies of the Pipley WI, and the men they'd conscripted to help them, had descended at dawn to erect the tents and set up the booths for the fête. Sofas and chairs had been brought out from the house for the guests of honour, and Miss Husselbee's favoured Union Jack bunting had been strung up to inspire an appropriate sense of patriotic fervour.

It was rather a grim day, but it looked as if the whole village had turned out en masse to get a peek at the new inhabitants of Peregrine Hall, together with some of the men convalescing at Merryweather House. They'd all been rather shy at first, but Harriet, proudly pushed along in her own homemade wheelchair by Jonathon himself, had quickly put them all at ease with her sincere thanks, quiet dignity, and obvious delight in their attendance. The familiar presence of Leo and Margaret had further broken the ice, and soon the festivities were in full swing.

There were paper hats, lawn games, a lottery, contests for best cake and most impressive squash, and even a children's costume parade, judged by Squadron Leader Max Dunn and members of his crew. With donated fabric scraps of red, white, blue, and gold, Violet Darling had fashioned RAF roundel broaches, which were being sold for a shilling donation to the Spitfire Fund; nearly everyone in attendance had one pinned to their lapels.

Olive was astounded by the mouthwatering assortment of cakes and jellies, the women having saved up their sugar rations for weeks. But better still, Harriet had had the marvellous idea that the booths should offer them for sale in servings of two, one to be shared with an attending hero of the RAF. Judging by the number of ladies—and even a few men—she'd watched eagerly bearing down on the unsuspecting guests of honour, a pair of plates in hand, the fundraiser was going like a house afire. She'd even heard a few whispers marvelling at the prospect of Miss Hussel-bee's ghost in attendance. She sighed happily and turned to see Jamie arrive with Danny Tierney in tow.

Jamie was handling the crutch quite dexterously and seemed to be in good spirits, but Tierney looked as downtrodden as she'd ever seen him. Marie had broken his heart. Olive smiled at the pair of them, hoping the day would be a pleasant distraction from recent events.

"Well, you've missed the children's parade, and some of the costumes were particularly imaginative. Jonathon dressed as a victory garden, and Tommy Prince's costume was billed as 'Make Do and Mend.' Between you and me, he looks the same as always, in torn jumper and trousers."

"You look rather fine, Olive," Tierney said, smiling shyly.

"Why, thank you," she said, smoothing her hands over her mauve jumper and tweed skirt. "It's nice to be out of that drab FANY uniform for a little while at least."

It was the sort of day—much like Margaret's wedding day—

that made her wish her heart was spoken for. But a bittersweet glance at Jamie served as a ready reminder that, as far as the village was concerned, it was.

Suppressing a sigh, she linked arms with both men. "Shall I introduce you round?" she said brightly.

She left Tierney in the capable hands of Jonathon, who, it seemed, was taking a break from haunting to play a game of lawn skittles. Jamie, she pressed into a seat positioned beside Max's wheelchair, then leaned in between them. "Squadron Leader Max Dunn, this is Captain Jameson Aldridge." The men shook hands. "Max is a bit at loose ends, and I thought he might be quite useful to the NPS," she said coyly. Presumably, Jamie still remembered the day he'd shown up at her loft on behalf of Baker Street, only to be mistaken for an NPS official. She raised her brows encouragingly.

Max's head swivelled, and he stared in confusion. "The NPS? Isn't that—"

"I'll let Captain Aldridge fill you in," she said. "I'll fetch tea and cake for the pair of you—my heroes." She smiled sincerely and set off across the lawn.

The shadows grew longer, and the lanterns winked on; a bar cart crowded with bottles was rolled out onto the lawn, and some guests settled in for a comfortable chat. Olive, who'd been pressed into service at various booths for the past few hours, was eager for a reprieve and a private conversation of her own.

Forever the romantic, Harriet had quickly agreed to her stepdaughter's appeal for the temporary use of the wheelchair. Olive desperately wanted a bit of time alone with Jamie—although not for the reasons her stepmother suspected—and his broken leg wasn't conducive to a leisurely stroll through the grounds. So, she intended to sweep him off his feet.

Harriet stalled her with a discreet finger, raised at Miss Danes's approach. Olive dutifully waited.

"Hello, Winifred," her stepmother said smartly. "How are you managing at the tea tent? Still have plenty of cakes and biscuits?"

"I made three trays of my jam tarts—strawberry and raspberry—and they were all bought up quick as a wink." Her smile was smug. "I suppose it should hardly come as a surprise—" There was a muffled thump, and Olive frowned as Miss Danes demanded, "What was . . . ?"

"Still using black market sugar, are you, Winifred?" This was punctuated by a loud harrumphing, and then a familiar strident voice went on. "I would hate for someone to catch you out. I suggest you redeem yourself with a very large donation . . ."

Olive felt the laugh bubble up even as her eyes glossed with tears. She would carry that voice in her thoughts forever.

"I'm sorry, Winifred. I see Lady Camilla is looking for me," Harriet interjected. "Olive," she added, glancing back, "would you be so good as to wheel me in her direction?"

Olive set off with the wheelchair at a brisk clip and stopped beside a large urn on the terrace.

"The coast is clear," she said, prompting Hen to poke her head from the skirting drape that covered the space beneath the wheelchair's seat. The girl climbed out, brushed off her Guide uniform, and stood, wincing a bit as she extended her legs.

"She's doing marvellously," Harriet enthused in a whispered aside. "It's uncanny, really. The more irascible her tone, the bigger the donation," she added. "Although, I must say, all those thumps are rather off-putting." She beamed at Hen. "It's high time for a well-earned break. Go and get yourself some tea and cake," Harriet insisted, dropping a few coins into the girl's hand.

"Now, then," she said to Olive, "if you'll help me to a seat on the lawn, you'll be able to use the chair to your heart's content." She smiled, glancing over to where Jamie sat with the other injured men, most of whom were surrounded by villagers eager to chat. "It was an inspired idea, Olive. We're, all of us, the better for it. And I think we're going to be able to make a sizeable contribution to the Spitfire Fund, which will help going forward. Although, with any luck, we'll be done with this beastly war before it's needed." They smiled encouragingly at each other, both knowing that the worst was still yet to come.

Jamie hadn't moved from his chair, and now Violet Darling was poised on its edge, smiling rather besottedly at Max Dunn. They all glanced up as Olive appeared with the wheelchair.

"It's on loan for the next quarter of an hour," she informed Jamie. He frowned. "From Harriet," she added with an encouraging smile.

"For whom?" he said carefully.

Violet and Max exchanged amused glances.

"For you, you idiot," Olive said, careful to keep her voice flirty, lest she be accused of insubordination. "I'd like to take a walk with you, but I don't want to have to drag your crutch along."

The whole business required no less than the teasing and bullying of a trio of RAF crewmen before Jamie finally agreed to let himself be taken off in the chair. Olive made a beeline for the edge of the property, anxious to be out of hearing. Jamie grumbled discontentedly the whole way.

"Oh, hush," she finally said sharply. "It's only temporary, and since Harriet is having a wonderful time with two dashing pilots, the least you can do is appreciate her largesse. I hardly think you have any reason for complaint." No sooner had the words left her mouth than she rolled the chair into a muddy patch, sending him lurching to the side.

"You were saying?" he said sourly.

"You're meant to be in love with me, you beast of a man," she said with some exasperation, battling with the chair. "There are plenty of men who wouldn't even have to work at the task. This particular cover story would be a breeze in their capable hands."

He twisted his head round to look at her, amusement having finally overtaken his grouchy mood. "Is that so?"

"It is," she ground out. "Now, tell me what was in that message Alice carried home whilst you shoot me adoring glances. Specifically, who is Elise?"

"All these men who're in love with you—they don't mind the bossiness?"

She swatted the back of his head, hoping that at a distance it looked like a playful ruffling of his hair.

"No more," he said, laughing, "or I'll be utterly besotted." He cleared his throat as she pushed the chair along the border of the victory garden, now sown with winter greens, Brussels sprouts, and other sturdy vegetables. "Elise is a local girl who caught Renauld releasing one of the pigeons."

Olive gasped involuntarily.

"Thankfully," Jamie went on, "she was working with the Resistance—right under the nose of her brother, a known collaborator. When the Nazis began closing in, she took the last pigeon . . . Alice, was it?" Seeing her nod, he continued. "And managed to send it home with intelligence collected by her own contacts."

Olive jerked the chair to an abrupt stop. "Well, that's marvellous news," she said brightly, laying her hands on Jamie's shoulders to give them a happy squeeze. Then she walked round the chair to face him, took in his grim face and Horace's sudden unwelcome appearance. Her stomach clenched. *What is it?*"

"The Belgian section forwarded us a transmission received from one of their operators, relaying a further message from Elise. Weasel has been captured and transported by train to a work camp in Germany. Rémi and Renauld managed to elude capture, and she's connected them with the organisers of the Comet Line, who are working to smuggle them back to Britain via Gibraltar."

Olive's shoulders slumped. They'd been too late to undo the full damage wrought by Marie. While the news of Weasel was heartbreaking, it was, in fact, the fate she'd assumed had befallen all three of the Conjugal agents. That two of them had eluded capture and were working their way back to Baker Street, despite Marie's perfidy, was nothing short of a miracle.

"And," he added, somewhat in the manner of a man bestowing gifts, "she's indicated that if we drop additional pigeons in the spot the message indicates—alerting her via the BBC broadcasts—she'll endeavour to return them with actionable intelligence." He rubbed a hand over his leg, and Olive wondered if it was paining him. "Leopold Vindictive remains elusive, but something tells me Elise will be indispensable."

Thrilled at this turnabout in the mission, Olive lost her head, bending over him to plant a quick kiss in the spot where Horace was just beginning to disappear from view. As she was pulling back promptly to explain, she found her movement thwarted by his hand cupping the back of her neck.

Startled, she met his eyes. He shrugged and said only, "I'm meant to be in love with you," before pressing his lips to hers.

Olive wanted to climb onto his lap, drape her arms round his neck, and let herself fall into the kiss for a few moments' escape from death and betrayal, worry and fear. But even more, she wanted a moment free of all pretense. More than anything, she wanted to trade this kiss, undertaken because someone was watching and would expect it, for one given freely because Jamie was so inclined. But she would take what was on offer. It was over much too soon, and she sighed, giving him a teasing smile as she looked into his eyes, startled to feel an odd little frisson of awareness skitter over her skin.

Neither moved nor spoke, both seeming to be seeing each other with new eyes, until Olive heard someone calling her name. She glanced up to stare bemusedly at the man who stood before her. She hadn't seen him in five months, and now, here he was, the same as ever, but for his Wedgwood-blue war service dress, newly decorated with sergeant's flashing and RAF wings.

"George," she exclaimed, poised to lunge for him, rather desperate for a real, honest hug, but she was pulled up short by the willowy figure standing just beside him, dressed in the uniform of the Air Transport Auxiliary.

"It was meant to be a surprise," George said eagerly. "Mum

told me about the fête, and I had a bit of leave coming, so we thought we'd make the trip down. But then the train was stopped on the line, and we were late getting in . . ." He trailed off, and wrapping his arm round the woman beside him, he nudged her forward and clutched her to his side. "This is the girl I wrote to you about—the best of the Attagirls, and the prettiest, as well. Bridget Nivens, this is my childhood chum, Olive Bright."

Bridget stepped forward, her hand outstretched. "It's a pleasure, Olive. George talks of you so much, I feel as if we're friends already."

Olive smiled at her, determined not to show the envy she felt not only at having been supplanted as George's best friend, but also in witnessing the true and honest nature of their relationship.

Before she could reply, George glanced at Jamie, who was watching them all from his borrowed wheelchair. "You're quite the odd man out," he said rather jovially, taking in Jamie's army uniform, which was rather homely compared to the crisp blue of the RAF. Recuperating in Merryweather House, as well, are you?" He added the last with sober respect.

Olive looked at Jamie, who appeared to be waiting for her to take the lead. But her typical introduction had lodged in her throat, and she couldn't quite decide what to say. She thought of their complicated relationship: the shared deceptions, frustrated arguments, unrepentant teasing, and the occasional, rather thrilling, amorous moments. She thought of the kaleidoscope of feelings he dredged up in her and found herself utterly tongue tied. How should she characterise his all-consuming presence in her life?

At the precise moment the silence had run on too long, Jamie took her hand, laced his fingers with hers, and said simply, "I'm Captain Jameson Aldridge." He glanced up at the woman beside him, an unreadable look in his eyes. "Olive and I are . . . complicated, but I would go to very great lengths to make her happy."

Olive's face momentarily went blank as she tussled with this unexpected answer. Present company was surely expecting doe eyes and a devoted smile, but her thoughts were prompting pursed lips and a considering frown. Jamie had sounded so sincere, so either he'd upped his romantic game or else . . . Or else what, exactly? For once, she didn't have a ready answer.

Most definitely a mystery. And she expected solving it could be rewarding indeed.

Author's Note

Historical fiction is constructed with a scaffolding of truth, and I did my best to ensure that this book was as sturdy as possible. I took a few liberties, but I hope they're sufficiently minor as to be unremarkable.

Operation Columba saw the Allies dropping thousands of pigeons into occupied Europe, in a wide swath running from Denmark south to France, from early 1941 through 1944. A great many were lost—to natural predators, to Nazi paranoia, or simply to desperately hungry citizens. To be found with a pigeon in a Nazi-occupied country was a death sentence. But some courageous men and women viewed the pigeons as hopeful reminders that they were not suffering alone, that the British were just across the Channel, tirelessly strategising for an Allied victory. These heroes risked everything to send the birds home with any intelligence they thought might prove a detriment to the Nazis.

Such was Leopold Vindictive, led by Joseph Raskin, a veteran intelligence gatherer of the Great War and missionary, who was able to travel rather inconspicuously throughout Belgium. The members of this Belgian Resistance network collectively amassed a tremendous amount of information regarding German infrastructure, potential bombing targets, and the ongoing preparations for the invasion of Britain. Raskin then carefully transcribed it all, complete with maps, onto two sheets of rice paper, each approximately three inches square, which were included, along with a pencil and some pigeon feed, with each pigeon dropped as part of Operation Columba. It was a tremendous feat, and I encourage you to have a look at an image of Message 37, as it was classified by MI14(d), Britain's 'Special Continental Pigeon Service.' (Gordon Corera's *Secret Pigeon Service* includes a marvelous photograph of Leopold Vindictive's Message 37.) Unfortunately, after this promising beginning, the British were not able to coordinate effective communications with Leopold Vindictive, and before long, Joseph Raskin was captured, sentenced, and put to death, along with several other members of the network.

Believe it or not, Operation Conjugal was not a construct of my imagination (and how could I resist including it?). But details are few. My research uncovered only that agents were sent into Belgium, intent on sabotage and liaison, and they were captured. But with the fate of those agents in my hands, I chose to alter the ending.

A fascinating, and little known, aspect of British intelligence during World War II is the work of MI9. It was the purview of this department to ensure that soldiers and downed airmen understood that their first imperative was to evade capture and, if that failed, to escape captivity. To facilitate this directive, MI9 mass-produced location-specific silk maps of Europe (and beyond), printed with cities and towns, frontier borders, and natural landmarks, to be carried by RAF crew members, soldiers, and Special Forces units. In addition, MI9's operations man, Christopher Hutton, devised all sorts of ingenious ways to get escape aids into the hands of Allied prisoners. Working through fake charity organisations rather than the Red Cross, so as not to violate the Geneva Convention, MI9 smuggled in board games, playing cards, badminton rackets, and vinyl records, concealing maps and blueprints, money and identity cards. An estimated 35,000 Allied personnel managed to meet MI9's directive to escape captivity, many thanks to these escape aids.

As to the details regarding the Royal Observer Corps, the various Women's Institute schemes, Station XVII training, and so on, I contend that everything is historically possible. . . .